"Ripley, dear boy, I am to monitor every penny of government money devoted to iceberg recovery."

"I don't believe it," Forte said, coloring.

"Don't grieve, Ripley," Jennifer Red Cloud said. "I'll grow on you."

Forte looked down at her. "You already have."

"I beg your pardon?" She seemed truly taken aback.

"I've loved you from the first time I saw you, the day you married Ned."

"But you—"

"Shut up and listen, Red. If I had met you a day earlier, I'd have killed him before I'd let him have you. Then, after Ned died, when I *could* have had you—"

"The *hell* you could," she flared. "I'd never—"

"Be quiet. I could have had you, but you'd have wanted to run the show, just as you ran Ned. Well, sister, I'm going to have you, but it's going to be on *my* terms. First, I'll break your company. Then I'm going to marry you!"

Also by Daniel da Cruz
Published by Ballantine Books:

THE AYES OF TEXAS

THE GROTTO OF THE FORMIGANS

TEXAS ON THE ROCKS

Daniel da Cruz

A Del Rey Book
BALLANTINE BOOKS • NEW YORK

A Del Rey Book
Published by Ballantine Books

Library of Congress Catalog Card Number: 85-91199

ISBN 0-345-31659-2

Printed in Canada

First Edition: April 1986

Cover Art by Barclay Shaw

For
Hayat Elbi Lina

TABLE OF CONTENTS

PART I
WATER

1. SCENARIO
11 SEPTEMBER 2004

AT TEN O'CLOCK ON SUNDAY NIGHT, SEPTEMBER 11, 2004, David D. Castle stood in the center of the big parking lot of a darkened, abandoned warehouse in Bailey's Crossroads, Virginia, seven miles from the nation's capital. It was bitter cold, and a sharp wind swirled about his bare head. Around his neck was wrapped a wool scarf, and beneath his suit jacket he wore a heavy sweater, but they did little to ward off the chill. What warmth there was came from the heat of the curses he heaped upon the head of William S. Grayle, but it wasn't enough to still his shivering limbs and chattering teeth.

At ten minutes past ten it began to drizzle, and Castle's curses multiplied. He briefly considered returning to the car for his umbrella but thought better of it.

As the drizzle turned to rain, Castle turned to philosophy. At least, he comforted himself, on a night like this he had nothing to fear from muggers. And that was no small consolation considering that the briefcase he was carrying contained more money than many men made in their entire lives.

He was examining his watch yet again when, at ten twenty-two, a long black limousine slid up out of the darkness and stopped in front of the sagging gate of the warehouse. Its headlights went dark, and a spotlight flashed on. Its beam made a leisurely circuit of the empty grounds and came to rest on David D. Castle, who stood unflinchingly squinting into the beam until finally it winked out.

The headlights flashed twice. David D. Castle splashed through the puddles toward the car with smoked-glass windows parked fifty yards away. The rear door opened at his approach. A dim floor bulb revealed a little leather jump seat facing the rear. He stepped inside and took the

3

seat, closing the door behind him.

As his eyes tried to penetrate the darkness, he heard the old man speak from the opposite side of the car.

"You brought the money?"

"Right here," replied Castle, patting the briefcase.

"Pass it to my driver."

Castle felt a slight current of air as the black glass slid down behind him. He passed the briefcase through.

"Count it," Grayle instructed his chauffeur.

Castle bristled. "I beg your pardon, sir. I am a member of Congress."

"I had forgotten. Count it twice, Brandon."

Castle sat in aggrieved silence, his occasional sniffles muffled by the riffle of bank notes and the steady drumbeat of rain on the roof.

"Two hundred and fifty thousand, sir," said the chauffeur.

"Drive on," Grayle instructed.

The communicating window whooshed shut, and the limousine moved off into the night. The two men sat in total darkness, the opaque windows admitting not the dimmest ray of light. It was all of a piece with Grayle's reputation for reclusiveness. Although he had been whispering uncannily prescient advice into the ears of the mighty for more than forty years, very little was known of the man beyond a name and a number—no address—in the telephone directory.

The tinkle of ice in a glass, the splash of liquids, and a glass was pressed into his hand. Castle, who had begun to shiver in his wet clothes, didn't care what it was so long as it was strong. He sipped it, then drank greedily.

A Bloody Mary, with Russian vodka, fresh lemon, and Tabasco, by God! In public, to preserve his image as a champion of local industry, Castle drank California wine. But in the privacy of his own study, a Bloody Mary was his evening solace, with Tabasco instead of Worcestershire. Somehow William S. Grayle knew. But then, why not? He was said to know everything worth knowing in Washington, D.C. It was for Grayle's knowledge that Castle had just paid the old man $250,000, and it was going to make him, Congressman David D. Castle, President of the United States of America.

As the dean of "public affairs consultants" in the nation's capital, William S. Grayle was believed to have retired more than a decade earlier, having molded national politics and the careers of some of the nation's leading power brokers as well as serving as special adviser to six consecutive presidents. According to gossip around the Hill, in recent years he had undertaken only the occasional "mission impossible," simply to add flavor to his declining years and to prove to himself that he had not lost his exquisite political touch.

Such a visionary project had been proposed to him by David D. Castle, congressman from California.

Castle had only one question: Did Mr. William S. Grayle think he could bring it off?

What a silly question, thought William S. Grayle. He acknowledged himself, without false modesty, the shrewdest political mind in the nation's capital, but still not quite God-on-High. Who the hell did this junior congressman, ordinarily good-looking but totally lacking in charisma, well-to-do but not excessively rich, with a sound but undistinguished record during five terms in Congress, think he was, anyway?

Yet the more he pondered the sheer magnitude of the challenge, the more irresistible it became. It could be a coup to make the history books.

2. GROWLER
23 OCTOBER 2004

HE'D SHOW THE OLD MAN.

Ripley Forte shoved the eight throttles forward until the indicator needle bit into the red. The eight powerful propfan engines answered with a banshee roar that surged out across the choppy waters of the Labrador Strait and then bounced back from the craggy blue-green sides of the million-ton iceberg.

Silent and sinister, its base shrouded in fog, the berg loomed above Forte and his jet sled like a Matterhorn suspended in space.

The sled responded to the engines' thrust. It shot forward, the eight fourteen-foot, ten-bladed propfans clawing at the frigid morning air. Behind the sled a braided-nylon cable, eleven inches in diameter, surfaced from beneath the frothing wake as the sled pulled away from the huge pinnacle iceberg. The cable drew taut, and suddenly the seasled, as big and unlovely as a Mississippi coal barge, lay dead in the water, shackled by the enormous mountain of ice.

His weathered face framed by bulbous orange ear defenders that only partially blocked out the din of the jet engines, Ripley Forte squinted through the icy spray at the inertial-navigation dial on the control panel. The readout was accurate to the hundredth of a second of arc: a little over ten inches of movement by the seasled would be discernible. But the dial didn't move.

The tension began to tighten around his sinewy neck like a strangler's hands. A wave of nausea rose from his empty stomach. He swallowed hard and choked it back.

"Move, damn you," he growled, and beat his fist against the dial with its frozen needle.

Suddenly he laughed.

Well, of *course* the damn berg hadn't moved. The 6,500-horsepower engines fighting the iceberg were analogous to the schoolgirl and the *Queen Mary* in that old physics puzzler: If she pushed long enough, would the ocean liner ease away from the pier? Of course, because the force exerted by the girl, having nowhere else to go, would be translated into motion. The same principle applied here: Those 52,000 horses straining to shift that mountain of ice were damned well *going* to move it.

But it was going to take time.

Meanwhile, in the barge's flying bridge amidships, high above the slipstream of the jet engines, Ripley Forte willed himself to remain calm. At the moment, the crew needed no orders. The cable tender had deployed the buoy-supported nylon towing line around the iceberg and sheered off. The line was secured to the two barrel-sized bitts on the seasled's fantail.

The shotman had fixed his explosive charge to the nylon towing line fifty meters abaft the barge's stern. From his cupola the shotman watched the berg and the seabirds resting there. Gulls and petrels instinctively took wing seconds before a berg capsized. This is a common fate of icebergs, for beneath the warmer sea waters cut into the submerged ice like a woodsman's axe. This ablation could cause the unbalanced berg to tumble forward, smashing down on the sled, and sending its crew to the bottom. If it *did* begin to capsize, the shotman would blow the explosive and sever the line, allowing the seasled to rocket out of harm's way.

The thick line from barge to berg, the nexus between an almost irresistible force and an almost immovable body, quivered faintly as the two forces contended. Should it part under the strain, the severed end would snap back like a gigantic rubber band, slicing through the bridge's steel superstructure. Forte turned back to the inertial navigation dial.

By God! They *had* moved. Only 130 centimeters, but they had moved!

He punched in numbers on his control console: elapsed time at full power, distance made good, relative water-current speed, wind speed, estimated iceberg mass, engine thrust. He plotted the distances which would be made good at five-minute intervals. The line on the screen started flat and then rose sharply, leveling off at 1,050 meters per hour. He laughed and smote his thigh in exultation.

He'd show the old man!

For as long as he could remember, that had been Ripley's overpowering ambition. But Gwillam Forte cast so long a shadow, it had seemed that his son would never get clear of it. Now, though, everything was falling into place. Soon Ripley Forte would be rich—richer than his billionaire father had ever dreamed of being. He had made it on his own. To be sure, he could never rival Gwillam Forte's feat of arms—single-handedly saving the Republic of Texas by destroying Russia's 17th High Seas Fleet—

but then, what mortal man could?

Certainly not Ripley Forte. Christ, it had already taken him the best part of his forty-three years even to get within striking distance of the lesser of Gwillam Forte's achievements.

Gwillam Forte was already a rich man when Ripley, his firstborn, became aware that his was no ordinary father. For one thing, Gwillam was a triple amputee as a result of the explosion of a Japanese kamikaze aboard the U.S.S. *Texas*, on which he had served as bugler during World War II. For another, he had surmounted his handicap by making a fortune in Houston real estate, investing millions of it in prosthesis research—bread upon the waters that returned to him in the form of an artificial arm and two artificial legs that in most respects equaled, and in some excelled, the performance of the limbs he had lost. An even more striking distinction was his father's fierce loyalty to Texas, to which he owed everything: three amazingly lifelike prostheses, five wives, seven children, a $1.3 billion fortune, the respect of his fellow Texans, and finally their reverence for sacrificing his life that the Republic of Texas might live.

Gwillam Forte's remarkable record of accomplishment was beyond the ambitions of Ripley's half brothers and sisters; they were content to graze the clover so fruitfully cultivated by their father. Ripley Forte was different. To him, Gwillam was a god, and Ripley would prove his devotion by walking in his footsteps; the stormier the path, the more worthy his emulation.

Just as his father had done before him, a bored and restless Ripley quit school in the eighth grade and hit the road, determined to meet life head on.

For the first time in his life, he breathed freely. No more English butlers standing behind his chair at dinner at El Cabellejo Ranch, no more riding lessons on purebred horses. Farewell to neckties, chamber music, formal dances with toothy young females, obsequious smiles from bank cashiers, ironed sheets, vitamin pills, visits to art galleries, cashmere sweaters, tiny sports cars, daily baths. He was out in the world Gwillam Forte, with two plastic legs and a steel hook instead of a hand, had taken on and conquered. Well, if Gwillam Forte could do it, so could he, by God!

One thing was certain: Young Ripley wouldn't get by on his looks. He had a barrel chest, arms made muscular from repairing range fence during summer vacations, too-big ears, and long spindly legs that no amount of running and bicycling had been able to develop to the proportions of the rest of his body. At fifteen his hairline was already receding; by thirty the loss would stabilize, leaving him hairless from his thick black eyebrows to the crown of his head. His nose had been broken several times in fights, but the loss of symmetry was compensated for by the knife scar from the earlobe to the corner of his mouth that gave him a perpetual and slightly sinister smile. In temperament, he was flexible, as a herd of stampeding longhorns is flexible, in that he wouldn't gallop over people and stomp them into the turf unless they happened to get in his way. Somewhere behind his deep-set dark eyes, full of intelligence and imagination, was a sense of humor, but it rarely showed, for he was a young man of purpose with little time to spare on idle laughter.

For the next four years he kicked around Texas, while Texas kicked *him* around. He worked as water boy on a road construction crew, graduated to tool-room assistant, worked as a short-order cook, roughneck, gandy dancer, shrimp-boat hand, door-to-door encyclopedia salesman, swamper in a mine, wheat harvester, supplier of ink and needles to tattoo parlors, partner in a tire repair shop, and inmate in the Jim Hogg County jail for throwing a deputy sheriff out of a bar and grill, through a door that he hadn't observed was closed.

He had been locked up for three of his 18-months sentence when Gwillam Forte got him sprung. Two days later, he again disappeared from his father's El Cabellejo ranch, angry because his father insisted he return to school, to prepare to succeed him in the management of his dozen oil companies, newspaper chain, and the 40-odd corporations in which Gwillam Forte had important share-holdings.

Instead, Forte joined the Marine Corps, and fought campaigns in Lebanon, Honduras, and Nicaragua. In Central America, the Texan-born and bred Ripley, speaking Spanish as fluently as English, led a platoon of contras, picked up two minor wounds, and developed a distaste for foreign wars.

Home after his four-year tour, his father's paternal hand weighed too heavily on him, so Ripley went to work for Mark Medina, one of Texas's leading contractors. Within six years he had begun his own contracting company and made a small fortune in fast-growing west Texas, establishing a name as a sound practical engineer and a man of his word—and a lousy businessman. His seventh year in business, he lost everything as a shareholder in a liquid-metal fast-breeder reactor, which bred only debt—but fast.

Back at El Cabellejo Ranch for a weekend on his way to Alaska, resolved to stay away from stockbrokers while working as subcontractor on a pipeline, he found his father had mellowed; he no longer gave orders, but advice. "The sea, my boy—that's where the promise of your generation lies."

"Since when? You've done pretty well on dry land: real estate, oil, newspapers and television stations, manufacturing, information systems. Why should it be any different for me?"

"Because," said Gwillam Forte, "my generation has done too well. In our passion to produce things, we've just about used up all the land's resources. We have poisoned what little remains with foul air and blighted cities and decimated forests and fetid rivers. The oceans, Ripley—they are your future."

Ripley Forte knew about his father's being recently commissioned a captain in the "Texas Navy," charged with rehabilitating the old U.S.S. *Texas* on which he had served as a youth and lost three limbs. The refurbished ship would be the centerpiece of the millenary celebrations Governor Tom Traynor had scheduled to inaugurate the year 2000 in Texas. Obviously, this sudden interest in the sea had stemmed from his father's new command.

Gwillam Forte admitted it. "In fact, Governor Traynor's proposition came just as I was considering buying out an ocean technology company with a long string of annual deficits but bright prospects."

"And what did you decide?"

"Not to buy. I had the capital, but I didn't have anybody to run it."

"What about Ned Raynes?" Gwillam's son by his second wife, Ned was thirty years old, had recently married a stunning young woman of mixed Norwegian, Scots, and Apache parentage, and was one of the cleverest corporate manipulators west of the Mississippi.

"Ned's a charmer, all right," said the elder Forte, "but son or no son, he's a schemer and a crook—must have inherited his stepfather's character. He'd work like hell to make the company a winner just for the satisfaction of stealing it from me the minute its balance sheet was in the black. And if *he* didn't, that Red Cloud girl would. She's smart and ambitious and as ruthless as old Chief Snake-in-the-Grass. I've left standing instructions to take her tomahawk away before she's allowed into the house."

"Then keep the stock and put him on the payroll, with the strict understanding that he handles the business side and nothing but."

"He wouldn't be interested unless he had a big chunk of the equity, Rip. Besides, who would run the operations, the technical side? The company has all the technology to recover manganese nodules, all the ships and personnel. The company also makes thermal energy units, but that operation is a shambles, and the efficiency of the OTEC equipment itself has to be upgraded to become commercially profitable. And there are 8,615 people in five major divisions to ramrod. No, my boy, I've looked everywhere, but I haven't found the man to tackle a mix like that."

"It's a tough assignment," conceded Ripley. "It looks like you want a man who's smart, flexible, and a whip-wielding son of a bitch to shape up an outfit like that. One with the clout to stiff-arm Ned when he tried to horn in on operations. And knowing Ned, he'd try. You need a lean, keen, clean, mean bastard."

Gwillam Forte sipped his brandy, apparently lost in thought. He studied the Remington oil over the mantel, a cowboy on a cayuse chasing a heifer across the prairie. He carefully flicked the ash from his evening Emperador and hummed a little tune. He examined his fake fingernails. He assiduously avoided Ripley Forte's eyes.

Ripley chuckled. "Getting subtle in your old age, aren't you, Dad?"

"I'm afraid I don't know what you mean."

"That being the case, I don't suppose you'd know the pay, either."

"Six hundred thousand a year," shot back Gwillam Forte. "That's to start. More when profits justify it."

"A free hand?"

"Absolutely."

"And when the company's in the black?"

"The stock closed today at 6 3/8. There are five million shares outstanding. I'll give each of you options—at eight—to buy half the shares, less one which I'll hold onto to keep peace in the family. Once you boys pull the company out of the red."

Ripley Forte thought it over. "Did you ever wonder what it's like to build shopping malls, Dad?" he asked finally.

"Can't say as I ever did, son."

"Don't ask."

The wind had picked up. Low-lying patches of fog eddied around the iceberg. Now only the tender's radar could warn them of its imminent capsize. The margin of safety was cut, but what the hell—roping icebergs was no more risky than taking a banker's word of honor, and besides, the air was cleaner than in lower Manhattan.

After the first ten minutes, the barge and its lassoed prey had slowly accelerated until, forty-five minutes later, they were plowing steadily through the waves at 880 meters per hour, at right angles to the Labrador Current. The mathematics was simple enough: Providing that a berg was small enough—few were larger than a million tons—and that radar detected its approach within seven thousand meters of a downstream drilling rig, there would be ample time to dispatch a propfan sled to rope and tow it away from a collision course with the platform.

Speed and power were the keys.

He hadn't understood this elemental fact when, in 1998, he had brashly made the winning bid to the Canadian government for the Yellow Rose Oil Field concession. More prudent investors, fearing rogue icebergs such as that which sank the *Titanic* in 1912, had declined to bid.

Forte planned tugboat intercepts of threatening icebergs as far as sixty kilometers north of his rigs up Iceberg Alley, and to tow them clear. His failure to do so had cost him his fortune and the lives of many good men. Icebergs, poor reflectors of radio waves, had slipped like eels through the radar net with disconcerting regularity. During the first four years ghostly mountains of moving ice had penetrated the radar defenses and sank one pedestal and two jack-up rigs, dragging nearly two hundred men to the bottom. Increasingly in hock to the banks—the rigs cost up to $200 million apiece—Forte in desperation strengthened his line of radar picket craft and tripled the number of oceangoing tugs. No more rigs were lost, but the huge revenue-draining fleet of tugs—idle for the seven iceberg-free months of the year—drove him even closer to bankruptcy.

Five years of incessant struggle and the tragic loss of so many shipmates had aged him, squeezed him dry. By 2003, he felt he had nothing left to give, no expedient left untried. Once again, he sensed, fate was about to push him over the precipice.

Nine years earlier, in 1994, it had seemed that nothing lay ahead but calm seas and smooth sailing. His father had given him, as promised, total control over operations of the new Forte Oceanic Resources. As Gwillam had foreseen, Ripley had driven his scientists, workers, and especially himself like galley slaves to dredge up the treasures of the deep.

The success of Forte Oceanic Resources, Forte argued, depended on developing radical technologies, and the most revolutionary were being discovered and perfected in university laboratories. He packed his bag and went on the road. He returned to Houston with a dozen crack scientists and a single idea: the concentration of mineral salts dissolved in seawater by means of microorganisms. The idea wasn't exactly new. For years bacteria had been cultivated commercially to break down plastic wastes or to concentrate such toxic substances as dioxin for easier disposal, but the extraction of mineral salts from seawater by means of bacteria had proved a dead end.

Fungi had not. One of Forte's researchers discovered a soil fungus that gobbled up cadmium in its normal metabolic processes. A genetically engineered mutant did the same for selenium. Starting on this hopeful base, in less than two years his genetic engineers had created fungi that concentrated titanium and monazite—source of thorium and cerium—from seawater. All three elements were extremely valuable. This development ended the United States's almost total dependence on Russia for titanium, indispensable for the hulls of deep-diving submarines. Even so, these metals constituted a mere fraction of the 40 million tons of dissolved salts worth $35 billion contained in each cubic mile of seawater. Reclamation of these mineral riches, together with mechanized recovery of the abundant phosphorite and manganese nodules from the seabed, put Forte Oceanic Resources in the forefront of American producers of rare metals.

By 1998, Ripley's energy and organizational skills, the fruits of his researchers' imagination, and Ned Raynes' financial acumen had turned the failing company around. Meanwhile, Russia's bloodless conquest of Europe, Asia, and South America between 1989 and 1993 had slowly choked off the flow of strategic minerals to the United States. As national stockpiles of metals dwindled in the mid-1990s, the price of minerals extracted from the sea by Forte Oceanic Resources skyrocketed. FOR was on its way.

But Ripley Forte wouldn't be along for the ride. On July 7, 1998, Captain Gwillam Forte went down with the U.S.S. *Texas* in the Houston Ship Channel, taking along to the bottom an entire Soviet fleet in what would be recorded as one of the most bizarre, lopsided, and ultimately satisfying fleet actions in history. In the aftermath, the State of Texas went its own way as the Republic of Texas, Gwillam Forte was enshrined in the Texas pantheon along with Stephen Austin and Sam Houston, and his vast estate was divided among his numerous ex-wives and their progeny. Ripley's portion was $37 million in securities and real estate and very near half of FOR's 5,000,001 shares. Near—and yet so far.

Driven by the pathological ambition of Jennifer Red Cloud, Ned Raynes quickly bought out the fractional shareholdings of his half-siblings, giving him a 6/7-share majority of voting stock, which he exercised by immediately reorganizing the privately held company. Before Ripley knew what was afoot, Ned had sold FOR's assets to a new company, Raynes Oceanic Resources, Ned Raynes, president, for $10 million. Ripley's 2,500,000.14286 shares came to $5,000001.35. Since the real assets of the company in four years had increased in value sixfold to more than $200 million, not to mention the tremendous profits that were just beginning to roll in, Ripley Forte computed that he had been diddled out of a round $100 million.

Up there somewhere, his father must have been laughing his head off. Here was Ripley Forte, thirty-seven years old, an accomplished hands-on engineer, yet so devoid of business sense that he'd been taken in by a crude stratagem that he should have anticipated years before.

Since then, to destroy the man, his wife, and his company had become the consuming ambition of Ripley Forte's life.

The Canadian offshore concession, an area of 7,223 square kilometers on the Grand Banks, would be Forte's bastion, from which he would engage Raynes Oceanic Resources and batter it into a smoking ruin. Exploratory drillings had indicated the field held reserves of 3.5 billion barrels of sweet crude with gravities averaging 27 API, on a par with the best of Indonesia, Venezuela, and Saudi Arabia, the latter two now in Russian hands. Because the Russians were holding back exports to cripple their capitalist enemy, U.S. production could barely keep pace with domestic demand and prices were steadily rising. If only Forte could solve the problem of the deadly icebergs, he would ride the wave of booming oil prices to riches beyond the dreams of even a Jennifer Red Cloud. And with those riches, he would crush his foes, and ROR would roar no more.

Between Forte and his goal were the icebergs that calved from Greenland's glaciers at the rate of ten thousand to

twelve thousand a year—about the same number, oddly
enough, produced by the vastly larger Antarctic glaciers,
although Greenland's icebergs were mere ice cubes by
comparison. Small though they might be, most were big
enough to smash and sink the biggest ship afloat or uproot
the sturdiest pedestal oil rig like a weed.

The solution to the iceberg dilemma came to him one
day as he chugged northward at eighteen knots aboard a
tug in pursuit of a 20,000-tonner, an hour's sailing away.
What a waste of time, he mused. A scaled-up bayou
buggy—that flat-bottomed skiff powered by a light-air-
craft engine and used by hunters in the Everglades—
would have made the trip in fifteen minutes. Heavier,
bigger, with a mighty power plant . . . More speed and more
power meant faster response, fewer vessels, fewer crew,
less overhead, fewer debts.

Within ten days simulation studies at the University
of Texas Computer Center were completed. Within weeks
a prototype full-scale seasled with eight forward-mounted
propfan engines, delivering half again as much power as
pure jets at 35 percent less cost, was undergoing trials.
Fitted with hydrofoils, the newly christened *Nola Ann*
could thunder along at 85 knots at 40 percent power. Ripley
Forte himself was in command on its maiden voyage to
the Grand Banks, where he immediately went in search
of the enemy.

Peering through binoculars, he could now discern the
first of two imperiled rigs through the mist at a distance
of six kilometers to the south. Free and adrift, the berg
he had roped would certainly have smashed into the other
within the next three hours. But under tow by the powerful *Nola Ann*, it was steadily being dragged off its collision course. In an hour he could cast it adrift, a menace
no more. Floating south, the berg would meet the warm
waters of the northward-flowing Gulf Stream and melt
away. After a day or two the ice giant would become a
"bergy bit," and with the passage of another hour or two
a "growler," a pussycat of an iceberg no longer able to
devour a 5,000-ton drilling rig in one bite, a mere scratcher
of paintwork.

The thunder of the engines faded from his consciousness as Ripley Forte, alone on the starboard wing of the flying bridge, contemplated the rosy future. On the credit side, he had an experienced, smoothly functioning crew, nine rigs with four more on order, and nearly four billion tons of sweet crude ready to gush up from the wellheads. On the debit side was more than a billion dollars in loans, not to mention another two hundred million that would still be needed to put the field into full production. But the bankers, lately fractious and inaccessible, fearing that icebergs would defeat Forte, would now come running, briefcases bulging with greenbacks, impatient to cash in at last. What with the rising price of oil, he figured to be free and clear within eighteen months.

More than five years in Arctic waters filled with peril and back-breaking labor lay behind him. Ahead lay the financial resources to build a corporate empire that would challenge, defeat, and devour Raynes Oceanic Resources. His day had finally come.

Forte's ideas of the hereafter were vague but absolute. Somewhere up there, he was certain, Gwillam Forte was looking down upon him, a proud smile on his lips. At last he knew what Ripley Forte was made of.

Too bad Ned Raynes had died of a heart attack three years before, depriving Ripley Forte of the pleasure of bankrupting him. On the other hand, Ned's widow, Jennifer Red Cloud, was still in business.

Forte smiled. Not for long, sweetheart.

3. CEMETERY
3 NOVEMBER 2004

"WAIT AT THE GATE OF THE NEW HOPE CEMETERY. TEN P.M., November 3."

Castle complied with the instructions. This time he was better prepared. He wore a raincoat and rain hat and carried a flashlight and umbrella, although the thick ground fog seemed to preclude rain any time soon. He switched on his flashlight and looked at his watch. A few minutes before ten, punctual as always.

Suddenly he sensed an alien presence and whirled to confront a large figure that had materialized behind him. An arm reached forward and gently disengaged the flashlight from his unresisting hand.

"You won't need this," said a voice he recognized as that of Grayle's chauffeur. "Follow me."

"You have a problem, Congressman," said William S. Grayle as the limousine, its interior dark as before, picked up speed. "You want to be President of the United States. That is not, of course, an uncommon ambition among politicians. However, the realists among them usually have something more specific to offer—I must speak frankly— than a hunger for preferment. You have no large popular following like former Navy pilot Pastor Dave Berg, the Flying Fundamentalist. You haven't the blazing rhetoric of our modern black messiah, Governor Randy Nixon of New Jersey. You have authored no significant legislation, proposed no new foreign or domestic initiatives, wed no beautiful movie actress, been involved in none of those juicy but endearing scandals which voters are so willing to forgive in their elected officials. Negatives, sir—all negatives. Now, then, can you give me one *positive* reason why the average American would favor you for President over, say the city recorder of Toledo, Ohio?"

Castle was silent.

"Just as I thought. You have none. As matters stand, therefore, no reasonable man would give you a Chinaman's chance of even getting nominated, let alone elected. But as you know, politicans are not elected on the basis of such qualities as reason, or integrity, or a compulsion to serve the public interest. If they were, the halls of Congress would be a lonely place.

"Nevertheless, I can conceive of one faint possibility: to seize the attention of the American people with an electrifying issue, one which will mesmerize, galvanize, terrorize them, a crisis which will so engage their passions that they will have no time for rational examination of its implications, an emergency pregnant with overtones of life and death for citizen and nation, for which only David D. Castle has a solution to lead the great American people out upon the broad sunlit uplands of prosperity and happiness."

"Yes, I thought—"

"You need a castastrophe-in-the-making, something that will scare the hell out of the American electorate. In the best of times, only fifty percent of our electorate exercises its franchise. These regular voters are captive to conventional appeals of party demagogues. Therefore, you must create a totally new constituency. Your issue will be simple, elemental. Your weapon—naked fear.

"America's problems are many, and they are pressing. But for your purposes we can straightaway eliminate most of them. First of all, forget diplomatic initiatives. Americans have never really been concerned with foreign relations. Besides, thanks to our two oceans and Russia's recent conquest of Europe, South America, and most of Africa, which appear to be as much as it can digest at present, we have achieved a temporary, if uneasy, truce. So long as it prevails, Americans just aren't going to get excited over foreign affairs.

"Domestic social and political issues? Worthless. American standards of living have never been higher. And when the people prosper, politics takes a back seat.

"Religion? Now, that's always an active possibility. Invent a new one and you can become governor of California. But of course the California vote alone won't put you in the White House. Neither will the votes of those fractions of the American population obsessed with parochial concerns—abortion, states' rights, drug abuse, education, health, women's rights, pollution, space travel, and so on. No one group's votes will be decisive. A single issue, therefore, must be found which will galvanize them all.

"Now, then, Mr. Castle," said William S. Grayle gently, "let me tell you exactly what your $250,000 has bought. Your needs required careful study by the best minds in many fields. To conduct that study, I selected a number of specialists, each to forecast developments during the next five years in his area of competence. What I sought was a crisis or problem that: *a*, will affect the vast majority of Americans; *b*, is presently unperceived by that vast majority; *c*, though of insignificant dimensions at present will grow at such a rate as to become a national problem with potentially catastrophic consequences within two or three years; and, *d*, be susceptible to solution within four years at the outside.

"They were to list the coming crises according to national priority. Some listed as many as nine which fit my guidelines, others only one. Their two-page appreciations of each potential crisis were delivered to me last week."

"Can I get a copy?" said Castle eagerly.

"Of course. The fee is one hundred thousand dollars."

Castle nearly choked on the Bloody Mary Grayle had mixed for him.

"By far the most intriguing and far-reaching issue we considered," Grayle continued, "was that of population. Cutting back our present 274 million population to, say, 50 million would solve nearly every social, political, and economic ill that now afflicts us.

"Think of it, Congressman Castle. Children would again become precious, and family life would be revivified. Our overworked farms would rest and regain their fertility. Pollution would disappear. Tomatoes would taste like tomatoes again, not like cardboard."

"Negative," said Castle emphatically. "I'd lose the Catholics, fundamentalists, Hispanics, and blacks, all in a lump. May I make a suggestion? What about the waste of our mineral resources?" Natural resources was a topic about which Castle was informed, as ranking member of the House Interior and Insular Affairs committee.

"Natural resources *is* an excellent issue. It is the best issue you can have—for your reelection campaign, since the curve of mineral resources exhaustion will peak about 2010. As President, you will be able not only to predict that crisis but have in hand a plan to cope with it, which I will be happy to supply."

"Meanwhile?"

"Meanwhile, Congressman Castle, I believe I heard the rattle of ice cubes. Allow me to refresh your drink."

Castle handed over his glass, wondering when Grayle would get to the point.

Grayle made invisible magic with his decanters and pressed the result into Castle's hand. "Getting impatient, are you, Congressman?"

"Not at all," lied Castle.

"That's good. Because we are on the verge of discovering the *only* crisis that can vault you into the presidency in 2008. Shall we drink to it?"

And about time, too, you old goat, thought David D. Castle to himself. He touched his glass to the other's in the dark.

He drank deeply . . .

He tried to scream, but the pain was too intense. Liquid fire seared his mouth, scorched his tongue, flamed down his esophagus, poured into his stomach like red-hot lava. *The son of a bitch had filled his glass with Tabasco sauce!*

"Water!" he croaked.

"Precisely," said William S. Grayle.

4. TAKEOVER
12 NOVEMBER 2004

"ICE?" ASKED YUSSEF MANSOUR.

Ripley Forte glowered.

Mansour laughed, a remarkably deep and robust laugh from so small a man, and filled the glass with bourbon. Had it not been for ice, in the form of icebergs, neither of them would have been in the main salon of Mansour's 1,600-ton yacht *Linno* to discuss the fate of the Yellow Rose Oil Company. Conferring a silent blessing on ice in all its myriad forms, Mansour dropped a cube into his own glass, added two fingers of Scotch, and smiled over the rim at the Texan.

"Cheers!"

Forte grunted and sampled the bourbon. It was the best. But then, everything about Joe Mansour was the best. Forte put the glass on the spindly little Louis XVI table beside him. He would drink no more, for he needed a clear head.

"I'm flattered that you found my loan request for a mere $300 million important enough to come all the way from Beirut," Forte said.

"I have been following your battle with icebergs for several years, Mr. Forte, and I'm happy for the excuse to make your acquaintance. Besides, Beirut is horribly crowded these days, what with the Russians and Germans and Poles flocking to our beaches and—"

"Beaches?" broke in Forte. "In *November*?"

"Why not? The water along their Baltic beaches in the middle of July is colder than our Mediterranean coast in midwinter." He glanced through the salon's picture window at the howling snowstorm that was sweeping the deck outside and shuddered.

Mansour's delicate gesture seemed to Forte right in character with his rather effeminate appearance. Short and rotund, he was resplendently dressed. His shoes came from his personal shoemaker in Milan, his silk shirts from his shirtmaker in Geneva, his foulards from an artisan in Lyon to designs by Miss Noon, his linen from Madeira, his suits from his tailor in Brussels, his belts from his Seville beltmaker, his hats from his Bond Street hatter.

What Forte failed to appreciate was that Mansour's sartorial elegance was only partly a matter of personal fastidiousness. For Mansour, it was a weapon: he had learned that his splendid attire inspired condescension in his adversaries, who imagined that a man so preoccupied with his appearance could spare little thought for business.

"Well," observed Forte, gesturing toward the driving snow, "as you can see, we sure don't have any shortage of rotten weather here. That, as I explained in detail in the loan application, is all that has been holding up the Yellow Rose Field. During the past twelve months we have had close to fifteen thousand bergs to worry about."

"Really?" said Joe Mansour, arching an eyebrow. "Strange, I thought that twelve thousand was the maximum."

Forte looked sharply at the little Lebanese financier, with his long nose and patent-leather hair. Clearly it would be best not to talk down to Joe Mansour. "Well, you're right, of course. Ten to twelve thousand *is* the usual figure. But for the past three years, a one-and-a-half-degree drop in global temperatures has fouled up rainfall patterns in the entire northern hemisphere, and the number has jumped to around fifteen thousand. If we hadn't thought of using high-speed, high-powered propfan seasleds to drag them away from our rigs, they would have beaten us."

The small Lebanese smiled gently. "They *have* beaten you, Mr. Forte."

"How do you mean?"

"My Phoenicia Holding Company is only one of four international banking consortia that you have approached for loans during the past thirty days. That sounds to me suspiciously like desperation, a last-ditch attempt to stave off ruin."

Forte forced a laugh. "Not desperation—haste. You see, my seasleds have solved the only real problem in extracting Grand Banks oil—icebergs. From here on in, it's smooth sailing. The oil's there. What I need now is financing for the gathering system, a tanker fleet, and certain downstream facilities. Then all I have to do is turn on the tap and watch the money pour in."

"Provided you have the $300 million, that is."

"Yes, sure. But there's no worry about my getting it. Our Grand Banks reserves have proved out at nearly 4 billion barrels. Rigs, tankers, and auxiliary equipment are available. Nearby American markets for sweet crude are getting better every day. No banker in his right mind would turn down a loan request under these conditions. The only area of negotiation is the rate of interest. And since you're the first on the scene, and known for quick decision, I am prepared to be flexible."

"Very good of you, I'm sure," murmured Mansour. He gazed out the window. The snow squall had ended as abruptly as it had begun. The masts and stacks of the other ships that lay at anchor in Argentia Bay stood out starkly against the Newfoundland snowscape. "But according to your credit application, the Fourth First National Bank of Houston, the Bank of Chicago, and Boston Federal all hold your notes totaling more than a billion dollars. If your prospects are so rosy, Mr. Forte, why don't you approach them for the relatively paltry sum you still need to put your field into production? Surely they would be more than happy to advance what you require."

Forte fidgeted in the period chair, which barely contained his spacious frame. He took a pull from the glass of bourbon, held it up to the light, and nodded resignedly.

"I *did* go to those three banks. They turned me down. I still don't know why."

"Maybe they have doubts about your management ability."

"I don't think so. After all, I have brought the company this far, from a standing start to the point where profits are about to take off into the wild blue yonder."

"But what if you—Ripley Forte—were no longer present? I speak of the unpleasant but ever-present possibility of accidents in this hazardous line of work. Where would *that* leave the Yellow Rose Oil Company?"

"Just where it is now—in top-notch shape. I've developed strong, experienced managers in every department. Any one of half a dozen men could replace me tomorrow."

"It's all very puzzling," Joe Mansour observed. "Tell me, what would be the situation if, for any reason, you were unable to negotiate this $300 million loan?"

Forte laughed bitterly. "Nothing, except I'd be wiped out for the third time in my life."

Mansour rose and walked across the big salon. It could have been an elegant eighteenth-century Parisian drawing room, with its Beauvias tapestry and works by Valesquez, Steen, Arthur Frick, and Cezanne on the walls, Boulle cabinet and desk, Louis XVI chairs and tables, Bohemian crystal chandelier, and enormous blood-red Bakhtiari carpet. From the desk he took a pink slip of paper. He handed it to Forte.

It was a bank draft for $300 million, dated this day, November 12, 2004, drawn on the Phoenicia Holding Corporation and payable to the Yellow Rose Oil Company.

Forte inspected it, bit his lip in puzzlement, and put it down on the table next to him. He picked up his drink and sipped it carefully. Bankers didn't do things this way.

"Don't think I don't appreciate your confidence in the Yellow Rose Oil Company," he began, "but it would be more businesslike if we discussed the interest rate and conditions of repayment before I accept this, Mr. Mansour."

"There is no interest. There are no conditions."

"I don't get it. I—"

"When I say there are no conditions, I am not being strictly accurate. In fact, there *is* one condition: that you turn over your responsibilities to any subordinate you select and come work with—observe that I did not say 'for'—me."

Forte pulled his nose and looked at Mansour suspiciously. "Doing what?"

"I will tell you in good time. But first you must have a rest, a vacation, to put yourself in the proper frame of mind to tackle the biggest project in the history of mankind."

"Sounds promising, if a little vague. I don't suppose you could be a bit more specific." Forte frowned thoughtfully as he said this, but actually he felt like laughing out loud at the little man and his pompous "biggest project in the history of mankind."

"I fear I cannot," replied Yussef Mansour, equally serious of mien. "But rest assured, this project will tax your abilities to the utmost, and the rewards will be beyond your wildest expectations. I will arrange for all the necessary financing, and you will have total autonomy in the execution of the project. And we will share the profits equally."

"Uh-huh. But will the government rent us the First Marine Division to knock off Fort Knox?"

Mansour nodded patiently. "Mr. Forte, I analyze everything in which I anticipate involving myself. I have studied this project and determined its feasibility in consultation with some of the most august authorities in the world. And I have studied you, from your days as a junior high school dropout to your present precarious situation as head of the Yellow Rose Oil Company. I know you have a preference for tall women, preferably leggy, dark-eyed, dark-skinned. I know you once beat a foreman half to death for making a remark about your late father's handicap. I know your taste in literature—Gibbon, Orwell, Henry Cecil, J.H. Parry, and Beryl Markham—and in music—Bach, Telemann, Berlioz, and Brahms. I know that you have $331 in your personal checking account as of this morning. And I know that you are going to tell me no—that you built this oil company and that, by God, you're going to run it as you please."

Forte smiled woodenly. "Right. On all counts."

"Wrong. On one. You no longer own the Yellow Rose Oil Company."

"That so?" said Forte, feeling the stirring of premonition in the pit of his stomach. "Then who does?"

"*I* do. I bought your notes—at a premium, I confess—from Boston Federal, the Fourth First National Bank of Houston, and the Bank of Chicago. I likewise bought the 15 million shares outstanding of the Yellow Rose Oil Company which you deposited with those banks as collateral for your long series of loans. Yesterday I took possession of the Yellow Rose as a result of your default in interest. You will receive official notification in the next mail."

Forte rose from his chair, his face suffused.

"You wouldn't do that," he said, his voice tight and menacing. "You say you know all about me. Then you know I'd kill anyone who tried to steal my company, destroy everything I've built these last six years."

"Nevertheless I did," replied Mansour.

Mansour didn't move as Forte advanced across the salon, his hands opening and closing, his eyes a little crazy.

Forte reached down and grabbed Mansour by the neck. With one arm he shoved the little Lebanese up against the bulkhead. He squeezed. A shirt button popped. He squeezed some more, and Mansour's eyes popped. He squeezed harder. Mansour's eyes rolled up, and he passed out.

Forte had never learned to kill a defenseless man. His grip around the man's neck eased, and the little financier crumpled to the floor, his face still cyanotic.

Forte nudged him ungently with the sharp toe of a size-12½ cowboy boot.

"Quit faking and get up, you little son of a bitch. You and me got things to talk about."

5. CHAOS
2 DECEMBER 2004.

ON DECEMBER 2, 2004, CITY TUNNEL NO. 1 COLLAPSED just south of Hillview Reservoir. Supplying Manhattan and the Bronx, it was one of two trunk tunnels funneling water from northern tributaries of the Hudson and Delaware rivers. Together they constituted the five boroughs' sole source of water. And more than half of it had suddenly vanished.

The loss was catastrophic. The system transported 1.7 billion gallons of water daily, enabling each man, woman, and child in New York to use an average of 230 gallons a day. Most went for manufacturing.

The steel in one washing machine took 4,500 gallons to fabricate. The refinery that produced sugar for New Yorkers' morning coffee gulped down 4,000,000 gallons per day. A ton of cement required 1,125 gallons. A cannery used 10 gallons for each can of beans or corn produced. The paper in the Bible, took 185,000 gallons per ton to manufacture. The rayon in an ordinary living room carpet cost 50,000 gallons to synthesize. A single plant that brewed beer gulped down 15,000,000 gallons a day.

In homes, a five-minute shower consumed 12 gallons, ten minutes of lawn watering 100 gallons. A total of 90 gallons a day flowed through the average family's faucets. That same family of four consumed twenty-four pounds of food daily, but the food itself cost 3,200 gallons—thirteen tons—of water to grow. That was enough to fill the backyard swimming pool every day.

The collapse of City Tunnel No. 1 was no accident, the result of the explosion of a ten-kilo charge of TNT. The previously unknown Freedom for Puerto Rico Militant Action Group claimed responsibility. City engineers estimated that it would take at least ten days before the flow could be fully restored.

Mayor Nancy Meyer immediately convened an emergency meeting of the city council. She proposed, and it ratified, draconian measures to ensure that Manhattan and the Bronx would survive with minimum inconvenience. Car washes were shut down. Block watches were organized for early detection of fires, cutting down on the use of water by the fire companies. Manufacturers were ordered to recycle water when possible. In the Bronx and Manhattan water was rationed—what water was available trickled in from cross conduits linking City Tunnel No. 1 with City Tunnel No. 2, serving Brooklyn, Queens, and Staten Island. Homes and apartments were limited to thirty-minutes of water daily.

Rationing meant an end to steam heating. Temperatures in apartments all over Manhattan and the Bronx fell below freezing, only a few degrees above the bitter cold outside. Water pipes froze and burst. Huddled beneath bedclothes to stave off the freezing cold, New Yorkers upon whom their fellow citizens were dependent for food, transportation, and other essential services called in sick. The streets were half empty, the roar of city traffic stilled, and an air of desperation settled over the city.

A brownout was decreed: Consolidated Edison's coal-powered electricity-generating facilities alone used up nine hundred gallons of water for every kilowatt hour of energy produced. This water could no longer be spared.

At night the city was dark, as if war had come. The use of cars was forbidden to all but physicians and emergency workers, and those of violators were confiscated. To conserve electricity, elevators were run for but five minutes every hour. Unused to such hardships, during the next five days an estimated 470,000 New Yorkers decided

to take their Christmas vacations early. Since many were
professionals and executives around whom much of New
York's economic life revolved, business in Manhattan
ground almost to a standstill.

On December 9, 2004, catastrophe became chaos: at
2 A.M., City Tunnel No. 2 was blown up.

The detonation slightly injured two New York national
guardsmen of the four thousand called up by New York's
governor to patrol the length of the pipeline, the shores
of the larger reservoirs, the banks of the tributaries, pumping plants and water treatment facilities, and the electric
generation grid supplying power to bring water into the
city.

Water, which before December 2 had been so taken
for granted that it wasn't even metered by the municipality—billing was on the basis of the street frontage a
building occupied—suddenly became a valued commod-
ity. During the first week, the price of water rose from
twenty-five cents to a dollar a gallon. The watershed, so
to speak, came after the second explosion, when quarts,
not gallons, became the medium of exchange—and the
price of a quart ranged from one to three dollars.

Providentially, snow blanketed the streets on December 11. In most places it didn't last long enough to turn
to slush. The city dwellers scooped up the stuff by the
shovelful, potful, even spoonful, and rushed indoors to
melt it on kitchen stoves and before fireplaces.

All traffic into the city was halted except for vehicles
carrying food, emergency supplies for hospitals, and water,
brought in by tank truck from as far away as Wilmington,
Delaware. Supplies were dispensed—at first free, then
for one dollar a gallon, one gallon per customer—on a
first-come, first-served basis. Tank trucks were stationed
at principal intersections throughout the city. Pressed
against the walls of buildings to shelter from the wind and
snow, the queues were reminiscent of breadlines in Soviet
Russia. Some entrepreneurs made queuing and water
scalping a full-time occupation. The price per scalped gallon shot to a high of $23 around Wall Street, and those
who managed to stand up to eighteen hours a day in line
were making more money than stockbrokers.

Others drove to neighboring cities, brought back cases of Clorox, and went into the business of disinfecting water from the Hudson or East rivers and selling it by the jerry can.

As great as was the turmoil in the city, the country scarcely noticed it amid the convulsions that had seized Wall Street and America's other financial markets. The exodus from New York had included so many brokers, financiers, bankers, and computer operators that the financial center had virtually ceased to function. At the Chicago, San Francisco, and lesser exchanges, the disaster had been a signal to unload one's holdings at any price, for if Wall Street went down in flames, the heat would consume all other American financial institutions along with it. The panic quickly spread to foreign markets. There American shares tumbled, the dollar fell to its lowest value in thirty-seven years, and the price of gold went over the moon.

Americans who first dismissed New York's plight as a local affair, and in fact welcomed the misfortune that had brought the proud city to its knees, rejoiced but briefly. They found that their checks were no longer honored; checks had to be cleared through the banking system's clearinghouse in New York City. Credit cards likewise became worthless, and when cash ran out, citizens across the land were reduced to barter. Economic life became a shambles, and in its train came the usual consequences: a breakdown in public order, a precipitate rise in robbery, theft, random brutality, rape, and looting.

Meanwhile, in the city itself, the incidence of communicable disease soared, and diarrhea became endemic. Hepatitis and cholera were also reported with increasing frequency, and dehydration became the most common cause of death among infants and the aged.

The epidemic scare caused a new stampede. Terminals were jammed with the panic-driven. Limited to one suitcase per person, passengers abandoned other belongings, created fast-rising mountains of luggage beside which foresaken children whimpered for parents who in the confusion sometimes lost them forever.

Soon the streets were crammed with cars crawling

bumper to bumper as their owners joined the hegira to any city or village with a water supply of its own. Bridges, tunnels, sidewalks, and footpaths were clogged with fleeing New Yorkers.

New York's fast-dwindling population was learning the meaning of anarchy. Police and firemen had joined in the general flight, leaving lawlessness in their wake. The mobs that attacked and ransacked warehouses where Clorox was thought to be stored were only the harbinger of widespread looting and violence.

Fires raged unchecked. Whole city blocks were consumed as the few remaining firemen, unable to reach fires through stalled traffic, watched helplessly from afar.

It was the New York National Guard that, descending upon the city in tanks and armored personnel carriers, began the immense task of bringing order to the city, fighting fires, shooting looters, and providing emergency services to the old, the afflicted, and the solitary.

The men in uniform blasted whole city blocks into rubble as firebreaks. Gas lines that had fueled the conflagration were shut down. By and by, the menace of fires burning out of control diminished, and the clouds of greasy black smoke that covered the city like an imam's robe began to dissipate.

By Christmas Day 2004, the City of New York was a city of devastation. Whole sections had been destroyed by fire. Streets were littered with burned-out cars and sidewalks with shattered furniture, television sets and children's toys, garbage, and waste paper. And here and there a huddled lifeless body testified to the ferocity of what had become a savage civil war.

6. HEARINGS
4 JANUARY 2005

"I CALL AS FIRST WITNESS DR. CARL GARBOLOTTI."

A husky man with a thatch of reddish hair and a bushy guardsman's mustache took his oath and a seat at the witness table.

"Would you state in what capacity you appear before the House Interior and Insular Affairs Committee, Dr. Garbolotti?"

"I am testifying as chief hydrologist of the Interior Department's Office of Land and Water Resources, Mr. Chairman."

"Do you wish to make an introductory statement?"

"In view of the widespread media coverage of the catastrophe which has befallen New York City, sir, I think it is by now common knowledge that the United States is facing water problems of gargantuan dimensions, so perhaps my testimony can be most useful in supplying specifics."

Congressman Castle nodded, making sure that his eyes did not meet the banks of television cameras clustered at the rear of the committee room. It was his first appearance on all four national networks simultaneously, and he must take care, as William S. Grayle had cautioned him, to project an image of calm, confidence, and control. Grayle had provided Castle and his witness with detailed scripts, which they had thoroughly digested but not memorized in order to preserve the illusion of spontaneity.

"Very well, sir," said Castle. "Of all the water problems that face the nation today, which would you characterize as the most pressing?"

"No question about it, that would have to be the exhaustion of the Ogallala aquifer."

"Kindly explain that, Dr. Garbolotti, in words a layman like me can understand."

Garbolotti studied his thumbnail.

"To start with, an aquifer is sort of nature's underground water reservoir, made mostly of limestones, sands, and gravels. This mixture is porous, and the interstices fill with water filtering down through the soil."

"Water from rains?"

"Rains or runoff. This water can be withdrawn by means of wells, drilled or dug. Now, a few million years ago when the Rockies were as high as today's Himalayas, the Ogallala was a vast alluvial plain created by silt runoff from the Rockies to the west. Rains and snows and glacier melt fed this plain. For thousands of years this plain, which today underlies the Republic of Texas panhandle northward through Oklahoma, Kansas, western Colorado, Nebraska, and southern South Dakota, soaked up water. During the next few million years, the plain was covered by a couple of hundred feet of soil deposits. Meanwhile, weather patterns changed. Rainfall dropped to less than thirty inches a year, sufficient for grass to support herds of antelope and buffalo but not enough for anything except subsistence farming.

"Then, late in the nineteenth century, sodbusting pioneers drilled wells and found water under that parched land. There was, in fact, a quadrillion—a million billion—gallons of it. They watered their stock, and irrigated their fields, on a small scale. But it wasn't until after the great drought of the 1930s that they began to mine this fossil water in a big way."

"Mine, you say?"

"To mine is to extract a nonreplenishable resource such as coal, iron, or water from the earth."

"But surely, rains replenish the Ogallala's—ah—fossil water."

"Unfortunately, very little. The Ogallala is capped with a layer of impermeable stone, and rains run off it right into the sea, along with huge quantities of topsoil. Its farmers have made the plains states the granary of the world, but the day is soon coming when the water will be gone, and the great plains will become a new dust bowl, this time for perhaps another million years."

"But that's, that's—"

"—a fact, sir. It's a disagreeable fact our farmers and the government that props up farm prices have known for years but refused to face. Back in the 1970s, hydrologists estimated that at the then-current depletion rates, the Ogallala will be dry by the year 2020."

"Surely things can't be *that* bad," protested the chairman.

"I'm giving you facts," said Dr. Garbolotti stubbornly. "If you want fiction, call in the economists."

"But what are the alternatives? Surely there must be some alternative to the depression you are forecasting."

"Not until we find new sources of irrigation water."

"And where will we find it?"

"I don't know. At present there aren't any."

The next day Congressman Castle called Assistant Secretary of the Interior for Land and Water Resources Jacob Jonas.

"Do you agree with Dr. Garbolotti's pessimistic vision of the future for the great plains, Mr. Jonas?" he asked.

Mr. Jonas removed his glasses and made a show of polishing the lenses. He smiled deprecatingly.

"Dr. Garbolotti sometimes gets carried away, Congressman. Actually, two projects, both eminently sound, are waiting only for congressional sanction and funding to solve this problem."

"Would you kindly describe them for the committee?"

Jonas pushed his glasses onto his balding forehead and opened a file.

"Alternative one proposes a series of canals, lined and covered to minimize losses through seepage and evaporation. They will be constructed by the Corps of Engineers from the headwaters of the Arkansas, Platte, Missouri, and Mississippi rivers to distribute those waters among the plains states. A favorable gradient would allow the water to flow southward and eastward by gravity; unfortunately, that gradient does not exist. Therefore, tunnels will have to be blasted through the intervening Rocky Mountains, intermediate reservoirs excavated, and pumping stations installed to raise the water to higher levels."

"How long would these canals be?"

"The shortest is 375 miles; the longest, 1,140."

"And the diameter of these tunnels and canals?"

"The canals will vary according to terrain and subsoil," said Mr. Jonas, "but the tunnels will be on the order of six meters in diameter."

"And the cost, in time and dollars?"

Jonas hesitated. As a high-echelon bureaucrat, he felt himself above such grubby details. He consulted his notes.

"Well, Congressman, this is a long-standing proposal. Back in 1970, cost estimates ranged from $3.6 to $22.6 billion. Today, thirty-five years later, because of inflation we would have to multiply the figures by nine, to the $160 to $200 billion range. If done on a crash basis, it would take twelve years."

"By which time," said Castle curtly, "the Midwest would become a new dust bowl."

"That, sir, is a matter of opinion. I myself—"

"You mentioned a second alternative."

"Yes, sir. NAWAPA."

"I beg your pardon?"

"NAWAPA: the North American Water and Power Alliance. This is a plan to use water, *currently completely wasted*, for irrigating the Midwest."

"That sounds promising. I wasn't aware any such water existed."

"Indeed it does, and this project to utilize it was first conceived back in the 1950s. The idea is to reverse the flow of rivers emptying into the polar seas, where it benefits no one."

"That is very imaginative, Mr. Jonas, but will it work?"

"Yes, Congressman Castle, it will, for it has already been done on a limited scale by the Russians, to irrigate their virgin lands. We propose a similar—"

"And how did the Russian project work out, Mr. Jonas?"

Jonas hesitated.

"Well, actually, there were a few snags."

"Such as?"

"For one thing, the Caspian Sea level has fallen because its historic sources were diverted."

"You mean it has dried up?"

"Well, not completely."

"You're saying, I believe," persisted the chairman, "that the Russians have destroyed the largest body of fresh water on earth and that we should follow their example."

"No, no," said Jonas, beads of sweat appearing on his upper lip. "We intend, naturally, to avoid their mistakes."

"Details," snapped Castle. "Details, Mr. Jonas."

"Yes, sir. Above the fifty-fifth parallel the Mackenzie, the Yukon, the Coppermine, and many other rivers empty into the Beaufort Sea in the Canadian Arctic. NAWAPA proposes to preserve these waters for mankind by means of a series of great dams, thus reclaiming some 36 trillion gallons of sweet water a year. Think of it—an amount equivalent to 6,000 gallons for every man, woman, and child on earth."

"Remarkable," said Castle dryly. "You will dam those rivers, then?"

"Exactly. The impounded waters will then be piped southward to create a reservoir five hundred miles long in northeastern British Columbia by damming both ends of the Rocky Mountain Trench."

"Canada gets the water?"

"Only a small portion. We pay for the project, we get the lion's share."

"How, pray tell? Between British Columbia and the plains states are Idaho and the Rocky Mountains. How do you propose to get the water over the mountains—by siphons?"

"Very shrewd of you to suggest it," said Jonas with an ingratiating smile. "Actually, though, a more feasible method is to drill a tunnel through the Rockies."

"The tunnel's dimensions?"

"Nothing the Corps of Engineers can't take in its stride, I can assure you."

"Assure me with numbers."

"The tunnel will be eighty feet in diameter and fifty miles long."

"Which is to say, the diameter of this committee room

and as long as the distance from here to Baltimore."

"Yes, sir."

"Requiring the removal—correct me if I'm wrong—of more than 1.3 billion cubic feet of solid rock?"

"I, uh, think that is substantially correct," said Jonas, his confidence ebbing fast.

"Through mountains charged with uncharted springs under high pressure, which if breached during drilling could flood the works instantly, killing hundreds?"

"Well, sir, as to that, I—"

"Go on, Mr. Jonas. What happens next, if our hundreds of workmen survive drowning?"

"The emerging waters," said Jonas hastily, "are channeled to the Great Lakes for distribution where needed and to the Missouri River, from which they can be withdrawn downstream."

"How very neat! And what will be the cost to the taxpayer of this little adventure in civil engineering?"

"I—ah—it is hard to compute, given the inflation over thirty years. I—"

"Let me help you," said Congressman Castle with a mongoose smile. "Would you say, for example, $900 billion, in round figures?"

Jonas mumbled something.

"Speak up, Mr. Jonas. We didn't hear your answer."

"I said," replied the miserable Jonas, "that that would be pretty close."

"In other words, an amount equivalent to our total social service expenditure for two years. On the other hand, we are buying a tremendous quantity of water, aren't we? Thirty-six trillion gallons a year I believe you said."

Jonas brightened. "Yes, it can supply six thousand gallons to—"

"—every man, woman, and child in the world. True, and Dr. Garbolotti told us that in 1964, 36 trillion gallons would have sufficed for our national needs for four months. But during the intervening forty years, as a result of the explosive growth of our population, manufacturing, and agriculture, water use has increased by a factor of seventeen—I'm quoting figures from your department, Mr.

Jonas. Now the question is this: How many days will
NAWAPA's new water suffice for the United States,
today?"

Mr. Jonas cursed Castle under his breath.

"Seven," he answered between clenched teeth.

"Therefore," said Castle, smiling wickedly, "we must
expend $900 billion and the labor of whole regiments of
men for two decades, we must transform the geography
of North America, we must dislocate whole populations,
and wreck the environment of the entire Midwest. And
at the end of all this, we gain *one week's* supply of water.
Is that the way you see it, Mr. Jonas?"

It wasn't, but Jonas hadn't gotten where he was by
contradicting congressmen.

"Something like that," he compromised.

"The committee thanks you for your candor, Mr.
Jonas," said Congressman Castle.

He banged his gavel.

"This session stands recessed until two o'clock this
afternoon."

Minutes before he was due to resume the hearings,
Congressman Castle received a telephone call from William S. Grayle.

"Have you heard the news?" said the sepulchral voice.

"What news?"

"If you don't know, you obviously haven't heard it.
You have a certain Delia Ann Mukhaiber scheduled to
testify at two o'clock, I believe?"

"Yes."

"Cancel her appearance and call Professor Scott Randolph."

"Who's he?"

"Oh, of course, you don't know. Well, he's the man
you're going to call," said Grayle, ringing off.

Another of Grayle's simpleminded jokes, thought Castle angrily, but knew better than to ignore his consultant's
instructions. So far they had worked perfectly. The hearings had gone smoothly, the press was unanimous in praise
of his handling of this complicated issue, and according
to the television polls, an unprecedented 24 percent of

the viewing public was tuning in to this public service program, nearly as many as were following *The Guiding Light*.

"I call Professor Scott Randolph," said Chairman Castle as the committee settled into its chairs shortly after two o'clock.

Professor Randolph, a very tall man with an air of amiable, scholary distraction, was sworn and took his place at the witness table.

"Professor Randolph, since some of the viewers of these proceedings may not be as informed of your brilliant accomplishments as we, perhaps you'd be good enough to tell us a little of your background."

"Distinguished Professor, particle physics, Stanford. Ten years' study of effect of human activity on stratospheric ozone layer. President, PTA, Palo Alto. California high jump champion, 1966. Oh, yes, Nobel Prize in chemistry, 1989."

Castle looked at him blankly, none the wiser for the professor's burst of telegraphese. Then he recalled Grayle's words.

"But it's the implications of the latest news that brings you here today, is it not, Professor?"

"Right."

Castle smiled and relaxed.

"Then perhaps you'll tell us all about it, in your own manner. From the beginning."

"August 2002?"

"Yes," said Castle confidently. "Not everyone will recall the background."

"True. August 15, 2002. Mount Kharjak blows top in Russian Kazakhstan. Five point five on Richter scale. United States yawns. Everybody forgets quick. Remember Krakatoa?"

"How forget?" said Castle, getting the hang of the language but wondering whether Krakatoa was an exotic tropical plant or the latest dance rage.

"Krakatoa. Javan volcano. Put up six cubic miles of fine dust in 1883, not so? Cloud envelopes earth for three years, cutting solar radiation. Kharjak no Krakatoa—then. But *second* explosion today equivalent to *five* Krakatoas.

Sound waves shatters windows in Moscow, tsunami—tidal wave—created in Mediterranean. Maybe wipe out Alexandria, Naples, Barcelona, Marseilles."

"Frightful!" acknowledged Castle. "But what will be the effect on the United States, Professor?"

"Frightful squared. Forty cubic miles of stratospheric dust. Ten years to settle. Solar radiation reduced in high latitudes by order of magnitude. Cooler ocean surfaces, less evaporation. Less evaporation, fewer clouds. Fewer clouds, less rainfall. Rivers and streams dry up. Meanwhile, less sunlight, reduced photosynthesis, less plant life. Synergism of reduced sunlight and reduced rainfall—catastrophic for food supply."

"Are you telling this committee, Professor," said Castle, the implications of his words sinking in, "that we're facing an imminent worldwide food shortage?"

"Yes."

"Many will starve?"

"Yes."

"Millions?"

"*Billions.*"

"But surely something can be done."

"Yes. Vastly increase water supply. Compensate for diminished rainfall. Only way to go."

"But that's impossible. You heard the past four weeks of testimony, didn't you, Professor?"

"Every word."

"Then you'll agree there just isn't any practicable way to increase the water supply."

"Not just no *practical* way—no way at all."

7. TURNBULL
11 FEBRUARY 2005

"BUT I'M TELLING YOU, MR. PRESIDENT, THE SON OF A bitch is killing us."

"Now, now, Pat," said Horatio Francis Turnbull soothingly, "don't panic. It's forty-five months to election day. Castle will run out of gas long before then."

Pat Benson, the President's national affairs adviser, shook his head glumly. "I wish I could believe that, Mr. President. I've been out in the hustings these past ten days, and never in thirty-eight years of taking the public's pulse have I witnessed such honest-to-God hysteria."

"Relax, Pat. You'll think of something. You always do."

The President tilted back in his tall leather chair and put his feet on the desk. He lit a nine-inch Emperador and silently commended his sagacity in repealing the embargo on Cuban tobacco. He was content. How many men could put their feet on a desk once owned by Abraham Lincoln, enjoy an unlimited supply of the world's best hand-rolled cigars, and have the fate of the nation in the palm of their hand—not to mention the undivided attention of a man like Dr. Sidney Bussek, lately the eminent chancellor of the University of Southern California, silently awaiting an invitation to speak?

President Turnball turned to his scientific adviser and smiled. "How about it, Sid—don't you think Pat is getting his bowels in an uproar over nothing?"

"On the contrary." Sidney Bussek was a tall man clad in black who looked rather like a professional mourner. "Congressman Castle is scaring the public witless. He tells them that the population bomb is about to blow up our water supply and implies that this crime must be laid at the door of the last four or five Republican administrations. He trumpets the dangers to our rivers of raw

41

sewage and industrial toxins and thermal pollution. He piles statistic on statistic—how it takes fifteen thousand gallons of water to irrigate the land to grow a bushel of wheat, four thousand gallons to produce a brace of chicken eggs for breakfast, and so on and so forth. But before scientific commentators can put into perspective those scare headlines Castle produces day after day, he hits us with new ones. I agree with Ben: The man's a menace. If we don't do something soon, he could be real trouble."

"What do you suggest?" said President Turnbull, adjusting his handsome features into an expression of concern.

Horatio Frances Turnbull looked the way a president should look. He was tall, substantially built, and ruddy-faced, with the silver mane of an antebellum southern senator. He had a pleasing baritone voice, the gift of sounding as if he were confiding a secret to a valued friend even when addressing an audience of thousands, and a patent sincerity of manner that won him friends and elections. He did not, it was true, adhere to any fixed principles but cast his vote with the majority, on the indisputably democratic premise that the majority is always right. Advice was a nuisance he endured: It made his associates happy, and Turnball liked to see happy faces around him. But when it came to political decisions, he relied on instinct, and it had never failed him yet. So he would listen to Dr. Sidney Bussek with attention, as he listened to all his advisers, and do precisely as his instincts had told him to do all along.

"That there *is* a water crisis," said Dr. Bussek, "cannot be denied. But a variety of simple measures can alleviate it. Every American could start in his own home, for example, and reduce water consumption by 50 percent by such simple means as putting a couple of bricks in the toilet's water closet. That would save 2.5 billion gallons a day. Installing the Clivus Multram composting toilet, a Swedish invention of thirty years ago which uses no water at all, would save 4.2 billion gallons."

"Forget toilets," said Pat Benson emphatically. "People don't vote for toilets."

"Tell you what you do, Sid," broke in President Turnbull. "Write me up a memo and lay it all out. Give me the problems, the solutions, their drawbacks and advantages, the time it will all take, what new agencies we'll need to create, if any, the people we should recruit to handle it, what political interests we've got to avoid alienating in the process—that sort of thing. Give it to me in the usual form—one page. Tomorrow."

He lowered his feet to the floor and rose. "I want to thank you for dropping in, Sid. I hope you'll make it a habit, because I need somebody to lean on I can trust in this era of rapid technological progress. Ben here is good in getting out the vote, but he can't tell a hawk from a handsaw."

He saw the two men out the door, massaging Dr. Bussek's arm as he went, considered a sure sign of personal regard by President watchers, and returned to his desk. He sat down in the big leather chair, folded his hands behind his head, and regarded the ceiling. He chuckled.

"Come on in, Mr. Grayle," he said.

The door opposite that through which his aides had just departed opened, and William S. Grayle entered. He was a tall, spare man with abundant wavy gray hair, a luxuriant gray beard, and dark glasses that obscured the rest of his face. He walked slowly and carefully, his steps rationed by old age.

"Did you hear?" said President Turnbull, coming around the desk to hold the chair for his guest.

"I heard."

"What do you think?"

"They suspect nothing."

"Exactly," said the President, nodding vigorously as he returned to his desk. "And if Pat suspects nothing, then *nobody* suspects nothing—anything. Well, Mr. Grayle, what now?"

Grayle stroked his beard with his gloved hand. "We let nature take its course. We're right on schedule. During the next three sessions, the committee will deal with ways, mostly visionary, to augment the nation's water supply. Castle will quite properly reject them all as too little, too late, or impractical. Only one possibility remains, he will intimate. And on that note he will adjourn the hearings to give a little time for public suspense to build up.

"When it peaks in about ten days, Castle will hold a

televised press conference. He will announce the solution to America's water problem."

"Beautiful," said the President, his eyes alight with admiration for the astuteness of William S. Grayle, who had quietly emerged from retirement recently with a scheme to guarantee his, Horatio Francis Turnbull's, reelection in 2008.

The plan was going to cost the Republican National Committee dear but would be worth every penny. Known only to Turnbull himself, Grayle's plan guaranteed that during the next four years, Congressman David D. Castle would receive so much favorable news coverage and deal with the nation's gravest crisis with such vigor and imagination that by convention time all other contenders for the Democratic nomination in 2008 would be steamrollered into obscurity. It was, as Turnbull admitted, a great plan. With David D. Castle as Democratic nominee, Turnbull could not possibly lose. Unless...

"But what if—" he began, a frown clouding his face.

"—Castle *does* succeed in bringing an iceberg into San Francisco Bay?" said Grayle. "If he does, he wins by a landslide, of course. But no, the drums will beat and the banners will wave until, just before convention time, it will become apparent that he has failed miserably. And you'll sail into office for a second term."

"Yes, yes," said Turnbull. "But if he *does* succeed?"

"Impossible. The California Current will defeat him. Castle doesn't have the chance of a snowball in Hades. *Nobody* does. Castle is living in a dream world."

8. HAMBURGER
22 FEBRUARY 2005

OUTSIDE THE HALLS OF CONGRESS THE AIR WAS COLD and dry, but inside, in the House Interior and Insular Affairs committee room, the atmosphere was hot and steamy, charged with the sweat and exhalations of some two hundred press and television reporters. Since 8 P.M. they had been jostling and shoving to get vantage points for Congressman Castle's press conference, which would be heard and seen by an estimated 145 million Americans.

At two minutes before nine, Congressman David D. Castle made his entrance and mounted the podium. He was dressed in black, and his expression was grave. He was alone and without notes.

At exactly nine o'clock, the red on-the-air lights blinked on above the lenses of a dozen television cameras, and the sober countenance of the representative from California's Sixth District appeared on 50 million screens.

"Fellow Americans," he began in a warm conversational tone, "on the way home at night after work I often stopped for a hamburger. No more. Why not? Well, in the hearings I have conducted during the past two months I have learned many things. I learned, for instance, that in addition to the flour that makes the bun, it takes nearly a bushel of wheat to produce the meat that goes into the hamburger itself. Some farmer in the Midwest expended twenty-two minutes to harvest that wheat, along with 655 grams of fertilizer and 15,000 gallons of water from aquifers that will not be replenished for another 10 million years. In effect, I was consuming a bushel of wheat and 15,000 gallons of water to wash it down. It was too much. I lost my appetite for hamburger.

"The hearings have been about our waste of water. There's a shortage. It is real, it is serious, and it is upon us. Solutions were proposed. They include conservation and redistribution of our present supplies and the creation of new sources through seawater distillation, reverse osmosis, reversing the flow of Arctic rivers, seeding the clouds with iodine crystals, and so on. All involve enormous expenditures and frightening environmental risks. We cannot afford to experiment with these new monsters, for experience proves they are more likely to destroy than to serve us.

"One solution remains. It is untried, but it is wholly feasible. It will provide the purest water in the world in unlimited quantities. It will be costly, but the cost is but a fraction of that of such environmental calamities as the North American Water and Power Alliance scheme and negligible compared with the alternative: chronic thirst, economic disaster, defenselessness against foreign aggression, and massive suffering.

"That solution is icebergs."

A murmur of surprise and disappointment rose from the assembled press. The iceberg idea had been kicking around since the 1970s, when Saudi Arabia's Prince Mohammed Feisal had launched a company to bring Antarctic icebergs to his waterless kingdom. But the scheme had foundered on the rocks of primitive technology, poor administration, and inadequate financing.

"That was exactly *my* reaction," said Castle grimly as the murmur subsided, "when I first heard of iceberg transport. But the facts, ladies and gentlemen—the facts are too compelling to ignore. Allow me to share some of them with you.

"The Antarctic is the world's fifth largest continent, at 5.5 million square miles almost double the size of the United States. It's a vast plateau averaging 7,500 feet above sea level. The uppermost 6,500 feet, containing seven million cubic miles, is almost solid ice. If melted, the water would equal the flow of the Mississippi for 46,000 years. If melted, it could provide the United States with water everlasting.

"But how do we get it here to melt? The answer is, we tow it, one iceberg at a time, as we tow a river barge. But before we hitch it to our tugboat, let's go back to the Antarctic uplands where those icebergs are born for a closer look.

"There, little snow falls. It amounts to only two inches a year, barely a third the precipitation that falls on, for example, Phoenix, Arizona. Compacted by its own weight over the years, the slow accumulation of snow turns to ice in temperatures that go down to more than −120 degrees Fahrenheit. Almost imperceptibly, sometimes at a rate of only inches per year, the huge mass flows downhill toward the sea as a river of ice. The glacier's journey to the sea may take up to 20,000 years. Along the way, high-velocity winds smooth its irregularities and plane it flat. It moves out inexorably across the face of the sea, until at last the wave motion of the turbulent sea boiling beneath it breaks off chunks of ice, and the new-born icebergs float away.

"They can be huge. In the late 1970s a 768-square-mile iceberg was sighted off the tip of South America. On November 12, 1956, the U.S.S. *Glacier* spotted a berg west of Scott Island in the Pacific; its area was an estimated 12,000 square miles, twice the size of Massachusetts. Ten thousand icebergs a year calve from five main ice shelves. Caught in the cold Circumpolar Current, they may survive for up to seven years, until warmer water melts them away, their superlatively pure water lost to the salty sea.

"Science can save these icebergs for us, bring them to our shores, and revitalize America. A single iceberg of optimum transportable size, that is, two kilometers long by one kilometer wide and one-fifth of a kilometer thick, contains a billion tons of water. That amount would supply every inhabitant of Manhattan, for instance, with water for his domestic needs for six years. Icebergs brought to our shores on a continuous basis would revive American agriculture and industry and lead us into a new era of national prosperity."

Castle paused and looked around the room at a sea of disbelieving faces. Somewhere a snicker was heard, then a cynical chuckle. Laughter rippled through the room.

Castle colored but managed to maintain his aplomb. He pulled a handkerchief from his pocket and wiped his brow.

"I, too, was a skeptic," he said when the laughter subsided. "But once it was made clear to me that there was no other alternative, I consulted leading authorities around the world: glaciologists, computer experts, ocean engineers, mathematicians, mechanical engineers, ship masters, hydrologists, and experts from dozens of other disciplines. They have provided evidence—*incontrovertible* evidence—that iceberg transport from the Antarctic to America is not only possible but practical. Furthermore, it will be economically feasible once the iceberg pipeline is filled, compared with the present costs of irrigation and industrial water—water which, I need not remind you, is scarcer, more polluted, and more costly every day."

He paused and looked out beyond the glaring lights into the phalanx of unconvinced reporters in the crowded chamber.

"This conclusion, ladies and gentlemen, is the verdict of science, based on some seven weeks of hearings by this committee. I know you will have some questions. I shall do my best to answer them."

A babel of shouting rose from the floor.

For the next hour and a half, as the klieg lights blazed hot and a steady barrage of questions rained down upon him, Castle, with cool logic, defended the accuracy of the report.

He was still going strong when, just before eleven, a flying wedge of Secret Service men plowed through the pack of reporters at the rear of the committee room. Behind them, grinning broadly, came the President of the United States.

Only momentarily at a loss, Castle descended from the podium and warmly grasped President Turnbull's outstretched hand. Concealing his ire beneath a deferential welcoming smile, he escorted the chief executive up the three steps to the bank of microphones.

It was obvious to the assembled media that President Turnbull had come to defuse Castle's rocket before it got off the ground. He would trot out some old nostrum, perhaps water desalinization with solar power or even plain conservation, to divert attention from Castle's scheme.

Such thoughts paraded through the cynical minds of those present as David D. Castle cleared his throat.

"Ladies and gentlemen," he said, "we are flattered and honored by the unscheduled appearance of the chief executive of the United States. It is obvious that he shares with all of us here a concern for our nation's plight, and like us invokes the intervention of the Lord so eloquently expressed in the Psalm,

'Oh God, thou art my God; early will I seek thee;

    my soul thirsteth for thee, my flesh longeth for thee
    in a dry and thirsty land, where no water is . . .'"

—let the old coot try to top *that*!—"to favor us with a
solution to this problem. I confidently expect he will now
present it to us, as I now present to you—the President
of the United States."

The chamber reverberated with applause. Castle nodded graciously, content to believe that it was for his adroit
volley of the water crisis into Turnbull's court.

The President, doubting not that the applause was for
him, raised his hands in the politician's victory salute and
stepped up to the microphones.

"I thank Congressman Castle for his kind words," said
the President, "and I thank him doubly for invoking the
name of the Lord. His reference is a reminder that, as
the Germans say, 'God does not give to all alike; to one
He gives the goose, and to another the egg.' In the matter
of water, in these first years of this century, as we all
know, He, in His infinite wisdom, has given us a little of
both: the goose egg.

"This evening, Congressman Castle has given us something else: an example—and hope. While the rest of us
were blithely oblivious of the gathering black clouds of
national disaster, the honorable gentleman from California
was measuring its awesome dimensions and implications
and sounding the alarm in this committee room.

"From the evidence he has presented this evening, it
appears that miracles have not yet ceased, that he has
indeed discovered the thread which will lead us out of
the Minotaur's labyrinth onto the vast plains of national
prosperity. So far, however, we have only the hope of
victory. Hard work, imagination, money, dedication, and
luck will be required to achieve our goal. Above all, leadership of the highest order will be needed to guide this
vast national enterprise to success.

"To this end, tomorrow I will submit to the Congress
draft legislation for the immediate establishment of a
Department of Water Resources."

Castle suddenly felt faint and put his hand on the edge
of the lectern to steady himself. He had neglected to con-

sider the possibility that Turnbull might go *along* with his proposal, steal the whole idea and make it his own, and freeze him right out of the picture. The hundreds of hours in the public eye, the millions spent for Grayle's services, the long sleepless nights rehearsing his lines, the dream of becoming President—all in vain.

He felt the President's arm around his shoulder. He could feel it coming—the Judas kiss. The old bastard was going to thank him on behalf of the nation and laud his true bipartisan spirit, or some such guff. He smiled through gritted teeth and swore he would somehow, someday make the old man pay.

"I am sure everyone will agree," the President was saying, "that there can be only one leader for this monumental project: the Honorable David D. Castle, Congressman from California."

9. JENNIFER RED CLOUD
24 FEBRUARY 2005

AS FAR AS THE EX-MARINE SECURITY GUARD IN THE SENtry tower could discern through his ten-power binoculars, Jennifer Red Cloud was without blemish. As she lay naked in the sun, her copper-hued skin seemed as soft as the feathery breeze that floated in off Montego Bay, her contours as smooth as the undulating hills beyond his eyrie, her hair sleek and lustrous, like that of a black panther at midnight.

He adjusted the focus and wondered what a woman like Jennifer Red Cloud would be thinking about. With a body like that, it could only be sex.

Jennifer Red Cloud was thinking about ocean thermal energy conversion. The theory was simple enough even for someone of her limited scientific training. The difference in temperature between warm surface waters of the ocean and cold waters of the depths was harnessed to drive a closed evaporation-condensation cycle and so generate electricity, like a refrigerator working in reverse. The warm surface waters contained enough heat to vaporize a compound such as ammonia. Then cold bottom waters would be pumped up to condense the vapor, to be cycled through evaporators using the warm waters to drive turbines linked to banks of generators.

Or something. She was a bit hazy about the details, but then, that was what engineers were for. More immediately important were the questions of scale and geography. Where ocean warm-surface–cold-bottom conditions prevailed, as in the midocean tropics, there were obviously no customers for electricity, or anything else. In coastal climes markets were abundant, but the water-temperature differentials were too small unless the OTEC facilities were huge, which made them noncompetitive with nuclear- or fossil-fuel-generated electricity.

With this in mind, her board of directors had strongly advised against the purchase of Sea Exploration and Development's OTEC patents and factories. Jennifer Red Cloud's instincts told her to ignore the counsel. She seldom argued with her instincts, for they were correct more often than her advisers. She had just resolved that if she could beat down SEAD's price another $5 million or so, she would buy, when a voice intruded on her reflections.

"Madame Red Cloud?"

"What do you want?" she said testily, holding up her hand to shade her eyes from the sun. The staff had strict instructions not to intrude unless it was a matter of life or death—hers.

"Mr. Dan Adamus is on the telephone, madame," replied Luis, her Filipino steward.

Mr. Adamus was Raynes Oceanic Resources vice president for governmental relations. Vice presidents for governmental relations were a dime a dozen, but a good suntan was hard to come by.

"Tell him he's fired."

"Yes, madame."

Luis trudged up the beach toward the house. It was bigger than it looked, consisting of a twelve-room main building with wings concealed behind rows of palms housing her staff, her offices, and her stables. The lawns on all sides were of a deep green as uniform as artificial turf, and the beds of tropical plants were awash with primary colors, blooming strictly according to Mrs. Red Cloud's schedule—or else. Around the periphery of the four-hundred-acre estate ran a high electric fence.

Five minutes after Luis's departure, he was back. Mrs. Red Cloud was now lying on her back, but otherwise her attitude was unchanged.

"Listen, you goddamn Hukbalahap," she hissed, "if I see your face once more today, I'm going to ship you back to Mindinao. Understand?"

"It's Leyte, actually, madame." The steward had been through it all before. "However," Luis went on, "it is not Mr. Adamus who is now on the telephone, madame, but Mr. Gustafson. He is very insistent that he speak with madame."

Jennifer Red Cloud sighed and rose, cursing subordinates who had the bad judgment to incite her to dismiss them. Still, it just *might* be something important. Randy Gustafson liked that $850,000-a-year salary as president of Raynes Ocean Resources too much to jeopardize it by bothering her with trifles. She strode up the beach, past the tennis courts and the saltwater swimming pool, across the broad veranda with its red-striped awning, into her study. There her secretary, Terence, was holding a white telephone. He pretended to avert his eyes from her still-nude body but failed to impress her: She was well aware he preferred male privates, preferably out of uniform, to female captains of industry.

"This had better be good," she said into the telephone.

"It is. The chance of a lifetime, if you move fast."

"Get to the point, Randy."

"You must come to Washington right away."

"You're not paid to tell me what I must do, Randy," she said frostily. "You may, however, tell me why I *should* come to Washington."

"I can't. A lot of big ears are probably tuned in to this conversation."

"That's true. Very well, if it's really important, I'll come."

"When?"

Washington, nearly two thousand kilometers distant, was two hours away in the Raynes corporate jet. "Meet me at Dulles in three hours."

"Sooner would be better," said Gustafson.

"Very well, make it two hours and a half."

It meant she'd have to ride shotgun in the converted F-15 courier plane. She hated the cramped rear seat. Worse, the oxygen mask mussed her lipstick.

10. MR. SECRETARY CASTLE
24 FEBRUARY 2005

THE CONVERTED F-15 TOUCHED DOWN WITH A SHRIEK OF burning rubber at Dulles International Airport at five past eleven, and taxied to the far end of the strip. There a helicopter, its rotors turning lazily, waited. ROR President Randy Gustafson, a hard-bellied man of middle age with chalk-white hair, hooked the aluminum ladder to the side of the plane as the Plexiglas canopy lifted up and back.

Jennifer Red Cloud punched the release button of the shoulder harness and pulled off her helmet. She stood, hiked up her skirt so she could extend a sculptured leg over the side of the cockpit, and climbed down.

She disregarded Gustafson's proffered hand and flounced across the tarmac to the Sea Drift helicopter, heels clicking on the pavement, white sharkskin dress molded against her body by the propwash, long black hair streaming in the wind. She climbed up the five steps, and moments later they were airborne for downtown Washington.

"I'm listening," said Mrs. Red Cloud, taking her seat before a bank of mirrors and a cabinet containing a complete array of the made-to-her-order powders, creams, ointments, lip rouge, unguents, blushes, and other magic substances waiting at her every port of call, in a futile attempt, in Gustafson's view, to improve on nature.

As her Filipino makeup artist Ernesto went about repairing the ravages of the trip, Gustafson told her apologetically that he had waited all the previous day for her telephone call, and only when none had come had he instructed Adamus to get in contact with her.

"Just tell me why I'm here."

"President Turnbull created a new Department of Water Resources Tuesday night and named David D. Castle as secretary."

Mrs. Red Cloud regarded Gustafson coldly in the mirror.

"Why wasn't I informed immediately?"

"Your phones are disconnected between 5 P.M. and 9 A.M.—company policy," he reminded her. "Yesterday, I figured you had must have already got—"

"You could have flown down."

"Your personal orders are—"

"I know my personal orders, Mr. Gustafson. You must learn when to disobey."

"I'll have to tell Dan Adamus that—if I ever see him again," said Gustafson wryly.

"Never mind Adamus. Did you make an appointment for me with Castle?"

"Yes, ma'am. It's for eleven-thirty."

"Well, at least you're not *completely* useless, Randy."

Randy Gustafson sighed. When she wanted to murder him, it was Mr. Gustafson. When she loved him, it was Randy. On the other hand, when *he* thought about *her*, he was Randy all the time.

"I did the best I could, Mrs. Red Cloud, but I'm afraid somebody got there before us. Brill tells me Ripley Forte has been in conference with Castle since ten-thirty."

At the mention of Forte's name, her head jerked as if she had been stabbed in the small of the back. The lipstick Ernesto was applying made an ugly smear across her cheek.

"Terribly sorry, ma'am," said the Filipino, wiping off the lipstick with a tissue. Under his fingertips he could feel her jaw muscle tighten.

"Is this as fast at this goddamn machine will go?" she demanded.

Ernesto noticed that her eyes were a little crazy. It was the kind of thing, as good as he was, no makeup could cover.

Mrs. Red Cloud was six minutes late, but it didn't matter, said Miss Brill, Castle's wan, middle-aged secretary. He was still tied up with his ten-thirty appointment, and would they please have a seat? On the wall behind Miss Brill a life-size portrait of President Horatio Francis Turnbull in a stainless-steel frame gazed down like Big Brother.

"No, thank you," replied Mrs. Red Cloud, her eyes coming to rest on the rotating spools of the tape recorder in the open side drawer. Miss Brill shot a quick look at Gustafson, who had taken the trouble to get to know the Secretary's secretary. He smiled and nodded.

Miss Brill demonstrated the decisive action that made her so valuable a civil servant. She rose, locked the outside door, and entered the five-number code that permitted her to transcribe a conference in progress. The voice of a man came through the desk-top speaker.

"...only in bare-bones outline, of course," Ripley Forte was saying.

"Some outline," marveled David D. Castle. "Your plan is remarkably like that proposed by the scientists whose report I commissioned, not only in scientific theory but in execution and projected production costs and goals. If I weren't a hundred percent sure that it couldn't be done, I'd think you had somehow gotten hold of it."

Ripley Forte smiled blandly. "There's less a mystery about my knowledge of the subject than there appears, Mr. Secretary. Remember, I have been battling icebergs for more than six years. When I started, I didn't know a damned thing about them. But when they began knocking over my rigs and killing my men, I learned fast. Within two years, I think it's safe to say, I knew as much about icebergs on the working level as any man alive. But it wasn't enough, because I was still losing money and men. Like you, I commissioned studies—mostly by Canadian, Norwegian, and Australian glaciologists, oceanographers, and cold weather experts. They—"

"Why not American experts?" broke in Castle.

"Good question. In the first place, Canadians, Norwegians, and Aussies, being nearer to Arctic regions, have more experience along those lines. Also, I was beginning to suspect that icebergs might play a role in solving the water shortage—a role that could make money, and I didn't want to alert American competitors."

"Go on, Mr. Forte."

"Well, the more I dug, the better it looked. Not for Arctic pinnacle bergs, of course—they capsize and are too small in any case. But if big tabular bergs from the Antarctic could be tamed and towed, I realized, there could be enormous returns. I intensified my researches, and naturally I came up with much the same answers as you did. Two minds with a single thought, you might say."

"Yes," agreed Castle, "that makes sense." It *had* to. There couldn't be any other explanation.

"What it all boils down to, Mr. Secretary," said Forte, "is that your research and mine have demonstrated, independently, the feasibility of transporting icebergs from Antarctica to America."

"That's true."

"And that I'm the man to do it."

"Ah, that is something else, Mr. Forte. This is a project of historic dimensions which—"

Forte raised his hand.

"Let me put it to you briefly, Congressman. This is a project which, if it succeeds, will give you as its father a very good chance of getting to the White House in 2008. If it fails—oblivion. It will take me, at my best estimate, no less than forty months to do the job. Pick anybody with qualifications inferior to mine and you'll miss the conventions and the presidency. It's up to you, Mr. Secretary."

Castle smiled wryly. "It's a good thing you're an engineer, Mr. Forte. You'd never go far in politics with so blunt a tongue."

"Does my blunt tongue pound home the point, Congressman?"

"It does. And my first instinct is to name you as prime contractor and get the show on the road at once. But as a lawyer, and especially as secretary of water resources,

I cannot. There are others in the running, and I must consider them. For instance, General Dynamics, Lykes Lines, Boeing, Bath Shipbuilding, and IBM are meeting at this moment to form a consortium, and I shall be seeing them tomorrow."

Forte rose. "They don't scare me. I'll have a berg halfway to America while they're still forming committees and arguing about executive compensation packages."

Castle came around the desk and shook Forte's hand warmly.

"I can't tell you how glad I am you came to see me." He meant it. There was no question in his mind that probably only Forte could bring an iceberg into San Francisco Bay in time to win Castle the presidency. Of course, he'd have to go through the motions of considering alternatives, but his mind was already made up: Forte was his man.

"You realize that with a prime contract like this, worth many billions of dollars, the competition will be fierce, and my decision as to the winner closely scrutinized. But if—I must emphasize—*if*—I should decide to name Forte Ocean Engineering as prime contractor, when could you begin operations?"

"I've already started."

In the outer office, Miss Brill switched off the speaker. A moment later, the door to the Secretary's office swung open and Ripley Forte emerged. Jennifer Red Cloud, who had been whispering instructions to Randy Gustafson, looked up.

"Why, hello, Ripley," she said with an amused look. "What's a man like you doing in a place like this?"

Forte hadn't seen her in five or six years, but if anything, she was even more lovely than when they had last met. More rounded, more mature, with the hint of lines at the corners of those big violet eyes.

Ripley Forte nodded gravely. "Well, well. If it isn't our little Indian princess! How are things back at the castle?"

"The castles I've got interest me a lot less than the castles I'm going to get."

"Pretty sure of yourself, aren't you, Red?"

"*Very* sure of myself. After all, if I can demolish a Forte, a Castle shouldn't give me much trouble."

Forte couldn't top that, so he wished her a very good morning and left. She watched him go and then turned to enter David D. Castle's inner office.

As she closed the door behind Mrs. Red Cloud and returned to her desk, Miss Brill reached over to turn up the tape recorder volume.

Gustafson shook his head. "I don't want to hear it," he said. "I don't want *anybody* to hear it—ever."

"Why, I can't do that," protested Miss Brill. "That would be against government regulations."

Gustafson cocked an eyebrow at her.

"Besides," she went on, "that's a voice-activated machine. There's no way I can turn it off so long as they're talking in there. It's all automatic."

"Think on your feet, girlie."

"I'm sorry, but there just isn't—"

"You'll wish there was, when Castle hears about that $20,000 with your greasy thumbprints all over it."

With a speed that surprised him, she crossed the room to the supply closet and returned with an aerosol can. She sprayed the revolving tapes liberally. They slowed, stuttered, and stopped.

Secretary Castle had never been able to shake the memory of Jennifer Red Cloud. Their paths had crossed frequently on Capitol Hill when they were both new to Washington—he as a freshman congressman, she as a bright television reporter. Like practically every man she interviewed, he had asked her out to dinner. Somewhat to his surprise, she accepted, ate sparingly, drank nothing, listened to his confided ambition to be *numero uno* someday, and kissed him chastely on the cheek as he deposited her on her doorstep. It was their first and last private meeting, but for weeks he thought about her constantly. His confidences hadn't been worth reporting, and some months later she had gone on to marry Ned Raynes. He wondered if she even remembered him. Nothing in her demeanor suggested she did. Jennifer Red Cloud, he knew, was a clever, conspiratorial, resolute, and dangerous woman. As chairman of Raynes Oceanic Resources, she had obviously come ready to do battle for the prime contract for the iceberg recovery project. There was no question that, as experienced and successful as her company had been, she could bring nothing like the depth of experience and expertise that Ripley Forte offered. But he would have to be deferential, for she was rich and well connected. And he would have to be firm, for his political career was riding on his decision.

Mrs. Red Cloud cut short his pleasantries. She wanted, she said, the prime contract to bring icebergs from the Antarctic to America.

"How much experience has your company had in handling icebergs, Mrs. Red Cloud?"

"None whatever."

"Well, then, I suppose your company has been doing research on the subject, and you have come to discuss a detailed plan to implement the project?"

"No, it has not, and I have not."

"Perhaps your company's considerable resources will be enough to fund the research, the purchase of the equipment, and the mobilization of the many experts who will be needed to bring the project to fruition," Castle suggested gently.

"My company's resources are considerable, not astronomical."

Secretary Castle regarded his visitor with a puzzled frown.

"Then, Mrs. Red Cloud, on exactly what basis do you propose to bid for the prime contract?"

"Let *me* ask *you* a few questions, and I think your answers will provide a basis."

"By all means," assented Castle.

"What's in it for you?"

"I beg your pardon," said Castle, drawing back.

"You can forget the public service routine, Mr. Castle. You want to be President of the United States. It sticks out a mile—has for months. And you believe that the iceberg project will be your springboard into the White House."

Castle smiled wryly. "Some such suggestion has been made."

"If the project succeeds, you will stand a good chance

of achieving your ambition. For its success, you need to organize the best scientific brains and the best operational talent available. The organizational framework already exists: Raynes Oceanic Resources. The brains, the brawn, and the hardware can all be bought. Raynes will put up a token sum, the U.S. government the remainder."

"Is that all?"

"That is my offer."

"Then I must regretfully tell you, Mrs. Raynes, that your offer is not irresistible. The gentlemen with whom I have just been in conference, Mr. Ripley Forte—"

"I know, he's just made an offer you can't refuse. And besides, he knows more about icebergs than anybody."

"Exactly."

"But you're losing sight of your objective. Forte is interested in bringing in an iceberg. You are interested in becoming the President of the United States."

"And you?" countered Castle.

"I am interested in getting the contract, and unlike Ripley Forte, I also want to see you President of the United States."

"I'm afraid I don't follow."

"I'll spell it out, Mr. Castle. If Forte brings in the iceberg, you may well become President. If he doesn't, you are nothing. If I, on the other hand, bring in the iceberg—and I can muster as impressive a list of resources as Forte, remember—you stand the same chance of sitting in the Oval Office. But what if I fail? *You shall be President of the United States just the same.* For I will put the entire weight of Raynes Oceanic Resources behind you. My company is worth $780 million, and every penny necessary will be used to convince the American people that they need a forceful statesman like you to lead them. Money has done it before, and it can do it again."

What she said was true, Castle had to admit. And no question about it, two chances were better than one. Why tie his fortunes to the delivery of an iceberg if he could gain the supreme office in the land whether he delivered it or not? But, to rephrase her own question, what was in it for *her?*

The answer was devastatingly simple, direct, and convincing, and he wondered why it had not occurred to him before.

"I want," said Jennifer Red Cloud, smiling for the first time, "to be First Lady of the Land. With you, David, as *numero uno*, I *will* be."

11. EMPIRES
4 MARCH 2005

A WEEK EARLIER MISS BRILL HAD BEEN SECRETARY CAStle's lone staffer. Now she was chief administrative officer, one of a whole battalion of legislative assistants, program officers, analyists, policy planners, legal counselors, associate directors, deputy associate directors, assistant deputy associate directors, and deputy associate assistant administrators. Her single outer room had mushroomed to a suite of offices, stiff with secretaries busily clicking away at word processors, its anterooms filled with milling reporters eager for a word, if not from Secretary Castle himself, at least from a deputy assistant assistant deputy secretary.

It was through this legion of spear carriers that Ripley Forte elbowed his way more than a week after his first interview with Secretary Castle. For the first few weeks of that week he had been on the telephone, contacting the men who would form the nucleus of his team from among the hundreds of specialists in many fields he had worked with over the years. On Thursday, he flew to Bermuda, where Joe Mansour's *Linno* lay at anchor, to make his progress report. It was now Friday, and he was back in Washington, ready to get rolling.

And in all that time, there was still no word from Secretary Castle.

Forte was not perturbed. He knew the ways of Washington well. It took time and effort to build empires, and Castle's was growing with unprecedented speed. He would be working day and night drafting the enabling legislation that would officially establish the Department of Water Resources and lobbying for the huge supplemental congressional appropriation to finance the research and development of iceberg recovery methods. Still, Ripley Forte had gone about as far as he could go without an official endorsement.

Miss Brill greeted him with an effusive bonhomie that should have put him on guard. "Oh, Mr. Forte," she gushed, "what a coincidence seeing you here. My secretary has been trying to contact you for days."

"Really?" said Forte, taking the lie at face value. "Funny, the girl who works for me never mentioned it."

"Well, you know how it is. We've been expanding our office force so fast that messages get lost in the shuffle, and I—"

"That's okay," said Forte with a wave of the hand. "I'm here now. Maybe you could tell Mr. Castle that I'd like to see him."

"Oh, I'm afraid that won't be possible this morning, Mr. Forte. As a matter of fact, I was calling to tell you that perhaps he could squeeze you in next week—*late* next week. Say Friday afternoon."

The coin dropped.

Forte flushed. He was about to speak but thought better of it. Before Miss Brill could interpose her scrawny body between him and the door, he stalked into Castle's office.

Castle looked up from his papers with annoyance. When he saw that the intruder was Forte, he rose and extended his hand. "Why, Mr. Forte," he said with his paste-on politician's smile, "what a coincidence. I've been trying to contact you for the past week. That will be all, Miss Brill," he said over Forte's shoulder to his secretary, who was dithering in the background.

The door closed behind her.

"Please have a seat, Mr. Forte," said Castle, taking his own.

"I'm not going to take up a lot of your valuable time, Mr. Secretary, but you'll appreciate that I've got to get cracking if we're going to bring that iceberg into port in time for the presidential convention. And money. As I mentioned last week, I can raise the $2 billion through conventional financing so long as I can assure the underwriters of the bond issue that it represents no more than 10 percent of the total investment, the other 90 percent being earmarked for the project in government funds. So all I need from you to start stalking on Wall Street is a go-ahead."

"Go-ahead?"

"It doesn't need to be anything final, understand," said Forte. "A simple letter of intent to name Forte Ocean Engineering as the prime contractor for the iceberg project will suffice. Something I can wave under the noses of the bankers."

Castle leaned back in his chair and drummed his fingers lightly on the arms. His expression was solemn, judicial. "The iceberg project—by the way, we have come up with a name for it, an inspiring name: *Salvation*—is not, you'll grant, one which can be awarded without some deliberation. During the past week I have been literally besieged by aspirants for the prime contract. Every one of them has powerful political backing I cannot ignore. Those who are putting pressure on me are the very men whose votes I will solicit for the funds needed to get *Salvation* off the ground and into the water, so to speak."

"Sure, you need to stroke a few backs," said Forte, "but the proof of the pudding is the eating, and there won't be anything on the menu unless I put it there. You as much as said so yourself."

"That was last week, Mr. Forte."

"What's changed?"

"As a matter of fact, I have been pleasantly surprised to learn that there are several candidates who could qualify for the prime contract, and their credentials are—I regret to have to tell you this—fully as gilt-edged as your own."

"There's no man who can do the job as I can do, and you know it," said Forte, his choler showing.

"Perhaps a man was not what I had in mind."

Forte felt his bones turning to mush. The ripe odor of double cross filled the air. "She got to you, did she?"

"I beg your pardon?" said Castle haughtily.

Forte regarded him with eyes like basalt. He leaned forward, his huge hands kneading his knees.

"Listen to me, Castle, and listen carefully. Jennifer Red Cloud put me through the grinder once, and I let her get away with it. It's not going to happen again. If you award the prime contract to her, I'm going to sink her without a trace, and that goes for anybody who happens to be along for the ride. Not only will I see, personally, that your *Salvation* never touches the shores of the United States, I'm here to guarantee that you'll never be President."

David D. Castle looked at Ripley Forte coolly. "Good day, Mr. Forte," he said, and returned to his papers.

When the door closed behind Forte, Castle abandoned his pretense of work and leaned back in his chair to review the situation.

Could Forte actually sabotage the *Salvation* as he had promised? Very unlikely. Every man connected with the operation would be run through the security sieve, and besides, the project was too big. It would be like trying to sabotage the Great Wall of China.

There was another danger: Could Forte cry foul when the award went to Raynes Oceanic Resources?

No, again. It could easily be demonstrated that Forte, despite his vast familiarity with icebergs, was a bad business risk. He had gone under in his first contracting business. He had been so inept that he was dismissed from Forte Oceanic Resources, accepting a mere $5 million in settlement for stock worth twenty times that sum. Only months previously, Joe Mansour, the Lebanese tycoon, had taken over Forte's mismanaged, debt-laden Yellow Rose Oil Company. And now this perennial failure wanted to take charge of the biggest engineering operation in the history of mankind! Nobody would listen to him, that was certain.

But what about the award of the contract to Jennifer Red Cloud's company, in competition with the various immense consortia that had been formed for the specific purpose of bringing *Salvation* into port?

Well, as she had pointed out, Raynes Oceanic Resources

was the leading established ocean engineering firm in the world. It had formidable cash reserves and borrowing power, which she was willing to commit to the project. As for any breath of scandal, she had cleverly deflected that possibility by insisting that they have as little to do with each other, publicly and privately, as possible while the operation was under way. There would be no paparazzi shooting pictures of them snuggling together, simply because they would never snuggle. Her personal fortune would finance a multitude of political action committees to work for his candidacy, so they would have no ostensible personal relationship. Their names would never be linked romantically until, as the result of their collaboration in bringing the *Salvation* home, they found that they shared a community of interests, especially in public service, and decided to marry, a very natural development. And with a running mate like Jennifer Red Cloud, wed at the crest of a tidal wave of national euphoria after the *Salvation* was docked and after sweeping away the opposition at the Democratic national convention in July 2008, how could he possibly lose? Never in the history of presidential elections would the American people be offered such a candidate—a man of proven ability, good looks, and accomplishment that included their literal salvation. Never in history would the people have such a capable, successful, and beautiful First Lady.

Only one cloud—a very small and insubstantial red cloud—hovered on the horizon: the possibility that Jennifer might double-cross *him* as she had unquestionably double-crossed Ripley Forte. He dismissed it from his mind. Every thought, every action, every dream of Jennifer Red Cloud was fired by a single ambition: the lust for power.

She thought she had convinced him that being First Lady would be her ultimate satisfaction. But Castle knew that a woman as ruthless and greedy for domination as Jennifer Red Cloud would never be content to walk in a man's shadow. What she really wanted was to run the United States of America, using him as her puppet on a string, just as she had run Raynes Oceanic Resources through her husband, Ned. Well, let her indulge her fantasies, he mused: time enough to wake her up once he became President.

12. ROOM 101
10 APRIL 2005

MAJOR GENERAL GRIGORIY ALEKSANDREVICH PIATAkov was, as befitted a senior officer of the *Raketnye Voiska Srategicheskogo Nazacheniya*—Rocket Troops of Strategic Designation—a man on his way up. But on the morning of 10 April 2005, he found himself moving in the opposite direction, via elevator 340 meters straight down to Room 101, the subterranean headquarters of the KGB's Foreign Intelligence Directorate beneath the Kremlin.

Room 101 was a child of the 1950s' cold war, when Russia's leaders lived in dread of an American nuclear strike. A 200-meter shaft had been sunk beneath the ancient fortress on Red Square, then a horizontal passageway 50 meters to another shaft, extending a further 140 meters down to Room 101. At each end of the passageway were steel blast doors two meters thick. It took only eight minutes to reach Room 101 from the surface, so that top political and military leaders had sufficient time to find sanctuary underground in the event incoming nuclear missiles were detected. There they could survive attack even by megaton H-bombs.

In the more relaxed 1980s, Room 101 had been converted into an unbreachable repository for the master files of the KGB's Foreign Intelligence Directorate going back to the days of the czarist Okhrana. For this purpose, the "room" was greatly enlarged to accommodate uncounted tons of dossiers and hundreds of clerks and custodians. Vast dank caverns illuminated by bare bulbs hanging from dripping concrete ceilings housed whole regiments of filing cabinets containing information on the basis of which the Soviet Union waged its relentless struggle against the imperialist West.

But in the 1990s, as Russia's iron shadow fell across the greater part of the world, the Kremlin's interests had gradually shifted. To keep the peoples of the new territorial conquests in line absorbed an ever greater share of Russia's energies. Whole cadres of former KGB field agents were transferred to the task of maintaining order and suppressing dissent in Russian satellites whose land area constituted well over half the earth's surface. Happily, the agents could be spared, for the KGB's target areas had meanwhile shrunk commensurately. The United States, Japan, and South Africa were now the only enemies who really mattered, and even they were no longer an active menace.

Room 101 became something of a backwater. Its Foreign Intelligence Directorate still went through the motions, but the sense of urgency had gone. Bright young men and women quietly transferred to the domestic KGB apparatus, and Room 101 slid grudgingly into obscurity, an elephant's graveyard for party hacks, a Siberia-in-Moscow for officials in disgrace. Once assigned to 101, staffers found their careers at a dead end.

Nevertheless, the masters of the Kremlin recognized that Room 101's neglected files contained information that, if properly exploited, would vastly accelerate the collapse of the United States and its puppets, Canada, South Africa, Japan, and Australia. It was to shake the dust off Room 101 that Major General Piatakov had been summoned.

As a management and systems expert, he was to suggest remedial action to improve the alarming drop in intelligence productivity in Room 101. Piatakov had been trained in America, receiving an MBA from Harvard and both a B.S. and an M.S. in systems engineering from MIT, avoiding the taint of contamination with capitalism by a sincere and committed membership in the Communist Party. His meteoric rise through the ranks of the *Raketnye Voiska* had been likened to the blasting into the stratosphere of an SS-27. Reaching the rank of major general at the age of thirty-six, handsome and outgoing, he was also fortunate in his personal life. He had recently wed the handsome and articulate Nadezhda Voznesenska Muravieva, outspoken assistant political editor for *Literaturnaya Gazeta*.

Piatakov's ears popped as he began his descent to Room 101. Eight minutes later, the doors whooshed open, and he was greeted by the senior officer present, Lieutenant General Ivan Vissarionovich Ogarov, a relaxed, sunlamp-tanned, jolly soul who pumped his hand and bade him welcome.

Piatakov looked about him. Everything seemed homey and informal, most unlike the KGB of his experience. General Ogarov was clad in white shorts, a rainbow-hued Hawaiian sport shirt, and run-down carpet slippers. Piles of tattered files littered tables and cabinets, the floor was cluttered with waste paper, cigarette butts, and crushed Pepsi Cola cans; coffee cups were balanced on stacks of reference books; and a thick haze of tobacco smoke like a low-hanging cloud partially obscured the banks of over-head fluorescent lights. The workers lounged at their desks, languidly leafing through documents or reading books with feet propped up on chairs, staring vacantly out into space, or, in at least two cases, sleeping stretched out full length on their desks. One was snoring fitfully.

General Ogarov noticed his visitor's narrowed eyes. He laughed.

"Socialist discipline is difficult to maintain in 101," he explained with a shrug.

"Yes, I suppose that's true," admitted General Piatakov. "But somehow we must increase your productivity. The current Five-Year Plan calls for a six percent increase, and you are running at a negative one-and-a-half percent."

"Can't be helped, I'm afraid, short of a miracle. We get all the worn-out equipment because nothing down here is on public display where the authorities can be shocked by its obsolescence. And we keep getting new responsibilities heaped on us before we can train men to handle them. Case in point: Presidium Directive 1/337/4 of 2 February 2001, transferring all Pentagon/State Department radio traffic decoding operations from Kiev Station to our section. Since that directive was issued, as you know, the state of the art in encipherment has gone into orbit. One of the *simplest* low-security State Department codes averages 3 million nulls per character of text. We don't have anything like the computer capacity to filter out all that crap. We—what do you say to a cup of coffee?"

"That would be most welcome," said Piatakov. "Do you mind if I remove my jacket and tie?"

"Remove anything you like," chuckled his host. "Down here, anything goes."

During the next sixteen hours, Piatakov was given the grand tour: the huge files department, dark and dank as an underground mushroom farm, wherein were kept dossiers on more than 300 million Russians, alive and dead; the Executive Operations Section, where the staff planned black operations against the enemy; the Collection Directorate; the Information, Analysis, and Evaluation Directorate, which received and assessed field reports from intelligence agents and open sources; and all the other sections, departments, and directorates for which the KGB had been famed and feared for a hundred years.

Finally the two men passed a door supplied with a tumbler lock. Piatakov looked inquiringly at Ogarov.

The general hesitated. "Well, why not?" he said finally. "They told me to let you see everything. If you take out paid space tomorrow in *Izvestia* to tell what you saw, it's *their* funeral."

He dialed in the combination and swung open a steel door. Inside, a pale young man rose from a high stool before a filing cabinet and stood approximately at attention. He was barefoot, and clad in a pair of shorts.

"This is Piotr Petrovich, General. Piotr Petrovich, tell General Piatakov what keeps you locked up here like a mass rapist on death row."

The young man turned, picked up a clipboard, and waited for General Ogarov to sign an official release. "This, sir," said Piotr, sweeping his arm around the small room, "is the 'Mole Hole.' It is accessible only to my co-worker Dimitri and General Ogarov, for it contains the most sensitive secrets in the Soviet Union: the identity of our most important agents."

General Ogarov, who was getting hungry, interrupted. "Piotr Petrovich, perhaps you could astound General Piatakov with a few examples of the family *Talpidae* burrowing into the soft underbelly of the bloated running dogs of Wall Street."

Piotr Petrovich opened a drawer and removed four or five thick folders. "I get copies of all reports and insert them into the pertinent files. Here, for example, is the leader of the current majority in the Lok Sabha—India's lower house of parliament, you know. A staunch 'enemy' of the Soviet Union.

"Here is another, the Canadian multimillionaire paper manufacturer, Mr. Caesar Lundquist. He is a patron of the arts, an intimate of the major politicians of both parties, and a noted peace activist. I'm afraid we'll have to transfer him soon to the dead files, though."

"Why?" asked Piatakov.

"He's going to die. At eighty-three, his heart can't stand the rigors of twice-weekly dialysis. Now, here is an interesting situation. This is an institution file, dealing with an important activity which affects the security of the Soviet Union. These five people whose pictures you see are all deeply involved in the project. They are William S. Grayle, Yussef Mansour, David D. Castle, Ripley Forte, and Jennifer Red Cloud. Any one of these five could sabotage this great project, on which the prosperity, perhaps even the survival, of the United States depends. We are therefore especially lucky, because we own one of them body and soul. Care to make a guess, General?"

General Piatakov examined the features of each closely and then placed his finger on the nose of one of the men.

"Wrong!" chortled Piotr Petrovich. "It's this one."

Ogarov and Piatakov lunched in the senior staff dining room, waited upon by young women who, though uniformly comely, went about their duties like zombies.

While waiting for their food, General Ogarov returned to the subject of his work. "Now, to get back to the problem of integrating GS-4 section with the Rapid Response Unit, I feel that . . ."

Piatakov was only half listening. His claustrophobia was beginning to assert itself, sitting at this little table in this little room with this little man. Room 101 was getting to him. The sooner he got out of here, the better he'd feel. This place was light-years from the real world, *his* world. He knew that even hourly doses of happy pills wouldn't prevent him from opening his veins after a week down here.

It was not until late in the evening that his inspection was complete. The inspection was far from comprehensive. One of the most important factors in determining Room 101's capacity for increased efficiency was the quality of the personnel, which would take an expert weeks of patient interviews to assess. But already Piatakov had come to some tentative conclusions, and he was eager to get back to his office to write them up and put this enlightening but disturbing day behind him. Next week he would be back on the ICBM test range beyond the Urals, and Room 101 would soon vanish from his thoughts.

Lieutenant General Ogarov accompanied him to the elevator. Piatakov had put on his necktie and donned his jacket and was thanking his host with an effusiveness he did not feel for his time and consideration, when the duty officer told him that Comrade Chairman Baliev wished to speak with him on the telephone before his departure.

Piatakov nodded and made the call from the duty officer's desk.

"Chairman's office," a female voice said.

"This is Major General Piatakov, calling the Comrade Chairman as ordered." Piatakov's voice was steady, but his heart was beating like a hummingbird's wings. A call from the chairman of the KGB could mean anything, but the timing was peculiar. Couldn't whatever Comrade Baliev had to say wait until morning? What if—

"Baliev."

"This is Piatakov, Comrade Chairman."

"Ah, yes, Piatakov, thank you for calling. I have been quite disturbed, as you can well imagine, by the productivity decline in Room 101 and have been waiting all day to hear your recommendations. You are the expert, everyone tells me, and I'm sure what you have to suggest will be constructive."

"That's very flattering, sir. I have, of course, come to some very tentative conclusions, but they need reflection and refinement. I shall give you a provisional report by this time tomorrow, if that is acceptable."

"Unfortunately, no. Tomorrow morning there will be a meeting of the Presidium, and Room 101 is on the agenda. I expect to get a lot of heat, and I'd like to have something in hand to douse the flames with. What can you tell me now?"

Piatakov considered. He could discuss Room 101's problems in generalities, but generalities would not appease the Presidium. On the other hand, specifics implied a commitment, and he must be careful not to get in over his head, suggesting solutions Ogarov could not implement. But there *were* a few improvements he could recommend without reservation.

"Well, sir, one of the major difficulties is overcrowding, due to the antique system of retaining paper files. I'd recommend the immediate conversion of these files to laserdisk, and disposal of the originals. We would save 99.7 percent of the file space now employed and vastly facilitate retrieval. The process will, naturally, take years."

"Noted. Go on."

"I further recommend the installation of a fiber-optic system to transmit Room 101's reports and recommendations to the chairman's office. The present system, though transmission lines are well guarded, is subject to possible interference or surveillance."

"Good point. Anything else?"

"Well, sir, I don't wish to seem critical, but I detect a severe morale problem, a malaise among the workers which I believe must be affecting their productivity. It cannot be cured with material incentives."

"How *can* it be cured?"

"By extending their horizons, getting them more intimately involved in operations, getting feedback from the field on the results of the operations they have planned. At present, they formulate the plan, nurse it through channels, and that's usually the last they hear of it. Above all, I'd like to see them be thinking on a strategic rather than a tactical plane. They plan mostly single, one-shot operations, usually without regard to their consequences on the Presidium's grand strategy. If, furthermore, the results of an operation can somehow affect, *improve*, the quality of their own work, it would be a huge morale booster."

"I don't follow. How can this be done?"

Piatakov hadn't the foggiest notion. Occasionally, under stress, his tongue ran away with his thoughts. But suddenly the recollection of the chaos of the information synthesis process and Ogarov's comment on the inadequacy of the deciphering equipment provided inspiration.

"I intended to dilate on this subject in my report, sir. I need—"

"*I* need, General, and I need it now!"

"Very well, Comrade Chairman. You are aware of the capabilities of the American Brown-Ash Mark IX computer. If we could get one, a single Brown-Ash Mark IX could supply the Presidium with much faster analysis of Pentagon and State Department communications. With the same computer, we could rationalize the present chaotic and slow information processing now done in Room 101 with no less than seventeen computer systems of various types. Why, we could even pump in our meteorological data from Weather Central and get accurate forecasts for eight to twelve hours beyond what we get today. The air force would love us—you."

"*That* would be a novelty," said Chairman Baliev with an edge to his voice.

"But best of all," went on Piatakov, warming to the subject, "we would be providing a concrete goal for workers in Room 101. Its acquisition would affect the motherland's entire strategic posture. Installed here in Room 101, the BAM-IX would be visible evidence of the value of the Foreign Intelligence Directorate's teamwork and discipline. Its could increase every worker's productivity by as much as 50 percent."

The chairman did not reply. Silence echoed from the plate-glass sides of the duty officer's kiosk. Piatakov waited. He waited for what seemed an awfully long time.

Finally the chairman spoke. "I shall look forward, Comrade Piatakov, to receiving your full report. Meanwhile, I want to congratulate you on your exceptionally perceptive analysis of the faults you have detected in 101. Such outstanding work demands commensurate recognition. Tomorrow morning, I shall recommend to the Presidium your immediate promotion to lieutenant general."

Piatakov was stunned.

"Don't thank me," Director Baliev said. "You have earned the rank. But that raises another problem."

"Problem?" Piatakov, bathed in the euphoria of his elevation, could see no problem. At the rate he was going, he would be Marshal of the Soviet Union before he was fifty. No problem there.

"Yes. You see, I can think of no assignment where a lieutenant general with your particular combination of talents would fit." He paused. "Unless..."

A curtain of sudden apprehension descended upon Piatakov.

"Sir?" he croaked.

"Unless you would graciously consent to serve, as you have served throughout your distinguished career, where your unique capabilities could best promote the vital interests of the USSR."

The apprehension turned to cold fear.

"I wonder if you would agree, Lieutenant General Piatakov," said KGB Chairman Baliev, "to put your stimulating and promising theories into practice as director of Room 101. After all, no one can convert theory to action so ably as its creator."

"But, sir," protested Piatakov, struggling to hold back his panic, "Room 101 already *has* a director."

Baliev chuckled. "No problem."

PART II
SNOW

13. SALVATION
19 JANUARY 2006

IT LOOKED LIKE SOMETHING OUT OF AN OLD NORSE EDDA: an enormous mist-shrouded floating white island of a magnitude to be peopled by Vikings as tall as pine trees, impervious alike to the raging waves churned up by Njord, god of the seas, and thunderbolts sent crashing down by Thor, son of Odin. For the moment, though, the seas around it were serene, the skies overhead were clear of storm clouds, and neither Viking nor other race of man had yet glimpsed its virgin surface.

But far overhead, an ever-vigilant satellite had witnessed its birth, when it calved some twenty hours earlier from the Ross Ice Shelf.

"It's what we've been looking for, Mrs. Red Cloud," announced Randy Gustafson, striding into the chairman's office with the computer printout streaming behind him. He spread the printout across her desk, cluttered by not so much as a paper clip.

"What's the berg's size?"

"Just about the perfect parallelepiped, Mrs. Red Cloud: 2 kilometers long, a shade over 1 kilometer wide, and 229 meters thick."

"Randy, you know very well that the metric system and I don't see eye to eye."

"About a mile and a half long, six-tenths of a mile wide, and 680 feet high, or about 130 feet higher than the Washington Monument, but only a hundred feet shows above the waterline."

"That's better," she purred. "And how much water does it contain?"

"Very roughly, 200 million tons. Close to 50 billion gallons. Enough for a tribe of thirsty Arabs."

"*And* their goats and camels. Its position?"

Randy Gustafson aimed a remote control at the wall opposite Mrs. Red Cloud's desk. The wall sprang alive, showing a smooth blue surface. Barely visible in midscreen was a white dot the size of a postage stamp. Gustafson did things with the control, and the postage stamp expanded to the size of a bedsheet.

"This tape was taken about ten minutes ago as the ROR satellite passed over in polar orbit. We'll have an update available in forty minutes. The berg's just the size we've been looking for, and it couldn't be better placed. It's at 77°40' S, 172°12' W."

He switched to a Mercator projection of the globe. "As you can see, that position is just south of the islands of Samoa and Midway, and Adak, Alaska."

"And where are our ships?"

"About fifty nautical miles to the north of the berg." A blinking red light indicated the fleet's position.

"It's not 'the berg' now, Randy. It's the *Salvation*. Instruct Dr. Lepoint to capture the *Salvation* at once and take it in tow."

"Roger," said Randy, and was on his way. Despite the fact that her presence automatically improved the quality of the scenery about a hundred percent, Gustafson never felt quite comfortable around her. She was a little too volatile for his taste, too ready to kiss or kill, with what seemed to him a natural predilection for the latter.

She stared morosely at the wall display, with its blinking red light now become an arrow, pointing at the stationary white light representing the *Salvation*.

Salvation. It had *better* be. When Raynes Oceanic Resources was awarded the prime contract, Castle had agreed that ROR would put up 10 percent of the capital. But after the letter of intent had been prepared, President Turnbull had overruled his Secretary of Water Resources. He had insisted that the prime contractor for such a potentially profitable enterprise must commit one-third of the funds, with the government supplying the rest. To back out now, after Raynes's publicity men had been portraying the company in the media as the best qualified to handle this historic project, would have made Jennifer Red Cloud a laughingstock. Ripley Forte especially would have laughed his head off, and that would have killed her. Her only course was to go discreetly to the banks and mortgage Raynes's future on the outcome of this one mammoth project. If she succeeded in bringing the berg into San Francisco Bay, ROR would automatically have a monopoly on iceberg recovery technology and within a few years dwarf Exxon and IBM. If she failed . . .

Dr. Valery Daniel Lepoint was a small man whose profile was that of an inverted turnip. He was rich in reputation, honors, diplomas, self-esteem, and energy. A Parisian, he had graduated from not one but two of *les grandes écoles*. He had published (though not, following academic custom, had he in every case written) some three hundred papers on glaciology and oceanography and was considered by many the world's foremost authority on the theory of iceberg recovery and transport. He held fourteen patents on devices designed for this purpose. At the University of Paris, he currently occupied the chair of theoretical fluid dynamics. That he had never led an expedition to the Arctic or Antarctic or, indeed, had even actually *seen* an iceberg in its native habitat—he had, to be sure, once seen a one-ton specimen at an iceberg symposium in Iowa—he considered no handicap as leader of the first-ever expedition to bring a commercial-scale iceberg into port. Whatever shortcomings he might have in practical applications, he felt, were more than compensated by his immense knowledge of theory, thorough acquaintance with the literature, and ripe Gallic intuition.

Within minutes of receiving news that an ideal candidate for recovery had been sighted, Dr. Lepoint's fleet was on its way, even before the order had been received from ROR's head office. As operational chief, Dr. Lepoint didn't feel that he needed direction from a distant headquarters, especially one headed by a woman.

His fleet was a heterogenous one. It consisted of a flagship—a converted U.S. Navy command ship bristling with radar antennas and other navigation and communications gear—six huge oceangoing tugs, five supply ships, a submarine mother ship, two tenders, two oilers, a small troop transport to accommodate the personnel who would work aboard the iceberg, a seaplane tender that had been converted into a floating laboratory and information-processing station, and a helicopter carrier with twelve personnel choppers and three huge transports with six-bladed counterrotating props capable of lifting twenty-five tons.

Within three hours the first of Lepoint's motley fleet had closed on the *Salvation* and the exploration group had been airlifted to its center.

Two hours later, the berg was pronounced free of man-eating crevices, and the seismographic party took charge. At intervals across the entire surface they planted rows of sensors and then set off calibrated charges of blasting powder in order to anaylze the reverberation patterns.

Forty hours later, the chief seismographer pronounced the *Salvation* "*aussi solide que le roc de Gilbralter.*"

Relays of helicopters were soon shuttling back and forth, discharging a steady stream of men and cargoes.

The mounds of equipment in the center of the berg grew in number and volume as the January sun rose feebly in the sky. First to arrive were the makings of eight twelve-man bunkhouses.

A galley and mess hall, an administrative section, three workshops, and an electrical generating unit big enough to supply a town of forty-five thousand quickly followed. Inflatable bubble structures warehoused the supplies that kept coming in a never-ending flow. The bunkhouses, aux-iliary buildings, and materiel depots were widely sepa-rated from one another so that a crevasse opening beneath their feet could swallow at most one or two buildings and their crews but would spare the rest.

Lepoint's first, major task was to take the *Salvation* in tow. For this purpose he had contrived a restraint sys-tem based on the net shopping bag traditionally carried by French shoppers. Consisting of interwoven straps of Strylene, a high-strength synthetic, each strand was fifty meters long, half a meter wide, and five centimeters thick. These were fashioned into a loose mesh a thousand meters wide and two kilometers long. Across the berg's midline, six leaders from the net were brought forward over the berg's forward lip and made fast to the six tugs that waited

there, barely making steerageway. The net's opposite end
was dragged to the rear and lowered over the afterportion
of the berg by electrically operated winches. At water's
edge the mesh, along with buoys and a Strylene leader
attached on either side, was taken in tow by net-tending
tugs and deployed in the berg's wake like a bridal train.
When the mesh stretched out behind by about a kilometer,
the buoys were released and the net sank, now restrained
only by its two outboard leaders. The leaders, made of
braided French-made *grimpalon* cable as thick as a weight
lifter's biceps, were brought by tug around to the forward
edge of the berg and the net hauled up snug against the
bottom. The restraining device was completed by bringing
the submerged lines forward to the surface and making
them fast around bitts on the six powerful tugs that were
to pull the *Salvation* north.

That Dr. Lepoint had anticipated every problem was
evident in the smooth deployment of the Strylene harness
and the making fast of the twelve hawsers aboard the tugs
less than fifty hours later. On the day of departure, Dr.
Lepoint made final rounds, personally inspecting arrangements, and pronounced himself satisfied. The men were
comfortably installed in their bunkhouses and looked forward to a dinner prepared by French chefs, a selection
of fine French wines, and old cognac and cigars. The
oceangoing tugs were operating well within their predicted performance envelopes. The steady pull on the
harness, now that maximum forward momentum had been
attained after four days under way, translated into a speed
of 1.3 knots, very close to the anticipated 1.46 knots.

At midnight, Dr. Daniel Valery Lepoint went to the
radio shack and dictated a message to be transmitted at
once to Mrs. Jennifer Red Cloud in San Diego:

> Madam: I have the honor and pleasure to inform
> you that today, January 19, 2006, the *Salvation* has
> been taken successfully under tow and is proceeding
> northward at the rate of approximately one and a
> half statute miles per hour. Barring misadventure,
> we expect to bring the *Salvation* into its berth in
> San Francisco Bay during the second week in July

2006. I look forward to presenting the *Salvation* to you personally on that historic occasion. *Bonne année! Vive les Etats Unis! Vive la France!*

/s/ Lepoint.

14. SOUTHERN EXPOSURE
14 MARCH 2006

A COUPLE OF OFF-DUTY CREW MEMBERS CLAD IN YELLOW wet suits were racing wind surfers. Others sunned themselves on a raft anchored near the shore of the frigid manmade lake. Fast motorboats, used for transporting workers, buzzed between the floating supply sheds and the work sites. Huge rubber lighters powered by outboard engines ferried supplies and equipment from the loading dock at the edge of the *Salvation* to warehouses spotted around the lake. The warehouses, like all the other structures on the lake, undulated gently on inflated rubber bladders.

There was little sound but the gentle slap and swish of waves against the base of the berg as it was drawn ponderously northward by its tugs, like a slumbering polar bear being dragged by six white mice. At midmorning another sound was heard, that of a distant plane approaching. Minutes later an amphibian Grumman TiltJet 301 appeared on the horizon.

The plane's pilot checked his instruments and then punched in the frequency of the *Salvation*'s homing device on the autoland system, flicked the switch, and lit a cigarette as the computers took over. A moment later the twin throttles eased back, and the two big fanjet engines began to swivel upward. The plane decelerated and descended swiftly as the engines rotated to the vertical, and the plane fought the battle against gravity it was programmed to lose, but only on its own terms. The thrust vectoring sent the plane sliding down through the sky like a bead on a string toward the homing transmitter floating atop a buoy in the center of a group of widely spaced aluminum-roofed buildings. An instant before touchdown, the jets roared at full power and then throttled back to idle as the aircraft settled in the water that covered the entire iceberg except for a ten-meter-wide Strylene border at the edge. The pilot snubbed out his cigarette and shut down the engines. The copilot pulled the handle that released the fore and aft anchors. In the rear, the stewardess pressed the main hatch button, and the door swung back to reveal a big rubber boat approaching.

The sixty-odd reporters of the media pool clambered single file down the steps into the boat. When all were aboard, the coxswain cast off, and the craft lumbered off toward the administration building two hundred meters away. The floating barracks and maintenance shed swayed gently as the boat passed by.

"Nothing like as bad as being aboard a destroyer," explained the boat's pilot to a reporter, "but some of the crew live on seasick pills, especially when they see the buildings rolling one way and the ships down below us pitching the other."

"Novel way to build," observed the reporter.

"Yeah. It was either put up the buildings on air suspension cells or sink deep piles into the berg. Dr. Lepoint figured, though, that pile driving might set up stress lines that could precipitate calving."

"Very perceptive of Dr. Lepoint."

"Yes, indeed," said the coxswain with conviction. "That's one smart hombre. He's thought of everything."

He hadn't, however, thought of this press conference to announce the imminent passage of the *Salvation* across the equator, when it would have completed more than three-quarters of its journey from the Antarctic to San Francisco Bay. That had been Mrs. Jennifer Red Cloud's idea. Although the iceberg had received a tremendous amount of publicity in the United States, until now the press had been forbidden to set foot aboard, for fear of infiltration by corporate spies intent on learning exactly how Dr. Lepoint had accomplished his miracle.

Mrs. Red Cloud, on her part, foresaw that a flood of news stories, generating an intense public interest on the eve of *Salvation*'s arrival, would pave the way for new bond issues, essential now that her liquid assets were so heavily committed to the *Salvation*.

"Welcome, ladies and gentlemen of the press," said Dr. Valery Daniel Lepoint from the podium of the small screening room into which the press had been crowded. "Welcome to the *Salvation*, and welcome to a new era in science and technology. What you will see here today on your inspection tour is a glimpse of the future, when man will alter the world's geography, its very weather and climate, for his benefit and survival. This first great step will provide a continuous supply of the purest water in the world to America's West Coast. Not only will it and those icebergs to follow provide water to the states of California, Nevada, Utah, and Arizona, but they will relieve the current pressure for supplies on the Colorado, Columbia, Missouri, Arkansas, Platte, and other rivers, allowing their waters to slake the thirst of the drought-plagued Midwest and plains states.

"The mechanics of this vast redistribution of American waters you must discuss with specialists in the United States. Here you will learn how we intend to fill this now-empty pipeline."

Dr. Lepoint, dapper and bow tied, was in the environment he liked best: the classroom. These were his students, and today he would teach them as much as they could absorb. He smiled, as if to give them confidence that the scientific wonders he was about to unveil were something any reasonably intelligent man or woman could comprehend. But before he saddled them with technicalities, they would need to have a concise, overall picture of the operation.

"The Stars and Stripes were raised over the *Salvation* as sovereign American territory on January 19, 2006. It was then taken under tow by a crew from Raynes Oceanic Resources. For the first thousand miles of its journey, the *Salvation* was hurried along by the winds of the Screaming Sixties, Furious Fifties, and Roaring Forties, the eastward-flowing circumpolar current, and of course, our fleet of oceangoing tugs. Together, the winds, currents and diesel power allowed us to make good an average of 42 nautical miles per day, that is to say, some 50 statute miles. The *Salvation* is about 2,000 meters long, 1,000 meters wide, and 229 meters from surface to bottom. Fortunately—perhaps miraculously—we have experienced no calving problems whatsoever.

"In all respects, the *Salvation* has been a resounding success. It was acquired, ablation-shielded, harnessed, and hitched to its team of six tugs with minimum difficulty. Two men were lost, it is true, when their clothing got tangled in a steel cable and . . . well, there is no use in going into this tragic occurrence—but otherwise everything has gone according to plan. The tugs succeeded in pulling the *Salvation* clear of the circumpolar current 380 miles west of Tierra del Fuego, on the tip of South America. For the next eight days we made good only 28 nautical miles per day. Then we caught the Humboldt Current, a cold current which sweeps up the coast of Chile and Peru, and made excellent time. Just off southern Ecuador, we pulled out of the Humboldt, which there swings west, and picked up the Peru Current, which will carry us almost to Panama. The *Salvation* will arrive in San Francisco Bay, where the basin to receive it is nearing completion, in early October.

"The ablation/friction shield is functioning flawlessly. Freshwater loss through tears in the ablation/insultion shielding and through evaporation will amount, it is estimated, to 17 percent by the time we make port. That will allow us to reclaim 800 million tons—180 billion gallons—of the purest water on earth, enough to float the United States on its way to national recovery along the maritime highway created by Raynes Oceanic Resources.

"And now, ladies and gentlemen of the press, before I have the pleasure of conducting you on a tour of our installation aboard the service barge, are there any questions?"

A hand shot up. It belonged to the correspondent of a stuffy scientific magazine, *Future Technologies*.

"Howard Foster," said the reporter, "*F.T.* My readers would like to know, Dr. Lepoint, what will keep the *Sal-*

vation from melting away now that it is in tropical waters?"

"A good question, Mr. Foster. Icebergs *do* melt fast in warm water. One, 400 feet long, reportedly melted completely in 36 hours in 80° Fahrenheit water. Fortunately for us, somewhat different conditions prevail. For the first thousand miles, of course, the water temperature was approximately zero degrees Centigrade, so we suffered little loss. The next 400 miles were through water of 4° Centigrade, then we encountered a 300-miles band of 8° Centigrade water, and finally the Humboldt Current, 12° Centigrade for 1,500 miles. We are now in the Peru Current, averaging 16°. Thanks to the protective insulation, the melt rate has been inconsequential, and the water that has melted on the surface itself serves as insulation."

"But from here on?"

"There *will* be a higher melt rate, but remember, we are already more than three-quarters of the way home . . . Yes?"

He pointed to a woman with upraised arm.

"Ginny Moyer, *Tuscaloosa Times*. You mentioned the California Current, Dr. Lepoint. As I understand it, the California Current shifts in the summer—very soon, in fact—from northwesterly to southeasterly. So instead of the current assisting, as it has up to now, it will actually *hinder* the iceberg's progress."

"Quite true, Mrs. Moyer," said Dr. Lepoint amiably. "This fact—and quite a crucial fact it is, too—has been taken into account. You may be interested to know that the timing of your visit has not been accidental. It was coordinated with the arrival of six additional tugs from Panama, which should be coming along at any moment. Supplementing the six now on station, they will add tractive power sufficient to increase our daily progress from thirty-nine to forty-one nautical miles."

"Will the harness be strong enough to bear the extra strain?" she asked.

"Yes, indeed. The harness and lines all have a 40 percent safety factor above any anticipated load applied by the twelve tugs."

*   *   *

As Lepoint spoke, his operations chief, Guy de la Chance, was hunched over a readout-spewing computer in the seismography shack. He had heard the whirr of the Grumman TiltJet's props as it came in for a landing, but it didn't register. His mind was on the perturbations in the seismic patterns that the readouts revealed.

He had observed, for instance, that the refraction and reflection patterns that were recorded from the daily but limited explosions picked by geophone arrays never seemed to be the same. Chief seismographer Elliott explained patiently that this was because an iceberg, unlike a section of Texas prairie, for instance, was always in a state of flux. Its passage through water of changing temperatures, through currents of varying speeds and directions, set up waves of internal pressure that disturbed the iceberg's crystalline structure. In effect, it responded to exterior influences almost like a living organism, something like an amoeba drawing back and rearranging its internal architecture when encountering a pointed object. The structural stability of an iceberg, therefore, did not depend on a completely rigid and unchanging solidity, like a bar of iron, but on its ability to absorb, transmit, refract and reflect, and finally dampen trillions of tiny shock waves, which in effect canceled one another out. Its stability was that of a bowl of Jell-O.

de la Chance was silenced but not convinced. Temperamentally, he preferred iron to Jello-O. And so, more on hunch than scientific evidence, he kept studying the seismographs, looking for changes in patterns long after the men responsible became bored. The most they would concede was that yes, accumulated random vibration *could* threaten the *Salvation*. That danger point was represented by a red line across the top of the bar graph on which they registered their daily readings. But so long as the plot of daily readings continued straight across the *bottom* of the graph, there was absolutely nothing to worry about.

de la Chance nevertheless worried. He worried while Dr. Valery Daniel Lepoint conducted the press on a guided tour of the various floating facilities. He worried as the newly arrived tugs took up their stations and their burden of pulling the *Salvation* against the adverse current. And,

on his regular morning visit to the seismograph shack
three days later, he finally found the reason for his worry:
There was a blip in that lower graph line where before
there had been none.

de la Chance pointed out that blip as the first item of
his noon inspection report to Dr. Lepoint on 26 May. Dr.
Lepoint did not respond. The next day the blip was still
there. Worse, it had a brother blip a notch up on the graph
paper. De la Chance immediately notified Dr. Lepoint by
telephone. Dr. Lepoint reassured him, saying that naturally, with the cavitation vibrations from the propellers of
twelve tugs instead of six, a new level of random vibration
must be expected; it was no cause for concern, since the
line would soon stabilize.

It didn't. On 28 May, a Sunday, when all but a skeleton
crew were off duty, de la Chance ordered the entire seismographic crew to report for a special assignment. When
they assembled, in less than hearty spirits, he instructed
them to run six surveys every hour, using full geophone
arrays. He signed the requisition order for the six hundred
pounds of high explosive that would be required for the
shots. The men put on their wet suits, grumbling audibly,
and slouched down the passageway to the motorboats that
would take them to their stations. Chief seismographer
Elliott, as annoyed as his men, stayed behind with de la
Chance to await the data.

Elliott sipped his coffee and flipped morosely through
the pages of *Playboy*, avoiding de la Chance's eye as they
waited, not speaking, for the first data to come in. When
they did, Elliott ran them through the computer and
reached for the graph. The base line—that line which had
not varied more than a tenth of a unit since the *Salvation*
had been christened and begun its voyage north—was 2.6
on the chart. de la Chance's blips of the day before had
been at 2.7 and 2.78, respectively. Elliott's new entry was
2.83. The next five tapes ranged from 2.76 to 3.01.

The average was now 2.92.

That was still a long way from the red danger line at
13.77, but it was edging closer. There was no reason for
it to do so. The new pattern of vibration should have been
well established by now, since the twelve tugs had been

pulling together for almost a week. Of course, there were no statistics on how long it took an iceberg's vibration pattern to stabilize. Such data didn't exist, but Elliott's guess was that three or four days should have been sufficient. Yet the plot line was steadily rising. He bit his lip and shot a sideways look at de la Chance.

The operations chief was impassive. He nodded and went back to his study of the computer printouts of the previous weeks. If they told him anything, he didn't share it with Elliott.

"Let's go to lunch," said de la Chance finally, stacking the printouts in a pile. He locked the graph in a desk drawer.

"Shouldn't we tell Dr. Lepoint about this?" said Elliott anxiously.

"Not yet. We don't want the good doctor to come down with the fantods."

"But he should know what—"

"We'll tell him tomorrow. One swallow doesn't a bummer make, you know. Unless we have solid evidence, he'll laugh at us. We have to have data Lepoint can't explain away."

"But—"

"Tomorrow."

The next day Elliott had his crew waiting in their small fleet of two-man craft when de la Chance tied up at the seismograph shack. Elliott held out the clipboard for his boss to sign the explosives requisition.

"Twelve hundred pounds?" asked de la Chance. "Do we need all that?"

"Cold turkey. Let's find out once and for all if this vibration pattern is an aberration or the real thing. We'll double the number of shot sites and nail it down. Okay?"

"You're the expert," de la Chance sighed.

At noon the results were in.

The point on the plot was 4.75.

"*Now* we talk to Lepoint," said de la Chance. He flicked on the intercom and asked the operator to ascertain Dr. Lepoint's whereabouts.

"He's in the auditorium, Monsieur de la Chance."

"Not another press conference?"

"No, sir. It's an awards ceremony. In fact, you're supposed to be there. I've been trying to locate you for the last—"

"I'm on my way."

Five minutes later he was striding down the aisle of the screening room, followed by Elliott clutching a file folder. On the podium, Dr. Lepoint was handing a check and a scroll to the captain of the *William Hellman*. There was a polite scattering of applause from the two dozen men who were awaiting their turn.

"Ah, there you are, Guy. And just in time to receive your citation and cash award from Raynes Oceanic Resources for your part in bringing the *Salvation* successfully across the southern hemisphere."

"Thank you, Professor Lepoint, but right now I'm thinking of the *northern* hemisphere."

"What do you mean?" demanded Lepoint.

"I mean, I think the *Salvation* doesn't have a hope of ever reaching the northern hemisphere."

"And why not, may one ask?"

"Because vibration—vibration caused by the propellers of the extra tugs, the prop wash of twelve tugs piling up against the *Salvation*'s leading edge, and the iceberg's pounding against the adverse California current—will shake it apart."

Dr. Valery Daniel Lepoint relaxed. For a moment he had thought he was facing a serious problem.

"And so now, Guy, you are not only an excellent project operations manager but a skilled seismographer as well. You are a man of unexpected, hidden resources." He smiled at his sally.

"Well, I have the good sense to call in an expert like Elliott to look into the problem, anyway. Tell him, Elliott."

Elliott nodded. "I'm afraid he's right, Dr. Lepoint." He produced the graph from the file and spread it on the lectern. "You'll note that the change in the pattern began, ever so fractionally, just after we hit the interface between the Peru Current and the California Current. We were caught in sort of a whipsaw, and a third component was added by the pull of the six tugs. But it really became noticeable only after we added the other tugs. The way

I see it, the inability of the tugs to maintain an absolutely even strain on the towlines, due to wave action, inevitably causes a jerking motion. That jerking motion by twelve tugs instead of six is not a simple arithmetical function. It's a *geometric* function. And this—"

Dr. Lepoint held up his hand in good-natured protest. "My boy, while I was still back in my laboratory at the Sorbonne I envisioned this problem and had a graduate student work out the solution. It's a matter of restabilization, a matter of contending forces achieving a new equilibrium. You don't suppose, do you, that—"

"When?" interrupted de la Chance.

"When what?"

"When does the new equilibrium become established?"

"By my computations—I checked my student's figures, of course—it should be within eight days of the initial perturbations. That is to say, within five days."

"In five days we'll all be in the drink," warned Elliott.

"I'm afraid I must agree," said de la Chance. "The curve is ascending toward the vertical. When it intersects the red line—perhaps within seventy-two hours—I don't want to be aboard."

"*Mon dieu*, Monsieur de la Chance." said Lepoint in exasperation. "*Ça c'est tres fort*—that's putting it a little strong."

"I'm afraid not, sir."

"Are you suggesting that we abandon ship, leaving behind the machinery, the supplies, installations worth millions of dollars?" said Lepoint contemptuously. "Abandon an iceberg without visible flaw, turn our backs on the plight of the United States which only we can alleviate, *throw away our jobs and the high honors and rich rewards which await us*?"

Elliott did not reply.

"That's right," replied de la Chance shortly. "Throw it all away, and save the crew."

Lepoint canvassed the faces of the two score men in the screening room. He was a shrewd judge of men. He had plainly scored with his thrust about jobs and high honors and, especially, rich rewards. These were men who, if they left now, would return to America without

jobs, to wives without pride, to communities that would
think them cowards and fools.

"I am in your hands, my friends and coworkers. Let
us put it to a vote. All in favor of renouncing our sacred
duty, betraying the hopes of our fellow countrymen, for-
saking our very handsome salaries and benefits, raise your
hands."

There was a pause.

Elliott raised his hand, but when he looked around and
saw that he was alone, he quickly lowered it again.

Dr. Valery Daniel Lepoint smiled smugly at Guy de la
Chance.

"Good-bye, Guy."

de la Chance shook his head sadly. He shrugged. "Good-
bye, Dr. Lepoint." He looked at the men. They looked
back at him, some with hostility, others with embarrassment or wistfulness. They were a good crew, and he would
miss them. "Happy landings, *mes amis*," he said. "And
keep your life jackets handy."

He walked up the aisle and out of their lives. That
afternoon he was aboard the courier plane bound for Panama City.

Six days later, Elliott, who had been plotting the vibration curve with mounting anxiety at six-hour intervals,
entered the latest figures. With this entry, the curve
breached the red danger line at 13.77. The latest average
vibration coefficient was 14.20 and still rising. And yet
the *Salvation* remained solid. Maybe Dr. Lepoint was
right, after all. Elliott breathed more easily.

But he didn't breathe long, for that afternoon he ceased
to breathe altogether. The *Salvation* suddenly fractured
into five major pieces, hurling men, machinery, and buildings into the water, crushing them as huge shards of ice
broke off and toppled in upon them. Not all the men were
crushed or drowned. Dr. Valery Daniel Lepoint, at that
moment aboard his flagship, the *William Hellman*, sur-
vived to tell the world how the villainous Ripley Forte
had somehow sabotaged his and the nation's *Salvation*
and sent it tragically into the depths of the Pacific Ocean.

15. SHOPPING LIST
7 JUNE 2006

"I COULD HAVE YOU SHOT, YOU KNOW," SAID PRESIDENT Horatio Francis Turnbull.

"On what charge?" said Ripley Forte.

"Oh, piracy on the high seas, high treason—after all, you *are* a dual citizen of the United States and Texas—accessory before the fact to murder, genocide—any number of things. That's principally why presidents have attorneys general: to answer questions like yours."

"Then why don't you, Mr. President?"

"You know the answer to that. You wouldn't have come here if you thought I had a chance in hell of getting a conviction before you dragged the entire administration down with you. A man like you doesn't come to play poker without having a marked deck up his sleeve. What kind of hand do you have, young man?"

"Pretty good, sir. Maybe unbeatable. And speaking of poker, your secretary of water resources must have thought he had a pat hand when he awarded the prime contract to Raynes Oceanic Resources. It doesn't take a genius to figure out that the Apache princess made some powerful medicine to change his mind about giving the prime contract to Forte Ocean Engineering. What it was, your guess is as good as mine."

"Presidents do a lot of guessing, Mr. Forte, but in this case I don't have to: Mrs. Red Cloud convinced him she wants to be Mrs. President and promised to back Castle to the hilt in his presidential campaign whether the berg came in or not, in return for the prime contract. They make bugs pretty cute these days. I suppose you thought if you could get an investigation launched, the truth would come out about Castle and Mrs. Red Cloud and everybody would forget about Ripley Forte in the ensuing scandal."

"Right on the money, Mr. President."

The President chuckled, went to the cabinet bar, and filled two glasses from the assortment of bottles on the glass shelves. He handed one to Forte, who sipped it and decided that President Turnbull wasn't quite the simple-minded good ol' boy he sometimes pretended to be. The whiskey was bourbon, straight, and his brand. The President was obviously well briefed.

"So did you?" asked the chief executive.

"Sabotage the *Salvation*? No, sir. Didn't have to. It was doomed before Dr. Lepoint ever set foot on it. I had some pretty clever boys run computer simulations of every inch of the route the *Salvation* would have to travel. They told me to anticipate severe buffeting somewhere off the coast of Peru, well below the equator."

"And yet he miscalculated. Why?"

"Trouble is, Lepoint's a Frenchman. Frenchmen are never wrong—if you press them, they'll admit as much themselves. Old Lepoint not only snowed Mrs. Red Cloud, he snowed *himself*. He actually *believed* his calculations left no room for error, or accident, or intervention by the swift hand of God."

President Turnbull leaned back in the chair, holding his glass of amber fluid up to the light. "Tell me, Mr. Forte," said the President. "If the berg hadn't foundered of its own accord, would you have sabotaged it?"

"You bet. Castle and Red Cloud diddled me out of the prime contract. I don't hate quick, Mr. President, but when I do, I hate hard."

"I would never have guessed," said the President, with a twinkle in his eye. "And speaking of guessing, I don't suppose *you* could have guessed that the news that the *Salvation* will never arrive in San Francisco didn't exactly break my heart."

"I didn't think it would, somehow," conceded Ripley Forte.

"And as a matter of fact, I knew it wouldn't even before *you* did," the President went on.

"Then why did you appoint Castle secretary of water resources? His failure will blacken your name."

"A little, maybe. But whereas it could wound me, it'll kill him. As presidential timber goes, he's been chopped down to a toothpick."

"But how about your own chances in 2008, Mr. President? If you don't solve the water crisis, the voters are going to turn you out."

"It could happen," the President agreed. "But I have twenty-five months until the conventions, and I have my people working on alternatives."

"Conservation, reverse osmosis, electro-osmosis, cloud seeding—things like that?"

"Things like that. Why, do you have any better idea, Mr. Forte?"

"I do indeed, Mr. President," and Forte spent the next half hour explaining it in detail.

So they wouldn't be disturbed by golf carts, people who wanted to play through, and distracting shouts of "Fore!" Joe Mansour had booked four hours for his personal use at the Acadia Beach Country Club in Hamilton, Bermuda, off which his great white yacht *Linno* rode at anchor. There were complaints from the irate members, of course, but the management brushed them aside. After all, Joe Mansour owned the club, the links, the bridle paths, and the stables, and if he could somehow have managed it, he would have owned the balmy breeze that rustled the leaves of the hibiscus and the palms as well.

"A four iron, I think, Rip," said Mansour, studying the lie.

Forte selected a club from among the three he carried in his bag, addressed the ball, and took a mighty swing. The ball dribbled down the fairway, bounched off a hummock, and came to rest five yards in the rough.

"You should have used a four iron," said Mansour.

"I have a driver, a five iron, and a putter, as you very well know," said Forte disgustedly. "If I bought all the clubs, I might learn to play the game and even grow to like it."

"Well, why not? Every man must have a vice, and you have far too few to be healthy."

"Hit the goddamn ball."

Mansour hit the goddamn ball. It went straight and high, seemed to pause in midair, and then fell to the green, no more than ten yards from the pin.

"You ought to be a golf hustler," said Forte sourly.

"I once tried it, actually. Match play at $10,000 a hole with three young New York investment bankers who had, they thought unbeknownst to me, been on the golf teams at Cornell and Harvard."

"Smeared you, did they?"

"Indeed they did. I kept losing to all three from noon until nightfall. They went away deliriously happy with $340,000 of my money, only to discover that during their absence from the office my men had bought up a majority interest that afternoon in a $200 million company they had been working for months to acquire."

"Joe," said Forte admiringly, "you are a character."

"I am a businessman. Businessmen have no character. To prove it, let me say at once that I have been beastly to a woman since I talked with you last week."

"Anybody I know?" said Forte, stamping down the grass in front of the ball and then teeing the ball up on a mound of dirt.

"Mrs. Jennifer Red Cloud."

Forte swung and missed. He looked up at Mansour, his lips a thin line. "Tell me about it, Joe."

"Nothing much to tell. As you know, Raynes Oceanic Resources is severely overextended. Mrs. Red Cloud, like the gambler she is, put about everything Raynes owns on the *Salvation*. She's borrowed from three institutions, spreading the grief around. So I followed in her footsteps with my little money bags and bought up all the notes."

"She doesn't know about this, does she?"

"Not the slightest suspicion."

"Keep it that way," said Forte.

He swung. The shot was a beauty, landing between Joe Mansour's ball and the pin.

On the clubhouse terrace, Joe Mansour added up his score. It was 83.

Forte, who had reached 110 before he stopped counting on the fourteenth hole, tore up the card and dropped it in the ashtray. "Enough of this kid's game," he said, before telling the waitress to bring them something as long, cool, and refreshing as her gorgeous legs. "Let's talk icebergs."

"Let us, indeed."

"Got lots of loose money laying around?"

"I'll tell you when you've overspent your allowance, Rip."

"Well, then, item one: a refrigerating plant, portable, capable of supercooling 5 million liters of water daily to −18° Centigrade. I'll give you the specs when we get back aboard the *Linno*."

"A refrigerating plant—for the *Antarctic*?"

"Check. Item two: Ultravac, the Alcor Company in Vestry, Alabama, makes material for ski suits. It's called Supervac. Buy the plant."

"Check," said Joe Mansour, wondering if his was going to cover to Ripley Forte's growing needs.

"Item three: Sol Brothers of San Antonio manufactures a photovoltaic panel that comes in rolls six meters wide. We need half a million square meters. I see no reason to buy the company if they'll supply it."

"I marvel at your consideration."

"Ever heard of a Japanese corporation named Masayuke Hara, Inc.? No? Well, it doesn't matter. Buy it."

"I don't suppose you could tell me what it makes?" said Joe Mansour plaintively.

"At the moment, oceans of red ink, but we'll turn it around."

"Sure we will," said Mansour without conviction. He raised the glass that the leggy waitress had brought and made a mental note to give Forte a crash course in finance.

"Item three—"

"Item *five*," amended the little Lebanese. "If you *must* think in millions, at least learn to count to ten."

"One of these days, Joe," said Forte with a shrug. "Item five: In Sandusky, Ohio, there's a rolling mill for specialty steels named, surprisingly enough, Sandusky Specialty Steels. It filed for bankruptcy two months ago. You should be able to pick it up cheap. Kindly do so."

"Anything to oblige. Any other little thing?" he said, prepared to cringe.

"As a matter of fact, no, unless real estate interests you."

"You aren't about to suggest I buy the United States, are you?"

"Later, maybe. Listen, Joe," said Forte, leaning toward him confidentially. "In south-central Australia lies the Nullarbor Plain. It's desert now, but in prehistoric times, the Nullarbor was a fertile land—"

"Sure, but what about harbors?" said Joe Mansour, already way ahead of him. The Australian government would own the barren land and be happy to unload any amount of it at any price. How much should he buy, 10 million acres? Twenty? As much, certainly, as he could afford. With world population increasing at 1.7 percent, or nearly the population of Japan, every year, one couldn't own too much irrigated wheatland.

Forte grinned. "There's a dandy little bay between Mount Arid and Cape Pasley." It was nice to have a partner you didn't have to draw pictures for.

But after Ripley Forte left for Texas, Mansour had second thoughts. Soon Ripley Forte would be fighting the powerful forces of nature. He would be fighting Secretary of Water Resources David D. Castle, who would now be his implacable enemy with the full weight of a government agency behind him. But his most formidable enemy would be Mrs. Jennifer Red Cloud. She was proud, single-minded, and unforgiving.

He tried to suppress the thought, but the businessman in Joe Mansour prevailed. He kept thinking, What a perfect time to take out a million-dollar life insurance policy on Ripley Forte.

16. PIPELINES AND PYRAMIDS
9 JUNE 2006

"YOU WERE PROBABLY TOO BUSY HAULING ICE TO notice," said Mark Medina, who had just greeted Ripley Forte at Houston International Airport, "but down here we're in deep trouble: oil wells dry, range lands dry, treasury dry. The only thing that hasn't dried up is crime. When the government couldn't stop it, vigilante groups took over, and we sort of got used to seeing rapists and robbers and crooked bank managers dangling from telephone poles when we went out in the morning. The legislators in Austin began to wet their jeans, thinking—with some justification—they'd be next, and voted Governor Cherokee Tom Traynor power to rule by decree."

"Yeah, I heard about that," said Forte vaguely.

"I'll bet you did. He drafted thousands of hard-assed vets into the police force and instructed them not to spare the rod. He made states attorneys bring the accused to trial within ten days, judges to sentence the guilty within two. He decreed hanging the day after sentencing for murderers, rapists, armed robbers, drug dealers, drunken drivers guilty of manslaughter, and white-collar thieves stealing more than $50,000. He put welfare recipients to work fifty hours a week on public works and cut *all* payments for those with more than two kids. He doubled insurance rates for smokers, drinkers, and fat bodies. He *quadrupled* gas taxes to encourage car pooling and public transport."

"That's Cherokee Tom, all right. Pretty impressive."

"Band-aids. He's merely stopped the slide. Right now he's walking a tightrope," said Mark Medina, opening the door to the limousine. "The only thing keeping him afloat is his evenhandedness: he's hurt *everybody*. But our economy is based on oil, grain, and cattle, and unless he can revive those industries, we're going to have us a nice little revolution."

"How long can he hang on?" Forte asked.

"Two, maybe three years. Why?"

"That'll be time enough."

That afternoon on the long veranda of El Cabellejo Ranch, Forte and Medina sat in rocking chairs and discussed strategy.

"I made a deal with President Turnbull, Mark. He's going to ram Forte Ocean Engineering as new prime contractor for the iceberg project down Secretary Castle's throat. As a cosmetic change to salve poor David's wounded pride, I've agreed to remove my name from the title. The joint U. S.–Forte Ocean Engineering project is going to be called Iceberg International, Incorporated—Triple Eye for short. Castle hasn't the leverage to object. He can only hope we come through with the berg so he can bask in our glory."

"That could be dangerous, Rip. The son-of-a-bitch could claim the credit and build up a national following on his California base."

"Not if he doesn't have a California base."

Mark Medina frowned. "I don't get it."

"Neither does David D. Castle. *We* get the berg, and *he* gets the finger, although he doesn't realize that yet."

"You mean you're going to bring the berg to *Texas*?"

"Yep."

"When did you dream up *that* hot idea?"

"I never had any other. What the hell do I care about California? What's California ever done for me?"

"There's that. But how are you—"

"Ah, there's the answer to your question coming up the road right now. Part of the answer, at least. As for the rest, Mark, my friend, all in good time."

A rusty pickup truck materialized out of the brown cloud that had whirled up the dirt road like a dust devil and rattled to a stop in front of the veranda. Forte and Medina greeted the driver, a big stooped man with face and arms stained a rich mahogany from years under the Texas sun, dressed in sweaty dungarees and shirt and a new Stetson of aching white.

"By God, Rip, it's good to see you," said the newcomer, working Forte's hand like a pump handle. "What is it, five years?"

"At least. You know Mark Medina, don't you, Phil?"

Phil Guthrie looked at the white-haired, white-mustachioed man—who could have stepped out of a castle in Spain and been entirely in character—and squinted. "Well, I *did* know a Mexican horse thief named Mark Medina once. Had him build me a products pipeline from Houston to Wichita. Cheated me, he did, and I can prove it—not a goddamn drop of oil is running through that pipeline today." He broke into a grin and grasped the older man's hand. "How the hell are you, Mark? Long time no see."

"I know. You're too busy running away from your creditors to see anything but the handwriting on the wall."

They all laughed and went inside, where it was cool amid the softening shadows of the Texas afternoon.

"So, how are things going, Phil?" said Forte. "Last time we met you were putting together the Texas-Southern consortium. You were going to get a stranglehold on oil distribution all the way from Texas to Chicago, maybe even to Denver."

Guthrie grimaced. "More like it's got a stranglehold on me, Rip. Mark here was right. I'm running away from my creditors. You know what they call my company now, don't you? T-S Corp."

"Bad as that?"

"Worse. A lot worse."

"What are Texas-Southern shares selling for right now?"

"You can have all you want for $1.25. Imagine, just two years ago they were going for $36, and I was a paper billionaire."

"Don't worry, Phil, you will be again."

"Oh, sure."

"Here's the deal. I want to buy your company. Or rather, I want *you* to buy your company, all the shares you can lay hands on, quietly, over the next year, so you won't run up the price. I'll bankroll you."

Phil Guthrie cocked an eyebrow at him.

"You're a friend, Rip. You *both* are. I don't diddle my friends. When I tell you to stay away from Texas-Southern, I'm telling you as a friend."

"Next," said Forte, "I want you to start a little collection—warrants for the purchase of other pipeline stock, preferably of companies whose right-of-way runs through wheatlands and big cattle spreads. I want you to put together a pipeline network that will blanket the Republic of Texas. That's first priority. After that, the Midwest, everywhere from the Mississippi River to the Rocky Mountains. I can put up to $1.5 billion into that little enterprise."

"You're kidding me, Rip. The word is out that your

banks pulled the plug on you. From what I hear, you'd be smart to climb in that jalopy there and join me in my fascinating flight from foreclosure. Why, there isn't enough oil being pumped in Texas today to fill Texas-Southern, let alone the network you're talking about."

"Who said anything about oil?"

An hour later, when Texas had absorbed all the heat it could stand for the day and was beginning to throw it back at the sky, Forte and Mark Medina were in a helicopter winging their way south. Some miles to the northeast of Corpus Christi, Forte pointed down to a small, almost landlocked body of water.

"Know what that is, Mark?"

"Sure, Matagorda Bay."

"Nope. That's where I'm going to berth my iceberg."

Mark Medina snorted and looked at Forte sideways. "How big will that berg be, Rip?"

"*Texas* big. About 1.6 by 3.2 kilometers—five times the size of the *Salvation*."

"And how thick?

"About 230 meters—750 feet."

"That makes you as thick as the berg, if you think you are going to get that berg into Matagorda Bay, unless you drag it on wheels." He pointed to the shoreline of the Gulf of Mexico beyond the Matagorda Peninsula. "There's the continental shelf, Rip. It slopes downward gradually. It starts at around ten meters deep near shore and is still only a hundred meters below the surface a hundred kilometers out into the gulf, before it drops off into water deep enough to float a berg that thick."

"The trouble with you and Phil Guthrie," said Forte, pulling the chopper around in a tight turn and heading down the coast, "is that you're thinking in traditional terms. This iceberg business is a whole new ball game."

A case in point, Forte pointed out, was getting the iceberg into Matagorda Bay. This aspect of the Triple Eye project alone would be by far the biggest earth-moving job in history. Enormous, undreamed-of quantities of sand and mud would have to be shifted. In shallow areas, conventional dipper dredges using grab buckets would haul up the spoil, to be moved by relays of barges until it was beyond the edge of the projected channel. In deeper areas, hydraulic dredges with 4.5-meter suction pipes moving behind rotary cutters would bring the overburden to the surface, to be carried away by floating slurry pipelines.

Mark Medina heard him out and shook his head.

"Do you have any idea of how much spoil you'd have to shift? Millions of cubic meters."

"Correction, *billions*. We've got to gouge out a 220-meter-deep trench through the shelf, which itself has a mean depth of 70 meters below the surface, in order to reach Matagorda Bay. The melt en route to Texas will, of course, make the berg ride higher in the water. The channel must be two kilometers wide, with sloping sides to accommodate possible cave-ins. The mud and sand that must be removed will come to 26 billion tons."

"Enough to fill a lot of sandboxes."

"To be more precise," said Forte, "it will be the equivalent of ten thousand Great Pyramids. On the other hand, the pharaohs used slaves. You will use machines."

"*I* will use. Oh, I see."

"Of course," said Forte, "that will be only the beginning of your labors." He eased the chopper around in a slow turn.

"For starters, Matagorda Bay must be dredged out deep enough to take the berg. That means continuing the trench right up to the shoreline. But once the berg's docked, it will have to be isolated from the gulf's seawater by an impermeable gate. Then we can begin melting operations with no worry about contamination."

Mark Medina shook his head disbelievingly.

"What you're saying is, we have to build a dam about a mile across and as high as the Eiffel Tower. Furthermore, we must be able to move it aside so the iceberg can be floated to its basin, and then move it back again, and what you been smoking lately, Rip?"

"I warned you it was a largish problem, Mark. The dam idea is out, of course. Instead, we build floating caissons in two-hundred-meter-long sections and anchor them off Palacios in the northern part of the bay. Basically, they'll be huge compartmented trapezoidal boxes with massive internal bracing. When the berg is tied up in its basin, we move the caissons into place, lock them together in a solid line, and flood 'em. They sink, forming a water-tight bulwark against the sea. We pump out the basin's salt water the berg is floating on. The berg melts, and the pure water is pumped to the farms and ranches and cities of Texas and the Midwest through all those pipeline networks Phil Guthrie is going to bust his ass putting together for us.

"By the time that berg is completely melted, we'll have brought another north, ready to tow into position. We flood the basin, tow the five floating caissons out of the way, and repeat the cycle. What could be simpler?"

Mark Medina groaned. Here was the big ugly Texan talking blithely about not one but *two* of the greatest construction projects undertaken since the building of the Great Wall of China. And he, Mark Medina, was going to have to scour the Gulf and Atlantic coasts for dredges, and recruit thousands of men, and build a shipyard in which the monster caissons could be constructed, and a small city to house the workers. He pointed out these home truths to the dreamer piloting the helicopter.

"But that's part of the plan, don't you see, Mark? Of *course* you're going to have to recruit tens of thousands of men to do the job. There are ten times that many out of work in the republic, and they'll come a-runnin'. Not only will we get the hungriest workers and put a dent in the unemployment problem, we'll inject huge amounts of money into the economy and, above all, bring our people something that poor old Lepoint couldn't: *salvation.*"

"You make it sound possible," said Mark Medina bitterly.

"And *you* made me *do* the impossible when I worked for you. Now that Joe Mansour has bought control of *both* our companies and is calling the tune, you and I are going to dance to it."

Medina sighed.

"Cheer up, Mark," said Forte. "I've given you all the bad news. Now comes the *good* news, the details."

"Like?"

"Well, there's the matter of the batteries of centrifugal

pumps we'll need to remove the seawater from the basin fast."

Medina scowled.

"And then we have to give some thought as to the best shroud to put over the berg once it's in place. That berg will contain the freshest, purest water in the northern hemisphere: no acid rain, no refinery particulates, no prairie dust, no bird droppings. We're going to keep it that way. And the shroud, being airtight, will not only prevent the water evaporating, but its greenhouse effect will accelerate melting."

"Shrouds I like. I'll be needing one for myself about then. Kindly proceed with the details."

"Well, we'll have to construct feeder pipelines to link up with Guthrie's network after he's run pigs through them and flushed them out. And then there's the transmission network, high-tension lines and substations and the like."

"To bring in power to run this operation, you mean."

"No, no, Mark—get *out* the power we're going to generate, to the consumer."

"So now we're in the power business, huh?"

"We're in everything. The power comes from ocean thermal energy conversion units. They're about the size of an apartment house. They take advantage of the temperature differential, in this case the hot Texas sun and the ice-cold berg, to generate electricity. There's going to be a big market for electricity now that crude production has dropped off. The twenty-six OTECs we need are going to produce enough electricity to light every house from here to Amarillo."

Mark Medina took out a handkerchief and wiped his face.

"Okay, let me see if I've got it," said Medina with mock humility. "We're going to dig a subterranean trench big enough to accomodate ten thousand pyramids, complete with mummies, construct five caissons as high as an Irishman on Saturday night and as long as an elephant's memory, build a city from scratch to accomodate the workers, not to mention a couple of dozen miles of pipeline and several hundred of high-tension lines. And the shroud—

I almost forgot the shroud. How the hell could I forget the shroud? And the OTECs, twenty-six of them. Have I left out anything, lord and master?"

"Nothing important."

"And what, pray tell, are *you* going to be doing while I'm working on these, ah, details?"

"Oh, I've kept the tough part for myself," said Ripley Forte. "I've got to go up against Jennifer Red Cloud."

17. CARMEL
10 JUNE 2006

RIPLEY FORTE FOLLOWED THE ROAD WINDING UP through the rustling pines until he came to a wooden gate with two big signs nailed to it. One said: "STOP—Private Property—Turn Back." The other: "Trespassers Will Be Shot Without Warning." He got out of his car, opened the gate, and drove in.

Around the next bend a much more substantial iron gate barred the way. He stopped. Men stepped out of the woods on his right and left. They were dressed in woodland camies and carried automatic shotguns in the crooks of their arms.

"Lost your way, sir?" said the one nearest him.

"I don't think so," said Forte. "My name is Ripley Forte. I have an appointment."

"Yes, sir," the unsmiling young man replied. From a patch pocket he produced what appeared to be a pair of binoculars with a short whip aerial. He handed it to Forte. Forte put it to his eyes and pressed the red button on top. There was a brief sensation of warmth as the EyeDentifier recorded his retinal pattern. Two seconds later, the house mainframe signaled that the subject's identity was confirmed as Ripley Forte and that he was expected.

"You can leave your car here, Mr. Forte. We'll park it for you."

Forte stepped out of the car and stood, hands aloft, as

the guard inspected him with a magnetometer. Five minutes later a jeep appeared around the curve, and the guard raised the gate to let him walk through. On the crest of the hill, Ripley Forte climbed out of the jeep and followed the path down to the house. At one point he could look down the coast almost to Big Sur and out across the blue Pacific. The air was crisp with the fragrance of salt spray overlaid with the musty scent of redwood and fir. It was so quiet, he could hear distinctly the trilling of songbirds in the valley far below.

His ring was answered by a small wrinkled Filipino who conducted him into a spacious and simply but expensively furnished room with a single huge plate-glass window overlooking the sea. He was asked to be seated, supplied with the wrong brand of bourbon without having been asked, and told that Mrs. Red Cloud would be along shortly. Forte was gazing out at the Pacific spread out below him like a smooth blue carpet when he felt rather than heard Mrs. Red Cloud enter the room.

He turned.

He kept forgetting just *how* beautiful she was. When younger, she had been supple and athletic. Now she was mature, commanding, regal. She was wearing a high-necked, long-sleeved, floor-length gown of white silk jersey, split up the thigh *cheong sam* fashion, and from the tightness of its fit it was pretty obvious that it was all she had on. She was barefoot, and somebody had spent a lot of time working on her toenails.

"Hello, Red," he said solemnly, advancing to meet her with hand extended.

She took it and stretched up to kiss him lightly on the cheek. Her perfume did things to his equilibrium that whiskey never could.

"What a pleasure, Ripley." She indicated a chair with a languid hand as she sank into the chaise longue.

Forte sat.

"I'm glad you stopped by. I've been wanting to have a talk with you for a long time."

"About what?" he asked guardedly.

"Business, of course. What else do we have to talk about?"

Forte didn't reply.

"Yes, I think it is time we came to an understanding. Some years back I was indulgent enough to buy you off for a rather extravagant sum—$5 million, I think it was— to ensure that I had no further interference from you in my affairs."

"I remember it a little differently, Red. You and Ned cheated me out of about $100 million and the prospect of a lot more."

"Apparently the warning not to meddle in my affairs didn't take," Mrs. Red Cloud went on equably. She leaned forward, her eyes narrowed, her skirt parting to reveal a disturbing length of thigh. "I'm afraid I cannot allow you to continue this way."

Forte dragged his eyes away. "What do you intend to do, Red, have me put out of my misery?"

"I don't think that will be necessary. Any day I can't outsmart you and take away all your marbles, my dear Ripley, I'll cut my throat."

"Yes, well, let's not talk right now about pleasant dreams but stern realities. I know your financial situation, Red. I have spies in high places. You're skating on the thinnest of ice. When *Salvation* foundered, so did Raynes Oceanic Resources. What saved you was three providential bank loans. But while you're engaged in your usual crooked maneuvers to recoup your losses, you're going to have to pay the interest on those loans, and your cash flow is practically zero."

"Don't weep for me. I'll recoup my losses. And when I do, I shall break you, if it takes the rest of my life."

"Sure," said Forte easily, "but meanwhile you have to get some money in the till. Those interest payments begin on the first day of 2007. What do you plan to do?"

"I'll think of something."

"Don't strain that beautiful brain of yours, Red. I've already thought of something for you."

"If you mean sell out to you and Joe Mansour, forget it."

"No, no, nothing like that. I'm talking about a straight business deal. Quid pro quo."

Mrs. Red Cloud felt a surge of relief. It was axiomatic in the ocean engineering field that there was no better

operations man and no worse businessman than Ripley
Forte.

"I'm listening."

"As you must have heard by now, President Turnbull
has ordered the Department of Water Resources to fund
an iceberg recovery program on the same terms that
Raynes Oceanic Resources received, with Forte Ocean
Engineering getting the prime contract."

"I *have* in fact heard the good news. I have heard, as
well, that you plan to bring your berg into Matagorda Bay,
Texas."

Ripley Forte whistled softly.

"You keep that beautiful ear close to the ground, I see."

"And you are going to fail, Ripley. I shall see to it
personally."

"I'm sure you'll try, Red. But meanwhile, those nasty
old interest payments. I was thinking, if you could maybe
dispose of that big inventory of OTECs that you planned
to use on the *Salvation* but are now sitting uselessly in
your dry docks, you'd be able to keep your head above
water. In the present depression, you have no other likely
customers for them."

"You are proposing to buy them, I gather."

"*Lease* them, all eighteen so far completed. And I'll
give you a firm commitment on a further eight if the terms
are right."

"Don't make me laugh."

Her cash flow problems were solved! The production
of power was going to be one of the essential factors in
determining whether iceberg transport would be an economically sound proposition. Forte obviously had failed
to find enough OTECs elsewhere. That meant that he had
to come to her, at *her* terms. She would charge what the
traffic—Joe Mansour's immense bank account—would
bear.

"I wasn't trying to make you laugh," said Forte.

"You never try, Ripley, but you amuse me all the same.
Very well, you may have the OTECs but the terms are
cash." She made some swift mental calculations and named
a figure.

Forte ground his teeth. It was more than double what

he had thought he'd have to pay. "It's too much."

"Of course it is. But if you don't buy them, I shall dismantle them and take a very large tax write-off. Either way I'm happy."

"It's a deal," Forte said hastily, as if afraid she'd change her mind. "But on one condition."

"You're not in a position to impose conditions, my sweet."

"Well, you'll have to accept this one or the deal won't go through, because without the Brown-Ash Mark IX I won't be able to bring an iceberg into port, and now's as good a time to settle that point as any."

Her first impulse was to give a peremptory refusal, but some instinct held her back. The thought of parting with the Brown-Ash Mark IX to Ripley Forte was, to be sure, anathema. Its computing capacity was so prodigious that there was no telling what an imaginative international operator like Joe Mansour, with his nearly unlimited resources, might do with it.

"And why must you have a Mark IX, not that there is the slightest chance that you will get it?"

Forte drummed his fingers on his knees and looked into her eyes as if trying to assess whether she could be made to understand. "Look, Red, the physical forces at work within an iceberg are almost, but not quite, incalculable. The external forces acting on it—the currents, the ocean waves, the salinity of the water and its resultant density, tides, the Coriolis effect, the strains on the tugboat lines, winds, rainfall, vapor pressure, atmospheric pressure, propeller vibration, the heat of the sun—dozens of factors—are even more complex. Unless we know the resultant of *all* these forces—the same forces, by the way, which destroyed the *Salvation*—we cannot counteract them to keep the iceberg intact. Towing an iceberg isn't like pushing an ice cube around in a highball. It's more like trying to drag a dipper of ice cream through a bowl of warm soup. There are billions of numbers to crunch every second of every day for six months, and only the Mark IX has the capacity to do it. Old Lepoint didn't appreciate that, and if it hadn't been for my firsthand experience, I wouldn't have either.

"So there's your choice, Red. You can make or break the *Alamo* right here, right now."

"The *Alamo*?"

"That's the name I'm going to give my berg."

"You'd better save it for your mobile retirement home, because you certainly aren't going to get a Mark IX out of me!"

Ripley Forte sipped at his drink and looked out the picture window at the placid Pacific. "I sort of thought you'd say that, Red. But you forget one thing: I've got the personal and official backing of the President of the United States. All I need to do is give him a call, and you can bet those lovely lynx eyes of yours that he'll have an official order on the way by return mail."

"I'll refuse. It's a free country. Brown-Ash is a wholly owned subsidiary of Raynes Oceanic Resources. And I own Raynes."

"But do you own the Lackland Missile Development Center?"

"Of course not. So what?"

"Well, when I mentioned to President Turnbull you might be a little shirty if I asked to buy a BAM-IX, he said he might be able to persuade Lackland to lend me theirs, seeing us how they needed it primarily for simulation runs on the Titan IV, and the Titan IV is now in production."

"I see."

Her expression was savage, but her heart was serene. Better and better. She'd provide Ripley Forte with a Mark-IX, all right, *after* several minor adjustments had been made to it. For the rest of his days he'd remember the *Alamo*. "You win," she said briefly.

"That was my intention."

"But only temporarily. I am going to destroy you, Ripley. I should have done so when I kicked you out of Raynes."

"So it *was* you."

"Of course. Ned was afraid of you. He got cold feet. And I had a moment of weakness and let you have the money to get back on your feet. This time I will be walking in your shadow from the moment you find your blessed *Alamo* until it floats away in little pieces."

"I hope you're better at walking on water than you are in shadows, because you aren't going to get near *my* iceberg, lady."

"Am I not?"

"Unless you're going to disguise yourself as a skua."

"A skua? What's that?"

"Never mind," said Forte, realizing that the parallel was uncomfortably close. "You're welcome to conspire from a distance. Do your worst. But if you get even within spittin' range of the *Alamo*, I'm going to fan your bottom good."

"*That* should be an experience," she said, fluttering her long black lashes. "But before you run off to chisel those words in stone, my dear Ripley, I must inform you that yesterday I was appointed assistant secretary of water resources for administration by Secretary Castle. David has assigned me to monitor, personally, the expenditure of every penny of government money devoted to water projects, especially iceberg recovery."

"I don't believe it," said Forte, coloring.

"There's the phone. Perhaps you'd like to check with David yourself."

"You can't do it, Red. No serving member of a corporation board can occupy an appointive post in the federal government. That's conflict of interest."

"Not at all. Two hours before the appointment became official, I resigned my directorships and put all my stocks in a blind trust." She smiled sweetly.

Ripley rose, his face expressionless.

"Don't grieve, Ripley," said Jennifer Red Cloud soothingly, sitting in her chair with her feet tucked under her. "Maybe I'll grow on you."

Forte looked down at her. "You already have."

"I beg your pardon?" She seemed truly taken aback.

Score one for Ripley Forte. It was the first time he had actually surprised her. Why stop now? "You must be pretty stupid not to know that I've been in love with you from the first time I saw you, the day you married Ned."

Her hand came up to her face.

"But you—"

"Just shut up and listen, Red. If I had met you a day

earlier, I'd have killed him before I'd let him have you—
that's what you did to me. Then, after Ned died, when I
could have had you—"

"The *hell* you could," she flared. "I'd never—"

"Kindly be quiet. I could have had you, but not on my
terms. You'd want to run the show, just as I finally realized
you ran Ned. Well, sister, I'm not the kind of man you
can dangle on a string. I'm going to have you, but it's
going to be on *my* terms."

She laughed a brittle, hysterical laugh.

"Oh, you *are*?"

"You're damned right I am. First I'm going to break
Raynes Oceanic Resources. Then I'm going to marry you."

"*Marry*?" She laughed hysterically. "An ugly, hairy-
handed, bourbon-swilling, tinhorn baboon like you?"

"Ever read the ethologist Konrad Lorenz?"

"Never met him, Ripley."

"But he met you, and all other females in the animal
kingdom who yearn to be dominated but often find no
one with enough balls to do so, and out of frustration and
rage try to take over the male's function. They used to
call it women's lib. What they call it now I couldn't guess,
probably something as obscene as the concept."

"I—I—"

"Lorenz learned about women by studying jackdaws.
He observed that at the beginning of each mating season
the males would fight to establish a pecking order, the
stronger male pecking all the others below him on the
ladder. Only then did the *females* chose their mates, and
the most beautiful always chose the man at the top of the
status ladder, even if he was old and ugly. The poor bird
at the bottom, even though he might be young and handsome, got the least attractive of the females.

"That's why we see so many rich, fat, disgusting old
men married to young, lovely, *satisfied* females. That's
why a beautiful Apache-Norwegian maiden promises herself to an anemic third-rate politician who imagines he
has a shot at the White House. It's the jackdaw itch,
beautiful. Until Lorenz came along, we always thought
she married him for his money. We were wrong. She mar-
ries him because he is the man at the top of the ladder,

the man everybody respects, the man who, when he speaks, makes people jump."

"And you think that when you speak, I'll jump." Jennifer Red Cloud was cold with fury.

"Not yet, my sweet. When I've stripped you bare, and taken away all your playthings, *and* become king of the hill, *then* you'll jump."

"Get out of here, you goddamn son of a bitch!" she screamed, leaping to her feet.

Forte turned and walked to the door. As he opened it and passed through, he looked at her over his shoulder.

"Just think, sweetheart, I'm going to be captain of the *Alamo*, and you're going to be my first mate."

She threw a counterfeit Ming vase at his departing back. It crashed into the door and shattered into a dozen pieces.

The Filipino Manuel materialized.

"You called, madam?"

"Yes, I did," said Jennifer Red Cloud without a trace of emotion. "You're fired!"

18. THE TWELVE WISE MEN OF OYO
15 FEBRUARY 2007

THE REGULAR WEDNESDAY MORNING STAFF MEETING at the Oyo Experimental Farm Cooperative offices outside Oyo, 175 kilometers north of Nigeria's capital, Lagos, was devoted entirely to the report of Meyer Horowitz on the iceberg *Alamo* operation.

Horowitz, a short, rotund man with a bald head and half-moon glasses, rose and cleared his throat. He opened a file and laid it on the table in front of him.

"Fellow members," he began, "I finally have the information requested. Its accuracy is beyond question. And I believe that if we utilize it to the fullest, we may be able to strike a blow at Russia from which it may never recover. More of that later.

"We have established that preparations for the capture and transport of the *Alamo* are proceeding on schedule, in some cases ahead of schedule. If that schedule is carried through, the *Alamo* will be berthed in Matagorda Bay, the Republic of Texas, shortly before the presidential conventions begin. Therefore, the fates of both the incumbent and his future opponent, David D. Castle—each of whom is very concerned that the project succeed so he can take the lion's share of the credit for it—rides heavily on the outcome.

"Now, from a study of reports of our agents, of logistical preparations now under way, of ocean currents and the berg's destination, we have come to the conclusion that the *Alamo* will be towed into the northward-flowing Benguela Current. The Benguela is cold, fast, and, fellow members, *it runs within several hundred miles of the Nigerian coast.*"

"Remarkable!" said OEFC Chairman Chiam Shitrit.

"God's will!" said Rabbi Israel Cohen.

"The opportunity of the century!" said Moshe Davi, chief of operations.

"Yes," agreed Horowitz. "It is all those things. And now we must agree on the best means of utilizing our great good fortune."

The other eleven men in the sparsely furnished room knew exactly what he meant: The *Alamo* must be destroyed.

When the Russians had, in the late 1980s, conquered as much of the world as they thought they could comfortably digest, they had conspicuously omitted the Benipic countries—Bangladesh, Egypt, Nigeria, Indonesia, Pakistan, India, and China—from their acquisitions. At first the reasons for this omission were not apparent, but gradually their reasoning became clear. The seven countries were veritable baby factories whose uncontrolled birthrates could not possibly be matched by industrial and agricultural production to maintain even a subsistence standard of living.

The United States, as Russia had foreseen, came galloping to the rescue. It poured thousands of experts, millions of tons of foodstuffs, and billions of dollars into these sinkholes of man's hopes, where they disappeared without a trace, except to generate even greater numbers of hungry mouths. As it strove to catch up with the ever-increasing demand, the U.S. itself grew proportionately poorer. Eventually the forty-nine states became little more than a vast plantation whose people worked overtime to feed a hungry world, an arms factory to supply the tin-pot dictators who used American weapons mainly against their own people, and a bank to finance the extravagances of foreign tyrants who ruled the masses.

But the United States was also propping up its enemies. Encouraged by subsidies voted by politicians in Washington greedy for their vote, American farmers were producing great surpluses of food. Once produced, the surpluses had to be disposed of. This was accomplished by dumping millions of tons of grain every year on Russia at below-market prices, in one stroke averting bread riots in the streets of Moscow and freeing rubles for investment in war industries to produce weapons with which to menace America.

In recent years, of course, chronic drought had cut deeply into American farm surpluses. This both raised the price of exported wheat and reduced its availability. Russia, whose own farmers had for eighty years failed to satisfy domestic requirements thanks to a stultifying collective farming system, was suffering badly.

In short, the *Alamo* project on which America was pinning its hopes for recovery was for Russia, and for communism as well, the promise of salvation.

"Therefore," said Horowitz, "it must fail. Our most recent diaspora from Israel, one step ahead of the Russians, must be only temporary. I know it is tempting to wish our present situation were permanent. We are living comfortable, secure lives. We have brought the Nigerians organization and technical expertise, manned their hospitals, universities, and law courts, invigorated their armed forces with combat-hardened veterans. And the Nigerians are grateful and wish us to stay. But we must not."

"Quite true," agreed Rabbi Cohen. "Next year—Jerusalem!"

"*Some* year, anyway," said Davi wryly. "But to get there it must be over Russia's dead body. And that's what it will be—dead—unless it gets America's grain. No *Alamo*, no grain. It's as simple as that."

In the Israel they had fled, the twelve wise men had worn other hats: engineer, politician, soldier, banker. Here, the "administrators" and "agronomists" formed the Planning Organization, the supreme, if covert, governing body of Jews in Nigeria.

By nightfall, a weary Meyer Horowitz gaveled his colleagues into silence. "Gentlemen, we have discussed Project Titanic in, I believe, sufficient detail. If the first alternative fails, one of the others will surely succeed. Any dissents?"

No one spoke.

"Then we begin the implementation of Project Titanic tomorrow."

Rabbi Cohen sighed contentedly. It was the final solution.

19. BLACK PRAXIS
17 NOVEMBER 2007

HE WAS NOT A DRINKING MAN, BUT AT THE END OF HIS working day, at four o'clock on the morning of 17 November 2007, Lieutenant General Grigoriy Aleksandrevich Piatakov felt that a toast was in order.

Piatakov's optimism was recent. His first reaction to the realization that he was facing a dead end, that his career of infinite promise had been cut short, had been livid anger. Then, during the ensuing weeks, he had passed through successive phases of resignation, despair, and the contemplation of suicide.

He finally pulled out of it. He'd always been a man of action, and action, not self-pity, was needed now. Everything had been taken from him but faith in himself. This exile to Room 101 was just another test of his strength and ingenuity. He'd won through before; he'd do so again.

Work had not paused in Room 101 during his emotional crisis. The stack of files awaiting his attention grew steadily, and after he rejoined the living, working through them took a full two months of concentrated effort before he felt free to begin the program of reform of Room 101 that had inspired his permanent assignment here.

The most pressing task was to convert the files currently on paper to laserdisk. Though tedious, involving hand feeding uncounted millions of pages into the hoppers of the automated optical character readers, it involved no special skills. All technicians were required to spend two hours extra a day manning the banks of machines until the operation was finished.

The fiber-optic system Piatakov had recommended was soon in operation as well, and the regular transmission lines were cut. No longer was there the faintest possibility of interception of calls between Room 101 and the Presidium switchboard.

But despite his very dramatic improvements in the morale and efficiency of Room 101, he had not been able to devise a plan to involve his personnel in really significant strategic operations. For one thing, the Presidium had entertained second thoughts about the wisdom of concentrating so many vital functions in a single department, no matter how secure. For another, the operatives in the field expressed outrage at the suggestion that their flexible prerogatives might be curtailed. The best bargain Piatakov had been able to strike was to be allowed the opportunity to plan and execute a *single* operation. Its fulfillment by Room 101 would prove, Piatakov argued, that its immense resources were underutilized, and would constitute the rationale for expanded future responsibilities.

The operation chosen was the theft of a Brown-Ash Mark IX, now in its fourth year of manufacture. Russian agents had seen it, and one had actually written a program for it, as a member of the Pentagon staff having access to a late model. But security had been tight. By law, four armed guards stood watch day and night over each of the eleven BAM-IXs, and the limited-access areas where they were located were at the centers of military installations. There was one exception: the BAM-IX that reposed

at the bottom of an old salt dome just outside Houston,
Texas. Built by the Texas multimillionaire Gwillam Forte
to house his ultrasecret defense manufacturing plant,
SD-1 was a city very much like Room 101 in its inaccessibility. It could be entered, so far as was generally known,
only by two elevators, one passenger, one cargo, that
descended 1,450 meters straight down to the hollowed-out salt dome. It was big enough to house a good-sized
town. In fact, it had been conceived to do just that: During
the wintriest days of the cold war, Gwillam Forte had
ordered it built to accomodate the Houston employees of
Sunshine Industries, safe from everything but direct hits
by megaton nuclear missiles. When he died, SD-1 went
to his heirs. They in turn sold it to Joe Mansour when its
manufacturing facilities, until then producing heavy armaments for the United States, fell into desuetude after Texas
again became a republic.

And now that Ripley Forte was a partner with Joe
Mansour in the commercial recovery of Antarctic icebergs, SD-1 had been revived as the R&D center and
communications base for Triple Eye. The BAM-IX was
as diligently guarded in SD-1 as on the various military
installations, but SD-1 had an Achilles' heel that General
Piatakov intended to exploit.

During the secret conversion of the U.S.S. *Texas*, which
had devastated the Russian 17th High Seas Fleet in the
Battle of the Black Channel on 7 July 1998, a 9.1-kilometer-long tunnel had been built to link SD-1 with the basin in
which the *Texas* was tied up. No longer needed, the tunnel
had been abandoned and bricked up. From the basin at
the San Jacinto National Monument outside Houston, it
would be necessary only for frogmen to breach the steel
underwater door to gain admittance to the tunnel. Some
night, a KGB *spetsnaz* force would be introduced into the
tunnel. Equipped with gas masks, they would drill a hole
through the tunnel seal and inject nerve gas into SD-1
proper. The salt dome's air circulation system would diffuse the gas through the man-made cave within two minutes, and within three not a soul would be still alive. The
commandos would then haul the Brown-Ash Mark IX up
the tunnel tracks and load it onto a fast boat for a run

down the Houston Ship Channel to rendezvous with a waiting Russian submarine in the Gulf of Mexico. It would be aboard and on its way to Murmansk before the alarm was sounded.

Maybe. The success of the plan depended on many variables, but variables were the daily bread of Piatakov's specialists. As his officers proposed different combinations and permutations of the basic plan, the revised edition would be turned over to the Black Praxis group for testing. Black, or clandestine, operations, involving the risk of the operations team being summarily shot if detected, were always subjected to rigorous full-scale praxis: practical exercise as opposed to theory. Only when the most feasible plan had been fully worked out would the Presidium give the go-ahead and the team be dispatched.

The eighteen-man team for Operation Armageddon, as Piatakov had named it in a moment of wry humor, was still being selected. It would take at least six months before it would be ready for action. To wipe out all margin of error had been Piatakov's goal from the moment Operation Armageddon was first conceived. He was, after all, a professional. The Presidium was counting on him to obtain the BAM-IX, and he promised himself that come what may, the Presidium was going to get it.

To that end, Piatakov demanded every scrap of information that concerned SD-1, the *Alamo* operation, and Ripley Forte and his associates, their relatives, the friends of their relatives, and the relatives of their friends. Masses of information inundated Room 101. Most of it was useless, but now and again a useful morsel in the boiling caldron of gossip, speculation, and hard fact drifted to the surface. Such a one was contained in the dispatch that came from his operative in Oyo, Nigeria.

Levi Ben-Zvi was a plant geneticist allowed to emigrate from Russian to Israel on the completion of his studies at Moscow University in 1981. He was a brilliant young man and one whose good manners and civility were tempered by what appeared to be an unbearable sadness, as though he carried the world on his narrow shoulders. At the Weizmann Institute of Science in Rehovot, he rapidly

rose to become chief of the Department of Plant Genetics.
Ben-Zvi's contributions to his science were continuous,
conspicuous, and valuable to Israel. His contributions to
Russian intelligence were equally outstanding, for Levi
Ben-Zvi was an agent of the KGB.

The conflict between his two lives was the source of
his suffering. Not until some years after he had been
allowed—with unexpected ease, he thought at the time—
to emigrate to Israel did he realize that from his school
days he had been recruited into the Russian intelligence
network. His great talent had been one factor. The other
was his large family, for which he had such a fierce love
and pride that most of his pay in Israel went back to
Leningrad to help support them.

One winter evening while walking back to his spartan
quarters, shortly after he had become head of department
at Weizmann Institute, he was joined by a tall thin man
wearing a trench coat, with a fedora pulled down over his
brow. He looked like somebody out of a spy movie. He
introduced himself as Pavel. He had come to Israel with
news of Ben-Zvi's family.

"Are they well?" asked a startled Ben-Zvi.

"For now." He stopped under a street lamp and produced a picture. It was of Ben-Zvi's father, Amos. "But
we fear that this one may fall ill..."

From that day onward, Levi Ben-Zvi was one of KGB's
most faithful respondents. He told them everything he
knew, had heard, read, or conjectured, and then went
home to pray for his family, his country, his religion, and
his immortal soul. He was a tortured man.

After he fled to Nigeria with so many other Israelis,
he thought that perhaps the KGB had lost track of him.
In fact, he wasn't approached all the first year, and he
began to breathe easier. But they were leaving him alone,
he realized later, only until he had established himself in
the heirarchy of the new diaspora. By 1995 they had come
calling again, and their visits had never since ceased.

And now he had come up with some interesting, some
really interesting information, thought Lieutenant General Grigoriy Aleksandrevich Piatakov, information that
justified all the care they had lavished on Levi Ben-Zvi

and all the extra rations and protection they had provided his family.

He had just told his case officer about the three options of Project Titanic.

The three options concerned the iceberg *Alamo*, which Piatakov surmised, based on the information in his files about the *Salvation*, must still be part of a glacier in Antarctica, as yet unseen by man. The options were contrived to ensure that the iceberg never produced a drop of water for thirsty America, never a grain of wheat that could be shipped to the Jews' implacable enemy, Russia. As Piatakov might have expected, the three options were ingenious, logical, and probably untraceable to the twelve wise men of Oyo or, indeed, to anyone else.

The first option, Piatakov believed, would not work.

The second, given the right conditions, just might.

The third would succeed, without the slightest shadow of doubt.

Regretting that he wasn't a drinking man, he toasted the twelve in his heart.

PART III
ICE

20. THE *ALAMO*
2 JANUARY 2008

ON 2 JANUARY 2008 MRS. JENNIFER RED CLOUD CHRIS-
tened the iceberg *Alamo* with a bottle of the mixed waters
of the Pecos, Rio Grande, Colorado, Brazos, Neches,
Nueces, Trinity, and Guadalupe, the principal rivers of
the Republic of Texas, which during the drought, now in
its fifth year, had dwindled to little more than muddy
rivulets. If successfully brought to safe harbor in Matagorda Bay, the *Alamo* would go far toward relieving the
mounting hardships of the republic. The thoughts of the
four hundred male onlookers, mostly Texans, should
therefore have been focused on the importance and solemnity of this historic occasion.

They weren't. Their thoughts—and their eyes—were
focused on Mrs. Jennifer Red Cloud's lithe and lovely
body.

Ripley Forte promised himself that she would wear the
form-hugging Ultravac publicly as little as possible. He
felt the annoyance natural to one who sees everybody
else ogling the body he covets, and worse, he feared that
her distracting influence around men working with dangerous machinery could cause a catastrophe that would
result in his loss of the *Alamo*. Of course, since nothing
would please Jennifer Red Cloud more, he would have to
keep her on a short rein.

Immediately following the christening, he got her away
from the crowd by saying that he was off to make an
aerial inspection of the facilities, a boring chore she
obviously would prefer to give the miss. Predictably, she
insisted on coming along.

The four-place chopper ascended in a low looping arc
that brought them to the *Alamo*. Forte cruised its length
slowly, on the lookout for trouble spots that might not

have shown up on the preliminary seismographic surveys. Turning a corner, he started up the short side, pausing in midair from time to time, bringing the chopper down almost to the waterline and then straight back up before going on.

The *Alamo* had been under satellite surveillance since Triple Eye had received official U.S. government sanction in June 2006. By means of satellite imaging, every one of the more than fifteen thousand bergs that had calved from the Ross, Shackleton, Amery, Filchner, and Larsen ice shelves during the ensuing eighteen months had been tracked and photographed as they circled the Antarctic continent and gradually melted away in the Circumpolar Current.

That it had not calved in its seagoing life of more than fourteen months was an indication of its internal stability. Its present size and position close to the southern tip of the African continent were other factors that prompted him to take it in tow and, on the second day of the new year, proclaim it the *Alamo*.

"It's not as rectangular as the *Salvation*," Jennifer Red Cloud remarked. "It's more like a—a *trapezoid*," she added, as if this were a damning indictment.

"I chose it for its absence of fault lines and its ideal volume, not to enter in a beauty contest. It may not be as purty as your berg, but at 3,210 meters long by 1,165 meters wide it holds more than five times the water. More important, it's 232 meters thick, which means its mean density is greater than yours, and the denser it is, the less likely it is to develop internal strains."

She sniffed. Mere technicalities. He as much as admitted it: *hers* was more beautiful.

"If that's the case," she said, suddenly realizing how she could put him in his place, "why didn't you get a *bigger* berg, ten thousand meters by five thousand, say?"

"This berg is already about as much as we can handle."

"Well, I don't see why it has to be so *fat*. If it were narrower, it would look better in pictures. Also, if it were more streamlined, it would be easier to tow."

Forte smiled. Well, there was a way to stop her nagging, anyway. "Good point. But remember, the narrower a berg is, the greater the danger of its rolling over. The metacentric height should be positive—right?"

"Metacentric?"

"The metacenter is the intersection of a vertical line through the center of a floating body at equilibrium with a vertical line through the center of buoyancy when the line is tilted. *That's* clear enough, I hope."

"Of course," she said testily. "What do you think I am, a complete idiot?"

"Certainly not! Now, as you know, ocean waves beating against and under the ice shelf break off bergs to begin with. In the same fashion, large tabular bergs with width-to-depth ratios in excess of ten will be broken up in the same way by long-wavelength ocean waves. That's why we picked the *Alamo* with that particular geometry. You see?"

"Yes, yes," she said, her eyes beginning to glaze over. "It's very simple once you— What in the world is going on down *there*?" She pointed to a ship that was just coming into view, thankful for the diversion.

Forte gained altitude until they were five hundred meters above the edge of the berg onto which a ship was unloading. He put the machine on automatic hover.

Below them the sun flashed off enormous whirling propellers as a Mi-21K cargo helicopter lifted from the flight deck of a supply ship. In a cable sling it bore a length of iron pipe four meters in diameter and sixteen meters long to the afterend of the berg, where the helicopter lowered the pipe to the surface.

"What the devil is that?" said Jennifer Red Cloud, pointing.

"A helicopter."

"Don't you think I know a helicopter when I see one?" she said, her face turning pink within the bubble helmet.

"Then why did you ask?"

"I have never seen a helicopter so big, that's why. I wasn't aware that such monsters existed."

"It's Russian. Made to open up Siberia, where the permafrost doesn't permit the building of roads. It can transport a three-bedroom house or two companies of shock troops—choose your pick."

"But *Russian*?"

"Hated to do it, but there's no American chopper that can do the Mi's tricks."

"What was it carrying?"

"Make a guess."

"I'm no good at guesses."

"Then think about it."

"I'm thinking," she replied. "Some kind of fuel storage tank?"

"No cigar. They're cable anchors. Old Lepoint used an elaborate harness. Not bad in its way, but this is a better approach. We drive those cylinders—there will be sixteen of them at regular intervals across the aft end of the *Alamo* by the time we're finished—into the snow by heating their leading edges. Their weight does the rest. Then the ice refreezes, and the anchors are held fast by the ice."

"Yes, but there's an energy loss in refreezing the ice," she said triumphantly. "That's bad."

Forte smiled. "You're learning."

"Don't patronize me, you big baboon," she snapped at him. "Well?"

"Good thinking, as I said, but your assumption is wrong. This ice *isn't* zero degrees Celsius, the freezing point of water. It's true that up to about ten meters deep, the snow temperature is a good measure of the berg's mean annual surface temperature. Right now, for example, that mean temperature is around $-22°$ Celsius because that is the mean for the Ross Ice Shelf, where this berg originated. On the other hand, below ten meters the ice in a berg gradually warms. At the bottom of this berg when it separated from the Ross, it was about $-12°$, although that part in contact with the salty sea is quickly raising its temperature toward $-1.8°$, the freezing point of seawater here."

"So what does all this tell me?"

"Simply," said Forte, "that we don't need refrigeration to set those cable anchors, because the berg still has a substantial 'cold reserve.'"

"Which," Jennifer Red Cloud pointed out, "will dissipate when we get into warmer latitudes."

"I'm afraid so, and that's just *one* of our problems."

It took Forte's crew three and a half days, working around the clock in three shifts, to bury the sixteen cable anchors aft and rig them with their harnesses. Each pair of adjoining cables, made of braided nylon line a hundred meters long and as big around as a weight lifter's thigh, was yoked to a steel I beam whiffletree, to which a thicker line was attached. The sixteen lines thus became eight and, repeating the process, four.

"Only four tugs to haul this enormous berg?" Jennifer Red Cloud said as they disembarked from the helicopter for the daily inspection tour on a brilliant Sunday morning, 6 January 2008.

"Not even," said Forte mysteriously.

"Then how—"

"All in good time.

The rest of the day Forte spent mainly on logistics and getting the permanent seismographic survey organized. Like Lepoint, he spotted the facilities checkerboard fashion at wide intervals to minimize human loss in the event of calving, although he was fairly sure he had *that* problem licked, at least. Unlike Lepoint, Forte didn't construct his facilities on inflatable bladders, for with the berg totally encased in Ultravac, the best and toughest insulation man had yet devised, there would be very little surface melt, even in the tropics. Much of the material had been stacked at preselected sites where it would be used. This included dozens of enormous white-painted steel cylinders that seemed to Mrs. Red Cloud identical to those used for the cable anchors but which Forte assured her had an entirely different function.

The permanent seismographic survey team's ten technicians were constantly on the prowl about the surface of the *Alamo*, planting strings of sensors like rare flowers and then, after a brief sharp blast of powder, uprooting them and moving off to repeat the process elsewhere. The masses of data they accumulated were beamed to a geostationary satellite and routed to SD-1 in Houston for analysis by the BAM-IX, the results being radioed back within seconds. He wasn't sure how much notice of impending disaster the seismographic soundings would give, but even an hour would be enough to evacuate the berg if necessary.

That evening they had cocktails in the wardroom of the S.S *Isobel Jordan*, the converted U.S. Navy hospital ship that served as Forte's floating headquarters. They were sitting in a corner apart from the ship's officers, who were noisily kibitzing a game of acey-deucy between the chief engineer and the boatswain. Forte was in clean but disreputable dungarees and docksiders, and Mrs. Red Cloud wore a long black-and-silver lamé gown nearly as revealing as her daytime attire, a diamond pendant, and matching earrings. Her long, black, upswept hair had been the object of two hours of painstaking comb-and-spray-can virtuosity by her Filipino hairdresser Rudolfo, who had interlaced it with what appeared to be about five meters of strung pearls. It would probably take him another two hours to extricate them later that night. Her open-toed silver pumps had spike heels long enough to nail railroad ties together.

"So far, so good," said the beast to the beauty as they sat opposite each other.

She raised her glass and gazed at him appraisingly over the rim. "To crime."

"Speaking of which, how's your little plan to sabotage the *Alamo* coming along?"

"Not well. Of course, it's early days, and I have—how many did you say?"

"About 185."

"Yes, I have 185 days to go. Plenty of time."

"True, but there's plenty of berg, too," he taunted her. "You just can't let the air out of the tires, you know. It's got to be something big and gaudy, like a cosmic ray gun, and cosmic ray guns take space. I mention this simply to remind you that down here on the high seas I own about the only space there is: that fleet of twenty-three ships out there, each manned by men I know and trust. I'm not sure that even if you persuaded one of my captains to fill up his ship with dynamite and ram the *Alamo* that it would sink. Bergs are like women—cold, hard, and unforgiving and tending to go to pieces when you least expect it."

"Don't worry about me, Rip," she said with a steely

smile. "I'll think of a way." But nothing she had seen this morning seemed very promising. She couldn't put a torch to it, push it off a high place or in front of a truck, blow it up, or sink it. If she could somehow, she thought sourly, procure the services of a couple of thousand little men with blow torches . . .

"I'm sure you will—you and your computer brain."

"Speaking of which," she said casually, "how is the BAM-IX working out?"

"Like a dream, according to the boys back in SD-1. We feed it lots and lots of little numbers, and it processes them into a million points on a graph, and we step back to look at it, and lo! instant Seurat."

Seurat.

Jennifer Red Cloud blinked. How could a man who had spent his life at sea and in boisterous tent camps know about a relatively obscure nineteenth-century post-impressionist French painter, a pointillist who fashioned masterpieces from tiny dots of color on a broad canvas, for God's sake? And he didn't say *Georges* Seurat, either, as he would have if he were trying to impress her. Even more disconcerting, he had *pronounced* it correctly.

She looked at him, *really* looked at him, perhaps for the first time in her life. She began to feel uneasy; perhaps she had underestimated him. It was a disquieting thought.

For some reason, she found herself thinking of jack-daws.

21. THE SUN KING
11 JANUARY 2008

"WHAT'S IN CAPE TOWN?" JENNIFER RED CLOUD asked as the amphibian jet tiptoed across the wave crests and into the air.

"Well, for one thing, there are a lot of shops where you can buy clothes," Forte said pointedly. She was wearing a tight-fitting, high-necked, long-sleeved wool dress. It might have been applied with a spray can.

"Yes, there's that. Anything else?"

"Sure. Giraffes, shantytowns, diamond mines, hamburgers and Afrikaans burghers, land sharks, great white sharks, pool sharks—you name it."

"You're certainly the one for sharing knowledge. How long a flight will it be?"

"Just under half an hour. Not time enough to figure out how to blow the *Alamo* out of the water."

He got up and opened the door to the flight deck, occupied only by a squat, bearded man in the left-hand seat.

"Mind if I get in a little twin-engine time?" asked Forte.

"It's your plane, mate," the pilot pointed out.

It was a short, uneventful flight. The sun was already high in the sky when Forte set the boat down, a bit too roughly for the pilot's taste, and turned over the controls for taxiing up to the dock jutting out into Table Bay.

Aft, with not a hair of her coiffure out of place, Jennifer Red Cloud had changed into something more befitting Cape Town's balmy summer weather: a canary-yellow silk halter and a matching skirt split up one side, with a good deal of tanned, taut flesh showing.

The chartered helicopter awaited them on the dock. By 10 A.M. they were high above Table Mountain and heading past Devil's Peak and Lion's Head toward Simonstown, twenty miles due south.

They were met on Simonstown Dock Number Three, a jetty projecting more than a kilometer into False Bay, by Dr. Konrad Honikman, the mayor of the municipality, and a delegation of generals, engineers, civic officials, and a lone Japanese. Behind them milled many of the two-thousand-odd men and women who had worked on the project, waiting for the ceremonies to get under way and doubtless praying for few and short speeches so that they could get at the long tables behind the reviewing stand piled high with food and hard liquor.

Dr. Honikman seated his guests in a place of honor in the stands adjoining a monstrous iron vessel. To Jennifer

Red Cloud, it appeared to be a vast black Frisbee floating
on the placid bay. The deck was featureless except for
the stanchions like a line of white pickets around the
periphery of the vessel, on which were strung three lines
to prevent the crew, she supposed, from falling the seven
or eight meters to the water below.

Her inspection was interrupted by martial music, as a
military band broke into the strains of "Die Stem van Suid
Afrika." A preacher from the Dutch Reformed Church
advanced to the podium and asked for the blessings of
heaven, she gathered, in Afrikaans.

Then came Dr. Honikman. His was to be the first of
several speeches that dragged on for the next three hours.

Elegant in cutaway and top hat, he addressed his fellow
townsmen at great length in Afrikaans and then repeated,
word for tedious word, the welcoming speech in English.

A general, his uniform resplendent in flashes and dec-
orations, shared a few well-chosen thoughts about the
importance of the project to the nation's economy and
national defense.

The ambassador of Texas affirmed that the project
proved yet again the strong ties between the Republic of
Texas and South Africa.

The chief engineer praised his crew for assembling the
largest floating craft in history, the first, he hoped, of
many.

Finally Toshikazu Okada, the president of Masayuke
Hara, Inc., dilated on the great difficulties that had been
overcome in constructing the components in Japan and
shipping them to Simonstown for assembly by stalwart
South Africans working around the clock for many, many
months.

It was Forte's turn. Looking as uncomfortable as he
felt, dressed in suit and tie, he gazed out upon the sea of
faces. He said that the success or failure of Iceberg International, Incorporated, and the survival of the Sovereign
Republic of Texas, were riding on their labors. He thanked
them for their hard work and sacrifices. He hoped they
were all hungry and thirsty, because it would be a shame
for all that good food to go to waste. He sat down.

He got the biggest hand so far.

Mrs. Red Cloud had endured the ceremonies in sullen silence, furious because she was obviously the only one in this crowd of thousands who had not the faintest idea of the function of the ship being so lengthily and fulsomely praised.

Ripley Forte leaned toward her and whispered: "You're next, Red."

"*Me*? What am I supposed to do?"

"What you do so well—you're to christen the ship."

"It might help," she said coldly, "if I knew the name of the ship."

"Try *Sun King*."

Dr. Honikman crossed the platform to present her with a beribboned bottle of Tulbagh champagne and in the name of the Republic of South Africa invited her to christen the largest ship ever built, a ship that would change the course of history.

She suddenly felt a great deal better. It wasn't every day a woman could christen the biggest ship ever built, a ship that would change the course of history. And to be sure, of all the eminent women in the world, Jennifer Red Cloud was the only logical person to do it. Perhaps Ripley Forte wasn't a totally unfeeling clod after all in insisting that she have the honor.

She stood, grasped the bottle in her right hand, said in a ringing voice, "I christen thee *Sun King*," and smashed the bottle against the ship's bow. At least that's what she guessed it must be. She couldn't be sure: it was indistinguishable from any other part of the circular ship.

The crowd gave a brief cheer and dispersed en masse. Within minutes the two-thousand-odd workers were grazing noisily among the trestle tables.

Leaving them to it, Hara's President Okada conducted the christening party aboard for its first official inspection.

The *Sun King*, he told them in excellent English, was 1,352 meters across and 370 acres in area and was assembled from sections bolted, of course—not welded—together. Having completed its dock trials successfully, it would begin its five-day shakedown cruise that very afternoon.

Jennifer Red Cloud stood on the bare deck and sought

some clue as to the function of the ship. The deck itself seemed to be tesselated in patterns approximately one meter square. Around each meter-square area was a narrow steel and neoprene ledge, apparently a watertight joint, logical for a seagoing vessel with such a low seaboard.

Suddenly, in front of them a periscope rose from a recess in the deck and swiveled to focus on them. A moment later one of the panels near the lifeline slid back, revealing a steel ladder leading down into the ship.

Mr. Okada descended first and raised a hand to assist Jennifer Red Cloud down the ladder. She ignored it and went down by herself, holding tight to the steel handrails. When all were assembled in a compartment with curving passageways leading off to the left and right, their guide addressed them in Japanese. It was short but sounded portentous.

"*Haiku*," explained Okada. "'Amusement verse' in Japanese. I'm sure you are all familiar with our seventeen-syllable epigrammatic three-line stanza. This one I composed to commemorate the epochal engineering achievement represented by the *Sun King*. I am honored to dedicate it to our distinguished and lovely guest of honor, Mrs. Jennifer Red Cloud."

He bowed deeply.

Mrs. Red Cloud had only half heard. She was trying to guess what possible relation this ugly iron monster had to do with icebergs. She felt Forte's elbow in her ribs, and bowed back.

"I now translate," said Okada.

> "The sun's rays pierce darkness,
> Like golden spears,
> To impale pain and sorrow,"

he intoned, adding apologetically, "Of course, it loses something in the translation."

Nobody thought to ask him precisely *what* was lost, though he was fully prepared to explain, so he smiled philosophically and led the way down a dark-green passageway. They had gone a dozen paces when he stepped over the combing of an inboard hatch, and they found themselves in a spacious compartment. Flow diagrams, levers, knobs, dials, meters, and other engineering exotica occupied one bulkhead. Facing it were six monitors with high-backed leather chairs for the technicians with responsibilities for the various departments. Other work stations with computer consoles, radio gear, and a big glass table with bottom illumination were manned by other ship's officers.

"We are now in the main control center, the bridge, if you wish. It is one of three, a necessary redundancy in the event of instrument failure, collision, explosion, or other major mishap. The captain commands from that elevated platform facing the main instrument panel. At a glance, he can ascertain the *Sun King*'s direction, speed calibrated to the hundredth of a knot, state of the sea—meaning, of course, wave amplitude—direction and frequency, air and sea temperature and gradients down to six hundred meters, water salinity, ambient current, location of piston malfunction, piston power output, cable tension, solar power output, and numerous other functions. He can order any adjustments that might need to be made by the maintenance crews, elevate or lower or rotate the panels, and so on by mere voice command. The computer recognizes only his voice pattern and has on file some twelve-thousand command sequences."

It didn't look like any bridge she'd ever been on. For one thing, there weren't any portholes to view the sea, though behind them a bank of large television screens supplied a panoramic, 360-degree view of the sea around them. That labeled "Main Periscope" provided a view of the huge deck from the center of the ship at varying magnifications. In addition, a comfortable leather sofa and, facing it, two leather wing chairs, with a smoked glass coffee table between, were clustered at one end of the compartment. Nearby stood a big polished conference table with a dozen chairs.

Mr. Okada explained the function of the various instruments in language too technical for her to follow and then led them through the door beyond the conference table into another passageway, painted a light green.

"Now, here to the right is Captain Kerry Powell's stateroom and office. Other officers have their own spacious quarters. The crew occupies individual compartments farther down. Between the two areas is the mess hall, recreation room with card tables, dart board, weight machines, and so on, the laundry, the library, and other service areas.

"And in this room," said Engineer Okada, opening the door to a compartment in which several large models were on display, "we have working models of the *Sun King* and its various components on a scale of 1:500. Every major element is duplicated here to show visitors exactly how the ship functions."

He picked up a wooden pointer and indicated the side of the vessel.

"Kindly observe that although the freeboard is only 614 centimeters, the *Sun King* draws 2,810 centimeters, or 92 feet, of water. While this may seem considerable— and in fact the harbor here at Simonstown had to be dredged to accommodate it—most modern tankers draw considerably more. Moreover, because of its great diameter, the *Sun King* at sea is approximately as stable as a small island."

Okada took hold of the rim of the model and flexed it.

"Articulated," he explained. "At seven-meter intervals. This is to prevent flexure in high seas that might cause metal fatigue, which eventually could tear the ship apart. It also allowed us to build each unit separately in Japan on an assembly line, for final fitting together here. And, it goes without saying, once it reaches its final destination, it can quickly be broken down into eight sections—like slices of pie—to be towed back here by oceangoing tugs for reassembly and reuse."

He moved on to the next exhibit.

"Now here see the *Sun King's raison d'être*. This piston is a scale model of one of the ship's 28,100 pistons. Each is of steel, hollow, 3.5 meters in diameter and 2 meters high. With their supporting frames, connecting rods, crankshafts, gimbels, and ancillary equipment, they take up most of the vessel's interior below this deck. Each piston moves independently of the others, transferring the power generated by its vertical motion of two connecting rods, thence to a crankshaft. I need not tell you," he added with a smile, "that the pistons derive their power from the up-and-down movement of the waves over which the *Sun King* rides. When wave motion is considerable, as during a storm, the pistons oscillate to the limit of their possible travel, which is 18 meters. Since they move randomly, unfortunately they cannot be linked to common crankshafts. This drawback imposes weight and efficiency penalties because as a result each piston must drive its own electrical generator."

"That's true," broke in Captain Kerry Powell, a ruddy-faced mustachioed son of the sea with a plug of tobacco in his cheek, who had entered the compartment behind them. "But don't forget to tell our guests that the penalties have compensations."

"Oh, dear, no," said Mr. Okada. "Allow me, Madame Red Cloud and gentlemen, to introduce Captain Kerry Powell, the commander of this historic vessel."

There were handshakes all around.

"Perhaps you will be good enough to continue the explanations, Captain. There's no one better qualified."

"Good of you to say so, Toshi. Well, then, as Mr. Okada was telling you, our cellular approach has certain advantages. If a single piston breaks down, it does not affect the others. We can repair it at our leisure. This circumstance, however, required the installation of a lightweight generator for *each* piston. The electricity thus generated is used mainly for the *Alamo*'s refrigeration and propulsion."

"*Refrigeration*?" exclaimed Jennifer Red Cloud in spite of her resolution to keep silent. "Why on earth would you want to refrigerate an *iceberg*?"

Captain Powell looked at Ripley Forte in embarrassment. Didn't she know? And if she didn't, would Forte want her to be told?

"Tell her, Kerry," said Forte. "No secrets here."

"Refrigeration," said a relieved Kerry Powell, "as you know, has two distinct applications as applied to the *Alamo*. I will consider only one of them, as demonstrated by the next model."

He moved across the compartment to a cutaway of a

series of enormous telescoping pipes installed at intervals
of fourteen meters across the midline of the *Sun King*.

"There are ninety-eight of these pipes," he went on.
"They can be lowered to a depth of 480 meters. In section
they are triangular, as that the knifelike leading edge offers
a minimum of resistance, while the flat trailing base of
the triangle provides maximum resistance."

Jennifer Red Cloud shook her head.

"Sounds self-defeating, doesn't it, Mrs. Red Cloud?
But it isn't. You see, if the *Alamo*'s course is *with* the
surface current, which is usually a couple of hundred
meters deep, we lower the vanes that distance to take full
advantage of the push against the flat surface of the vanes.
In effect, they act as sails. As you are aware, beneath the
warmer surface current there is often a layer of colder
water which may range anywhere from 200 to 1,500 meters
in depth. Often it is a countercurrent, but sometimes, as
with the Benguela Current flowing up the west coast of
Africa, both currents go in the same direction. When this
happens, we lower the vanes still farther to profit from
the additional propulsion of the deep cold waters.

"*Colder* waters, you will observe. That is the reason,
beyond the structural strength of triangular forms, the
vanes double as pipes. You see, the surface of the Benguela Current is about 12 degrees Celsius just to the west
of Cape Town. Farther north, off Mocamedes Province
in southern Angola, it warms to 16 degrees. Off Cunza
Sul Province 300 miles still farther north, it becomes 20
degrees. Now observe that beneath these warm, northward-flowing waters there is a second layer with a temperature of 10 degrees, and a third below that of 5 degrees.
Both also flow northward, the lowest layer only 450 meters
below the surface. When we encounter such ideal conditions, we lower the vanes to their fullest extent to get
the extra push. And something else we get"— he said,
passing on to the next model —"is this. Here you see the
sternmost 180 degrees of the *Sun King* with a series of
water-discharge ports along the periphery. I won't insult
your intelligence by telling you what *they're* for."

"Please *do*," said Mrs. Red Cloud. "Of course I understand their significance in a general way, but you make

the details so *fascinating*."

"Well, of course, if you say so, ma'am," said the flattered Kerry Powell. "You'll remember from the *Salvation*'s tragic experience that the greatest menace in iceberg transport is catastrophic calving. The *next* greatest danger is the effect of wave action on the berg's leading edge, the accumulation of stresses which eventually pound the berg to pieces. The stress and ablation naturally intensify in tropic waters, which melt the berg's outer shell ice and destroy its crystalline integrity.

"Enter the multipurpose vanes. They suck up cold water from the depths, pass it through the Claude condensator to generate electricity, then out through the ninety-eight stern vents. They thus lay down a curtain of cold water that cools the warmer upper layers, retarding melting on the surface. Furthermore, since cold water sinks, the discharge water also inhibits melting and ablation across the entire leading edge of the berg."

"But the pumping of such enormous amounts of water must require correspondingly enormous amounts of energy," Jennifer Red Cloud pointed out.

"Which are provided by the constant wave action on the piston array."

"But what about the calm waters of the horse latitudes around the equator?" she persisted. "There the sea is often as smooth as glass."

Captain Powell looked at her with grudging respect. He had begun to believe she had no conception of what he was trying to explain. Obviously, she had just been leading him on.

"Next exhibit, ma'am," he said. "As you say, the horse latitudes, that is, between 30 degrees north and 30 degrees south of the equator, frequently have a high barometric pressure and consequent calms. As a compensation, there is usually little cloud cover to obscure the equatorial sun. This model shows the *Sun King*'s weather deck, made up of one-meter-square solar panels. Each computer-controlled panel rotates so that the sun's rays strike perpendicularly, capturing solar energy and converting it to electricity about 21 percent more efficiently than power derived from waves of 140-centimeter amplitude."

"What do you use at night, moonlight?" she said archly.

"No, ma'am. We use the surplus electricity stored in banks of cryobatteries. Any more questions?"

There were none.

Captain Powell cupped Mrs. Red Cloud's elbow in his hand and guided the inspection party down a candy-striped corridor toward the interior of the ship.

"Did I mention wake dampening?"

Mrs. Red Cloud shook her head. She tried to visualize how one dampened wakes—by dousing the Irish mourners with holy water?

"I should have. That's one of the *Sun King*'s most important functions. The constant beating of the waves against the berg's leading edge, as I said earlier, is as destructive as a jackhammer. But the passage of the *Sun King* flattens out the waves like an oil slick, producing a wake as smooth as the water in your backyard birdbath."

After lunch in the officers' mess, the inspection party prepared to return to shore. But one question remained uppermost in Mrs. Red Cloud's mind when Captain Powell had brought them through the labyrinth of passageways back to the dock.

"This has been most interesting, Captain," she said, "But I wish you had had time to show us the engine room. Judging by what I've already seen, it must make that of an ocean liner look like a wind-up toy."

"Engine room? Oh, I'm afraid we don't *have* an engine room, Mrs. Red Cloud."

"No engine room? Then how do you turn the propellers?"

He chuckled.

"The *Sun King* doesn't have propellers, either."

"Then how are you going to make it go? Are you going to get out and *push*?"

"No," replied Captain Kerry Powell, smiling, "*pull*."

22. MERMAIDS
15 JANUARY 2008

THE AMPHIBIAN PUT DOWN ON MODERATE SEAS NEAR THE
S.S. *Lupe Allen*, lying in Saint Helena Bay 150 miles up
the west coast of Africa from Cape Town. The 22,300-ton
submarine support ship dispatched a motor launch, and
a few minutes later Jennifer Red Cloud and Ripley Forte
were clambering up the accommodation ladder to the main
deck. There they were met by Captain Steve Brawley, a
tall, scholarly man wearing glasses, shorts, baseball cap
with "Navy" embroidered across the crown, and smudges
of grease on his face and forearms. He wiped his hands
on cotton waste and greeted Jennifer Red Cloud warmly.

"Welcome aboard, ma'am," he said, shaking her hand.

"Mrs. Red Cloud is assistant secretary of water
resources for administration," Forte explained. "She's
riding shotgun on Triple Eye aboard the *Sun King*."

"It's a real pleasure to greet somebody besides politicians trying to get their photographs in the papers and
public relations men trying to keep them out. What would
you like to see?"

Jennifer Red Cloud was wearing a dress of gauzelike
chiffon that stirred in every breeze. Cut up into strips, it
would have served to bandage a sizable scratch on the
elbow. Most of the crew seized the moment to pause in
their labors for a cigarette, with all eyes, without appearing to do so, managing to focus on the same spot.

"The works," she said. "I'm ecumenical—a little of
everything."

"Why don't we go up to the chart room on the bridge?
There we'll get a bird's-eye view of the fleet and a look
at the maps." He led the way up the ladder from the well
deck, followed by Mrs. Red Cloud, Forte, and a hundred
envious eyes.

On the bridge, Brawley pointed to the southeast. "The point of land you see is Cape Columbine, and about 150 kilometers down the coast is Cape Town. Over to the west, riding at anchor, are five of our supply ships. As fast as we empty one, it is replaced by another coming down from Houston or Galveston."

He stepped over the combing from the wing into the empty pilot house and on to the chart room behind it. The four bulkheads were covered with maps, as was the chart table.

"I understand Raynes Oceanic Resources works mostly Pacific waters, Mrs. Red Cloud. Are you familiar with the Atlantic as well?"

"I'm afraid not, Captain."

"Well, because of the Coriolis force, Atlantic waters in the southern hemisphere tend to veer to the left, in the northern hemisphere to the right. These so-called gyres are basically what is gong to bring the *Alamo* into port. The South Atlantic Gyre moves counterclockwise, sweeping up the west coast of Africa, across the equator going west, and south again down the Brazilian and Argentinian coast, then joining the Antarctic Circumpolar Current going east again. The *Alamo* will follow the Benguela Current north along Africa's west coast, then due west with the South Equatorial Current. You see?"

"I see it reaching almost the coast of Brazil and veering off toward the south."

"Well, yes. There's the critical area. There we have to nudge the *Alamo* at that point into the Guiana Current that flows up the northern Brazilian coast. Once we get there, we pick up the *clockwise*-flowing North Atlantic Gyre, and the Carribean Current takes the berg south of Cuba and along the coast of Mexico right into Matagorda Bay."

"Where's that critical area again?"

"Right here." Captain Brawley pointed at a spot in mid-Atlantic.

Jennifer Red Cloud exulted. If that northward "nudge" were somehow nullified, the *Alamo* would be swept south by the slow, warm Brazil current and melt to the size of an ice cream cone within weeks. Score one for the visiting team. "How fascinating! Do you mean that the *Alamo* is going to float all the way from the Antarctic to Texas on *ocean currents*?"

"Yes, Mrs. Red Cloud," said Steve Brawley. "Not wholly, of course. For one thing, it would be too slow. Now, the frigid Antarctic Circumpolar Current which is presently pushing the *Alamo* eastward toward us is moving at a sluggish two nautical miles a day; that figures when you consider that it's the biggest current in the world, moving 165 million tons of water a *second*. The Benguela Current in which we're anchored, on the other hand, is also cold, but *fast*. The South Equatorial and Guiana currents are even faster, but warm. As for the Carribean and gulf currents, they're *slow* and warm. Now, these currents, except for short stretches where they split up, can carry us all the way to Matagorda Bay."

"That's convenient." Jennifer Red Cloud's mind was on those short stretches.

"In fact, there's no other economically sound way. Still, the currents meander around the shores of the continents, and by the time the *Alamo* reaches this point, it will still have 9,300 nautical miles to go. Figuring the current carries the *Alamo* at an average thirty-two nautical miles per day, it would take us 290 days to reach our destination."

"Much too long," put in Ripley Forte. "The melt would be totally unacceptable after so many summer months in tropical currents. Not to mention the political angle. I've promised President Turnbull that it'll be in port by the opening of the Republican national convention in July so he can take credit for it."

Another point for the visiting team, gloated Jennifer Red Cloud. It wouldn't even be necessary to *destroy* the *Alamo*. Just to delay it would ruin Ripley Forte. He would never see another penny of government subsidy. And without it, Forte Oceanic Engineering would be ruined. She did some quick mental arithmetic.

"Then you have to get the *Alamo* to Texas in about 180 days."

"More like 185."

"Which means you have to make good at least fifty nautical miles a day."

"Right."

"In other words, the average thirty-two nautical miles the current will provide, plus another eighteen."

"Right," said Forte, "but we figure we can average an extra twenty-three nautical miles instead of eighteen."

"How?"

The two men looked at each other.

"Why don't you show her, Rip?" said Steve Brawley. "The *Mako*'s ready to go, and you're checked out on it."

"Come along, Mrs. Red Cloud," said Forte. "Let's take a dip."

She and Brawley followed him back through into the pilot house and down a steep iron ladder with greasy chains for handrails. She had to step very carefully to avoid getting her heels caught in the iron grating that formed the treads. They walked forward and then down three more levels to a lock opening into the Atlantic itself.

A few minutes later there was a burst of bubbles, and a yellow, cigar-shaped submersible broke the surface.

Rip Forte observed her bemused look. "Yep, it's one of your Raynes Rovers, Red. We believe in nothing but the very best."

"How did you get it?" she said, with an effort keeping her voice under control.

"*Them*," he corrected. "We have six. By we I mean the Coral Gables Oceanographic Institute, a wholly owned subsidiary of Forte Ocean Engineering."

"I see." She made a mental note, cast in concrete: She'd fire the whole Rover sales division for selling equipment to Forte's stooges that he could use to bankrupt her.

"Want to go for a spin?" Forte challenged her.

"That's what I'm here for."

"Then you'd better change," advised Brawley. "Your dress is very pretty, but I don't think it would do a couple of hundred meters down. I'll have one of the men provide something more appropriate."

Ten minutes later Jennifer Red Cloud rejoined them. She was barefoot and wore a tight white T-shirt and a pair of black satin swimming trunks. They belonged to Tulsi Ram Sharma, an oceanographer from Bombay so thin he had to stand twice in the same place to cast a shadow. Captain Brawley sighed and shot a glance at Forte. Some people had all the luck.

The two-man navigation crew, having completed their surface check, opened the hatch and emerged.

"The cabin thermostat is a little temperamental today, sir, but otherwise the *Mako*'s working fine," the craft's skipper reported. "The back-room crew just reported aboard."

"Very well," said Brawley. "Recharge the oxygen tanks, check the air scrubbers again, and see that there's fresh coffee and sandwiches aboard."

"Aye, aye, sir."

"It's a beauty," said Steve Brawley to Jennifer Red Cloud, "and you and your engineers deserve high marks for developing such a craft."

The Raynes Rover was essentially five transparent glass and ceramic spheres, each 315 centimeters in diameter, locked in tandem by a massive steel frame festooned with skids, grabs, probes, air tanks, battery pods, extendable legs, compass dome, sonar housing, whip antennae, crash bars, TV cameras, high-intensity lights, propellers, maneuvering jets, and two long retractable swept-back wings like those on supersonic fighter planes.

The motors and other operating equipment were free-flooded outside the pressure-hull spheres and controlled by titanium-encased fiber-optic cables, the only break in the surfaces of the smooth spheres aside from the personnel hatches and service umbilicals.

Mrs. Red Cloud descended into the Rover, followed by Forte, who reached above his head to dog the watertight hatch down tight. He was turning to the pilot's seat when he found it already occupied by Jennifer Red Cloud.

"I'll drive," she said, buckling her belt and handing him the clipboard with the getting-underway checkoff list.

The Rover's controls were very similar to those of an airplane, and they operated analogous control surfaces. The craft could do everything that an aircraft could do— barrel rolls, sideslips, Cuban eights—and it had the added virtue that it could not stall and fall out of the sky.

"Surface communication aerial," read Forte.

"*Deployed*," replied Jennifer Red Cloud, fingering the switch.

"Navigation transponder."

"*On.*"

"Emergency flash and flare."

"*Armed.*"

"Underwater communications transducer."

"*On standby.*"

"Ballast tanks."

"*Neutral buoyancy.*"

"Ballast tank pumps."

"*Idling—disengaged.*"

"Battery charge level."

"*Ninety-seven percent.*"

"Autopilot status."

"*Off.*"

"Cabin check."

"That's your department," she said.

He looked back at the little toilet, operated the flush mechanism, and put a check after it on his list. The narrow bunk above and behind them had the regulation two pillows and three wool blankets on it, folded neatly. He inspected the small fridge: ten sandwiches, wrapped in foil; twenty bottles of mineral water; ten bars of plain chocolate. Enough to cross the Atlantic on. All interior lights were operating. Ventilating fan and air scrubber ditto.

"Cabin check okay," Forte reported. "Cabin pressure?"

"*Seven hundred sixty millimeters.*"

"Temperature.

"*Thirty Celsius, even.*"

"Intercom."

"*Off.*"

"It should be on."

"Why? said Jennifer Red Cloud, surprised. "Are we carrying crew back there?"

"That's right. The schedule's too tight for a joyride. This is a working run. We'll be down below for nearly ten hours. It's not too late to change your mind. A reserve nav crew is standing by to take over if need be."

"Don't be silly," she said. "I came here to see what's going on, and I can't think of a better way than this." *Tight schedule*. Oaf! she thought. No wonder he had never gotten married: He didn't need a wife; he needed a mother. At the rate he was dropping bombs, by the time they got back to the *Lupe Allen* she would have figured out fifty ways to sink his stupid iceberg. She's make sure he remembered the *Alamo*.

She flipped on the intercom switch.

"Crew status report."

"Ready to go," came a voice through the cabin speakers. "Not *raring* to go, mind you, but ready. And say, what have you been munching on during your off-duty time, anyway, old buddy, estrogen eclairs?"

"I beg your pardon?" said Jennifer Red Cloud coldly.

"Yep. Just as I thought, I've been out to sea too long. I could have sworn you'd become a soprano, Tom."

"I am not Tom. I am Jennifer—Mrs. Red Cloud to you," she said, enunciating each word. "I am the captain on this descent, and unless you want to be looking for another job when we surface, don't you forget it, buster!"

There was a stunned silence while the drivers in the sphere to the rear digested the fact that their ultimate boss had somehow assumed command of the mission.

"Aye, aye, Captain," replied the one.

The other merely sighed.

In the command sphere, Ripley Forte read off the other items on the checklist, received the appropriate responses, and announced: "Raynes Rover *Mako*, ready to dive."

Jennifer Red Cloud reached up and gripped the knurled knob of the flood lever and eased it forward.

"Flooding one and two," she said.

"Four meters per minute," reported Forte, his eyes on the speed of descent gauge.

She pushed the lever a notch farther forward.

"Seven meters per minute."

They dropped past the clamshell hatch of the *Lupe Allen* into the open sea. Jennifer Red Cloud applied forward power, and the *Mako* went into a shallow dive.

"Clear to deploy diving planes?" she asked.

"Clear, but do not—repeat do *not*—deploy," said Forte, glancing over at her.

"Why not?"

"We're just beyond the continental shelf. Our target is

only 365 meters deep. Just activate the sonar-tracking device and the autopilot and set the speed for six knots, and we'll be at our destination in four or five minutes."

He shucked off his shoulder straps and turned in his seat. He pressed the coffee machine button and waited while coffee beans for a cup were ground to powder, mixed with boiling water, and decanted. He handed her the steaming porcelain cup and repeated the process for himself.

By now, the last vestiges of daylight had disappeared. The sunlight's reds had been completely absorbed by the water at 20 meters. Beyond 45 the yellow wavelengths could not penetrate. At 100 the green would go, and at 200 the blues. But here, as they passed the 50-meter mark, the light was already so dim that Jennifer Red Cloud had to turn on the high-intensity lights. Even so, the water so effectively absorbed light that in the depths, with the strongest beam, they would not be able to see beyond about ten meters.

What she was supposed to see, Jennifer Red Cloud could only guess. Something that could tow a billion-ton iceberg? Nonsense.

And yet Ripley Forte, however ugly, however infuriating, was no fool. He had not spent literally billions of dollars for something that did not at least have a good *chance* of pulling an iceberg the nearly ten thousand miles from the Antarctic to Matagorda Bay in the Republic of Texas. It had to be big. *Very* big.

She sipped her coffee and thought big.

Submarines couldn't be made big and powerful enough, obviously. But big could mean numbers, not size. How about a thousand whales yoked together? she thought, letting her fancy run wild.

Mermaids?...

23. THREADING THE NEEDLE
15 JANUARY 2008

JENNIFER RED CLOUD POINTED TO THE DOPPLER distance-to-target indicator. It read 330 meters.

Forte nodded and lay back in his seat, hands folded behind his head.

"Tell me when to slow down," she said.

"You're the driver. Use your own judgment."

"You're a lot of help."

At one hundred meters to target she was about to pull back on the throttle, when the submersible began to slow.

"Programmed?"

"Of course. This is a routine operation which will have to be repeated several thousand times without a hitch. We can't afford pilot error."

"I see."

She took her hands off the controls and lifted her eyes from the instrument panel to scan the sea around them. In the bright lights of the high-intensity beams she could make out the fleeting forms of slow-cruising fish, and she knew even without looking at the digital sonar readout that they must be near the bottom. Pelagic species inhabit the hundred meters closest to the surface, where they feed upon sunlight-dependent plankton. Below a hundred meters or so, though, sea life is scarce in the watery desert where neither plants nor animals find sustenance. But near the bottom, where edible debris floats slowly down from the surface, demersal fishes now appear, like the ugly customer with the jutting bony jaw that was crossing their bow.

"But still no mermaids," she said half to herself.

"How's that?" asked Forte with an absent air.

"I was just thinking about how krill go for Band-Aids," she returned smoothly.

"Uh huh," Forte said, having understood nothing. "Disengage the autopilot and I'll take it from here."

As she executed the order, he took the control stick to the right of his seat in one hand and brought the *Mako*'s nose up level. With his left hand he eased back on the throttle until the submersible was barely making steerageway.

Jennifer Red Cloud glanced down at the fathometer. It showed they were barely a meter above the seabed. Next to it the depth indicator registered 344 meters.

"Where are we?" she asked.

"About fifty kilometers off the African coast and"— he pointed at the depth indicator —"about 350 meters down."

"On the continental shelf, then?" she asked casually.

"No, the continental shelf is behind us. We're about seven or eight kilometers from its outer limit down the continental slope."

"And what happens here?"

"*That*," he said, pointing.

Dead ahead was what seemed to be a mammoth black cylinder extruded from the seabed at an angle of about thirty degrees. Forte pulled a red lever overhead, and two rigid arms slid out from their recesses on the bottom of the *Mako* and made fast with a *clang* that reverberated through the ship.

"Magnetic clamps," Forte explained. "Keeps us firmly in position to use the mechanical arms and maintain leverage and equilibrium. It was either this or use torque wrenches like the astronauts."

He depressed the red intercom button on the side of the control column. "This is Forte," he said. "Who's back there?"

"Hi, Mr. Forte! This is Pastorelli, and Gibbs is here with me."

"Glad to have you aboard. How is the job shaping up?"

"A piece of cake. It took four days to get the first anchor down, but now we're in the swing of it, eight hours is the average we're shooting at."

"Eight hours," mused Forte half aloud. "Four mother ships leapfrogging. Five nautical miles between anchors.

That works out to a line of anchors sixty nautical miles a day. The *Alamo* needs to make fifty to stay on schedule. That leaves a cushion of ten miles ... barring accidents."

Barring accidents, thought Jennifer Red Cloud. Easier and easier. It wasn't quite clear just what part the anchors played, but it *was* clear that without them the *Alamo* would never arrive on schedule.

"Permission to lock out," Pastorelli was saying for the second time. Forte was looking at her.

"Permission granted," said Jennifer Red Cloud.

In the fifth sphere to the rear, Pastorelli and Gibbs had suited up in Ultravac gear, fins, and oxygen-neon closed-circuit breathing apparatus. They wriggled through the narrow aperture into the lockout area and closed and dogged down the watertight door behind them. One after the other, they dropped through the open hatch on the bottom of the lockout sphere into the water, illuminated now by their helmet lights and the *Mako*'s high-intensity beams. Disengaging their big box of tools from its receptacle on the skid, they opened the compressed gas valve that blew the box's built-in tanks just enough to provide neutral buoyancy and dragged it behind them to the base of the big cylinder. The divers then returned to the submersible to focus its spotlights on the area where they would be working.

"All set?" said Forte when they resumed their stations beside the tilted column.

"All set."

Forte depressed a toggle switch on the instrument panel.

"Topside," came a voice over the intercom.

"All clear below."

"Stand by," said Topside. And a moment later: "It's on its way."

Forte pointed up. Jennifer Red Cloud's eyes followed, but she couldn't see anything.

"Keep watching," Forte said.

After a moment, Jennifer Red Cloud could discern a wire cable that rose vertically from the anchor.

"Guide wire," explained Forte. "It's lower end is attached to that semicircular arch on top of the cylinder. The other is supported on the surface by a boxcar-sized buoy. The line that is being lowered, which we are now going to attach to that arch by a mooring swivel—we first considered a large-sized bending shackle and a section of heavy-duty die-lock chain—will be supported by that buoy and a Jew's harp."

In the most elementary terms, Forte's men had stuck a needle at an angle in the continental slope. Now they were going to put a thread—the anchor rode—through the needle's eye and make it fast. The other end would be tied to a float. When the *Sun King* was maneuvered into position five miles away, an oceangoing tug would carry a line from the circular craft to the float, where the suspended line would be tied to it. The *Sun King*'s winches would take up the slack and pull the boat forward—kedging—by means of the anchor. The line to the next anchor would be made fast to the *Sun King*'s second winch before the first was released. The *Alamo*, harnessed behind the *Sun King* by four lines, would be dragged along behind. And so the two gigantic craft would proceed up the line of anchors like a man who hauls in his small boat by pulling on the mooring line, hand over hand.

The lines were gigantic, as big around as a barrel. In fact, the scale of *everything* connected with the project was gargantuan. But in essence the operation was childishly simple.

And vulnerable.

Jennifer Red Cloud considered a number of attractive alternatives. In order to sabotage the anchors, she would need only to have her men plant explosive charges; two hundred kilos would probably suffice. To destroy the shackling assembly, a thermite bomb could be used to melt the retaining pin. The braided nylon line could be fatally weakened by injecting the core with nitric acid so that it would part from the strain of pulling the *Sun King* and the *Alamo*. It was all so very elementary.

"Well, if you want *my* opinion," Jennifer Red Cloud said when the operation was concluded and the two divers were on their way back to the lockout, "it's a very uneconomical approach."

"How do you figure?" said Forte.

"I know something about diving at these depths. It's very, very expensive."

That was most definitely true. Before each eight-hour

shift down below, the divers had to spend three days in a compression tank, and then on reaching the surface again, eleven days decompressing. Anchor-embedment operations were being carried out around the clock. That meant eighty-four divers for each support ship, or nearly four hundred men, counting backups for accidents, sickness, and those who couldn't take the rigors of the deep and quit. It meant forty-five decompression chambers per ship, each at a different stage of decompression. And because the decompression took eleven days, room-sized tanks with full amenities had to be provided: bunks, exercise equipment, small galley, bathroom with shower, closed-circuit video. Servicing these men and facilities required a large medical and logistical staff. Divers' salaries, at $900 per day, alone cost Triple Eye nearly $2 million a week. Altogether a ruinously expensive method, above and beyond the costs of the anchors and ancillary installations and supply ships and crews themselves.

"How many anchors did you say?" she asked.

"A thousand one hundred and eighteen. There are none in midocean, of course. Too deep."

"Well," she sighed, "I guess you know what you're doing, but for what you're spending you could get a hundred oceangoing tugs."

"That's right. But look at it this way: Once planted, these anchors will serve for years. For kedging from one to the next, the waves and sunlight supply the motive power. Once we fill the pipeline, icebergs will be coming this way every four weeks. You'd need 140 tugs to supply the same power during the year. *And* you'd have to pay crews, buy oil, risk them running each other down during storms, and especially worry about them tearing up the bergs through random vibration, which destroyed your *Salvation* off the cost of Ecuador.

"Besides, the mechanical efficiency of a winch is nearly 100 percent. And you can develop high forces with modest power. For instance, at 1 knot the pull/power ratio is about 1.944 N/W (326 lbf/hp), or about ten times greater than the best pull/power ratios for screw-driven tugs. Moreover—"

"Spare me."

"Sure," said Forte, hurt that the expert knowledge he

had acquired at the cost of much study was not wanted. "It's just that I thought you wanted to know what was going on."

"I know all I need to know."

"Suit yourself." Forte lapsed into a morose silence that lasted until they were back on the surface.

By contrast, Jennifer Red Cloud was positively ebullient. On this brief dive, she had come up with no fewer than three airtight methods of sabotaging the *Alamo*. The steel and concrete anchor, the retaining pin, and the anchor rode to the buoy were all vulnerable. There were going to be 496 of them, Forte had said, spaced at fifty-nautical-mile intervals along the African coast as far north as the equator, and another 622 on the eastern Atlantic coast all the way to the Republic of Texas. How easy it was all going to be.

24. CAMP DAVID
15 JANUARY 2008

OUTSIDE, THE WIND HOWLED THROUGH NAKED BRANCHES, rattling the eaves of the log cabin and sweeping the needles of the barberry bushes across the windowpanes like fingernails on a blackboard. The snow was already piling up against the front door, and the storm was just beginning. Inside, the fire in the hearth blazed as hot as the August afternoon sun against the cheeks of the two men who sat staring into the flames, their feet propped on a big Moroccan leather ottoman, their liver-spotted hands clutching tall glasses as a shipwrecked man clutches a piece of driftwood.

"Frankly, William, I'm more than a little worried," said President Horatio Francis Turnbull.

The bearded William S. Grayle made a dismissive gesture with his hand. "Trust me, Mr. President. I haven't let you down yet."

"That's part of the trouble: I don't know whether you

have let me down or not. Things are coming to a head, and I sometimes fear, despite your assurances, that the head will roll, and it will be mine."

"God's will be done," said the other sententiously. "Over some events man has no control, nor can he see them coming. But to the degree that forethought, money, organization, imagination, and infinite pains can influence the course of U.S. political history, you have nothing to fear."

President Turnbull shook his head. "I wish I could share your optimism. This cancer business, for instance, is—"

"*Your* type of cancer," Grayle chuckled, "no matter what the *Washington Post* medical columnist would say if he got wind of it, is curable. Mark my words, two years from now, when you're well into your second term, you'll *thank* me for bundling you off to the Naval Medical Center."

"Sure I will, if I'm still around."

"You will be. William S. Grayle says you will, and his mother made him promise never to tell a lie."

President Turnbull heaved himself out of the chair and paid a visit to the decanter on the big oak sideboard. He wished he could share Grayle's optimism, but the formidable bipartisan following his secretary of water resources, David D. Castle, had built up during the past three years made it impossible. Of all the threats to Turnbull's reelection, David D. Castle was the most dangerous.

And Grayle had told him not to worry!

Ironically, Castle had proved a tower of strength largely owing to the counsel of William S. Grayle, who had continued to provide the secretary of water resources with advice, contacts, press handouts, ghosted articles, convention addresses, technical information, and revised organizational charts for his new department. He even vetted the applicants for all positions down to the assistant deputy to the deputy assistant secretary level, warning him away from job-hopping bureaucratic deadwood and cast-offs from other Washington agencies and suggesting men and women who could and would actually do a day's work.

No question about it, David D. Castle had surprised everybody with his success as secretary of water resources. William S. Grayle had, to be sure, mapped out for him the path to power, but it was a path that Castle himself had followed with energy and determination.

The first step, of course, was Iceberg International, Inc. For David D. Castle it was a no-lose situation: If Forte brought in the iceberg, its waters would irrigate the Midwest, and Castle would collect the political credit—and the Midwest's votes. If Forte failed, the *Salvation* and *Alamo* fiascoes would be scientific evidence that iceberg transport was not feasible.

Jennifer Red Cloud, who was along for the ride with the *Alamo* in hopes of learning how it could be made to succeed—and then sabotaging it—would have no further hope of recouping the fortune she had lost with the *Salvation*. She would, therefore, be even more eager to hitch her wagon to Castle's rising star and become First Lady of the land. Then a dummy company responsive to her remote control would be established. Her knowledge, an amalgam of years of leadership of Raynes and her first-hand observation of Forte's handling of the *Alamo*, would make the company easily America's most expert in iceberg transport. It would be a simple and straightforward matter for Castle, as President, to see that the new company obtained a monopoly on supplying Antarctic water to a thirsty America. And by the time he left the presidency in 2016, he and his lovely wife would be in control of what would certainly be the world's most profitable enterprise.

Meanwhile, Castle launched a frontal assault on the water problem by cracking down on industrial pollution, enforcing compliance with laws already on the books to eliminate poisonous industrial discharges into rivers and streams, and successfully lobbying for laws that gave tax credits to factories that installed antipollution and water-recycling equipment. Then he announced nationwide competitions for designers of truly water-efficient household equipment, and federal legislation was passed offering manufacturers of such devices a five-year tax holiday. Estimated *household* water saving was 65 gallons per day, more than 4.5 billion gallons a day nationwide, or a whopping 1.7 trillion gallons a year, enough to fill 420 million backyard swimming pools.

But water economies were only a partial and interim solution. Castle also encouraged progressive adoption of efficient household water-recycling systems by offering similar tax breaks to producers of equipment and those who used it.

Working closely with the now-autonomous Department of Health, Castle launched a drive to replace heavily sugared carbonated drinks with sparkling pure water, both bottled and canned. With the slogan "Satisfy your thirst, not your dentist" looking down from every billboard, he declared war on the Coke and Pepsi generations. Government-sponsored television ads made the consumption of sugar in soft drinks a matter of national defense by claiming—with just a whiff of hyperbole—that each Coke or Pepsi consumed cost enough Cuban sugar to buy a communist bullet to kill an American soldier.

And still, that was only the beginning, since household water accounted for only 5 percent of the total used by Americans. Industrial water used amounted to more than *six times* that figure. Water-intensive processes such as automobile manufacture, costing 100,000 gallons per car, and coal-powered electricity production, using 900 gallons of water for every kilowatt-hour produced, were heavily taxed, resulting in both decreased consumption and increased efficiencies.

Neither the household nor the industrial water revolution Secretary David D. Castle was spearheading, however, had quite the impact of his most important offensive: persuading farmers to abandon flood irrigation for drip irrigation. This measure alone could reduce by 90 percent farmers' water requirements, which used up 83 percent of the nation's entire supply.

Secretary Castle pushed solutions and pushed them hard. Their cumulative effect was a startling drop in national water consumption and in water costs and a corresponding rise in farm production and David D. Castle's popularity in the politically powerful Midwest. Concrete accomplishments in the wheat belt, furthermore, gave hope to city dwellers that his reforms would ease their lot as well, and they too climbed aboard the Castle bandwagon.

"And you tell me not to worry!" said the President to his guest.

"That's right, Mr. President. Every contingency has been foreseen."

The President snorted. "That's what you said about the iceberg project. And yet, it begins to look as if Ripley Forte is going to bring it home, after all."

"Yes," Grayle granted. "I didn't overestimate the difficulties, but I certainly did underestimate Ripley Forte. From what my spies tell me, he has a very good chance indeed to bring the *Alamo* into Matagorda Bay."

"There you are!" said President Turnbull triumphantly. "You have admitted that the great William S. Grayle is fallible, after all."

"I *have* been known to make mistakes. It's a practice, however, that I've never allowed to become a habit."

"Still, if you can be wrong about Forte, how can you be so certain you aren't wrong about Castle, too?"

"I'm not," said Grayle imperturbably. "I've taken out insurance, as you know."

"But if he *is* nominated?" Turnbull persisted.

"Then I shall see that he is not elected. You have my word."

25. THE MAGNUS EFFECT
16 JANUARY 2008

FROM THE CARGO COPTERS THAT SHUTTLED FROM SUP-port ship to iceberg, the *Alamo* looked like a big piece of angel food cake aswarm with ants on a picnic table, for in this most critical phase of the entire operation, Forte had mustered every available man from his fleet of support ships, and he was keeping them on the run.

According to wind and current data radioed to Houston and cranked into the Brown-Ash Mark IX computer in

SD-1, the *Alamo*'s closest approach to the Benguela Current would come in seventy-one hours, at 39°51' South and 10°06' East. Here the *Alamo* would effect its first man-made maneuver: a northward diversion from the West Wind Drift and insertion into the Benguela Current sweeping up the west coast of Africa. If it missed the Benguela, it was doomed to continue circling the Antarctic continent until it melted away. Triple Eye would be triple X'd before it got started.

Forte wasn't worried. He had every confidence in the sails that would propel the *Alamo* to its intercept position with the Benguela. His aerodynamic engineers had computed that all seventy-eight sails, taking advantage of the prevailing winds of the West Wind Drift, would be sufficient to nudge the *Alamo* into the Benguela, but with only a 12 percent margin of error. He couldn't take any chances: if the wind dropped by only eight knots, he would need every one of the seventy-eight.

"So that's why you're so curt and grouchy this morning," said Jennifer Red Cloud as she followed in his footsteps on this sunny Wednesday and listened to his terse explanation of the intense activity aboard the iceberg. She was in the best of spirits. The evening before, after returning from the *Lupe Allen*, she had thought up no fewer than six ways to sabotage the *Alamo*. She had then encoded her instructions to Randy Gustafson and sent them off before going to bed. She had slept the sleep of the just, knowing that given six swings, even Randy could not possible strike out.

"But I'm probably worrying for nothing," Forte said. "These men are the best there are, and—tell me, Red," he said, raking her from head to toe with his eyes, "don't you own anything but *flesh-colored* body stockings?"

"I picked the most unobtrusive color I could find," she said with an impudent smile.

"You're about as unobtrusive as a sledgehammer between the horns."

Jennifer Red Cloud shrugged and looked into the hole in the ice where Forte had led her. "What the hell *is* it?"

"An ice shaft," said Forte. "It goes down somewhere between a hundred and two hundred meters. They've been drilling them for ten days. You must have noticed."

"Of course," she said, "but I thought they were shot holes for the seismographic surveys."

"Let's go have a cup of mud," Forte said briskly, taking her by the arm and leading her toward the nearby seismo shack. "I'll tell you all about it."

Seated on a stool at a drafting table as she sipped the freshly brewed coffee, she studied the diagram of the berg Forte had just drawn for her.

"If we weren't a bit behind schedule, those holes would be filled up as fast as they were drilled."

"Filled up? Filled up with what?"

"Ice."

"*Ice*?"

"Mostly."

She laughed a nervous little laugh of incomprehension. "You drilled holes almost all the way through the berg, removing ice to make the holes, and now you're going to fill them up with *ice*?"

"Yep. That's about the size of it."

"I've never heard anything so ridiculous in my life."

"Sure *does* sound ridiculous, doesn't it?" Forte agreed.

She looked at him balefully. "Whenever you're ready to stop talking to me like a child, Rip," she said finally, "I'm ready to listen."

"I'll go back to the beginning, Red, and you can figure out the answer for yourself. Remember how the *Salvation* came to grief? She calved, cracked up, collapsed. The cause was the constant incalculable billions of tiny pressures every second from waves, wind, temperature differentials, sonic stresses, and so on that a dozen BAM-IX's couldn't keep track of. And these conflicting pressures create, even as we are conversing here, lines of weakness within the berg.

"Now, you know that seismographic surveys can detect the existence of lines of differential stress, fault lines, the places a berg'll crack apart, given time. Lepoint didn't pay enough attention to these fault lines, and he bought trouble. My boys think that treating them with respect is the key to bringing icebergs back alive."

"Uh huh," said Jennifer Red Cloud noncommittally.

"Remember how the ancient Babylonians made sun-baked brick?"

"I'm afraid my childhood memories are rather dim. Refresh me."

"They mixed straw with the mud, making the bricks many times stronger. That's what we're going to do."

"I see. You're going to fill those holes with ice."

"Right, but we're going to use the ice removed from the holes, melted and *mixed with a very long chain polymer*, and reinjected into the hole. The resulting crystalline structure has a high compressive strength and damn good tensile strength."

He pointed to the diagram. "Thanks to the Brown-Ash and virtually instantaneous satellite communications with SD-1 in Houston, we can process millions of seismic readings every hour. The Mark IX will pinpoint locations to drill the holes and tell us how deep and at what inclination they must be in order to neutralize the stress before it can magnify the fault line, causing calving. Within an hour of the seismographic reading, crews will have drilled the holes through strata of incipient stress, pumped the supercooled polymer-treated water back into them at the proper temperature for the local gradient, and gone on to the next."

"Next? How long is this process going to go on?"

"All the way to Matagorda Bay, probably. The internal structure never really stabilizes, you know."

"But what about the enormous power that you're going to need to supercool water down to the minus twenties that you encounter in the center of the berg?"

"Have you already forgotten about the wave and solar power that will be generated by the *Sun King*?"

She had, indeed. And that left today's score: Forte, 1; Red Cloud, 0.

Forte watched her. He could practically see the wheels and gears and levers of her mind at work. He chuckled.

"What are you laughing about?"

"You—you and those vicious little thoughts I can see parading behind those beautiful blue eyes."

"They're violet, and which vicious little thoughts on parade did you have in mind?"

Forte leaned back in his chair, laced his fingers behind

his balding head, and regarded the ceiling acoustic tile.

"Well, let's see. You were thinking about all those holes in the ice, and those precious little fault lines, and what interesting little sheer forces could be developed with a ton or two of dynamite dropped down one of them some dark night. Too bad, Red—that dynamite shed is under round-the-clock guard. Also, in about six hours the refrigerating crews will have finally caught up with the drilling crews, and there won't be any unguarded shafts to stuff with high explosive. How'm I doing?"

She looked at him venomously. He was nearer the mark than she would admit.

"Don't be mad, Red. Think of the trouble I'm sparing you." He rubbed his hands together briskly. "Now, then, since you can see you won't get any mileage trying to sabotage the drilling and refrigerating operations, how do you propose fouling up the sails?"

He was uncanny. The moment she had realized that sabotaging Forte's mud and bricks scheme was impossible, her mind had proceeded directly to the matter of the sails. Forte had emphasized that in order to insert the *Alamo* into the Benguela Current, all seventy-eight sails would be needed. They had not actually rigged the sails yet, but the enormous white cylindrical steel masts were already in place. She would only have to set fire to three or four sails, say, and the *Alamo* would never make its rendezvous with the Benguela.

"But before you decide," said Forte, rising and donning his fishbowl helmet, "let's have a closer look at them."

They were arranged in a rectangular pattern, six rows of thirteen tall columns spaced evenly across the huge expanse of the *Alamo*. From a distance they appeared to be factory smokestacks painted in white enamel, a measure, Forte told her, to minimize solar-heat absorption. They were perfectly cylindrical, their six-meter diameter varying not a millimeter from top to bottom, except for a regular pattern of spheroidal dimples over the entire surface. Their tops were covered by flat discs projecting around the entire circumference four meters or so like hat brims.

As they approached the nearest cylinder, Jennifer Red Cloud noted that at its base was a powerful engine, big enough to drive a tugboat. That made sense. A lot of horsepower would be needed to raise the gigantic sails such masts would carry. But where were the booms? Or would the sails be deployed as spinnakers? And where was the rigging and the blocks, cleats, and winches needed to handle it? These and other questions she addressed to Ripley Forte, who answered them all with the same infuriatingly bland reply.

"What you see is what there is."

"What do you mean?" she remonstrated. "I may not be the old salt you are, Rip Forte, but at least I can tell masts from sails."

"Apparently not. What you're looking at *are* sails—Flettner sails, invented by the German aeronautical engineer Anton Flettner, the man who conceived the trim tab for aircraft. As far back as the 1920s he had installed these weird chimneylike sails on boats, and one of his large craft had nearly succeeded in crossing the Atlantic before a sail collapsed from structural failure."

"These things are sails?"

"That's right. What *is* a sail, after all? Simply an air foil with the air pushing against it. Most people think the push is what makes the boat go, but that's only partly so. The wind creates pressure on the windward side, all right, but at the same time it creates a vacuum on the *leeward* side, thereby pushing *and* pulling. That's what is happening here—an application of the Magnus effect, named after another German, who discovered that a spinning object moving in a fluid such as water or air curves away from a straight path because of pressure differences in the fluid, resulting from velocity changes induced by the spinning object. Clear?"

"Oh, sure," said Jennifer Red Cloud a trifle too quickly.

Forte decided to try another approach. "Look, you play golf, don't you?"

"I have a six handicap. Want to play?"

"Very much, but not golf...and not right now. Okay, I suppose you hit a slice or a hook once in a while."

"Seldom."

"But when you do, it's because of the Magnus effect. Unless you hit it absolutely squarely, your club puts a spin on the ball. The ball, in spinning, drags some of the air around with it. As this air meets the oncoming air, it piles up and retards the ball. On the opposite side of the ball, the opposite occurs, and a partial vacuum develops. The net effect of the two forces causes the ball to veer with respect to the wind. Hitting it so that it spins one way produces a hook; making it spin the other way results in a slice. Hitting it absolutely squarely—no spin at all—and you have a shot down the fairway and maybe no bogey after all. Got that?"

"I—I think so."

"Good. Now you recall that a golf ball is dimpled. That magnifies both high- and low-pressure effects. That's why we have semispherical indentations over the mast's entire surface. Now you know all there is to know about the Magnus effect and the Flettner sail, except that they are approximately ten times as efficient as traditional sails of the same area."

She pointed upward to the disc atop the sail. "What's the little hat brim for?"

"That? Well, that disc increases efficiency by preventing spillage of accumulated pressure and vacuum over the top of the cylinder. If you're interested in statistics, the sail is 83 meters high, and the maximum load we expect to impose on it is 115 rpms. With full power and a 20-mph wind, the berg should develop a forward speed of 2.1 knots."

The sail's rotation was imparted by diesel power applied to a gear train. The sail itself revolved on huge roller bearings resting on a circular steel base embedded in a plug of ice, much like the anchor moorings. Depending on the direction of the wind, the computer program regulating the movement of the sails would make them turn in unison clockwise or counterclockwise. If a turn in the direction of the *Alamo* was required, this could be effected by rotating certain sails clockwise, others counterclockwise.

"I suppose you've tested this system?" asked Jennifer Red Cloud.

"In the lab, yes."

"Not full scale?"

"Nope. Never had the time."

"Then how do you know it's going to work?"

"Because," he said, "if it doesn't, I won't become a billionaire. And if I'm not a billionaire, I won't be able to marry an expensive woman like you."

"Oh, *now* I see," she said lightly. "You believe in miracles."

PART IV
SMOKE

26. MINE OVER MATTER
24 JANUARY 2008

THE PRESS BLIMP *ORANGE FREE STATE* OUT OF CAPE TOWN
was filled with reporters, photographers, the best booze
Triple Eye could supply, pretty South African hostesses
in short skirts, raucous conviviality, and anticipation. The
representatives of the world's press and television had
been mightily affronted by Forte's refusal to allow them
aboard the *Alamo*, but his explanations and alternative
arrangements had quickly assuaged their outrage.

He was thinking only of their welfare, he assured them.
After all, many fine men had perished aboard the *Salvation*, and he had too much regard for the media to
expose them to similar dangers.

The holdouts became believers when he took them on
a tour of the *Orange Free State*. Its usual mission was to
fly tourists at very low altitudes over Kruger National
Park and other game reserves, where they could goggle
and photograph in comfort and safety the area's few
remaining wild animals. The passenger section had been
remodeled to make provision for the usual facilities of a
modern media center, providing instant communication
with news capitals around the world by satellite. International, Chinese, and French cuisine was available at
any hour of the day in the dining room. The bar was open
from morning takeoff until 9 P.M., and it was stocked with
a gratifying assortment of liquors.

Of the representatives of the press, six stood apart.
They didn't smoke. They drank, but only mineral water
or fruit juices. At the breakfast table they ate sparingly.
They were all male, young, and hard-muscled and wore
their hair short and their trousers long. Among their sport-
shirted, sloppy-shorted, sandal-wearing colleagues, they
would have been instantly noticeable had it not been for

the fact that all eyes, including theirs, were on the *Alamo*, which came into view off Cape Columbine an hour after takeoff at seven.

As the huge silver airship lifted slowly into the sky, Gary English, Triple Eye's press officer, shepherded his guests toward the breakfast buffet, pointing out that very shortly the *Orange Free State* would be arriving over the area of operations. The press, ever hungry, needed no second invitation.

Half an hour later the correspondents, by then replete with food, began to gravitate, as if drawn by an irresistible force, toward the bar. Behind it was a large television screen, and to one side Forte's press officer had placed his lectern. Fifteen rows of folding chairs faced the bar and screen so that the reporters could combine business with pleasure.

"Ladies and gentlemen, please distribute yourselves evenly along both sides of the ship," English called. "The *Orange Free State* does, of course, have trim tanks, but. . . ." He smiled and left the consequences of a sudden disequilibrium of the ship unsaid.

He nodded toward the screen, which showed a medium-distance shot of the iceberg and its escorting vessels. "The *Alamo* is making rather better progress than we dared hope. In fact, because the current, wind, and Flettner sails brought it nearly ten miles farther north than we anticipated, we will bypass Anchors Nos. 1 and 2."

From his lectern he manipulated the cursor control. "That little yellow blob at which the arrow is pointing is AN-1. From where we are, at our present altitude of a thousand meters, it lies about six miles away on our port quarter. At about the same distance on our port bow," he said, shifting the cursor, "is AN-2. Beyond AN-2 you can now make out the Flettner sails silhouetted against the sea, and just off our bow—you can see it on the screen but not from the observation windows—AN-3. Between us and the anchor, getting ready to make contact, is the *Sun King*."

A reporter who had been scanning the seas below with high-powered binoculars came back from the angled plate-glass observation windows and slumped in a front-row seat.

"Question!" he said, holding up his hand.

"Shoot."

"Name's Milbrand. *Sydney Morning Herald*. What are chances of getting the blue-plate special instead of the full twelve courses?"

"I beg your pardon?"

"I can just about make my deadline if I can find out what's going on down there without listening to an hour-long lecture or plowing through this five-foot shelf your PR flunkies handed us when we came aboard."

"My briefings range from the terse to the interminable, from words of one syllable to the sesquipedalian," said English loftily. "Name your poison."

"Five minutes, basic English."

Gary English scanned his audience for signs of dissent, saw none, and for a moment busied himself reprogramming his lectern lantern slide.

A still picture appeared on the screen.

"Typical anchor, buried in the continental slope at an average depth of 450 meters, at least 10 kilometers from any point along the continental shelf less than 230 meters deep. This allows for liberal lateral motion without danger of berg's grounding. The resulting line of anchors is approximately 100 miles offshore.

"The anchor post is a column of prestressed concrete three meters in section, cemented in the slope's basalt, granite, or reef rock. In the few areas where the slope is not exposed rock, but instead is covered with unconsolidated sediment, as in the alluvial fan of the Congo River, we plant the anchors by propellant-actuated embedment procedures. However embedded, the anchor is attached to a braided nylon lead line, or anchor rode, 244 centimeters in circumference, supported on the ocean surface by a large buoy. Next picture."

"A 244-centimeter line looks pretty flimsy to drag a five-billion-ton iceberg," Milbrand observed.

"Page 122, press kit spec list," said English crisply. "'Line has a safety factor of 2.76.' Now, this artist's rendering shows the *Sun King* being towed by its tugs to AN-1. Only, of course, the rendering is obsolete, as the *Alamo* is actually at this moment approaching AN-3."

He pressed a frame-advance pickle, and a close-up

appeared on the screen.

"Here is a diagram in plan, simulating a bird's eye view from two thousand meters. Two tugs are on either side of the *Sun King*'s centerline. From above, we see that the tow-line tender, really a converted oceangoing tug, has inserted itself between the four tugs, two on each side. The winch on the tender is lifting the steel eye, to which the tow line is attached, from the *Sun King*. It will then be secured to a bitt on the tender's fantail."

Click!

"Now, the tender has now steamed ahead of the four tugs, unreeling the tow line from its capstan aboard the *Sun King*. Here you see the *Sun King*'s crew attaching a big yellow buoy to the line as it is dragged in the tender's wake. Tied on at kilometer intervals, eight buoys will keep the line being unreeled from the *Sun King* to the tender from sinking. Clear so far?"

Milbrand nodded. He was listening intently but wasn't, Gary English observed, taking notes.

Click!

"Now the tender reaches the anchor buoy. The steel tow-line eye is removed from the fantail bitt and shackled to the anchor rode. The tender moves to one side. In the port chain locker of the *Sun King*, the capstan crew awaits the signal to reel in the line."

English now switched to satellite imaging. The monitor showed the *Alamo* curving, so slowly as to be almost imperceptible, toward the smooth wake of the *Sun King*.

"It's going to take about three hours or more for the linkup," he said, "but meanwhile I can tell you what's going to happen next. The *Sun King* will begin to slow so that the *Alamo* can close. When they are one thousand meters apart, the skipper will signal the *Sun King* to start reeling in the tow line attached to AN-3 until reel speed is exactly equal to berg speed. The berg and the *Sun King* will thus be stationary with respect to each other.

"Two tugs will then deploy directly in front of the *Alamo*. The winches tending the four lines of the iceberg harness will be standing by. The innermost lines, numbers two and three, will be lowered over the forward end of the berg and secured to bitts on the stern of the respective tugs. The tugs will then move forward and transfer those lines to the respective bitts on the *Sun King*'s fantail. The tugs transfer lines one and four to make the linkup complete. The *Alamo* is now firmly secured by four strong lines to its escort and will remain so all the way to Matagorda Bay."

Click!

"And finally, here's an artist's impression of the whole mule train under way. Reading from bow to stern or, if you prefer from front to back, you have: *a*, the anchor; *b*, the anchor rode from anchor to buoy; *c*, the *Sun King* reeling in the tow line attached to the anchor rode; and, *d*, in the smooth wake of the *Sun King*, the *Alamo*, attached to its escort by an umbilical of four lines. Two lines, by the way, would be sufficient from an engineering standpoint. But splitting up the load among four weight-bearing cables is a safer bet."

He looked at his watch.

"Will that help you make your deadline, Mr. Milburn?"

"Milbrand—of the *Sydney Morning Herald*. I guess it will have to do, but there's just one thing: What happens when the *Sun King* reels in its five miles of tow line? It'll lie dead in the water until—"

"Mr. Milbrand, I said the tow line was attached to the reel in the *Sun King*'s *port* chain locker. There are port and starboard chain lockers. While the port tow line is being hauled in, the tender will be deploying the *starboard* line to the anchor beyond, in this case AN-4."

"Yeah, yeah, I get it. That should about wrap it up."

He levered himself out of the chair and made his way aft to the console assigned to him. Within thirty seconds he had hooked up his pocket tape recorder to the SPEECH RECOGNITION jack on the keyboard and hit DISPLAY. Gary English's words began to scroll onto the screen. When the readout was complete, Milbrand ad-libbed bits of color, such as the snapping of one of the *Alamo* tow lines (two men injured, one severely), the fire in the tender's boiler room (quickly extinguished), and the man overboard (rescued from the jaws of a great white shark), as he went. Fifteen minutes later, he touched the TRANSMIT button. Within seconds, his copy was on his editor's operating table in Australia, ready for radical surgery.

Milbrand, the heavy work done for the day, heaved a sigh of relief and headed for the bar.

The six young men, on the other hand, sat through press officer English's detailed explanations of the day's events, taking notes and frequently consulting the even more clinical text provided by the press kit. They spent time at the observation windows taking notes and pictures, especially when the *Orange Free State* hovered at low altitude over AN-3 as the tender bought up the tow line for linkup.

By early evening, most of the rest of the press corps had lost interest in the proceedings. They had dutifully observed the various linkups, interviewed by radio those of Forte's staff aboard the *Sun King* and the *Alamo* who could impart information he thought might do Triple Eye some good, filed their stories, and gotten down to the serious business of drinking as much as they could hold before the *Orange Free State* headed back to Cape Town.

On 6 February 2008, the tramp steamer *Elmira* put in at Lobito, Angola, for bunker fuel, water, and fresh provisions. The next day, at dawn, it set sail on a southerly course. On the morning of 8 February, off Palgrave Point in the Kaoko Veld, in that part of South-West Africa that once aspired to be Namibia but didn't quite make it, the *Elmira* turned due west. By nightfall it was some 225 kilometers from land, above the continental slope where the water was 462 meters deep.

The *Elmira* anchored, and six young ultra-deep-sea divers struggled into wet suits in the ship's decompression chamber, where they had been slowly subjected to rising pressures for the past thirty hours. They squirmed through the hatch into the submersible decompression chamber and dogged down the hatch behind them. Darkness was falling as the SDC, under 43 atmospheres within, was winched up from the hold.

Inside, the six men went through their predive checklist. The check complete, the leader gave a thumbs-up sign through the quartz-glass port and confirmed it with an "All clear!" over the intercom.

The SDC was hoisted over the side and lowered into the pitch-black sea.

According to the calculations of the skipper of the *Elmira*, they were precisely above AN-145. Three hundred kilometers to the south, just off Walvis Bay, South-West Africa's major port, the *Alamo* was forging steadily northward through the turbulent seas that had made that stretch of the Atlantic a graveyard of ships. According to radar plot and satellite scan, no other ship was within ninety kilometers. If all went well, therefore, they would be able to incapacitate Anchors 145, 144, and 143 by daybreak and be well on their way out of the area, their presence never having been observed.

Somewhere to the north another ship, the *Blakely*, would be disabling Anchors 146, 147, and 148.

The descent was swift. The divers switched on the high-intensity SDC lights, but they revealed little but swirling gray waters. At four hundred meters, the winch operator on the deck of the *Elmira* slowed the rotation of the cable drum, and the SDC drifted to a stop.

The senior diver activated the side-scan sonar. Immediately the anchor came into view as a blip on the sonar screen.

"Right on the money," he reported to topside control.

The SDC hovered almost directly above the anchor, buried at a 30-degree angle in the seabed. The lead diver gave the order to the winchman to lower the SDC another twenty meters to bring the submersible right alongside the anchor. The fifteen meter umbilicals supplying heliox to the two divers would now reach wherever their work would require. He checked the pressure gauge and made sure the assistant leader logged it to determine decompression time.

He adjusted his mask and climbed down the ladder, through the open hatch, into the stygian sea. A moment later his partner followed.

The high-intensity beams lit up the water for a good ten meters. Above the SDC was the big wire basket attached to the support cable. It contained three long, sausagelike plastic bladders filled with cyclotol, 60-40 RDX-TNT.

Detaching hand-held lamps from their brackets on the side of the SDC, the two men swam down toward the base of the concrete monolith. As they swam closer, however, they observed a strange sight. Attached to the plain square column of gray concrete and undulating in the current were dozens of bright yellow streamers. Every square meter of the column seemed to sprout them, as though a mammoth exotic seaweed had taken root in the anchor and proliferated overnight.

The men paused and looked at each other through the murky waters, apprehensive with a fear neither could define.

The leader shook off his hesitation and slowly swam closer, until one of the fluorescent yellow ribbons was only inches from his face mask. He extended his hand and took hold of it gingerly. He put the beam of his lamp on it. The foot-wide yellow plastic ribbon contained rows of printed script and something else—what appeared to be twin wires embedded throughout its length.

He scanned the printed legend. It was written in seven or eight languages. He could identify French, German, Spanish, Russian, characters that looked Chinese, squiggles that might have been Arabic or Farsi—and English, his native tongue. Apparently the same terse message was repeated the length of the plastic ribbon.

While his partner held the ribbon steady, he flashed his light on it and read: "The material on which this warning is written is extremely light-sensitive. Its exposure to visible radiation of the order of one-hundredth of a lumen will trigger a delayed-action fuse. The fuse will ignite charges which will be lethal to anyone within the vicinity. You have precisely ten minutes to get clear."

He tapped the other diver on the shoulder and signaled an immediate return to the SDC. Less than a minute later they were inside, the leader grabbing the phone from the hand of the startled duty communications man.

"Benny, get the captain!" he shouted.

"Captain's down below, having dinner," came the reply from above.

"Well, get him topside, *on the double*! This anchor down here is wired to blow us all to kingdom come. We've got to get clear within ten minutes—make that seven."

"Well, can't you disarm them? You're an old bomb disposal man."

J.B. felt his heart thumping but tried to keep a grip on himself. "The mine—mines—we can't see them. Just get that goddamn scow *moving*. If you don't, we're dead—understand?" J.B. looked at his watch. Six minutes.

"Sure, J.B., but you know nobody can order the ship under way but the... Here he comes now."

"What's up, J.B.?" said the captain, plainly annoyed.

"Captain, you've got to get underway at once."

"So Benny told me," the captain replied coldly.

"This anchor down here is rigged to explode in"—J.B. looked at his watch—"two minutes."

"What makes you think so? Is there a sign down there reading 'This anchor will explode in three and a half minutes'?" He laughed at his pleasantry. "Now suppose you settle down and tell me what the hell is going on down there. You know we can't afford..."

J.B. stopped listening. There was a block of ice where his stomach should have been. Eighty seconds.

"J.B.?"

"Yes." J.B.'s voice was a whisper. No matter what happened now, it was too late.

"You *really* think I should haul you up?"

J.B. shrugged. What use was a reply now?

"Okay, okay," said the captain. "But we'll have to reschedule the operation for tomorrow night, and God knows what—"

A shock wave from far below jolted the ship, knocking him off his feet, rolling the *Elmira* over on its side, and dislodging the loose gear on deck in a lethal avalanche that crushed half the crew then topside. At that moment, the tackle supporting the starboard lifeboat gave way, and the boat lurched from its davits and crashed down upon the captain, killing him instantly.

The *Elmira* rolled crazily in the water, burying first the port rail beneath the waves and then the starboard. But slowly the oscillations subsided, and the ship steadied. As the battered crew struggled to their feet, in the engine room oil from a ruptured fuel tank trickled toward a boiler.

* * *

Far to the south, the pilot of a commercial aircraft en route from Johannesburg to Freetown, Liberia, made a wry face.

"Meteorologists!" he remarked to the copilot.

"Huh?" said the other, looking up from his comic book.

"Didn't you see that flash of lightning?"

"Nope."

"And the idiots said it wasn't going to rain."

27. KING NEPTUNE
21 FEBRUARY 2008

"NICE TRY, RED," SAID RIPLEY FORTE TO JENNIFER RED CLOUD as he held the chair for her in the number one wardroom aboard the *Sun King*.

"Thank you very much," she replied as she took her seat and sipped her cold fresh orange juice. She scanned the breakfast menu.

"I'm not very hungry this morning," she told the white-jacketed steward waiting to take her order. "I think I'll just have half a pink grapefruit, two duck eggs over light, four rashers of bacon, crisp and well blotted, a stack of thin cakes with honey, whole-wheat toast, and a pot of your Ethiopian coffee. Oh, and home fries on the side, of course."

"Yes, ma'am. And yours, sir?"

"The same will do for me," said Forte. "I'm not hungry, either."

Mrs. Red Cloud was reading the headlines of the faxed international news section of *The New York Times* that had come in during the night. There was nothing new this morning: race riots in Kansas City; famine in central Africa; the announcement of the Nobel peace prize to Ecuador's Minister of Justice Enrico Perez-Padilla, a former urban guerrilla; floods in China; drought in Mexico; and the prospect of new missile meltdown talks between Russia and the United States. She put the paper aside and took another sip of juice.

"And just what is the occasion for your backhanded congratulations?" she enquired.

"The *Elmira*."

She looked at him blankly. "What is supposed to be my response to this incomprehensible utterance? Is it the opening sally in some new kind of word game?"

"The *Elmira* and the *Blakely*, names of the ships you sent to sabotage my anchors."

"How could you possibly know that?" Jennifer Red Cloud said.

Forte declined to rise to the bait. She was guilty, all right, guilty as hell. And if she tried once, she would certainly have no compunction about trying again if she saw a better chance of success. Forte had no intention of giving her that chance. If she learned that an integrated defense system surrounded every anchor installation and sent telemetry via satellite back to SD-1 in Houston, she and her stooges might find some way to get around it, although for the life of him he couldn't imagine how.

"How did we know there had been intruders? Well, because when the *Sun King* linked up with AN-146, while passing over AN-145, its demersal-water intakes pulled up some debris that clogged the filters."

"Debris? What kind of debris?"

"Parts of two frogmen, still in wet suits."

"How charming."

Although her appetite had fled, she carved the stack of pancakes into bite-sized bits, wishing it were Ripley Forte's heart. Her hand grew moist. Her concern had always been with the big picture, and unlike Forte's, her staff had never bothered her with the gory details.

After breakfast, Mrs. Red Cloud had been promised the usual traditional ceremony to celebrate her first crossing of the line on a surface craft. She was still a pollywog; at a few minutes past ten o'clock, when the *Alamo* passed from the southern hemisphere to the northern, she would become a shellback.

"What should I wear?" she asked Forte after breakfast.

"As little as possible, I should imagine—which won't cause you any distress."

Captain Eric Wills, skipper of the *Alamo* and senior man afloat, would act as King Neptune and dictate the tenor and tempo of the ceremony. A bewhiskered old salt, he had often been observed giving the eye that was glad to Mrs. Red Cloud. According to venerable naval custom, King Neptune and his court would try the two score initiates aboard the *Sun King* and *Alamo* and find them all guilty of being—horror of horrors!—pollywogs. Appropriate punishments would follow.

When he crossed the equator near Brazil in 1832, Charles Darwin had observed that among the initiation rites one "most disagreeable operation consists in having your face rubbed with paint and tar, which forms a lather for a saw which represents the razor, and then being half drowned in a sail filled with seawater." Wills and his merry company of shellbacks, even though dressed in bizarre costumes and disguises, probably wouldn't chance anything hazardous or off-color with Mrs. Red Cloud, but you never could tell with an imaginative old man like Captain Eric Wills.

Jennifer Red Cloud appeared at nine-thirty on the main deck of the *Sun King* in a demure—for her—outfit of virginal white shorts and a matching halter and not-so-virginal white pumps with three-inch spike heels. Forte, himself an old shellback, was rigged out as a seventeenth-century pirate, in floppy boots, ragged pants, black handlebar mustaches, a cutlass and brace of wheellock pistols tucked in a broad red sash, rakish black hat with a peacock feather and the brim turned up, and black eye patch. Mrs. Red Cloud observed that the costume could not be more appropriate to their respective characters, that is, beauty and the beast.

It was a brilliant summer day, and already Forte was sweating as he led her down the passageway between the raised solar panels to the docking station of the aerial tramway.

The tramcar was rigged on number two tow line between the *Sun King* and the *Alamo*. They took their seats aboard with twenty-odd other participants in King Neptune's coming trial and were swiftly borne up and away. The drive wheels of the power train sang against the big braided nylon cable as they propelled the vehicle at a shallow angle up toward the *Alamo* a kilometer astern. On both sides of the iceberg the seas ran high and choppy as the Benguela Current collided with the eastward-flowing Guinea Current, moving counterclockwise around the western bulge of Africa. Below them, though, the ocean was as smooth and level as a Texas prairie, ironed flat by the passage of the *Sun King*.

King Neptune's motley gang of cutthroats greeted the pollywogs with whoops and howls as the tram car glided to a stop. One was a barber pole painted with alternating diagonal stripes of white and red. Another was a cannibal with a spear in his hand and a bone through his nose; a third was Abe Lincoln in morning coat, stovepipe hat, and chin whiskers. There was even an ambulatory can of Campbell's clam chowder. Surrounding the pollywogs in a milling, shouting, shoving crowd, the costumed men hurried them across the ice to where King Neptune awaited them on his golden throne, a gilded barber's chair.

Ripley Forte, caught up in the mob, was craning his neck to get a view of the proceedings, when he felt a piece of paper thrust in his hand. He looked around to see who could have put it there but realized it might have been any one of the dozen jeering, shouting, laughing men who were jostling him from every side. He held up the paper and read:

> "Forte: there is a bomb in the radio-shack gear
>   locker. It is set to go off at precisely 10:10."

The words on the note were typewritten, except for the time: that was inscribed in pencil.

He looked at his watch. It was 9:53. The communications shack was half a mile away, near the midline of the *Alamo*.

Again he scanned the faces—or what he could see of them through their disguises—of the excited men around him but knew he was wasting his time.

He jogged over to where half a dozen motor scooters were parked nearby, mounted one, and switched on the engine. He went flying over the Ultravac-covered ice toward the radio shack. Nobody was in sight in any direction across the wide flat expanse except for the crowd he had left behind him.

He braked to a stop at the flimsy aluminum structure and mounted the three wooden steps. Inside, the radioman was trussed up with adhesive tape like a man with multiple fractures. Over his head was a paper bag. Forte pulled it off, saw by the frantic eyeball gestures that his man was alive and indignant, and stripped the tape off his mouth.

"Where's the gear locker?"

"There." The bound man nodded toward a bank of metal lockers along the bulkhead opposite radio equipment. "The first locker."

The locker was standing invitingly ajar. Forte picked up a flashlight from a desk and inspected the slit for wires of a booby trap. There didn't seem to be any. He eased the door open.

He saw a foxtail and dustpan, a damp and dirty swab, a broom, a bucket with some rags on top, an assortment of soap powders, and a couple of dog-eared magazines. Under the rags in the bucket was the bomb. It weighed in at about five kilos, probably enough to destroy the radio shack and certainly enough to knock out all the communications gear and kill the hapless radioman. The timer indicated that six minutes remained before the bomb would be detonated. Forte, who had seen explosive devices like it during his guerrilla days in the Marine Corps, disarmed it by cutting one of the contact wires.

He examined the bomb. It was of the simplest construction: three canisters of blasting powder used for seismic surveys, to be triggered with a standard industrial timing device. Taped to the canisters was an envelope with "Forte" typed on it. He held it up to the light, looking for the faint wires that might indicate a letter bomb. There were none. He ripped it open.

"Say, Mr. Forte," said the radioman plaintively. "Would you mind getting this damned tape off of me?"

Forte paused. "Did you get a look at who did this?"

The radioman shook his head. "Didn't see a thing. I'm transmitting the nine o'clock weather report, and then the lights went out—my lights."

"Be with you in a minute," Forte said, unfolding the single sheet within.

The typed message read:

> For breakfast this morning, Mrs. Red Cloud had orange juice, half a grapefruit, two eggs over light, home fries, four rashers of crisp bacon, a stack of wheat cakes with honey, and coffee. Mr. Yussef Mansour had for breakfast this morning a pear and a bunch of grapes, a *menouchi* with *lebni*, and oolong tea.
>
> At 3:35 this afternoon, the *Alamo* will be attacked by three aircraft which will deposit a layer of carbon black over the entire surface. You are expected to believe that the carbon black is for the purpose of absorption of the sun's rays, to cause a catastrophic melting of the berg. As you realize, this is a useless exercise, as the melting would be minimal, even without the iceberg's Ultravac covering. Your natural reaction will be, therefore, to dismiss the attack as frivolous. This would be a mistake: the carbon black is impregnated with anthrax bacilli.

There was no signature.

"Hey, Mr. Forte," came the radioman's plaintive voice. "What about me?"

"Shut up!" snapped Forte, thinking hard.

He strode over to the radio panel, switched on the radiotelephone circuit, and punched in the code of Joe Mansour's ship, the *Linno*.

A few seconds later came a voice: "This is the *Linno*."

"Ripley Forte here. Switch to scramble code 9178." He punched in the numbers on his own set.

A moment later came the voice again. "Do you read me, Mr. Forte?"

"Five by five. Where's the *Linno*?"

"We are off the coast of Antakya, Turkey."

"Get me Mr. Mansour, on the double."

"Aye, aye, sir."

There was another pause, and then the voice said: "Mr. Mansour is swimming off the fantail, sir. He'll be aboard in a moment."

"Then give me his steward."

"Yes, sir."

"This is Godolphin, Mr. Forte," said a British voice after an interval.

"Godolphin, what did Mr. Mansour have for breakfast this morning?"

"Sir?"

"Breakfast. What did Mr. Mansour eat?"

"Oh. Well, sir, Mr. Mansour had Magdouche grapes, a pear from Ashkelon, and a *menouchi* with some of my own *lebni*, sir," he replied with the aplomb of one who answered such a question every morning. "And oolong tea."

"Is that his usual breakfast?"

"No, sir. He always has oolong, of course, but rarely a *menouchi*, as he finds it fattening. As a matter of fact—"

But Forte had ceased to listen. He put his foot against the radio console and pushed, and his wheeled chair went scooting across the radio shack to the computer on the other side of the room.

He entered the access code for E1 Mundo Data Bank and then the single word "Anthrax."

One second later there appeared on the screen several options. Forte chose "Brief Description—Cause, Effect, Prophylaxis, Cure."

The screen filled with print. Forte entered the "scroll" command and mentally registered the passages that interested him as paragraphs passed in review.

"Anthrax, a.k.a. splenic fever, malignant pustule, woolsorter's disease . . . acute, specific, infectious, febrile disease caused by *Bacillus anthracis* . . . highly resistant spores capable of maintaining virulence for many years . . . in acute forms in man there is excitement and rise in body temperature followed by depression, spasms, respiratory or cardiac distress, trembling, staggering, convulsions terminating in death within a day or two...in humans can be a cutaneous, pulmonary, or intestinal infection...in pulmonary form, inhaling anthrax spores causes disease to run rapid course, usually terminating fatally...prompt diagnosis and treatment imperative.... Antianthrax serum, arsenicals, and antibiotics used with excellent results."

In the background, he heard a voice calling his name. He shuttled back across the room.

"This is Joe Mansour, Rip," the voice was saying.

"Joe, we've got a little problem."

28. BLACK SNOW
21 FEBRUARY 2008

ABOARD THE FOURTEEN-PLACE PIPER TILTPROP LIAISON plane headed for Swedru, Ghana, just six hundred kilometers to the north, Ripley Forte had time to reflect on the significance of the two messages he had received.

For one thing, there was the disquieting fact that *somebody* had at least two agents among his crew. One would have had access to the breakfast menu of the *Linno*, the other the opportunity to receive the message from agent number one, tie up the radioman, type up the two notes— both had been written on the radio-shack typewriter— plant the bomb with its message, and then hurry to the disembarkation of Forte and his party from the *Sun King* and slip him the monitory note. Not only was the organization impeccable, the timing was perfect. Somebody knew exactly what he was doing.

But it wouldn't be somebody from Raynes Oceanic Resources. In the first place, he doubted that ROR would have been able to plant an agent aboard the *Linno*. Joe Mansour had confirmed that his crew was the same that he had before Raynes and Forte had collided over Triple Eye, and until that moment ROR would have had no reason to be interested in Joe Mansour's activities. More germane was the fact that if the note about the sowing of anthrax spores was true, among the victims would probably be Mrs. Red Cloud herself.

The more he thought about it, the more he dreaded that the threat was real. It was the sort of two-edged sword a smart and determined enemy might conceive to decapitate Forte and cut off the Republic of Texas from the water it needed to survive. Under the guise of enveloping the *Alamo* in a shroud of black so that it would melt away in the tropical sun—a sophomoric scheme Forte would be sure to laugh off—the saboteurs would infect the crew with anthrax, which would kill them all before the cause of their sickness was even suspected. The unmanned iceberg would run aground or drift away in the vagrant tropical currents to its quick destruction somewhere in the warm midocean waters, far from the anchors on the continental slope that kept it moving on course.

Worse, even if the crew were somehow spared, the damage would still be catastrophic: The hardy anthrax spores would infect, potentially, every drop of water the *Alamo* produced, and a terrible death would await anybody who drank it or used it to water his crops or livestock.

It was a diabolical plot, and it had KGB written all over it.

Or did it? The Russians were pathetically dependent on American grain imports to make up the shortfalls on their own state farms. If Triple Eye failed, the USSR faced famine, and famine meant revolution. So who had warned him of the plot?

Such questions were frustrating and, moreover, impossible to answer. Forte was sick of being a puppet on a string. Ned Raynes had pulled those strings once, and Joe Mansour, David D. Castle, and Jennifer Red Cloud had ham-handedly been trying to do so for the past three years. He had had enough. From now on people would dance to *his* tune.

The show would begin in just one hour. Forte had picked ten men, all like himself with combat experience, all sagging with the weight of the new Russian RFK-12 automatic rifles, combat knives, RPGs, smoke and stun grenades, plus several bags of needle-sharp caltrops that Forte's armorer had laid in along with the other weaponry when he was setting up the *Alamo*'s defenses many months ago. But he had overlooked surface-to-air missiles, and now Forte and his men were on their way to make up that desperate deficiency.

Forte and Joe Mansour had first considered asking South Africa to dispatch fighter planes, but geography was against them. The *Alamo* was more than three thousand kilometers from the nearest base, beyond their range.

The only alternative was for Triple Eye to improvise its own defenses. *Jane's All the World's Military Bases* suggested three possibilities, of which Forte chose Swedru, Ghana, on the basis of the entry's excellent map and satellite photos. It was garrisoned by 122 Ghanian soldiers, officered by three Russians: a major and two lieutenants. Among the ammunition stores were SP-9 "Skidder" SAMs. A shoulder-launched, wire-guided, short-range missile designed to shoot down ground-attack bombers, they had been obsolete for at least ten years, which was the reason Russia had given them to the Ghanian armed forces. But with a range of four thousand meters, against low-flying aircraft they were the best available within striking range of the *Alamo*, and Ripley Forte had no choice but to liberate them.

At 10:50 the Piper tiltprop took off with Forte and ten volunteers. All but Forte and two others were dressed in jungle camies, their faces streaked with green and black greasepaint. Forte was still wearing his rakish pirate costume. The other two were dressed in the costumes they had had on when Forte called for volunteers: one a Santa Claus suit complete with a bag of colorfully wrapped gifts, and the other his knee-length Campbell soup can.

Fifty kilometers south of the Ghanian coastline, flying at one thousand meters, the aircraft was challenged by Accra Control. The pilot identified the plane as the personal aircraft of the Cameroon minister of state transport, out of Youanda bound for Dakar, Senegal. After an interval, he was given permission to proceed, since he was only transiting Ghanian off-shore airspace.

The pilot opened the cockpit door and said over his shoulder to Ripley Forte: "Stand by."

Forte opened the map he'd hard-copied from *Jane's* along with the information they would need for the raid. For the third and last time he ticked off the phases of the operation, the number of minutes scheduled for each, and the mission of each member of the raiding party.

"Now remember, we don't have time to work out a fallback plan, so we've got to do it right the first time," he said as the plane lost altitude. "If a glitch occurs, you'll just have to improvise. We're slightly outnumbered, but on the other hand we know what we're going to do, and they don't."

The pilot opened the door again. "Ready, Mr. Forte. Hold on, everybody.!"

The plane lost altitude rapidly. At two hundred meters the pilot could plainly make out the control tower at Winneba, which meant the Ghanese controllers could see him, too. He pulled the two cords that were jury-rigged to smoke flares under the port and starboard engines. They ignited, emitting sparks and an impressive trail of flame and smoke. He did a soft-shoe dance on the pedals, causing the plane to fishtail in the air, giving a convincing imitation of an aircraft in distress.

The Piper continued to lose altitude, passing out of visual range of Winneba, and the pilot flattened out, applied throttle, and made for the saddle fifteen kilometers farther on, separated from the Swedru ammunition dump by a tangled growth of trees and brush. Flying at treetop level over rolling range land, he pinpointed the landing site about a hundred yards from a dirt road snaking between the hills. When laser spot-sighted on the touchdown point, he flicked the autoland switch. The aircraft shuddered as it slowed. Its nose lifted slightly as the twin engines swiveled back until their blades were rotating horizontally and then settled on the sere savanna as smoothly as a falling leaf.

The door opened, and men poured out.

One of them ignited a large smoke bomb directly beneath the plane. Others ignited magnesium flares placed in a ring around the plane. In a moment, the plane was all but invisible in what seemed from a distance to be a roaring inferno. The men in camies jogged off to take up positions in the grove of trees fifty meters away. Forte and his two costumed companions, and the pilot, remained in their seats, waiting.

It wouldn't be long, Forte decided. The ammo dump was very near, and the dirt road passed close to the main gate. A patrol should show up in about five minutes, guided by the tower of smoke and the noise of the exploding satchel charges his men had just set off in the bushes.

Minutes later, two jeeps raced around a curve in the road and made for the plane. Both were filled to overflowing with troops—no fewer than fifteen in all—festooned with rifles, pistols, machetes, and bandoliers of ammunition.

The jeeps braked to a stop, and the men piled out, jabbering excitedly in Twi and Fanti, waiting for somebody to tell them what to do. As they milled about, out of the fire and smoke walked three figures the like of which they had never seen.

They fell silent and looked at each other, stupefied. Their jaws went slack. Their arms fell to their sides. And while they stood like so many statues carved of stone, from both sides of the plane came eight men, automatic weapons at the ready. In their eyes was a message, and the Ghanian soldiers did not require an interpreter to discover it. Thirty hands reached for the sky.

Swiftly, efficiently, the soldiers were stripped of their outer garments and trussed with adhesive tape. Then they were thrown into the plane like so many bags of fourth-class mail.

While Forte and his ten men were exchanging their clothing for the soldiers' uniforms, the Piper's engines coughed to life and quickly rose from a throaty whisper to a banshee wail. The plane lifted vertically from the ground to an altitude of fifty meters, hovered there as the engines tilted forward 45 degrees, and went scudding forward at treetop level toward landing point number two some twenty kilometers to the north. In that deserted area the pilot would unload his human cargo and wait for the radio signal from Forte to proceed to the rendezvous.

Forte and company piled into the jeeps, lugging their RPGs, grenades, and other weapons. Two blacks drove while the others darkened their faces and hands with shoe polish. They wouldn't pass close inspection, but then, close inspections weren't part of Forte's plan.

They drove at high speed through patches of thicket and forlorn stands of trees, but mostly over rolling countryside denuded of vegetation by centuries of overplanting and soil erosion, until the guard tower next to the main gate came into view. Then they slowed, as if their errand had been of no importance. The gate, a single iron bar across the road, was down. For a moment he thought they'd have to crash through, but at the last moment the sentry in the guard tower, apparently reassured by the sight of familiar uniforms in the two jeeps that had just left the compound, raised the bar, and the jeeps roared through.

According to *Jane's*, the administration building was down the road to the right, a hundred meters or so beyond the main gate, overlooking the parade ground. Driving sedately along the potholed street, the two jeeps passed a platoon of men in ragged ranks drilling on the dusty parade ground and another group under an acacia tree listlessly watching a sergeant disassembling a heavy machine gun. Nobody paid them more than cursory attention as they slid to a stop in front of the single-story building of whitewashed cinder block.

Forte climbed out of the jeep and entered the building, followed by his men. Two stood on either side of the first door on the right, which bore a plaque that read "Commanding Officer," while the others rounded up and bound the eight enlisted men in the building and deposited them in the orderly room. Forte then posted men at strategic points in the passageway, detailed one to keep watch on the communications room, and knocked on the door.

A voice barked: "Come!"

Forte opened the door and went in, followed by half a dozen of his men with their rifles at the ready. Unlike the other rooms in the low building, this was deliciously cool. The windows giving onto the parade ground were shuttered, and high in the wall an air-conditioning unit hummed contentedly.

Sitting behind the desk in an ample but neatly tailored tunic that splendid breasts strained to fill, straight golden hair reaching just to her shoulders, and imperious dark eyes framed by high cheekbones, Major Elena A. Maksimova—unless the nameplate on the desk lied—was the best argument he had yet seen for women in the service.

Two men, Soviet lieutenants, had frozen when Forte came through the door. One was a peasant at his desk on the left, the other a slender, dreamy-eyed fellow bending over some papers on the major's desk.

"Good morning, Major," said Forte politely. "You have SP-9 'Skidder' surface-to-air missiles on this base. I am here to relieve you of some of them. When I get them, you will all be released unharmed."

"You will never leave this base alive," the major promised.

"Want to bet?" He pulled a silenced pistol from his belt and grabbed the woman roughly by the hair. He shoved the pistol under her ear.

Forte looked at the two lieutenants. The tall, dreamy-eyed one—his name tag said Karlinskiy—paled.

"I'm going to count to three: one—two—"

"No!" cried Karlinskiy, coming out of his trance. He threw himself at Forte but was pinioned by two of Forte's men.

"You want to see her die, *tovarishch*?" sneered Forte.

"No, *please*!"

"Idiot!" screamed the major, and took a deep breath for a shout that would have brought the walls down.

Forte clamped his hand around her face, and her cry died aborning. She bit him, scratched at his face, and stomped on his foot with her service boot. From the pain, which brought tears to his eyes, Forte guessed it must have been about size eleven and hobnailed.

One of the men came to his aid with the adhesive tape, and a moment later she was firmly bound in her chair.

Lieutenant Potato-face hadn't batted an eye. He sat in his chair, stolid and unconcerned.

"You seem like a reasonable man, Lieutenant Karlinskiy," said Forte. "Now here's the way it's going to be: We get six 'Skidders' and everybody lives. We don't get the 'Skidders'..." He nodded toward his men-at-arms.

Karlinskiy swallowed hard and tried to avoid his superior's maddened eyes.

"Just six?"

"Just six," Forte assured him. "Take two of my men to help you load them in the jeep."

Twenty minutes later, through the shutter louvers, Forte observed the discreet thumbs-up sign of his squad leader. A minute later he took a last look at the two Russian officers, gagged and bound to each other back to back.

In the corridor outside he mustered his men. "Radio?"

"Totaled," said the man detailed for the job in the radio shack. "All the telephone lines cut and the PBX smashed."

"Enemy situation?"

"Most of them are in the mess hall having lunch."

"Let's go."

Forte led them out onto the veranda and down the steps. Without haste, they arranged themselves and their weapons in the jeeps and set off toward the gate. There Lieutenant Karlinskiy obediently signaled the sentries to raise the barrier as the jeeps approached, and they passed through without even slowing down.

At the junction with the dirt road by which they had come, the two jeeps took a right instead of a left and picked up speed as they passed from view of the guard tower. In the rear, the man in charge of the caltrops now began to distribute them liberally in the wake of his jeep.

They bounded down the rutted road, across dry streambeds, and around knolls burned clear of vegetation by brush fires and the searing sun, toward their rendezvous point seven kilometers on the other side of the camp from which they had landed.

Suddenly the road ahead of them blossomed with puffs of dust, and an instant later a MiG-23 thundered past, made a wing-over at two thousand meters, and came back at them head on. One jeep dashed to the left into the inadequate shelter of a shallow gully. Forte's vehicle bounced off to the right and stopped under the spreading branches of an afzelia tree. The men dispersed, seeking cover wherever they could find it.

The MiG returned, its machine guns stitching the road they had been traveling seconds before.

Forte, prone behind a rotting log, looked at his watch. They were due to rendezvous with the Piper at 12:15. It was now 12:01. Unless they got out, and fast, other MiGs would come, and one of them would spot the Piper in its clearing in the forest and cut it to pieces. Their line of retreat would be cut.

"Jackson," said Forte to the black who was lying under the jeep with the Russian officer, "you're supposed to know how to fire these things."

Jackson nodded.

"Well, do your stuff!"

Jackson clambered from his refuge and, with Forte's help, quickly withdrew one of the "Skidder" missiles from its tube. He adjusted the sights, armed the propulsion charge and the missile, and balanced the launcher on Forte's shoulder, facing back the way they had come. The MiG's next run would come from that direction and would probably be low. Jackson aimed at the break between the hills, took a deep breath, and released half of it. His finger rested lightly on the trigger.

The MiG appeared without warning. It was going only five hundred kilometers per hour or so—any faster and he would be past his target before he saw it—and his relatively slow speed gave Jackson the fraction of a second he needed.

For an instant the MiG was in the cross hairs less than a kilometer away. He pulled the trigger.

Half a second later a shower of flaming debris rained down over fifty acres of countryside. Part of a wing whistled down through the air, slicing through a branch of the afzelia tree. In falling, it raked Forte and Jackson across the face and arms.

Karlinskiy ran for the bushes.

"Let's go!" yelled Forte, brushing blood out of his eyes with his sleeve.

The jeep broke cover and lurched toward the road. The other jeep was already barreling down the road ahead of them.

Two minutes later they were loading the SP-9s aboard the Piper, which was waiting in the clearing with its props already turning over lazily.

Then they were airborne, hedge-hopping due west,

flying as near to the ground as the pilot dared in hopes that they would not show on the MiGs' look-down radar. The sea was just ahead, breakers foaming along the palm-fringed shore. The pilot descended still farther, to wave-top level, and firewalled the throttle.

"I've got two bogies at 170 degrees, range 18 kilometers," he said to Forte, who was standing tensely behind him. He pointed to the radarscope.

"Then we'd better give them something else to think about," said Forte.

He took the small transmitter from his pocket and pushed the red button.

They were too far away by now to hear the explosion or even to see the black mushroom rising in the sky as the Swedru ammunition dump erupted in flames, ignited by the radio-controlled charge planted by Jackson.

"They've turned away," reported the pilot.

"Good. What's our ETA?"

The pilot punched numbers into the calculator on the instrument panel. "If we can cruise at nine thousand meters, we should touch down on the *Alamo* at 1:33."

"Radar's clean. Take her up," Forte ordered. "But keep your eyes peeled for the nasties."

Forte went back to the passenger compartment, where he allowed one of the men to tend to his cuts. They weren't much, and even as the iodine burned into them Forte's mind was on other things.

If they reached the *Alamo* on schedule, they would have two hours to make preparations before the three enemy planes were due to sow carbon black and anthrax over the *Alamo*. That is, if the whole damned thing wasn't a hoax. The time was sufficient for all the action necessary; the problem was that the means no longer were.

In his haste to lay hands on the antiaircraft missiles, he had neglected to consider one of the most important factors of all. He had thought that six of the very reliable "Skidder" missiles would be more than adequate to shoot down three planes. In any case, he had little choice, for six was the maximum number his small raiding party could load aboard the two jeeps without leaving one of the men behind. But one "Skidder" had already been fired. Worse, he could only guess the *direction* from which the enemy planes would be coming at the iceberg. Five missiles would be enough to shoot them all down, but shooting them down wasn't his only worry. The enemy had to crash into the sea with their deadly cargo instead of on the *Alamo* or *Sun King*.

If they were shot down over either the *Alamo* or the *Sun King*, his crew would be fatally contaminated. To be sure, they could be administered anti-anthrax serum or antibiotics—and Joe Mansour had promised to send medical teams and serum winging south immediately—but what about the berg's own ice? No matter how meticulously the *Alamo* was decontaminated, some microscopic spores would penetrate the Ultravac shield and poison the pure crystalline water beneath.

The *Alamo* came into sight. Aboard it, two helicopters were standing by. Forte had still not made his decision. He delayed it until the Piper was on deck. Hedging his bet, he ordered two of the five men Jackson had checked out in the missile's operation to get aboard one of the choppers. The other three with their missiles climbed aboard the other.

He borrowed a coin from someone—he'd almost forgotten what money looked like, it was so long since he used any—and flipped it.

Heads.

He nodded to the helicopter pilot who would take the three missile men to support ships already fanned out west, five kilometers ahead of the *Sun King*, in case the enemy should attack out of the sun.

"Max, I want you to put one man down on the *Blaney*, another on the *Cochrane*, and the third on the *St. Vincent*."

To the men, his orders were equally simple: "If they approach in echelon, the man on the right takes out the plane on the right, and so on. If in line, the man on the right takes out the first plane, the man in the middle the second, and the man on the starboard ship hits tailend Charlie. Got it?"

"Yes, sir," said the three in unison. "But how do we know they will be attackers and not on some peaceful errand?" added one.

"If they come in your sights, they'll be hostiles. Shoot 'em down!"

He gave similar instructions to the men in the other helicopter and ascended the *Alamo* control tower, where he could gnaw his fingernails in solitude, awaiting the moment. From the glassed-in eyrie he could observe the cargo helicopters loading personnel for transfer to the ships that would take up station well off the flanks of the *Sun King* and the *Alamo*. No one would be left aboard either craft who wasn't absolutely indispensable to their operation. Within half an hour, the *Alamo* was nearly deserted.

At 3:18, a blip appeared to the east on the radar screen, followed a moment later by two more. They were sixty kilometers away, coming in slow—no more than five hundred kilometers per hour.

Forte flicked on the TBS—talk-between-ships. The laser's line of sight beam would be impossible for anyone in the planes to intercept.

"Max!" he said, calling the helicopter pilot he had sent forward. "Where are you?"

"Aboard the *Cochrane*," came Max Cooley's immediate reply.

"Get Bob Schooner and his missile aboard on the double and transport him to the *Carleton Wright* astern. Got it?"

"Roger."

Forte left the TBS channel open so that everybody listening would be informed about what was going on and flicked on the 8150-kilohertz guard band.

"This is Ripley Forte, aboard the iceberg *Alamo*, calling three unidentified aircraft on a course of 272° true, present position"—he squinted to read the coordinates off the radarscope—"0°7' North, 0°55' East."

There was no reply.

Forte repeated the message and added: "This is to inform you that the *Alamo* and the *Sun King* are sovereign territory of the Republic of Texas and as such interdict all intrusions on their territorial waters, which extend for twelve miles on all sides in accordance with international law. Any penetration of these waters or airspace will be considered a hostile act, and you will be shot down. Acknowledge."

Silence.

On the radarscope digital readout, Forte observed that the planes, while maintaining their course, had speeded up. They were now making 580 kph.

Forte shut down channel 8150 and requested a position report from Max Cooley aboard the *Cochrane*.

"Just lifting off, sir," came the message.

Forte groaned. They'd never make it in time.

"Flank speed, Cooley," he ordered.

"Roger," said Cooley, who had been redlining ever since takeoff.

Forte checked the enemy on radar. They had descended to five hundred meters and were now making 610 kph. "What's your altitude, Max?"

"One triple zero meters."

"Maintain that. Our friends are at five hundred. Ask Schooner if he thinks he can hit his bird on the wing."

"Don't have to, Mr. Forte. He's already opened the door and buckled up his harness. When we get within range, I'm going to cut power, turn broadside, and drop like a rock. I'll level off at five hundred meters. After that, it's up to Bob."

Max was going to put his chopper in the path of the enemy. If Schooner managed to shoot it down, well and good. If he missed, then the enemy would ram him, and they'd both go down in flames. Forte wouldn't forget what Cooley and Schooner were doing. But he hoped their reward wouldn't be posthumous.

"Tell Bob not to hurry his shot," Forte said, keeping his voice steady.

"Whites of their eyes, eh, boss?"

"Right."

Forte switched back to the international frequency and repeated his message to the three intruding planes.

Still no reply.

"Okay, men," he said, shutting down the 8150 channel for the final time, "it's all yours. They're coming in at five hundred meters. Wait until they are within fifteen hundred meters and let 'em have it."

He swiveled the tripod-mounted Questar around to the east. He could just make them out, three black spots coming toward them, low and in a loose echelon formation. That could make things difficult for his missile men. If the first plane was shot down before the others came into range, they could peel off and attack from another angle. And the other angles weren't covered.

Forte bit his lip and kept his eye on the lead plane.

Suddenly it blossomed like a Fourth of July rocket in the sky, and its smoking carcass spiraled in a graceful curve into the sea.

The other two aircraft wavered.

Then the first straightened out and resumed its deadly course.

A second shot, a second sunburst.

Forte stopped breathing.

Two down, one to go.

But that one was peeling off to the south.

It did a shallow wingover, and in doing so exposed its inviting underside.

Max Cooley's helicopter slewed in midair. From its open door came a flash, followed by a streak of smoke in the sky. The missile curved in a smooth arc toward its target. A third sunburst lit the sky, and the enemy plane distributed its flame-blackened pieces upon an indifferent sea.

The helicopter did a little victory dance in the air.

29. POSTMORTEM
22 FEBRUARY 2008

CHAIRMAN CHAIM SHITRIT DIDN'T NEED TO TELL HIS eleven fellow members of the Planning Organization the bad news. It was written in the deepened lines of his face and across his slumped shoulders.

After some minutes he looked up. There were tears in his eyes. One rolled down his nose. He rubbed it aside with a soil-stained hand. "The news has been confirmed," he said. "All the Hercules were lost."

The other men looked at one another grimly.

"And all the crew?" asked Rabbi Israel Cohen.

"Yes."

"And the *Alamo*?"

"Untouched."

"But how can that be?" asked Moshe Davi, the former Israeli Air Force vice-chief of staff. "There were no anti-aircraft defenses aboard the ships of Forte's support force."

"Nevertheless, the planes did not return to base," said Shitrit. "Perhaps Moshe can entertain us with alternative hypotheses, having eliminated the possibility that the *Alamo* shot them down."

Moshe Davi nodded. Who could say that the Nigerians who had taken the bribes to allow three C-130s to disappear did not sell the information to the Russians? Russian forces, including fighter aircraft, were based in every one of Nigeria's neighbors: Benin, Togo, Ghana, and the Ivory Coast to the west, and Cameroon, Rio Muni, Fernando Po, Gabon, and Congo to the south. All were within fighter range of the *Alamo*'s position the day before.

"True," Shitrit agreed. "And there is no question that KGB agents are operating in Nigeria. They are everywhere."

"Including the oil refineries at Ibadan from which we obtained the carbon black."

"But they can't have penetrated the pharmaceutical laboratory where we manufactured the anthrax bacillus," said Levi Ben-Zvi, the plant geneticist. "A picked team of Jews performed that phase of the operation."

"And a Jew could not be in the service of the Russians, I suppose?" said Davi sarcastically.

"I hope that you are not suggesting," Ben-Zvi began angrily, "that—"

"That's *exactly* what I'm—"

"Gentlemen, gentlemen," said Shitrit plaintively, "I want to hear the rest of Moshe's hypotheses about how the planes could have been lost."

"A waste of time," said ex-bank director Solomon Molcho in exasperation. "I say let us bury our dead, double our security precautions, and get on with the next phase of Project Titanic."

Shitrit didn't take a vote. His colleagues' faces told him that agreement was general. "Very well. Haim," he said, turning to the chemical engineer, "as project manager on phase two, perhaps you will be good enough to review for us the—"

The printer next to the word processor began to beep. Shitrit punched in the day's key sequence. The printer began to stutter. "Explosion which wiped out ammunition dump at Swedru yesterday was not rpt *not* accident as reported in national media. Reliable sources say that force of commandos in company strength infiltrated camp Wednesday night 20th, stole weapons including recoilless rifles, mortars, heavy machine guns, SAMs, and RPGs, and made their escape overland. Immediate counterattack by squadron of MiGs which strafed and pursued enemy into bush to the north. Force said to consist of black dissidents seeking to destabilize Russian puppet government. Recommend we make contact with dissidents and lend all possible support. End message."

"If I may speak," said Davi, when they were again seated around the table.

"Of course," replied Shitrit.

"Isn't it an amazing coincidence," said Davi thoughtfully, "that this raid, which among other items of armament included SAMs, was carried out hours before our planes were shot down? That the raid occurred within easy range of the liaison aircraft aboard the *Alamo*? Isn't it interesting that ex-Marine Forte has all manner of ex-soldiers, ex-sailors, and ex-Marines among his personnel?"

"You think it is Forte and his men who have, as our agent puts it, 'disappeared into the jungle to overthrow the Ghanian puppet government'?"

"I'm convinced of it."

"The important fact is that our planes were shot down within hours of the theft of SAMs from Swedru. That means that Forte must have been informed only a few hours earlier."

"How so?"

"Because if he'd have known as little as a *day* in advance, he would have had time to get SAMs from Texas."

"Granted. But where does all this get us?"

"It tells us that we've been penetrated—not by the Americans, certainly not by the Nigerians. The Russians are the best bet. And if the Russians knew about phase one, they may know about phase two. They can't know about phase three because we haven't finalized it yet. They knew, also, about the *timing* of phase one. So they will know about the timing of phase two, won't they?"

"Yes."

"But they won't know if only I—or another one, and I stress *one*—of us is put in charge, to determine both the time and the place of phase two."

"You're assuming that one of us in this room is a traitor."

"That is an assumption which, I'm grieved to say, must be entertained."

Some of the men at the table met Davi's eye as he looked at them one after another; some didn't. An amateur psychologist, he suspected those who did more than those who didn't.

Shitrit spoke. "Moshe has made a grave, a *very* grave, charge. It is not one, however, we can safely ignore. Therefore, until we can investigate this charge, I move that we adopt his suggestion that he alone be made responsible for the timing and site of phase two. All in favor?"

All hands were raised.

"Phase two is now your total responsibility, Moshe," said Shitrit. "I sincerely hope it succeeds. But if it fails, at least we will know that eleven of us can be eliminated from the list of possible traitors."

Five chairs were ranged in a semicircle before the desk in the Oval Office that afternoon at two o'clock. They were occupied by Presidential Scientific Adviser Dr. Sidney Bussek, National Affairs Adviser Pat Benson, Director of the Central Intelligence Agency John Broadman, Chairman of the Joint Chiefs of Staff General Moe Sill, and Secretary of Water Resources David D. Castle. As President Horatio Francis Turnbull entered, lighting a fragrant cigar, all stood.

He motioned them to their seats and took his place behind the desk, all business.

"We'll hear first from Pat."

Benson cleared his throat and sat up in his chair. "The facts are these: Ripley Forte was warned yesterday morning that an attempt would be made to saturate the *Alamo* with anthrax spores. He improvised a commando squad from his ex-service employees and raided the Russian ammunition dump at Swedru, retrieving a dozen or so 'Skidders' with which he clobbered the attacking planes, all of which were shot down. Thus endeth the reading."

"Where did those planes come from, John?"

"They could have come from any of several places," began the CIA director.

"That is to say, you don't know."

"No, sir, not yet."

"Did you have any advance information that such an attack would be launched?"

"No, sir."

"Do you know who had any reason to launch such an attack?"

"Well, sir, that we do. The Russians—"

"Damn it, John, with you CIA types the Russians are always behind everything. Do you have *proof* that the Russians did it?"

"As to that, sir, the answer must be, in the present time frame, a qualified—and here I must emphasize the word 'qualified'—subtrahend. But—"

"Jesus," said President Turnbull. "Moe?" The President turned brusquely to the Chairman of the Joint Chiefs of Staff. "What's your reading, preferably in Anglo-Saxon words of one syllable or less?"

"We don't have a clue, sir, beyond what Pat here just told you."

"An honest man. Remind me to ask you sometime how you made general.

"Secretary Castle?"

"I can add nothing, Mr. President, except to express my apprehensions about the fate of Triple Eye. The benefits of iceberg transport are so enormous, so obvious, so universal that I cannot imagine who would want it to fail. Certainly not the Russians, who stand to gain most."

"I agree. This project must not fail. The fate of this country rests on its success." So did Horatio Francis Turnbull's prospects of reelection, but he didn't think this was the moment to say so.

He glanced at the clock on the desk. It was 2:17. "I'm sorry that I cannot give more time to this vital matter, gentlemen," he said, "but the fact is I am already late for an important meeting. Normally I'd appoint a committee to study the situation, but we need action now, not a report in two months. Accordingly, I'm asking General Sill to get to the bottom of this criminal conspiracy. We will meet in forty-eight hours, when he will tell us what we must do to protect the *Alamo*."

He stood and nodded dismissal.

The presidential advisers filed out.

A moment later two dozen well-fed citizens filed in, prodding a neatly combed boy of ten or eleven years ahead of them.

President Turnbull glanced down at his appointments calendar, with the names and pictures of three of the leaders of the delegation. Julia Bacon, the Gay Activist Coalition leader, would be the woman with mottled skin and flower-basket hat. State Senator Jacob Friskin had a wart on his nose and had been a minor league baseball player. Fred Johnson, the Teamster vice-president, who could also be identified by his nose, repeatedly broken and ripely veined from fruit of the vine, fancied himself an expert on labor trends.

"Julia!" said President Turnbull, sliding a file folder over the calendar and coming around the desk to grasp her hand warmly, "you must tell me the name of your milliner so I can tell my wife . . . and Jake—what a pleasure! I was just recalling the other day that home run you hit off of—of—"

He tapped his forehead as if to suggest fast-approaching senility.

"Baker—Stan Baker," prompted a beaming Jacob Friskin.

The President snapped his fingers.

"Baker, of course."

He slid an arm around Johnson's meaty shoulders and whispered confidentially, "Fred, I need your input on a possible reorganization of the Department of Labor. Could you call my secretary so he can set up an appointment?"

Before the flattered Teamster could reply, Turnbull turned and leaned over to shake the hand of the newly elected governor of the Illinois Youth Congress.

"Governor," he said gravely, "I want to congratulate you on your election—and ask you a favor."

"Sir?"

"Do you think you could deliver Illinois come November?"

Forte had had a long if fitful night's sleep, filled with nightmares that fortunately he could not remember upon awakening, but a quick check with the captains of the *Sun King* and the *Alamo* assured him that everything was going routinely. Still, with leisure to digest yesterday's events and assess their significance, he had the uneasy premonition that the new day wasn't going to be an unalloyed pleasure, either.

Jennifer Red Cloud was waiting for him at breakfast.

"Where on earth did you disappear to so suddenly yesterday?"

"You don't know?"

"If I knew, would I ask?"

She might be telling the truth. Forte had never encouraged loose talk among the crew, especially within Mrs. Red Cloud's hearing. "Later," said Forte, remembering with what accuracy the note had reported what she had eaten the day before. There was at least one spy aboard—perhaps several—and what he had to say to Jennifer Red Cloud was for her ears only.

He ate in silence, and nothing she said could get a word out of him.

After breakfast, Forte suggested she join him in his morning helicopter inspection of the fleet. She agreed.

"How was the crossing the line ceremony?" he asked when they were winging their way toward the head of the fleet, which, now that the installation of the refrigerating gear and Flettner sails was complete, was reduced to fewer than twenty ships.

"It was fun, innocuous, and only slightly bawdy, if you discount forty horny hands clutching at my backside."

"So now you're a shellback."

"Yes, now I'm a shellback. And if you are through with the small talk, perhaps you will tell me what happened yesterday."

Forte told her everything, from time to time sneaking a sidelong glance to see her reactions.

She had none.

"And where were you when all this was happening?" he asked when he had concluded the tale.

"At about eleven-thirty when the initiation was over, I returned to the *Sun King*, had lunch, a nap, did some paperwork, and put in an hour and a half of hard labor on my suntan. Why do you ask? I hope it isn't because you think *I* had anything to do with it."

"No. You're sneaky, and ruthless, Red, but I don't think you're suicidal. On the other hand, if I found by searching your cabin that you had a stock of antianthrax serum stashed away—"

"You wouldn't dare!"

"I already have. I sent my men in while you were at breakfast."

"You really have a wonderful opinion of me, don't you?"

"I'm working on it, Red. I believe a man should always have a good opinion of the woman he's going to marry."

He only half heard the sound of her lilting laughter, for already his thoughts were far away, on the attack: Where had it originated, who was behind it, and why had it been launched?

A good Christian could not but grieve over the deaths of the crews of the three Hercules planes shot down in the wake of the *Alamo*, and over the anguish the attack caused the wise men of Oyo who had sent them, and the fears of Forte and Mansour, and the consternation of Turnbull and Castle. But then, Lieutenant General Grigoriy Aleksandrevich Piatakov was not a Christian, and so he rejoiced. His planning of three years was beginning to pay dividends.

He could not take credit for the fieldwork that had

planted agents aboard Joe Mansour's ship *Linno* or in Forte Ocean Engineering and Triple Eye, at the experimental farm in Oyo, or in various high circles of the United States government. This had been done over the years before he had ever become involved with the KGB. But the rest—the grand strategy, the painstaking assessment of the strengths and weaknesses of the players involved, the minuet to which he made his unsuspecting players dance—all this was pure Piatakov, and he was proud of his handiwork.

Like all artists, Piatakov yearned for an audience. Yet that was the one thing a clandestine operations professional must do without. There would come a time, within months, perhaps...

Piatakov had rehearsed the entire operation many times, taking into consideration difficulties Forte might encounter. Piatakov's only miscalculation was that Forte had done his work with more expedition than expected, and with more than an hour to spare.

General Piatakov calculated that three days hence would be the best time to make his approach to Ripley Forte. He would have had time to recover physically, think things through, and realize how lucky he had been to have received a warning from a friend. He would naturally be eager to reward that friendship, which had saved his life, his reputation, and the prospects of his beloved Republic of Texas.

And Piatakov would show him how he could do it. He pulled a tablet toward him, unscrewed the top of his old-fashioned ink-filled pen, and wrote:

My dear Ripley Forte:

I have just had the honor and pleasure of saving your life and those of your shipmates, the *Alamo*, and, not incidentally, the farmlands on which the future prosperity of your nation depends. I am not a mercenary man, putting a price on services which I am only too happy, in the name of common humanity, to extend to one whose main desire is to embellish the luster of the family name you bear.

I am conscious, however, that your generous spirit

would resist the suggestion that the salvation of an iceberg worth, in monetary terms alone, more than $2 billion should go unrewarded. To relieve you of this embarrassment, I would like to point out that the humanitarian work of the research organization which was able to assemble the information which assisted you a few days ago would be much facilitated by the acquisition of a Brown-Ash Mark IX, should you happen to know where one might be obtained. The exchange of a $36 million computer for a $2 billion iceberg might seem to you ridiculously inadequate, but believe me, it's the thought that counts.

The Brown-Ash Mark IX, if you should happen to stumble across one, should be shipped to Messrs. Al Ross-Al Ein, 15 Sharia Kamil el-Abd, Tripoli, Libya.

If I can ever be of further service, you can be sure I shall.

A sincere friend.

30. CHOKE POINT
12 MARCH 2008

FOR WEEKS, EVER SINCE THE ABORTIVE AIRCRAFT ATTACK on February 21, Jennifer Red Cloud had been in irrepressibly good spirits. And the happier she was, the more depressed it made Ripley Forte. It was his own fault. He had made the mistake of showing her the notes he had received: the one warning him of the imminent attack and the other demanding a Brown-Ash Mark IX in payment of the information.

She had been enveloped in a cloud of euphoria ever since.

There was no question in Forte's mind about the reason for her joy. He got an inkling of it with her first question, after having read the note about the computer, the day after the attack.

"You're not thinking of *giving* him the Brown-Ash, I hope?" she had said.

"I'm thinking about it, of course."

"That's ridiculous, and you know it. In the first place, without the Mark IX doing your navigating, your precious *Alamo* is liable to end up in the south China Sea. Furthermore, according to our contract, that computer can be resold only to the original vender: Raynes Oceanic Resources. Not to mention federal law: It is absolutely forbidden to show, much less demonstrate, lease, lend, or ship a Brown-Ash to any foreign power."

"You sold it to me," he reminded her. "I'm a Texan."

"You are a Texan *and* an American, a dual citizen, as you yourself reminded me when I first refused to sell."

Obviously, she still didn't realize that Forte's request for the machine had been purely a defensive ploy. It was true that alone the Mark IX could have handled simultaneously all the myriad computational problems involved in the transport of the *Alamo*. But for the *Alamo* operation, the BAM-IX was not an absolute necessity. Nine IBM-7200 series main-frames in tandem were doing the work quite as well, if rather less speedily, with the same raw data being fed into the BAM-IX as a backup. So far, no discrepancies had appeared in the two sets of calculations, but knowing Jennifer Red Cloud and her conspiratorial little mind, he was sure that one of these days, when least expected, the BAM-IX would start spewing out instructions that, if followed, would probably ground the *Alamo* in Minot, North Dakota.

As a defensive measure his ploy wasn't any great shakes, but where Jennifer Red Cloud was concerned, any defense was better than none.

No wonder she was so cheerful. With the Mark IX in reserve, she doubtless had been cooking up other plans to disable the *Alamo* since her scheme to blow up the anchors had gone sour. But what really brought the rose to her cheeks was the heartwarming realization that another powerful and imaginative enemy of Triple Eye was intent on doing her work for her. One of them, she thought, would have to succeed.

Forte was pretty sure he knew when and where the unknown enemy would strike next.

Two days after the attack, on February 23, at 0°31′ N, 18°30′ E, the *Sun King* had cast off from Anchor No. 496, the last anchor on the eastern side of the Atlantic. At that point, they had left the cold but slow Benguela Current over the African continental slope and passed into the deep water of the warmer but faster-flowing South Equatorial Current, which pours 6 million tons of water a second across the equator in its surge toward the American continent.

In this free-floating phase of the journey, the *Alamo* was propelled mainly by the current, moving the berg at an average of thirty-seven nautical miles a day. Its Flettner sails added another twelve. As before, the *Sun King* preceded the *Alamo*, smoothing the waters for the iceberg, but instead of kedging forward by means of anchors, the *Sun King* was pulled by four 32,500-hp tugs, sufficient to keep taut the lines between the *Sun King* and the *Alamo* but adding little to the latter's forward progress. Most of the electrical power generated by the *Sun King*'s solar cells under the equatorial sun now went to maintain the refrigeration of the iceberg that followed.

They were now making the best time of the voyage, averaging 49 nautical miles per day as against 47 nmpd while on the Benguela Current leg. The distance to the Brazilian coast, where kedging would be resumed, was 2,640 nautical miles, a journey of 54 days. The broad ocean lay before them, with land no longer visible on any quarter. Except for the comforting proximity of the auxiliary ships, they were alone.

About halfway between the African and South American continents, at 0°56′ N, 29°22′ W, lies the St. Peter and St. Paul Rock. A collection of upthrusting rocks from the midocean ridge, scarcely a quarter of a mile across, St. Peter and St. Paul is near the confluence of three great Atlantic currents. If the *Alamo* stayed on its computed course, it would pass just south of St. Peter and St. Paul Rock and join the Guinea Current flowing up the northeast coast of Brazil. Should the iceberg wander just ten miles northward, it would be seized by the powerful Equatorial Countercurrent, flowing back toward Africa at 22 nautical miles a day, too great a speed for its Flettner sails to fight. Were the *Alamo* to deviate the same distance south, it would be dragged down toward Argentina and the Antarctic by the Brazil Current at the rate of 48 nautical miles per day.

Whoever was intent upon destroying the *Alamo* was clever, resourceful, and very well informed. If Forte knew these things, so must the enemy. Therefore, the attack, when it came—and it was sure to come—would take place shortly before the *Alamo* passed below St. Peter and St. Paul Rock.

But *how*?

On the morning of March 12, he discovered the answer.

He rose, as usual, at 6 A.M., when, rubbing the sleep out of his eyes, he went to the head. There, taped to the mirror, was a typewritten note:

Dear Mr. Forte:

Since these days you probably have saints much on your mind, perhaps you recall that St. Luke said (chapter 10, verse 7): '. . . the laborer is worthy of his hire.'

If, therefore, your Brown-Ash Mark IX is en route to me within twelve hours, you will have complete details of the imminent threat to the *Alamo* and how best to combat it. Until then, I can only remind you, as an ex-Marine, of the last words of the first stanza of your celebrated hymn.

Your sincere friend.

Last words? How did they go? He couldn't remember without starting at the beginning.

"From the Halls of Montezuma,
to the shores of Tripoli,
We will fight our country's battles,
on the land as on the sea."

On the sea.

So the attack would come by sea.

The only two navies that counted in the twenty-first

century were those of the United States and Russia. The American navy certainly wasn't a threat. And this supposition confirmed Forte's belief that he was dealing either with two Russian factions, with the aggressor being unaware of the existence of his "sincere friend," or a single enemy trying to whipsaw him.

But none of that mattered now. What mattered was that the threat was plain, and he had to deal with it.

At 6:20 that Wednesday morning in March, Forte requested an urgent meeting with the President of the United States, Secretary of Water Resources David D. Castle, and the Navy and Air Force chiefs of staff. By 6:35, when the confirmation of the appointment came in, Forte was already airborne. At 2:40 that afternoon Forte landed at Washington National, where the President's personal helicopter was waiting to take him to the White House.

Horatio Francis Turnbull rose from his chair to greet Forte as he strode into the Oval Office. The other three men, two of them resplendent in uniforms sagging with ribbons miraculously accumulated during thirty years of peace, were waiting for him. Forte shook hands all around and was invited to take a seat.

"First thing," said Turnbull, taking his own and propping his feet on an open drawer, "is not to worry. We want to bring that berg home. The Russians want us to bring it home. Anything or anybody that gets in the way is going to be squashed like a beetle. Now, then, before we get down to the specific threat, Mr. Forte, I think we might profit from a run-down of the voyage as planned so that we can anticipate further troubles up the road. If I read you correctly, you think more attempts will be made even if this one fails."

"I'm sure of it, Mr. President. May I?" he asked, displaying a map, which, at Turnbull's nod, he proceeded to unroll on the President's desk. Turnbull himself put inkstand and coffee cup at the corners as the others crowded around.

"The red line represents our course from pickup point off Cape Town to the *Alamo*'s berth in Matagorda Bay.

The 9,220-nautical mile voyage is scheduled for 185 days, and we're bang on target almost to the minute so far. When we land, we should have an immediate melt available of 110 million tons, thanks to the warm waters which we will encounter from now on.

"Now, as you see, the trip is broken into five phases from acquisition at Anchor No. 1 to Anchor No. 1118—the last. We spent 47 days in the Benguela. In the South Equatorial, where we are now, we'll spend 54 days. In the Guiana Current, we'll spend 25 days. In the Caribbean's deep waters, we'll make only 25 mpd. And finally, in the gulf we'll be able to use all three forms of propulsion, giving us 48 mpd from kedging, 6 from the weak current, and 17 from the sails."

"Arriving?" asked President Turnbull.

"On 27 June."

The President was plainly pleased. The Republican national convention would be held from August 11 to August 14. This would give him more than six weeks to milk the state committees for unanimous support on the first ballot as a result of this epochal achievement.

"As I see it," said U.S. Chief of Naval Operations Admiral Michael "Iron Mike" Devin, "you're vulnerable every single mile of your journey. In the open sea, you can't stray out of the mainstream of the current for fear of losing your forward momentum or getting diverted into another gyre. And when you hug the coastline, you're like a puppet on a string so long as you're kedging, unable to move to either side."

"That's exactly the problem, Admiral. That red line represents not only our course but the track we must make good. Any deviations of more than a mile or two would be fatal."

Admiral Devin nodded, his eyes glinting behind his granny glasses at the prospect of a knockdown fight. "So you'll not only need protection from our surface forces, you'll need antisubmarine forces and a reconnaissance in strength by our minesweepers to guard against magnetic or moored mines."

"I need all that, and I need it quick, because in 48 hours we'll be at the choke point, where the *Alamo* is at greatest risk. Will I get what I need?"

Admiral Devin looked questioningly at the President.

President Turnbull nodded. "That goes without saying. This iceberg must come in on schedule. The fate of the nation, no less than credibility of the administration, depends on it. Your *jobs* as well as my own depend on it. Now, then, Admiral, what do you need from me?"

Devin straightened. "Merely your authorization, sir, to the secretary of defense to go ahead with the deployment. I will order the formation of a task force from elements of the north and south Atlantic fleets. They will be on station within thirty-six hours."

"That quick?"

"Well, sir," said Devin with a puckish smile, "we've been keeping an eye on the *Alamo* since the incident off Ghana. We have six antiaircraft cruisers, twenty destroyers and frigates, and a dozen assorted other ships within strike range right now. Within thirty-six hours we'll have the *Alamo* so well boxed in that an enemy won't be able to get a rowboat through our lines."

"But we're right in the middle of the Atlantic shipping lanes," Forte reminded him.

"Sure, I'll admit that a merchant vessel could launch a couple of surface-to-surface missiles, but we'll shoot them down with our Gatlings before they can reach the *Alamo*. What I'm really concerned about is surface units."

"And subs?" asked the President.

"We're on top of that, sir."

"So, gentlemen," said Turnbull, "what do we have? Intruder surface warships will be intercepted at what distance, Mike?"

"Eighty miles, sir."

"Mines?"

"The course of the *Alamo* will be swept clean beginning tomorrow evening. I can't do better than that."

"Very well. And the submarine threat will be contained?"

"God willing."

"Well, that should be no problem, as God is a Republican." He turned to his Air Force chief of staff, General John O'Sullivan.

"Jake, are you going to let the Navy collect all the kudos?"

"Not if we can help it, Mr. President."

"And how do you propose to avoid that catastrophe?"

"An AWACS will go aloft the moment this meeting ends. Until the *Alamo* is safely in port, it will have maximum air cover. The AWACS overhead will be accompanied by four F-111 attack craft equipped with air-to-air and air-to-surface missiles."

"Any comments, Mike?"

"No, sir. I don't see how any enemy force can penetrate, especially as I shall be sending up combat air patrols from the task force flattop, and shore-based antisubmarine reconnaissance aircraft as well."

Turnbull turned to David D. Castle, who had been listening without comment to the service chiefs.

"I have nothing to contribute, Mr. President. It seems to me that the experts have the situation well in hand."

"They'd better," said President Turnbull. "It's the Legion of Merit all around if the *Alamo* comes safely to Matagorda Bay, gentlemen—"

The chiefs of staff looked at each other with ill-concealed pleasure.

"—but early retirement if it should fail," the President went on. "And if the stick seems to be mightier than the carrot, well, that is just what I had in mind."

Back aboard the *Sun King* the evening of the following day, Forte was having a drink on the weather deck with Jennifer Red Cloud. A beach table and two comfortable leather club chairs had been brought up for them to observe the sunset on the broad expanse of the black deck, whose solar panels had been lowered for the night. There were just the two of them, the sea, and the sunset.

This evening the long sweep of cirrus clouds was painted a pale purple across the sky, while closer to the horizon the rays of the setting sun had erupted in a burst of brilliant reds and yellows among the towering cumulus that heralded a coming storm. The southeast trade winds blew gently against their cheeks, and only the occasional whitecap disturbed the smooth and easy swell of the sea in the distance.

Jennifer Red Cloud was talking—she hadn't shut up for days—excited about the prospect, apparently, of the coming attack. As she chattered on, his thoughts were engaged in speculation as to what quarter the attack would come from. For the life of him, he couldn't imagine how any surface attack could succeed. The satellite surveillance, the combat air patrols, the high-flying F-111's, the antisub squadrons all reported no unusual air or sea activity. Merchant shipping—mainly breakbulk and ore ships and ULCCs—ultra-large crude carriers—was proceeding on courses usual for the time of year and the international markets. Naval officers had inspected their log books as well as their holds as they entered the hundred-mile cordon of naval steel that ringed the *Sun King* and the *Alamo*. So far, boarding parties had found no armaments more menacing than pistols and shotguns. Undersea activity had likewise been absent.

"—don't you?" Jennifer Red Cloud was saying.

"Don't I what?" He hadn't heard a word she had said for the past five minutes.

"Don't you ever listen to a word I'm saying?"

"I guess I was thinking about something else." Why the hell didn't she stop talking and go below?

"Hey!" he said, suddenly sitting up and cupping his hand to his ear.

"What is it?" She looked around her. The sun had sunk below the horizon, leaving only brilliant reds and yellows slowly draining out of the clouds. She couldn't hear a thing.

"I thought I heard a bell," said Forte.

"Bell?"

"Yeah. The telephone. I think it's David calling you."

"I see," she said stiffly, rising. "If you don't want my company, a simple statement to that effect would suffice. Allow me to bid you good evening and a night filled with horrid dreams, may all of which come true."

Forte gestured wearily with his hand. "Go fall overboard, Red," he said, wishing she were a man so that he could give her a push.

After she had gone below, not overboard—she never did anything he told her—Forte took a turn about the deck of the *Sun King*. It took some time to do this, as there was 370 acres of it, its perimeter enclosed by a wire-cable lifeline and footrope with running lights at five-meter intervals. Below him he could see the phosphorscent glow of the plankton as the swell of the sea broke against the side of the huge iron vessel. Astern, directly to the east, the *Alamo*'s running lights illuminated its forward edge. Above him the stars, which in these latitudes always seemed three times as big as they should be, flickered like fireflies in the sky. Somewhere below the horizon the crescent moon was lurking like an Arab's scimitar poised to cut through the night.

He made two full circuits of the deck, nearly two miles in all, and was none the wiser. Keyed up more than ever, as if he had drunk a dozen cups of coffee, he walked back toward the glow of the hatch in the center of the vast black expanse of the deck. Down below, he collected a sleeping bag and brought it up and unrolled it on the deck. It was too hot to crawl inside, so he lay down upon it just as he was, fully clothed. A minute later, his eyes still half open, he was snoring softly.

He dreamed that in a dream some nameless horror was upon him. He awoke with a start and sat up. He looked down at the luminous dial of his watch. It was 3:07.

He searched the horizon.

Behind him, to the east, the reassuring lights of the *Alamo* were displayed like shining beads on a string paralleling the horizon. To the north and south, except for its stars, the sky was black velvet. To the west, the faintest blush of false dawn announced the coming of a new day. In an hour, at most, the sun would be up.

He lay down again. He let his eyes close. He would be up with the sun, but meanwhile he was still exhausted from the work and worry of the past three days.

He *wanted* to sleep, yet sleep wouldn't come. Every time he slipped toward the timelessness of slumber, a tug of wakefulness pulled him back to the present. Something was wrong, something he had seen.

The glow of false dawn? No, this was the time of day the sun came up like thunder out of the east. Perhaps it was the—

Out of the east.

But the Alamo was to the east. Astern. The sun was rising in the west.

He leaped to his feet.

There it was, the light to the west, glowing brighter.

He felt his heart thudding against his ribs, for as he looked at the false dawn, more luminous every second, he realized that it was spreading out along the horizon in front of him. And not only in front of him to the west, but now the glow appeared on the horizon to his right and to his left. He swung around. Behind the *Alamo*, too, the horizon was aglow.

He was rooted to the spot, not knowing whether he was asleep or awake, hoping it was just another nightmare.

But it wasn't.

They were surrounded by a sea of fire.

PART V
FIRE

31. TRIANGLE OF FIRE
14 MARCH 2008

THE THREE SHIPPING COMPANIES HAD MUCH IN COMMON, had anyone been interested. But of course no one was.

Each company owned a single ULCC. Each tanker had a capacity of a million tons of crude oil. Each ship was of a very similar design, having been built by the Daewoo Shipbuilding Company of Korea in the mid-1990s, when international oil economics favored megaton tankers. Each had been scheduled for the breaker's yard now that they were old and uneconomical. All three companies had been in existence only since January 2008, when they had bought the ULCCs from, respectively, firms in Norway, Hong Kong, and Singapore. All three tankers were highly automated, requiring crews of only fourteen.

The captain of each ship was a Jew.

On March 3, the *Selwa* left Oran, Algeria, with a full cargo of crude for Recife, Brazil, some thirty-thousand nautical miles to the southwest. The trip would take just two weeks at an economical cruise speed of twelve knots.

Two days later, the *Maryam* departed the port of Lobito, Angola, with a full load of crude for New Orleans. It, too, was cruising at twelve knots.

On March 7, the *Samira* took on a million tons of crude at Maracaibo, Venezuela, and set sail for Port Elizabeth, South Africa, steaming at twelve knots.

The courses of all three ships, by no coincidence, would intersect those of the others on March 14, just to the southeast of St. Peter and St. Paul Rock in the mid-Atlantic. A plot of those intersections would form an isoceles triangle on a chart of the area, a triangle that was some eighty-five nautical miles on each side.

On March 13, the three enormous tankers—at 1,700 feet long they were so big that travel between the bridge aft and the forecastle was by motor scooter—were still more than 400 miles apart. But since they would be coming within the 100-mile cordon around the *Sun King* and the *Alamo*, the U.S. Navy dispatched boarding parties to confirm their cargoes and inspect their logs.

The old frigate U.S.S. *Fanning* was detailed to check the *Maryam*. The captain of the *Fanning*, Commander Dan Doon, a rangy black-mustachioed man of thirty-two with a no-nonsense air about him, climbed aboard by Jacob's ladder, saluted the quarterdeck, and was escorted to the bridge. There he had a cup of coffee with the *Maryam*'s captain, inspected the log, and received a report from the chief petty officer in charge of the detail checking the cargo. Everything seemed to be in order.

By nightfall of March 13, when darkness brought an end to visual but not radar surveillance, the task force commander was able to report to the White House and Pentagon that so far all was well.

As he spoke, the three tankers had nearly reached the points which had been determined by the Planning Organization, not absolute map coordinates but rather positions at the vertices of that imaginary triangle in the center of which the *Sun King* and the *Alamo* were being borne by the South Equatorial Current, Flettner sails, and ocean-going tugs toward South America.

The sun had set at 8:01 for the westernmost tanker, and by 8:40 sea and sky had melted together in nearly total darkness.

This was the moment.

The captain of the *Maryam* ordered the gate valves on the eight cargo manifolds, four port and four starboard, opened full. He ordered the manifold discharge pumps run up to maximum rpm. Oil gushed through eighteen-inch rubber hoses rigged across the scuppers, arcing in a graceful curve, black against black, into the sea. At the maximum pumping rate of 165,000 tons per hour, the ship would be emptied by 2:30 A.M. By then, lightened of its load, the tanker would be moving through the sea at full speed.

Well before daylight the tanker would have passed through the cordon of U.S. Navy ships. And shortly after it did, the captain would press the red button on his remote-control radio, igniting the floating magnesium-thermite flares he had dropped overboard just before midnight.

And the scene would be repeated simultaneously aboard the *Selwa* and the *Samira*.

Each ship would be empty just as it passed the point at which another of the three had begun to discharge its cargo, enclosing the *Sun King* and the *Alamo* in a triangle of fire from which escape was impossible.

Other men would have run to give the alarm. Ripley Forte stayed where he was. He knew that any action he took now would be a waste of time. The origin of the fire was obvious enough. He himself had scanned position reports of all shipping within five hundred miles before coming up on deck with Jennifer Red Cloud the night before.

Sirens began to sound aboard the *Sun King* and the *Alamo*, and high-intensity lights flashed on from stem to stern, turning the ebbing night into day.

Forte forced himself to walk calmly across the deck to the easy chair he had occupied the night before and sit down. He took three deep, slow breaths and by an effort of will walled off the wail of the sirens from his consciousness. Then he concentrated on the problem.

The problem was, he admitted to himself at once, probably insoluble. Action would be taken by his skippers and those of the navy ships, imaginative and perhaps heroic action, but it would not be enough.

Nothing could be done to arrest the forward progress of the two behemoths. They could be slowed by reversing the Flettner sails, perhaps, and by warping the *Sun King* into a circular course. But the torque developed in a turning maneuver would probably put unbearable stresses on one side of the *Alamo*. It would break up before it could be turned in any reasonable span of time.

And turn *where*? He recalled that the three tankers that had been pinpointed on the chart during the evening briefing were all megatonners. If their cargo was discharged inside the hundred-mile cordon, each side of the flaming triangle would be somewhere between seventy and ninety miles long. But the carpet of fire would spread in all directions, the viscosity of the oil decreasing in direct proportion to the heat of the fire. After three or four hours, each leg of the blazing triangle would be something like eighty miles long by three miles wide. No ship afloat could possibly get through that curtain of fire, much less the *Sun King* and the *Alamo*.

Such were Ripley Forte's somber reflections as the senior officers of the *Sun King* pounded up the metal ladder and out on the deck. The five men drew up short as they took in what they would always remember as one of the most incongruous sights of their lives: the horizon ringed in flames and Ripley Forte sitting in an easy chair, apparently relaxed and unruffled.

"What the hell is happening?" said the skipper.

Forte told them. "Now that you know what we're up against," he said, "we can spare ourselves wasting time on half measures. There's one chance. Let's go below and look into it."

He led the way down to the main deck and along the green passageway to the communications room.

"I want you to get President Turnbull and Navy Chief of Staff Devin on the horn," he told the communications watch officer. He turned to a radio officer at an adjoining console. "And while he's doing that, get me Vice-Admiral Hodge." Vice-Admiral Ramsey Hodge was the commander of the task force charged with guarding the *Sun King* and the *Alamo*.

A moment later Hodge's voice, hard and brittle, came over the speaker.

"Hodge here."

"Ramsey, this is Rip. What's the situation?"

"Air recon indicates a triangle of fire with you very near the center. In fact, you're only a shade over twenty miles away from the leg of the triangle toward which you are drifting. You have about eight hours before the flames will engulf the *Sun King*. May I make a suggestion?"

"That's why I called you."

"Then abandon ship. I've already ordered the U.S.S. *Swordfish* to stand by to evacuate your crews. It should be surfacing at your position in about forty minutes. It's a 3,800-ton Trident sub. Plenty of room for everybody."

"Good thinking, Ramsey. I'll get them mustered and aboard as soon as possible."

"'Them'? I hope you're not thinking about honoring that old tradition by going down with your ship?"

"Maybe I won't have to. It may depend on you."

"Shoot."

"What have you got near the leg of the triangle of fire toward which we are drifting?"

"My flagship and the bulk of my task force—my carrier, four cruisers, and seven destroyers. Why?"

Forte explained one of the two ideas that had occurred to him.

"It could work," Hodge said, not believing it for a moment.

"It had better. Unless you've got a brighter idea."

"I wish to hell I did. I'll deploy the ships at once and issue orders for the recall of all the ships that can get here in time, in case it works."

"Many thanks, Admiral."

"Keep your fingers crossed." Hodge signed off.

Forte turned to the *Sun King*'s captain. "You heard it all. Make your plans accordingly."

"On the basis that we're going to get through?"

Forte shook his head.

"On the basis that we're not. I want all personnel unessential to the operation of the tugs and communications gear readied for evacuation within thirty minutes. Nobody else remains except volunteers. When the *Swordfish* arrives, I want the other hands put aboard immediately. That way it can get back to the carrier, disembark our crews, and have time to come back for us if needed."

The officers thought he should have said "when" needed, but didn't think it wise to say so.

The executive officer handed a cup of black coffee to Forte as he headed out the door to muster his crew.

"Good luck, sir."

"Don't take a strain," Forte said with a cheerfulness he didn't feel. "You and your men will be back aboard busting your butts scraping the soot off this old scow before we see another another sunrise."

"It's the President, sir," broke in the radioman, swiveling in his chair.

"Mr. President," Forte began, depressing the button on his handset, "sorry to—"

"No apologies, Rip," the President said briskly. "You have troubles."

"Yes, sir."

"What can I do?"

"Is Admiral Devin on?"

"Yes," said Devin, speaking for himself.

"Good. I—"

The *Sun King* started to shake like an aircraft caught in sudden turbulence, and two seconds later the deep-throated rumble of a cascade of bursting high explosives reverberated from the iron hull.

"Is that gunfire I hear?" demanded the President.

"It's everything Admiral Hodge can throw at it, sir. I've requested a two-minute bombardment with shells, missiles, and bombs dropped from his carrier-based planes. The idea is to blast a path through the flaming oil so we can pass through."

"I see."

"I don't," put in Chief of Staff Devin. "How will you be able to keep the flaming oil from flowing right back across the break?"

"Well, sir, while the firing is underway, Admiral Hodge is going to maneuver his carrier, four cruisers, and five destroyers into two lines, in right and left echelon. If a pathway is cleared, he's going to ram his ships through the break. The wake of the first ship in line will push back the oil a hundred yards or so, the second another hundred yards, and so on, clearing a path for the *Sun King* and the *Alamo* to pass through when it reaches that point in the line of fire in about eight hours."

"And once the ships are through the first run, they'll turn 180 degrees, increase the separation between the echelons, and go back, widening the breach?"

"That's it."

"But what if it *doesn't* work?" said President Turnbull.

"We'll know in a minute. I'll have Admiral Hodge patched into this circuit while I go topside to see what's going on."

He nodded to the radio operator, who had been listening in. The operator flipped switches, and a moment later Vice-Admiral Hodge's voice acknowledged the call.

"The President and Admiral Devin are on the line, Ramsey. Any luck?"

"Can't tell yet, Rip. The shelling is still in progress, but the visibility is degrading as the fire builds, and I can't be sure of a break until I actually see it. One of my destroyers is standing by to make the first run."

"Ramsey," he said into the handset, "have you sent in the tin can yet?"

"Just gave the order to execute," Admiral Hodge said.

"What does aerial reconnaissance estimate the width of the oil track now?"

"The smoke is too dense to take a visual reading, Rip, but infrared detectors aboard the AWACS say it's 1,050 meters."

"How long will it take that destroyer to penetrate and report?"

"It should take forty-five seconds at flank speed to come out on your side. Any second now."

They waited, keeping the voice channel clear for the destroyer commander's report.

Suddenly a new, raspy voice came through the speaker.

"Captain U.S.S. *Pratt* speaking, sir. We're through."

"Great!" said Admiral Hodge.

"No, sir, not so great."

"What the hell—" Hodges began angrily and then, as if suddenly realizing that someone may have been hurt during the dash through the fire, went on solicitously, "No casualties, I hope, Captain?"

"Couple of guys are groggy from smoke inhalation, sir."

"Then what—"

"The flames are pretty hot, Admiral, and the hull paint ignited. We're aflame from stem to stern."

32. EXPERTS
14 MARCH 2008

IT WAS A BUSY TWENTY MINUTES FOR FORTE AND THE three radio officers who had volunteered to stay behind.

At 0337 Forte rousted Al Seifert out of an all-night poker game in San Antonio.

At 0343 he located Benjamin J. Rockwell, who was superintending operations at the scene of a forest fire in northeastern California.

At 0344 he caught up with Lieutenant General Fritz Habner, deputy commander of the military air transport service, on an inspection tour at an Air Force base near Topeka, Kansas.

After a brief discussion with Seifert and Rockwell to learn who was the top fire theoretician, Forte ran Professor Jerry K. Smith to earth at a singles bar in Cambridge, Massachusetts.

The four men were instructed to stay on the open line by presidential order, which Forte had taken upon himself to issue in Turnbull's name.

Meanwhile, at 3:44, the captain of the U.S.S. *Pratt* reported that the fire, which he had anticipated and prepared for by mustering all hands at fire quarters before committing his ship to the flames, had been extinguished.

At 3:51 the U.S.S. *Swordfish* surfaced on the starboard beam of the *Sun King* and was now boarding crew members who could be spared.

Just before 4 A.M. Admiral Hodge reported that the three tankers had been intercepted, but all three captains had come up missing.

For the moment, Ripley Forte had done all he could do. Several hundred nonessential personnel would be out of danger within the next half hour. They would be transferred to Task Force 71 Able by 0600. Then the *Swordfish* would return, standing by to evacuate the other personnel when it got too hot to remain aboard.

Three minutes now stood between him and the fateful decision. There was only one way now to save the *Sun King* and the *Alamo*. But Forte knew instinctively that he couldn't push the President; he would have to be gently shepherded in the right direction so that, in the end, Turnbull would believe that he himself had been father of the idea.

As he watched the clock running down to the moment of truth, he became aware that he and his three busy radio operators were no longer alone in the big communications room.

By the door stood Jennifer Red Cloud.

She was dressed in white sharkskin coveralls with a flaring collar and white high-heeled shoes. Her hands nursed a cup of coffee as she leaned against a bulkhead with an air of quiet amusement as she regarded Forte making his last-ditch effort to save the *Alamo*.

Well, the hell with her. He had more important things on his mind than Jennifer Red Cloud.

"Stand by, Mr. Forte," said one of the officers monitoring the circuits. A red light above the main console blinked on.

"Mr. President, this is Forte again."

"It's your party, Mr. Forte," replied Turnbull. "But I have taken the liberty of adding to the guest list by asking my scientific adviser, Dr. Sid Bussek, to be with me."

Dr. Sidney Bussek was an ace in the hole Forte hadn't counted on. Suddenly things looked brighter.

"Dr. Bussek is most welcome, Mr. President," said Forte. "First off, I'd like to have Mr. Al Seifert of San Antonio give us his opinion on the best way to handle a fire like this."

"Well, Rip," came a gravelly voice. "I've been up against a lot of oil fires but never one like the one you've described. From my experience, I'd have to say that if there's really three million tons of crude afire down there, it's going to have to burn itself out."

"That's not the problem, Al. We don't give a damn

about the fire, only about blasting a path which will be kept open by the wakes of ships cruising back and forth at high speed until we can slip the *Sun King* and the *Alamo* through."

"Yeah, I got all that the first time round, Rip," said Seifert dryly. "But if you want *me* to blast your way out, I'll need at least 3,500 liters of nitroglycerine."

"Will that do it?"

"It'll blast a half-mile path, no question about it."

"Can *you* do it?"

"Could, but can't."

"Why not?"

"Time factor. It would take at least twenty-four hours to get that much liquid thunder together. Then I'd have to have a cellular container constructed—couldn't have all that nitro sloshing around, you know—and that could take forty-eight hours from a standing start, and then there's transport time, plus the tricky business of placing the charge, and even if—"

"You're saying it's impossible to create a path through that burning crude within eight hours, right?"

"Sorry, Rip. Now, if I—"

Ripley Forte made a slashing motion with the edge of his hand against his throat. The radio operator cut off Al Seifert's voice in midsentence.

"Mr. Rockwell?"

"On the line, Mr. Forte, but speak up. My fire's a lot closer than yours, and it's pretty noisy."

His own voice barely came through the crackling and popping of a forest being consumed, according to Rockwell, at better than an acre every fifteen seconds.

"You've heard the problem, Mr. Rockwell."

"If it were up to me, I'd use several relays of five or six aircraft crossing the fire low and at right angles, dumping bentonite clay slurries on it. It could cover a large area, and we could keep it up indefinitely, provided we had the aircraft."

"Is the bentonite slurry available in large enough quantities?"

"What with this five-year drought and an average of three major fires in the northwest every week, we could drown you in the stuff. At a guess, eight hundred or a thousand tons would do the trick."

"If you had the transport," Forte prompted.

"That's right, if I had the transport."

Forte signaled Rockwell's circuit cut.

"Well, General Habner?"

"I wish to hell I could help, Mr. Forte, I really do. Now, if it were bombs, it wouldn't be a problem. But slurry requires continuous discharge. Even if we could somehow rig our aircraft to handle a liquid discharge, we'd have to install the proper tanks. That could take weeks."

"Why can't you use the same type aircraft that Rockwell uses? There should be plenty around, what with all the forest fires. It would only mean borrowing them for a day or so."

"True. But how are you going to fly them from the U.S. several thousand miles down to the equator without wing tanks? Wing-tank racks will take days to install."

"How about aerial refueling?"

"Hopeless. Rockwell's planes don't have the equipment."

"The answer is no, General Habner?"

"The answer is no, not with slurries, anyway."

"Stand by. Professor Smith?"

"Present, more or less," came a muzzy voice against a background of clinking glasses, strident voices, and loud music. "What's on your mind, keed?"

"General Habner says he can't dump bentonite slurry. Can you suggest any alternative?"

"Sure, get yourself another general." There was a peal of idiot laughter.

"Professor Smith, *please*. We've got three million tons of crude burning down here, and we're depending on you for answers."

"Wha's it worth to ya?" slurred the professor. "Money on the line, ass on the bed, or no dice—that's what my old daddy always used to say."

"You'll be well compensated. You can depend on it."

"I wanna million dollars—cash—or I'll take my business elsewhere."

President Turnbull broke in.

"Listen to me, you drunken son of a bitch!" he said savagely. "This is Horatio Francis Turnbull, the President of the United States. In about three minutes a couple carloads of F.B.I. agents are going to descend on that bar where you're lushing it up and take turns beating the shit out of you unless you give us answers and give them quick. Understand me, Smith?"

There was a slight pause while Smith considered whether to treat it all as a joke. But a lifetime spent in fear and trembling of saying the wrong thing and thus imperiling his chances for tenure asserted itself. Suddenly he was dead sober.

"What do you wish to know?" he replied in well-articulated Cantabrigian.

"If bentonite slurry won't put our oil fire out, what will?"

"Well, there's always the halogenated hydrocarbons, of course," said Smith crisply. "The Halon series is quite efficient, you know. Halon 1301, for instance, is at least ten times as efficient a flame retardant as carbon dioxide. Halon 2102 is even better for oil fires, of course."

"Is it readily available?"

"I'm afraid not, not in the quantities you'd need. Have you considered wet water?"

"Now listen here, you little—" began President Turnbull, but was quickly silenced by his scientific adviser, who assured him that something called wet water really did exist.

"Or more properly," Professor Smith hastened to say, "a fluorochemical wetting agent. The Navy uses it for extinguishing flaming fluids."

"The distribution problem," objected General Habner. "We can't get the right planes in sufficient numbers in time."

"Then use plain dry sand. It will bind the oil particles, and their combined weight will make them sink."

"Better, and it might work if I had twenty-four hours to organize it," sighed Habner. "But I don't."

Forte smiled grimly and motioned to the radiomen to sever all circuits but that of the President and the Navy chief of staff.

He waited. He had played his cards. From here on he had to trust to luck. It was fortunate Dr. Sidney Bussek was with the President. Forte was pretty sure Admiral Devin would drop a broad hint if the President didn't suggest it first, but with the President's own scientific adviser at his elbow, maybe even that fallback position wouldn't be necessary.

A discreet cough was heard in the background.

"Sid?" said the President.

"Well, sir, if you want my opinion, Al Seifert had the right idea about blasting the fire out."

"The right idea, maybe, but he couldn't deliver."

"No, sir, but Admiral Devin could."

"Is that right, Mike? You can deliver the nitro-glycerine?"

Admiral Devin hesitated.

"Well?"

"I don't think that nitroglycerine was what Dr. Bussek had in mind," said Admiral Devin slowly. "Or was it, Sid?"

"Of course not, Admiral. I was thinking of an atom bomb."

33. FLAMEOUT
14 MARCH 2008

0840 *ALAMO* TIME, 0540 WASHINGTON TIME, WAS ZERO hour.

The bomb had to be detonated over the burning crude oil by then, at the latest. By then, all the surface ships in Admiral Hodge's task force would have arrived on station seven miles to the west, close enough to dash through the blowout zone and keep it clear before the burning oil began to spread back and heal the breach in the triangle of fire.

When the *Sun King* and the *Alamo* got clear, along with their auxiliaries and the U.S.S. *Pratt*, now trapped with them, the task force would proceed at full speed out of the area and begin a thorough scrub-down of the ships to remove any trace of radioactive contamination.

The bomb itself would be a small thirty-kiloton device set for airburst above ground zero. The final altitude of detonation was as yet the subject of intense discussion. A compromise had to be struck to find an altitude at which the blast would be most effective against the flames and least injurious to the ships of the task force and, especially, to the fragile *Alamo*. Only when the B-2 was over the target at twelve thousand meters would the altitude for detonation and the order to drop be given.

If it was given.

Everybody was going ahead as though the decision had been made, but in fact only the President of the United States had given his permission. As one consequence of SALT III, two-thirds of Congress had to concur with any presidential decision to explode a nuclear device—anywhere and for any reason—except in the case of unprovoked attack on the United States.

Within two minutes of President Turnbull's assent to the use of an atomic bomb, the switchboards of the White House, Pentagon, State Department, CIA, and National Security Agency were summoning the 535 members of the U.S. Congress into emergency session. It was going to be a formidable job, for March 15 was a Saturday, and excellent spring weather had been predicted. One by one, the congressmen had to be run down, for the legislation that White House staffers were even then preparing required a quorum.

And run down they were. The first of them arrived on Capitol Hill shortly after 0200, Washington time, less than an hour after President Turnbull had made his decision. But they were few. Another surge of solons came along around 0300, escorted through empty Washington streets by park police cars, their sirens in full cry.

Still the chambers were less than half full. The first arrivals, apprised of the reason for the emergency session, formed tight little knots in the cloakrooms, exploring with men of like minds the possibilities that the President's urgent request had opened up. The ripe aroma of deals a-cookin' filtered through the corridors.

Not until 0400, when the speaker of the House and the president pro tem of the Senate called their respective chambers to order, was a quorum in prospect. The legislators came by cab, by subway, in squad cars, in Air Force helicopters. Many were rumpled and bleary-eyed, and a number were obviously drunk, but all were fully conscious of the gravity of the emergency. The sentiments of the vast majority were clear: If they failed the *Alamo* now, their thirsty constituents would remember it in November. The only question was whether the vote would be unanimous.

The bill, two paragraphs long, was presented in the Senate by the majority leader, a Democrat, and quickly read aloud by the Senate clerk.

A motion made that an immediate vote be taken was, however, blocked by Senator Davidson.

"Just before I entered this chamber," said the senior senator from New York, "I was informed by sources in the State Department that representations—serious representations—were made less than an hour ago to our government by the Soviet Union, protesting that the detonation of an atomic device would be construed as a unilateral abrogation of SALT III and that retaliatory action would be taken."

The Senate broke into uproar.

The president pro tem let his charges get the predawn bile out of their systems and then gaveled the house into silence. "We will not have the luxury of full debate on this issue, ladies and gentlemen. Perhaps the gentleman from New York will tell us whether his information came from the secretary of state."

"No, Mr. President, it did not. But—"

"If it did not, then it cannot be construed as official information. To be a factor in these particular deliberations, in any case, information bearing on foreign relations would have to come from the President himself."

"But surely, sir," protested Senator Davidson, "the issue of war or peace transcends—"

"Will the gentleman yield?" came the voice of Senator Winthrop Lukar of West Virginia, a tall young man of great wealth and greater ambition from whose fund-raising talents Senator Davidson had greatly benefited in the past election campaign. Davidson yielded with a gracious smile.

The president pro tem looked at the clock on the opposite wall. It was 4:13. He had been informed by the White House that 5:40 Washington time was zero hour for the bomb drop. By then, both houses would have had to approve the bill. It would then be sped by helicopter to the White House, where President Turnbull was waiting to sign it into law.

Senator Lukar rose to his full six feet seven inches and adjusted his horn-rimmed glasses. "Ladies and gentlemen," he began, "you will remember with what travail and soul-searching SALT III was negotiated, signed, and approved by this chamber. Are we now going to turn our backs on it? Are we now going to turn the clock back to those days—days of unbearable tension and fear—when the cold war for decades froze amicable relations between our nation and the USSR?

"I certainly hope not, and that we may place this extraordinary request of the executive branch in proper perspective, I should like to review a few salient facts concerning the relationship between our two countries which I feel sure you will agree with me must be carefully considered before we act.

"First of all, I call your attention to the abortive SALT II negotiations of President James Earl Carter. He—"

The president pro tem couldn't credit his ears. The son of a bitch was filibustering.

The President picked up the telephone. *"Filibuster?"*

"Yes, sir. Senator Lukar."

The President slammed down the phone. For long minutes he sat, staring into space, oblivious to the fact that he was grinding his teeth again. Suddenly he smiled and reached for the telephone.

"Get me the DCI."

A moment later the voice of the director of the central intelligence agency came on the line.

"Yes, Mr. President?"

"What's your latest reading on Soviet harvest prospects this fall?"

"The same old story, sir. We estimate the grain shortfall to be somewhere between thirty-five and forty million tons, worse than last year, in fact."

"And if they don't get it from us, where—"

"They won't get it at all. The world drought has—"

"That's all I wanted to know." President Turnbull cradled the receiver and reached for the red telephone.

Aboard the *Sun King*, the crew could only wait.

Forte had signed off his conversation with President Turnbull in a confident mood. The President would have his legislative assistant frame the resolution, which would be waiting for both houses when they convened.

Meanwhile, the B-2 bearing the thirty-kiloton bomb was winging southeast from Eglin Air Force Base in Florida, just over three thousand miles away, at an economical Mach 1.3. A second B-2 carrying a backup bomb had taken off behind it twenty minutes later.

Forte made sure his captains were taking all necessary measures, had another look on deck at the inferno raging afar, and descended to the deserted galley, where he cooked himself bacon and eggs.

He ate his breakfast at one of the stainless-steel galley tables and was pouring himself a second cup of coffee when Jennifer Red Cloud bounced in.

She was radiant. There was spring in her step and summer in her eyes. "I'm ravenous," she proclaimed as she strode into the galley in a hip-hugging cocktail dress of sky-blue silk. "Isn't it amazing what good news will do for one's appetite?"

"Sure is," said Forte, keeping a tight grip on his cup. "But if that's the good news, the bad news is that you'll have to fix your breakfast yourself. The cooks have been evacuated."

"Even better," she burbled. "I've never wanted to hurt their feelings, poor dears, but they're really not very good. This will give me a chance to have a decent breakfast for a change."

"Oh, so now you can cook?"

"My dear man, I think it only fair to tell you that before I met Ned Raynes, I spent six months in Paris mastering cordon bleu techniques."

"Your talents are endless."

Forte observed her art with interest. She prepared her breakfast con brio and with a lot of wrist, but he noted with malicious satisfaction that the eggs were overdone, the toast singed around the edges, and the bacon soggy.

"I take it," she said, pitching into her home cooking with a will, "that we have only until 0840 to evacuate. What a pity! Just when I was getting used to the dear old rust-bucket."

"I hate to ruin your day, Red, but it doesn't look like its going to work out that way. Weren't you there when the President agreed to drop the bomb?"

"I was there." she smiled.

"Well, it'll snuff out the fire like a candle."

"Really, Rip, if you'd spent less time on the high seas and more in Washington, you'd know it will never happen."

"Turnbull will—"

"Turnbull will propose, but the Congress will dispose. The Congress is 515 men and women with minds—well, at least concerns—of their own. They have a couple of hours to act. They'll spend those hours in wrangling, each trying to wring some advantage from the national peril."

"No," said Forte, shaking his head. "The nation needs the water. The *people* need the water. Those 407 congressmen and 98 senators are the people's voice. For them not to vote for dropping the bomb would be treason."

"If for any reason I'm wanted, I'll be in my stateroom," she said, "listening to the radio reports of the *Alamo*'s last hours. One must gather in life's little pleasures where one finds them, you know."

She strode cheerfully out of the galley, head back, heels clicking on the metal deck, hips swinging.

Quite a woman, Forte mused. Of course, she needed a daily application of what comes to the drum on feast days, and he was the man to do it, but that would have to wait. Time enough when he got the *Alamo* into port.

Back in the communications room, he received a situation report. Admiral Hodge's twenty-five ships were now deployed approximately seven miles beyond the belt of fire, ready to move at flank speed toward the firebreak the moment the fire was snuffed out. The U.S.S. *Pratt* had made contact with the first of the *Sun King*'s tugs and was distributing radiation-protection gear. Forte's skippers reported they were ready to take their craft through the break in the fire line as soon as the bomb created it. The lead B-2 was now passing over the Virgin Islands, on course and on schedule. The White House radioed that the special session of Congress was under way and that no problems were anticipated.

Forte remained in the communications room until 0700. Everything that could be done to prepare for the breakthrough he had done. After reviewing the drill once more with his commanders, he sensed that they were getting restive. So, indeed, was he. He put down his clipboard and went topside.

Forward, the four oceangoing tugs were straining just hard enough on their lines to the *Sun King* to keep them taut and to maintain steerageway. Astern, the *Alamo* rose out of the sea like a great white mountain, so still and huge that it seemed impossible that it could actually move—*was* moving—at 1.56 knots, reduced from 2.25 knots now that the Flettner sails had been shut down. On both sides were arrayed Forte's support ships, inboard closer than usual, practically dead in the water. Ahead, the U.S.S. *Pratt* prowled. The U.S.S. *Swordfish* was down there someplace, too, ready to surface the instant it was summoned to remove the remaining crew.

But beyond that small radius of familiarity, there was nothing to excite optimism. To the east, behind them, only a wall of smoke was visible. So, too, on either side. But dead ahead to the west, a streak of wavering red smeared across the horizon, and boiling up from it a roiling mass of black smoke reached up to merge with the clouds. The wind was hard and hot and dry. Although he had been sweating copiously below decks, up here his shirt dried within seconds, rough and scratchy, as if freshly starched and ironed on his body. The stink of burning oil quickly permeated his clothes and hair and assailed his nostrils, reminding him of the acrid warmth of the flaming tar buckets he had hunched over during bitter winter days while on the Hardin County road gang.

It was that tar-bucket smell that alerted him. He looked about and realized that history was about to repeat itself: firestorm, just like Dresden, 1945. Smoke swirled up from every quarter. The inrushing wind was whipping the surface of the ocean into froth, and the bulky easy chair he had been sitting in only hours before went ghosting by him on the deck, propelled by the mounting gale. Overhead, the smoke had cut out all but vagrant rays of sunlight.

He lurched toward the hatch, bending against the wind. He went through, slamming the hatch behind him, and rattled down the steel ladder. He staggered along the passageway to the communications room and seized the mike from the hands of a startled officer.

"All hands! All hands! Now hear this: The firestorm is depleting the oxygen supply within the fire perimeter, and it's going to get worse fast. All hands will therefore don Ultravac suits with bubble helmets at once. I repeat, all hands will don Ultravac suits with self-contained breathing apparatus on the double. Each skipper will acknowledge on the auxiliary channel."

Forte consulted a chart and then called the skipper of the *Amethyst* and ordered him to rendezvous with the *Pratt* and see that the men remaining aboard the Navy ship were outfitted in Ultravac and instructed in its use.

He looked at his watch as the first two of his communications officers hurried to comply with his order. It was 7:18.

It was 7:52 when he returned to his post, outfitted in the fishbowl helmet and the skin-tight insulating gear he hadn't worn since they had left the Antarctic. He was happy to note that the equipment was just as comfortable in the heat—the temperature had climbed three degrees in the past half hour—as it was in the cold.

"Everyone suited up?" he asked the senior officer on duty.

"Everyone but a few of the *Pratt* crew. They'll be

squared away in five or ten minutes."

"Mrs. Red Cloud?"

"I helped suit her up myself."

"I'll bet you did."

"The *Swordfish* will level off at sixty meters and stand by the *Pratt*."

"Good. What's the word from Washington?"

"Nothing, sir," said the officer worriedly.

"I knew it. Get me Pat Benson at the White House."

A few minutes later Pat Benson's flat midwestern drawl was coming across the line. "Simmer down, Rip," he said by way of greeting. "Everything's under control."

"Is that legislation signed?"

"Just about."

"What do you mean just about? What the hell's the holdup?"

"Capitol Hill politics, Rip. We'll all have a good laugh about it someday."

"Right now I'd settle for a little information."

"Sure, if you've got time to listen."

"If that bomb doesn't blow out that fire within the next forty minutes, I'll have all the time in the world."

Benson chuckled.

"Seems Senator Lukar got a bright idea: He'd filibuster about the Russian threat to do something nasty if we dropped the bomb. Of course, he don't give a damn about Russia, but it looks good in the *Congressional Record*. What was really on his mind, as everybody knew at once, was what happens to the *Alamo* water."

"It goes to the Midwest dust bowl, of course. With the water distribution system almost in place, where else could it go?"

"That's the point, see? Only the Midwest profits directly. What about the Far West? What about the South? The East? They want their pound of flesh, too. The midwestern senators didn't know they'd been outflanked by an impromptu caucus of Democratic senators from those other regions, though, and when the midwesterners called for cloture and a quick vote, they failed to get the necessary two-thirds majority. Then came some frantic whispered negotiations on the floor, a couple of calls to the

White House, and just a few minutes ago, agreement by the President to yield to their demands."

"Which were?"

"That Iceberg International, Incorporated, backed by additional federal funds if necessary, construct docking facilities in the East, the South, and the West and receive icebergs to come in strict rotation."

Forte exploded.

"That's crazy. That'll take years to accomplish. We'd have to start all over from the beginning if we lost our momentum now. Besides, it doesn't make engineering or economic sense. To get a berg to the East Coast means using the Gulf Stream. The berg will melt within days in that warm water, despite Ultravac."

"Yeah, I know. But that was the deal, and the President agreed to it. He made a condition, though."

"Condition?"

"He said that if by some miracle the *Sun King* and the *Alamo* did get through without our air force dropping the bomb, the deal was off."

"*Jesus!*" breathed Ripley Forte. "The old man's gone senile."

"I call your attention to Matthew, thee of little faith," said Pat Benson unctuously.

"How's it go?" Forte's mind was on Turnbull's apparent belief that political gimmicks were more powerful than A-bombs.

"Like this, and I quote: 'And behold, there arose a great tempest in the sea, and His disciples'—read 'voters'—'woke Him, and He said "Why are you fearful, O thee of little faith?" Then he arose and rebuked the winds and the sea, and there was a great calm.'"

"Sure," said Forte in a daze. He switched off the circuit and slumped into a chair.

For the next thirty minutes his mind was in another world. He had worked a lifetime for the biggest prize fate could bestow, and in half an hour it would all disappear before his eyes. He would plod like an automaton off the *Sun King*, down the companionway to the *Swordfish*, and be carried to safety while the achievement for which he had labored melted in hellish flames beneath a canopy of black smoke, never to be seen again by man.

From time to time one of his officers spoke to him, but he didn't bother to reply. He sat in the swivel chair as lifeless as a stuffed raccoon, staring at the green deck, not even responding when Jennifer Red Cloud entered the communications room and addressed him.

The officers remained at their posts, working out with the skipper of the *Swordfish* final plans for the evacuation of the various ships' crews.

At 8:39 the three men looked at each other and at Jennifer Red Cloud. "Better hang on to a stanchion, ma'am," one of them advised. "It may be a waste of time, but—"

There was a sudden roar, as if all the storms that ever were had loosed their thunder in a single blast. A moment later the *Sun King* was born up on a huge wave, hung there for a moment, its strained beams and plates creaking like the floorboards of a haunted house, and then descended again. It rocked gently and then was still.

The three officers, as one, bounded for the passageway and the ladder leading topside.

A minute later one returned, his face flushed with excitement inside his fishbowl. "Mr. Forte, it worked! That bomb must have blasted a hole ten miles wide through the fire. You can see daylight out there to the west, and Admiral Hodge's ships are signaling that they're on their way in."

Forte didn't answer.

The officer thought that Forte must not have heard him. "We made it, sir!" he said exuberantly.

Forte turned slowly, his expression vacant, his eyes in another world.

"Made what?"

34. EPITAPH
7 JUNE 2008

PENETRATING THE TRIANGLE OF FIRE WAS ALMOST AN anticlimax. The immense heat of the blast had flash-vaporized beneath it the layer of crude oil that coated the sea, producing a secondary explosion that, though tremendous in itself, was drowned out by the thunder of the atomic bomb burst. When the air cleared a few minutes later, there was a path through the flames more than five miles wide, so free of oil that Admiral Ramsey Hodge's flotilla, poised to keep the channel open, was never called into action.

By noon, its Flettner sails rotating at 145 rpm, the tugs' gas-turbine engines straining, and the South Equatorial Current pushing at a steady 1.54 nautical miles per hour, the *Alamo* left the triangle of fire behind.

The A-bomb had knocked out all radio communications aboard Forte's flotilla, and it wasn't until his ships were well clear that they were restored. Forte immediately put in a call to the White House. But President Turnbull was meeting with the press to proclaim that the *Alamo* had reached safe waters. Pat Benson took the call.

"I want you to convey my heartfelt thanks to the President, Pat."

"I'll tell him, Rip, and I know he's delighted that everything all worked out so well."

"Is that the way you see it?" said Forte, unable to restrain his bitterness.

"Sure. Don't you?"

"Hell, no. He's made Iceberg International, Incorporated, hostage to politics. It'll cost at least another $200 billion to build ports that aren't needed, create pipeline distribution systems where none exist, dredge—well, there's no use in my telling you all this, Pat. By the time his inauguration rolls around, even the politicians who forced him into it will see that the crazy scheme won't work. In a year or so they'll have to back down in the face of taxpayer pressure. But by then the cost of maintaining our unused facilities will have plowed Triple Eye under."

There was a pause and then a chuckle. "Any other bellyaches you want to get out of your system?"

"No."

"Good. You're not only wrong, but you've grievously underestimated the man in the Oval Office."

"Yeah? What does he plan to do, welsh on his promise? *That* should win him a lot of votes come November."

"Your memory must be failing, Rip," chided Benson. "His promise was exactly what the Congress had demanded, but he made a condition. Remember?"

"No."

"That's what I thought. The condition was that if, *by some miracle*, the *Sun King* and the *Alamo* did get through without the Air Force dropping the bomb, then the promise was null and void."

"Come on, Pat," said Forte angrily, "he can't get away with that. There were a couple of thousand witnesses aboard Admiral Hodge's task force."

"Right. And what do you think they saw?"

"They saw a B-2 drop an A-bomb—that's what they saw."

"They didn't. They saw an A-bomb burst, all right. But it wasn't a B-2 that dropped it. In fact, it wasn't dropped at all. It was an air burst, at 1,500 meters altitude, of a Nagasaki-grade atomic missile launched from a submarine. A *Russian* submarine."

That the Russian premier had been able to have an A-bomb delivered at the right time, on short notice, by a submarine, was to Ripley Forte more than providential. It seemed merely part of a gigantic conspiracy between the President and the Congress, the Russian premier and the Russian navy, to manage the *Alamo* project without reference to Ripley Forte. Things were happening as the result of invisible forces he didn't begin to understand. He had lost control.

That ego-shattering realization plunged him into black

depression. He still went through the motions, but the sharp bite of command became toothless. From that fourteenth day of March, Jennifer Red Cloud watched—at first with disbelief, then with alarm, finally with compassion—as Ripley Forte slowly sank into apathy. He spent most of his time alone in his office performing meaningless paperwork, as if motion were somehow a measure of accomplishment. That Forte, a man of quick decision and resolute action, might have a breaking point was an idea that had never occurred to Jennifer Red Cloud. That he might already have gone beyond it she steadfastly refused to consider.

Fortunately, the state of Ripley Forte's mind had no observable effect on the operation of Triple Eye. So thoroughly had he indoctrinated the men, and so much experience had they accumulated in handling the *Sun King* and the *Alamo* during the previous six months, that his abdication of active command little affected the operation.

The Flettner sails, with a slight nudge from the *Sun King* and its tugs, eased the *Alamo* out of the South Equatorial and into the Guiana Current on schedule on 1 April, 18 days after they had pierced the triangle of fire. On 2 April they made fast to Anchor No. 497, which would pull them into the New World. On this leg of the voyage, with generally fine weather, they made the best progress of the voyage. The Guiana Current carried them along at twenty nautical miles per day, to which was added another forty-eight, on an average, by means of kedging. With an average of sixty-eight miles a day being made good, Forte's engineers were able to shut down the Flettner sails in order to replace their roller bearings, which were suffering the effects of metal fatigue under the immense weight of the great steel sails.

For twenty-nine days Forte's flotilla sailed northwest along the slanting northeast coast of Brazil and then, casting off from AN-899, again became free-floating in the Caribbean Current, where the sea was too deep to use anchors. From the continental slope of the northeast coast of Venezuela, the *Alamo* now traversed the warm Caribbean, still traveling in a northwesterly direction, to a point midway between Cuba and the Yucatán peninsula. During this leg, where the current provided twenty and the Flettner sails sixteen nautical miles of the distance made good, they made the slowest progress of the entire run, an average of only forty-three miles a day for thirty days.

Meanwhile, the waters had been getting progressively warmer. The Benguela's 12-degree Centigrade waters had given way to the 20-degree temperatures of the eastern portion of the South Equatorial. Midway across the Atlantic, the South Equatorial rose to 24 degrees, which held for both the Guiana and Caribbean. But on Day 159, as they prepared to swing southwest around the Yucatán peninsula into the Gulf of Mexico, the temperature shot up again, to 28 degrees centigrade, where it would remain until the *Alamo* reached its berth. Each increase in water temperature required a corresponding increase in maintenance refrigeration to preserve the structural integrity of the iceberg as well as to keep melting at a minimum. As foreseen, the *Sun King*'s wave-actuated generators and solar panels provided the needed power, although the refrigerating crew had to be more than doubled to keep up with the work.

The accelerated pace of work aboard the *Alamo* was more than matched by the U.S. Navy's activity close in, beyond the horizon, in the sky overhead, and in the deep waters beneath it.

President Turnbull had staked his political survival on the successful docking of the *Alamo* and the production of household, industrial, and irrigation water that would soon flow from it. Vice-Admiral Hodge was promised a fourth star on his shoulder boards if he succeeded in delivering the *Alamo* safely to port.

With his Task Force 71-Able of twenty-six ships augmented by a battle group from the Pacific Fleet, Hodge constructed two concentric rings of steel around the *Alamo* and the *Sun King*, one at a distance of five miles, the other a hundred miles away. No craft of any type was allowed within those concentric rings of ceaselessly patrolling ships.

Still, Admiral Hodge was too wise an old salt to let his guard down. Ahead of them lay the most difficult leg of the journey, the sixteen days and 1,100 nautical miles between the tip of Yucatán in southern Mexico and Matagorda Bay. Leaving the deep Caribbean, the *Alamo* would again be kedging along the continental slope. Anchors No. 900 to 1118 lay between them and their goal. Each was to be temporarily disarmed and inspected by Navy frogmen before the *Sun King* was made fast for its five-mile haul. The thousands of tiny inlets and river mouths along the Mexican shore would have to be inspected, double-checking on the puppet Mexican government whose Russian masters had issued stern orders to see that no harm to the *Alamo* came from its shores. And finally, a small flotilla of minesweepers was to clear the path in advance of the *Sun King* and the *Alamo* of any obstructions that might harbor an explosive device.

Admiral Hodge had done all he could do except pray. He wasn't a praying man, so as he always did when he wanted something done right, he called in professionals: the chief chaplains of Task Force 71-Able. He told them what he wanted and confidently left them to it: the odds were that at least *one* of them had a direct line.

On the morning of 6 June the *Sun King* tied up with AN-900 on the Yucatán peninsula's continental slope. Two hundred and seventeen more repetitions of the now-familiar routine would bring them into port in Matagorda Bay, and Forte would take his place in the books along with Magellan, Vasco da Gama, and Columbus for an historic feat of seamanship and discovery.

The last leg of the trip would be in the weak embrace of the Gulf Current, which flowed clockwise in the basin of the Gulf of Mexico at a leisurely six miles per day. To this would be added approximately forty-eight miles a day by kedging. Another seven mpd would be picked up by the Flettner sails rotating against the lighter winds of the gulf. Barring accidents, they could expect to arrive in Matagorda Bay on 24 June after a passage of 178 days, about a week better than Forte's scientists had originally anticipated. In all, they would have covered 9,200 nautical miles, a distance equal to three crossings of the Atlantic from New York to England.

The sixth of June—eighty-four days after the atom bomb had blown out Oyo's fire—started like any other for Ripley Forte. He had awakened at 0600, shaved and bathed with slow deliberation, read the overnight reports from the captains of his various craft, and ordered breakfast, which these days he took at his desk. When it arrived, he poured a cup of coffee and opened the folder of operations reports on the *Alamo* for the past twenty-four hours. The log was routine stuff: ice melt rate, fissure and fracture estimate, linear meters of refrigeration shaft excavated and filled, condition of the Flettner sails, harness, towing cables, and Ultravac sealing, personnel changes, sick list, and the like. He went systematically through the log, initialling each page until he came to the place where the accident report should have been. In its place was a brief typewritten note.

Dear Ripley,
Really, I have been very patient with you, but even my patience has limits which have, alas! been reached. I offer you one last chance to deliver to me—at once—the Brown-Ash Mark IX in your possession, failing which your epitaph will read: "Like father, like son."
> Your sincere friend.

35. THE SLEEPER AWAKES
7 JUNE 2008

A FEELING OF RELIEF WASHED OVER RIPLEY FORTE. He was a Lazarus entombed seeing the first ray of new morning's light, a sleeper awakened by a trumpet blast from on high. Banished were his feelings of helplessness, of hopelessness, of fatigue and disaffection. Here, at last, was something he could grasp, something he could act on, confirmation that another attack was coming. Thank God for foes who thought themselves cleverer than they were.

The coming assault would be the last. The letter implied it, and the fact that only eighteen days remained before the *Alamo* would gain the sanctuary of Matagorda Bay meant that it would be difficult to mount another major attack in time, should this one fail.

Why now, after nearly three months, when Admiral Hodge had steadily been refining his security measures, closing one by one the chinks in Task Force 71-Able's armor? The reason had to be related to place, not time. *Any* time would have suited the enemy to destroy the *Alamo*, and in fact on two previous random occasions he had tried to do so. The interval between the previous two attacks had been twenty-one days. Since then, 84 days had elapsed. Unless there was a good reason to delay the next attack, a determined enemy would have launched one long before now so that if it failed, he would have yet another chance. But he did not. Why not?

Forte thought he knew.

He pulled out a chart showing the *Alamo*'s track from pickup near the coast of South Africa to its present position off the tip of the Yucatán. A dotted line indicated the course of the *Alamo* from that point to Matagorda Bay. Some difference, some discrepancy between the intended course and the track actually made good, would account for the long delay. Was there one?

There were, in fact, several. Up to this point, the *Alamo* had traversed open sea—the Atlantic Ocean and the Caribbean Sea—over deep water; from here on, there *was* no deep water. It had also transited, and would again, relatively shallow waters over the continental slope; these elements, being noncontrastive, canceled each other out. But one feature of what lay ahead differed sharply from all that had come before: the trench that had been laboriously dredged out of the sea bottom, connecting the deep waters of the Gulf of Mexico with Matagorda Bay. It was unique. Over the continental slope, as in the open sea, the *Alamo* was, to a certain extent, maneuverable. With as little as six hours' warning of danger ahead, by means of tugs and Flettner sails, it could maneuver to one side or another and perhaps save itself. The chance was small but significant.

In the newly dredged channel that possibility vanished. The forward momentum of the iceberg could not be checked. Therefore, even if danger was detected ahead, they could do nothing to avoid it. Once it entered the channel, anyone with a pocket calculator could compute just where it would be at a given moment. The three-kilometer width of the channel and the momentum of the berg itself made it hostage to a well-planned assault, which could be launched at the moment the aggressor deemed most favorable to success.

The assault would take place in the channel. Forte felt it in his bones.

But the feeling in his bones was not enough. Was there solid evidence, and if so, of what? Forte believed there was. With the sky and open sea under constant surveillance, the greatest danger to the *Alamo* was from the unseen ocean depths. Yet surface and subsurface hydrophones, attack submarines, satellites, agents' reports— all had produced exactly nothing. The complete absence of submarine traffic was another indication that while the attack would come from below, *it would not come from a submarine*. Forte believed, in fact, that the attack had already been launched and that when the *Alamo* was in the proper postion, it would take place. He based his belief on the evidence so far adduced, together with the words his "sincere friend" had said would be his epitaph: "Like father, like son."

One: The writer of those words was most probably a Russian.

Two: His Russian "friend" would therefore be well acquainted with the story of his father Gwillam Forte's 1998 victory over the Russian 17th High Seas Fleet in the Battle of the Black Channel. There, single-handed, with the aid of particle weapons aboard the antique battleship U.S.S. *Texas* and a man-made tsunami, he had sunk an entire Russian fleet, but at the cost of his own ship and his own life. When the *Texas* sank to the bottom of the Houston Ship Channel, its atomic reactors blew up, creating an immense column of water that engulfed the enemy flagship.

Three: The *Alamo* in less than two weeks would enter a similar channel, and Forte's son would be aboard. The Russians had already tried and failed to subdue the *Alamo* with a plague of anthrax and three million tons of flaming crude oil. In this escalation of destruction, nothing was left but a nuclear weapon.

Four: To blow up Gwillam Forte's son as he himself had been blown up would have a vast appeal to the Russian sense of drama, for it was a punishment that exactly fit the crime, poetic justice personified.

Five: Since the U.S. Navy had made surreptitious attack by land, sea, and air virtually impossible, the bomb was probably already in place in the gulf channel, had been perhaps for months.

As Forte saw it, there was one flaw in his reasoning. If the Russians had been so cooperative in helping save the *Alamo* from the pestilence and the fire, why did they now wish to destroy it with a nuclear bomb? The question disturbed Ripley Forte only briefly. He put it down to factional infighting in the Kremlin.

Forte was sure that a bomb had somehow been sequestered in the channel, that the Russians had planted it, and that it would be detonated when the *Alamo* passed over.

Forte consumed one cup of coffee after another, pacing up and down the cabin, piecing together a plan of action. He had two objectives: to recover the bomb, preferably without detection by those who had been watching him on behalf of the Russians, and to dispose of it, preferably without blowing up the western hemisphere. To accomplish either purpose, he had to disappear, but in such a way as not to arouse suspicion.

Then there was the question of the Brown-Ash Mark IX.

At 1100, he sat down at the keyboard to translate the plan into action.

His communications program had been devised by the National Security Agency and was restricted to a limited number of addresses. He entered his cipher password.

Forte's plan called for the enemy to intercept and decode

some of his messages but not all.

He checked the sick call roster once more and jotted down the name Frank Gilbey.

Then messages in cipher began to flow to Tokyo, to the *Linno* in the South China Sea, to Houston, Washington, D.C., New York City, and other places.

Before he was finished, replies began to appear in swift lines on his printer-decoder.

The first was from the Texas Medical Center in Houston, from a kidney specialist.

The second was from Joe Mansour, who promised that the equipment and teams Forte needed would be ready in Corpus Christi within twenty-four hours.

The third, from SD-1 in Houston, said that the BAM-IX had begun to churn out data that didn't quite jibe with the data produced by the mainline computers.

The fourth—the only message received in the fairly low-grade OXX-7 cypher—was from the chairman of the Joint Chiefs of Staff at the Pentagon.

Mr. Ripley Forte, on the *Sun King*:

The spectacular success of the *Sun King* and *Alamo*, due to the courage, determination, and skill of yourself and your crew, is applauded by all Americans and Texans. Your success, nevertheless, I am sure you will agree, would have been problematical without the computational capabilities of the Brown-Ash Mark IX. This is yet another testimony to the remarkable power of this machine and its unique position in the nation's strategic arsenal.

According to published information, you will not be in need of these capabilities until the capture of your next iceberg, at the beginning of Antarctic summer in late October. Allied defense planning, on the other hand, requires this capability by mid-July for a new installation—I'm afraid, for security reasons, I cannot divulge its nature—in Japan.

Presidential authority (after consultation with the President of Texas) has been granted, accordingly, to transfer the Brown-Ash Mark IX computer in your possession at SD-1 in Houston to the Japanese

Defense Forces. The transfer is to be effected no later than 22 June 2008, the estimated time of arrival of the *Alamo* in Matagorda Bay. Delivery instructions follow. You will receive compensation for *force majeure* repossession as stipulated in your contract with Raynes Oceanic Resources. You are also authorized to purchase the next-but-one Brown-Ash (Mark X), scheduled for delivery in mid-November.

I regret any inconvenience this may cause you and Iceberg International, Inc., and thank you in advance for your cooperation.

/s/ N. Danilchik, General, USAF
Deputy Chairman, Joint Chiefs of Staff

Forte smiled and then reread the message from the Texas Medical Center.

The instructions were simple. Two tablets of any of the listed antihistamines. He went to the head and opened the medicine cabinet. Among the drugs he found a bottle containing Pertussamine. It was on his list. He took three tablets.

His next stop was the sick bay. Frank Gilbey was alone in a two-bed room. Forte walked in and closed the door behind him.

"How'ya doing, Frank?" said Forte to the man propped up in bed, reading a science-fiction novel.

"Hey, Mr. Forte," said Gilbey cheerfully. "What brings you down this way?"

"Heard there were complaints about the food. Wanted to see for myself."

"Hell, whoever complained about the chow must *really* be sick. It sure wasn't me."

"What's yours?" asked Forte.

"Bum kidneys. Doctor says I gotta go back to the States for tests. Leave this afternoon on the courier plane."

"Sorry to hear that, Frank. Painful?"

"The only pain is in the ass—every six hours I've got to piss in a bottle." He pointed to a full specimen jar on the bedside table.

"I'm going toward the lab," said Forte. "I'll drop it off."

Ten minutes later Forte was sitting in the office of the young ship's doctor, Dr. David Nasrallah.

"I've been having these pains, Doc," he said. "Nothing much, but today I noticed that my piss wasn't the usual color, and I thought maybe I'd better check."

"Pains? What kind of pains?"

"Well, I feel like a couple of cops with nightsticks have been encouraging me to confess with a kidney massage. But I probably just pulled a muscle."

"What about micturation? Does it hurt?"

"Yes, now that you mention it, it does. Doesn't exactly hurt. More like burns."

"I see. Let's have a look at your blood pressure, Mr. Forte."

Forte submitted.

Dr. Nasrallah took it twice.

"What's it read?" asked Forte.

"It just might set an altitude record," said Nasrallah gravely. "One hundred and eighty-five over one-fifteen. I'd like you to leave a urine specimen, Mr. Forte, and I'll get back to you this afternoon."

"Anything you say."

Two hours later, as Forte was working in his cabin, there came a knock on the door.

"It's open," he called.

Young Dr. Nasrallah walked in, his expression grim.

"Have a chair, Doc," said Forte, swinging around to face him. He noted the look on Dr. Nasrallah's face. "Anything wrong?"

"A lot. There must be an epidemic going on here."

"Epidemic? Of what?"

Dr. Nasrallah forced a smile. "Bad joke. What I meant was, you're the second in two days."

"Get to the point, Doctor."

"Of course. I'm sorry, Mr. Forte, but the results of your urine examination are very disquieting—blood, red cell casts, high albumin, fat bodies—not good at all."

"That doesn't mean anything to me," said Forte shortly. "Say something I can understand."

"I'm afraid you're a sick man, Mr. Forte, a very sick man, indeed."

"Don't be silly. I feel great except for those little things I mentioned this afternoon."

"Allow me to disagree. You're a sick man, and you need immediate attention at a major hospital."

"I don't suppose you could maybe confide in me what the hell you think I've got?"

"That's the trouble, Mr. Forte. I don't know. It could be systemic lupus erythematosus. It could be acute glomerulonephritis. It could be a number of things."

Ripley Forte leaned back in his chair and regarded Dr. Nasrallah uneasily.

"Are they as bad as they sound?"

"Worse."

36. CIGARETTE BOAT
21 JUNE 2008

THE PLANE THAT DELIVERED HIM TO HOUSTON TOOK OFF from the *Sun King* in midafternoon of the eighth. At 5:30 P.M. he checked into TMC's kidney clinic. He was assigned a private suite outside of which two muscular ex-paratroopers disguised as orderlies were stationed to exclude unwanted visitors. During the evening a troop of consultants, residents, and interns stopped by his room on grand rounds. When they left five minutes later Forte was among them, attired in a long white coat, with a stethoscope stuffed in his side pocket.

An hour later he was in Corpus Christi, where he proceeded to a waterfront warehouse upon which the men and materials he had asked Joe Mansour to send were already converging. By noon the next day, all six four-man teams and their special equipment were aboard a U.S. Navy hydrofoil speeding south to rendezvous with the support ship *Stephen F. Austin* thirty miles to the southwest of the *Sun King* and *Alamo* over the continental slope off Yucatán.

The next fourteen days were a nightmare of back-breaking labor and frustration.

The search had begun six miles ahead of the *Sun King*, on the evening of June 8. With the *Stephen F. Austin* serving as mother ship, all the Raynes Rover undersea craft his fleet could muster had been assigned to the task of combing and sifting the seabed inch by laborious inch before the *Sun King* and the *Alamo* hove into view. Forte had no illusions that if the submerged bomb were detonated by remote control, the *Alamo* might somehow be saved. Even at a distance of a hundred miles or more, the enormous iceberg would be upended and smashed into a million pieces by the tsunami produced by the underwater blast of even a small atom bomb. But Forte was hoping that the Russians would want to exact a storybook revenge. Their own flagship *Karl Marx* had been destroyed by such an atomic blast; they would, Forte hoped, rig their nuclear device to detonate just as the *Alamo* passed above it. That would be in character, but more important, Forte would have time to find it so long as he managed to stay ahead of the advancing iceberg.

That the bomb was there and that they would find it he never doubted for a moment. And if it *were* there, the odds, indeed, were against their missing it. The Raynes Rovers swept a swath of seabed fifty meters broad. Magnetometer arrays towed by each submersible detected metal masses as small as tin cans. The strength of the signal, its bearing, and other data were relayed by telemetry to the *Stephen F. Austin*, where computer analysis filtered out sightings of metal spars, oarlocks, oil drums, and other such jetsam. Everything else had to be investigated.

That was done by a pair of Rovers equipped with nuclear magnetic resonance gear developed by the Brookhaven National Laboratory for Nuclear Research to be used if and when the SALT-IV treaty ever became a reality.

Unfortunately, only one set of NMR gear for use at sea was available, and a multitude of big metallic objects littered the sea floor. Thus Forte and his men were able to gain less than fifteen nautical miles on the iceberg and its escorts before the Rovers entered the Matagorda Trench itself.

The Trench was simple, and they made short work of

it. It was only fifty-five miles long and a mile and a half wide. Most important, it was newly excavated, and only two vessels, a motor schooner and a small coastal craft, had sunk there. Both were innocent of any traces of plutonium. Forte's teams worked on, through Pass Cavallo and into Matagorda Bay, past the line of enormous two-hundred-meter-long floating caissons, right up to the end of the anchorage.

No A-bomb.

During Forte's futile search, the great white berg had been forging northward along the continental slope toward Texas, on schedule. It had entered the Trench, and in thirty hours it was due to enter Pass Cavallo. The *Alamo*, having slowed to half a knot, would then be drifting under its own momentum. Twenty-four hours later it would be nudged into its berth. The immense floating caissons were then to be winched into place behind it, and their buoyancy chambers flooded. By then the *Sun King* would be moored in its special dockyard in Palacios inlet. There, as each pie section was detached, it would be towed back separately to Simonstown Bay, there to await reassembly and another journey north.

On the marshy banks that two years before had been the refuge of heron and water moccasin, muskrat and mosquito, the boisterous, brawny town of Gwillam, Texas, had taken shape. Despite its seven thousand inhabitants, schools, churches, and paved roads, Gwillam was still raw and unfinished. Construction crews worked round the clock to build housing for the technicians who were still pouring in. These specialists would monitor the melting down of the berg, and man the huge pumps to send the pure cold waters coursing toward the parched plains to the north, and install the fifty-meter-high ocean thermal energy conversion units that now stood like great iron sentinels in a line on the edge of the basin, waiting to generate electricity to power the oil-starved industries of the Republic of Texas.

The town's lights were visible in the distance as Ripley Forte wearily boarded the *Stephen F. Austin* on the evening of June 20. He climbed the ladder to the bridge, feeling the weight of his forty-seven years.

"Any luck, Rip?" asked Captain Ramirez, who already knew what the answer would be.

"None." Forte pulled off his knitted blue cap and poured a cup of coffee. He climbed into the watch officer's high swivel chair. "What's the *Alamo*'s status?"

"She's closing in. Right now she's seventy miles astern. They'll reduce power in about two hours so the berg won't keep on going and end up in Peoria. Just talked with the skipper, and he says no problems are anticipated."

"Yeah," said Forte glumly. "Any word on Hurricane Nadja?"

"The meteorologists say it's a pussycat, so you can bet your ass it's a roaring tiger."

Forte finished his coffee, skipped dinner, and went below for a hot shower and the sack. He left a call for 0400. His crews, exhausted from fourteen days in the deep under intense pressure, weren't going to like it, but he intended to make another sweep of the final forty miles of the trench before the *Alamo* got there. That would be about the time the storm was due to strike, but it wouldn't affect the Rovers because they'd be nearly forty fathoms beneath the turbulent seas. As for the *Alamo*, it had weathered much worse in the Antarctic.

At 0335 he was awakened by a call from the watch officer in radar plot. "Yeah, what is it?" said Forte muzzily, squinting at the clock.

"I'm not quite sure, sir. It's moving fast and entering restricted waters. I spotted it coming out of a cove below Jones Creek, a-shittin' and a-gittin'."

"Speed and distance from the trench?"

"Speed: fifty-three knots; distance from the trench— ah—forty-seven nautical miles."

"Stay with it," said Forte. He cut the line and called the bridge.

"Yes, sir," responded the watch officer immediately.

"I want all SEALs to suit up immediately and every available Raynes Rover prepared to be put in the water."

"Aye, aye, sir."

Forte punched 11 on the phone and a moment later was talking with Admiral Hodge. "You got the word?"

"Just now, Rip. We've got a fix on him from shipboard

radar and airborne search-and-rescue planes. He probably thinks that we can't see him through all that low cloud cover."

Forte thought a moment. "Instead of intercepting him, Admiral, let's let him think he's undetected. Let him dump his bomb over the side and get away in the rain and darkness."

"And then?"

"*Then* you can pick him up and reason with him. Or you can save everybody a lot of bother."

Five minutes later Forte was lowering himself into the cockpit of the *Mako*, the Raynes Rover he had taken down off Cape Columbine with Jennifer Red Cloud— Christ! Was it six months ago already? And he'd hardly given her a thought these past two weeks. Well, there'd be time for her later, if there *was* a later.

At two hundred meters the *Mako* leveled off. Bill Makepeace, his copilot, slumped in his seat, fast asleep. The cabin was quiet except for the whirr of the exhaust fan. The only movement was of the two needles across the autonav recorder. One, marking the position of the *Mako* in the middle of the trench five miles from Pass Cavallo, was nearly stationary. The other, of the intruding craft, was moving fast toward the *Mako*. In five or six minutes, the two lines would intersect.

Enhanced radar imaging had established that the target was a "cigarette boat," an oceangoing craft that could crash through heavy swells at ninety-five miles per hour. Infrared detectors aboard the surveillance aircraft circling in the black clouds overhead indicated that in addition to a pair of very hot engines the boat carried two warm bodies.

At 0428 Ripley Forte nudged Bill Makepeace awake, jabbing his finger toward the sonar plot on the starboard side of the cabin.

Makepeace massaged the sleep out of his eyes and recited the figures from the digital readout: "Surface target bearing 269 degrees true, speed six knots and slowing, range 420 meters." The *Mako*'s position and that of the target nearly overlapped. "Maybe you'd better ease over to the port a bit," he was saying, when suddenly the target above them became two.

"Hard a-port, flank speed!" he shouted, and, not waiting for Forte to react, himself seized and firewalled the twin throttles. The craft shot forward, slamming them back in their seats, and slewed around as Forte swung the helm all the way over.

A deep boom reverberated through the little cabin. At the same instant the submersible careened over on its side, almost capsizing before Forte applied rudder and helm to right it.

Forte and Makepeace looked at each other numbly. Forte could feel a vein throbbing in his forehead. Well, he guessed, when nothing happened, they had a right to panic: They must have been the first people ever to be hit by an A-bomb—and live. With a shaking hand, he pulled the throttles back to idle, wishing it were that easy to slow down his racing heart. He sat still for a moment, taking slow and measured breaths.

After a time he switched on the intercom with the lockout in the rear. "Everything okay back there?"

"We thought you'd never ask. Was that what we think it was?"

"Affirmative," said Forte. "Also, yes. And you're the boys who are going to bring it back alive. All set?"

"As all set as we'll ever be. Permission to lock out."

"Granted."

Five submersibles had clustered around the black cylinder resting on the bottom of the trench, 222 meters down. Each cast high-intensity beams on the bomb from a different angle. The bomb had settled in the silt, nose first. Sheared rivets showed where vanes had been removed, presumably to save space. It was small—no more than 70 centimeters in diameter by about 170 long. It could have served as the coffin for a moderate-sized man—or half the population of Texas.

Although the SDCs carried a total of ten SEALs between them, only two would work at a time. More could not comfortably maneuver around the small nose cone.

The first two out, Lieutenant Commander Mahosky and Lieutenant Peloquin from the *Mako*, inspected the bomb with slow deliberation, relaying their findings over voice circuits to the eighteen men in the SDCs.

An esoteric discussion about the use of electromagnetic devices to contravene a possible booby trap ensued, during the course of which Forte, utterly exhausted, fell asleep.

It was 0740 when he awoke with a jolt.

"What's happening?" he said. Two men were floating languidly in the water less than three meters away. "What are Mahosky and Peloquin doing, anyway?"

"I guess they're asleep aft." Makepeace laughed. "Those guys you see out there are O'Sullivan and Hartline. And they may be sleeping, too, for all I know."

Forte shook his head and rubbed his eyes. "What the hell's going on?"

"They had a committee meeting and decided the only really safe way to handle the bomb was to immobilize the whole damned inner assembly."

"Gel?"

"Right. They've drilled something like seventy holes in the body and around the nose cone so far in order to inject their gunk."

"It's taken them long enough."

"Well, Mr. Forte, the problem has been to remove the drill bit and insert the gel nozzle before any seawater could seep in and complete a circuit."

Forte nodded. "I'd forgotten about that. How much longer?"

"Another ten injections should take care of it."

At 8:15 John O'Sullivan pronounced the bomb temporarily disarmed and ready to travel. "We've neutralized the fuse, probably a gravimetric device to be triggered by the passage overhead of the *Alamo*. Then we enveloped the bomb in polystyrene foam against knocks and shocks. On top of that we've sheathed it in heavy lead foil to prevent accidental detonation by ultra-low-frequency radio waves."

A team of six wrapped the lead-shielded bomb in a heavy nylon harness and strapped it by a sling to the *Mako*'s skids. The SEAL leader gave Forte the thumbs-up sign and returned with his men to their respective SDCs.

It was about 175 nautical miles to Houston via the Houston Ship Channel, a trip that would take ten hours at the eighteen knots Forte considered the fastest prudent speed, considering the cargo he was carrying. Only two other SDCs would be needed—one to lead, the other to follow in case of problems. He ordered the others to report to the *Stephen F. Austin* and called up Admiral Hodge on the scrambler.

"Admiral, we're ready to move."

"So are we. You'll have killer-sub escorts fore and aft all the way up the ship channel, submerged. I'm detaching four tin cans to give you surface cover. Overhead we'll have the usual combat air patrol. Think that'll do it?"

"If it doesn't," said Forte fervently, "we're in real trouble. Out."

Forte spent much of the next ten hours reviewing his plan for disposing of the bomb now that he actually had it. Of the main outlines of his solution he found no self-argument. But there was one aspect of his plan on which success would stand or fall. It was only a detail, but if he miscalculated, he would fail.

Whether he won or lost the next and final round depended possibly on whether the Russians had been able to see through his fake hospitalization, certainly on whether they had been able to penetrate SD-1. He was gambling that they had been thwarted in trying to place an agent in the old salt dome outside Houston where his father Gwillam had maintained a vast underground industrial complex.

To sweeten the odds, a week earlier he had devised an "accident" in SD-1. A slightly toxic gas had been released in the salt dome, precipitating the mass exodus of his hundreds of researchers and technicians. The forty-odd men his A-bomb operation depended on remained behind to "decontaminate" the man-made cavern. They'd stay until the operation was finished.

They were there now, waiting in SD-1, 1,450 meters below the surface. The elevator shafts to the surface were already sealed with huge steel bombproof blast shields. The central telephone exchange was inactivated. Only the navigation channels to the *Alamo* remained a link to the outside world.

There was still one way in, though, and Ripley Forte was one of the few men still alive who knew about it.

37. SHELL GAME
22 JUNE 2008

THE LAST TIME THE AIRLOCK HAD BEEN USED HAD BEEN ten years earlier, just before the U.S.S. *Texas*, Gwillam Forte, Captain, had sailed from its slip on its fatal voyage. The slip was now empty, but the turgid brown waters concealed the *Mako*'s stealthy passage as it glided up to the open airlock ten meters below the surface and was manhandled into its interior by waiting frogmen. They slid the big watertight doors back into place, and Ripley Forte switched on the lights.

He couldn't see the frogmen as they carefully disengaged the bomb from its sling, but after a few minutes they came into view, pushing it on a dolly ahead of them.

"All clear," came the voice of the team leader over the *Mako*'s loudspeakers, and he gave a thumbs-up to Forte inside the SDC by way of confirmation.

"Start the pumps," Forte ordered.

A high-pitched whine penetrated the tiny cabin, and the zero-buoyant SDC began to settle toward the floor of the airlock as the water was pumped out. A few minutes later it made contact with a gentle bump, and hands got busy undogging the forward hatch.

Forte climbed out and stretched his cramped and aching limbs, followed by Bill Makepeace, who lit up his first cigarette in what seemed like a century.

The inner door of the airlock was opened, and Gunnar Nielson, the chief of the Meta Unit, which would supervise the conversion, walked through. He was a stolid, unemotional Swede who seemed perpetually on the verge of falling asleep, but under his shaggy gray brows his eyes moved fast, and behind them his brain moved even faster.

He looked at the bomb and favored it with an unaccustomed smile.

Forte heaved a huge sigh of relief. If Nielson had scowled or remained expressionless, that would have been bad news indeed.

"It'll fit?" said Forte, to whom no reassurance about this particular matter would be excessive.

"Like Laurel and Hardy," said Nielson, his face reverting to its usual impassivity. "Shall we?"

"We shall," responded Forte.

He spread himself out on a wooden bench in the little passenger car that had brought Nielson and the *Mako*'s relief crew. The new pilot and his mate had already climbed down the SDC's hatch and buckled up. As soon as the bomb was secured to a flat car behind the miniature electric locomotive, the inside tunnel door would be closed and the airlock flooded. The frogmen would then open the outside door, and the *Mako* would start the long return journey down the Houston Ship Channel to the *Stephen F. Austin*, out in the Gulf of Mexico. There the exhausted SEAL divers, Lieutenant Commander Mahosky and Lieutenant Peloquin, who would by then have been under twenty-one atmospheres of pressure in the lockout and in the water for something over twenty-four hours, would at last be able to start their eight-day decompression.

"Ready to rumble," said a technician who had just finished tightening the last bolts on the steel webbing making fast the bomb to its carriage.

Nielson checked each fitting in turn and pointed his chin at the engine driver.

"Main braking system?"

The driver put his foot on the brake pedal and pushed. The brakes went on with a metallic snap.

"Auxiliaries?"

The driver reached down and jerked back on the long steel lever. Another *clank* as the shoes grabbed the brake drums.

"Ten kilometers per hour," Neilson ordered.

And at that jogger's pace they were off down the steeply inclined tunnel, 9.1 kilometers long, that led to the vast cavern that was SD-1, nearly a mile below the surface of the earth. It was 2100 hours when they arrived in the ion-drive engine assembly room, cleared for Team Meta two weeks earlier, when Forte had been ordered by the Pentagon to surrender the BAM-IX for transfer to the Japanese Defense Force.

The Brown-Ash Mark IX was already there, in the middle of the clean room, which was still under slightly positive pressure. The appearance of the Brown-Ash Mark IX was considerably less impressive than its performance. To Forte it looked like nothing so much as a big mechanical pineapple or a strange kind of electrical transformer bristling with cooling vanes wherever one could be tacked onto it. It stood three meters tall, and three big men could almost encircle it with outstretched arms. The barrel-shaped body rested on a squat base that contained a small built-in CRT and keyboard from a Lemon home computer, whose sole function was to confirm the status of the tens of thousands of interlocking systems and programs. The real work was done by a constellation of peripherals.

The sun had long since set, but lights still burned brightly in SD-1 when the work was done, the bomb secreted within the Brown-Ash Mark IX, and the Trojan horse computer carefully wrapped in layer after layer of Styrofoam and airtight plastic sheeting, crated in wood, and then packed with additonal dunnage in an iron minicontainer. All joints were welded tight, and the container was stenciled in bold black letters: COMPUTERIZED MILLING MACHINE—FRAGILE!

Shortly after midnight, four men wrestled a dolly bearing an iron container stenciled with that legend into the cargo elevator. At the surface the blast shield slid back on its rails, and the four men found, as expected, an empty tractor and trailer parked next to the darkened loading dock. By the light of hooded lanterns, they loaded the trailer. Two of the men, carrying shotguns, were locked with it inside. The other two, also armed, climbed into the tractor and moved off, headlights extinguished, toward the main gate. There they were met by unmarked cars, each carrying men with automatic weapons.

The procession moved out onto the main highway

toward Route 612 and the Houston International Airport, two cars in front, two behind. After a few minutes a helicopter appeared overhead and kept under surveillance the five vehicles moving at well beyond the legal speed limit, and yet unchallenged by the occasional passing police cruiser, all the way to the airport. There the trailer truck and its escorts proceeded to a far corner of the field and transferred the shipment to a Texas Air Force transport. The plane took off shortly thereafter with a flight plan filed for Haneda Airport, Tokyo, with refueling stops at Johannesburg and Dacca.

At 0300 on the morning of 23 June, the airlock of the tunnel through which the A-bomb had been admitted to SD-1 less than twenty-four hours earlier opened once more, and the dripping wet minicontainer with the Brown-Ash Mark IX and its lethal cargo was hoisted onto a barge that had been anchored in the slip during the night. The barge, without lights showing, moved out into the Houston Ship Channel and proceeded some miles downstream, where it tied up alongside the 4,300-ton Turkish breakbulk carrier *Kara Deniz*. The minicontainer was loaded aboard, the ship's anchor was raised, and it headed south toward the Gulf of Mexico. In the hold, among its nondescript cargo, was the minicontainer, the bill of lading of which called for delivery to a Mr. Miramura, c/o The Oki-hiko Co., Osaka.

The *Kara Deniz* made stops in New Orleans and Tampa before setting out across the Atlantic for its next stop at Lagos, Nigeria, en route to the Far East.

The Turkish merchant ship was slow and dilapidated, crewed by nonunion seamen from a dozen Asian and African nations, but its captain was meticulous in the observance of the rules of the road and international health regulations. It was, therefore, with some surprise that in mid-Atlantic, on the ninth day out of Tampa, he was ordered to heave to by a signal from a surfaced submarine displaying American colors. At the submarine skipper's request, he sent a boat, which returned with a handsome young lieutenant commander, two ratings, and the ship's doctor.

"No trouble, I hope," said the Turkish captain worriedly when the naval officer conveyed his respects and asked to examine the ship's log.

"No, no." The American smiled. "Just routine. We've just had a message saying that state public health authorities in Florida have issued an alert."

"Alert?"

"Pneumonic plague. They've already picked up two dead infected rats on the docks, and they have seven people under observation, including a bartender, two whores, and a couple of sailors." He leafed back through the log. "But so long as you didn't hit Tampa, you'll be all—oh, I see that you *did* put in there."

"Yes, a little over a week ago. Nine days, to be exact."

"Oh, well, you're all clear, aren't they, Doc?" He turned to the round-faced man with medical corps insignia and lieutenant's bars.

"I should think so," replied the doctor. "The incubation period is usually from three to six days. On the other hand, it can be an unpredictable disease—sometimes takes ten days for its symptoms to appear."

"Oh, for Christ's sake, Glenn," said the Navy commander impatiently, "I hope you aren't going to tie us up here. Nine days, the captain just said. And we're supposed to be on a patrol."

The medical officer shrugged. "The captain has to make the decision," he said, nodding toward the Turk.

The Turkish captain was uneasy. "Is there anything I should be doing?"

"I don't think so. Any respiratory problems among your officers and crew?"

"A couple of men have colds. Is there anything we can take—pills or shots or anything?"

"'Fraid not, Captain. Once the symptoms appear, that's it. Of course, vaccine administered before onset of symptoms is a hundred percent insurance."

"Do you have any of this vaccine?"

The medical officer chuckled. "Why do you think we're here?"

Twenty minutes later, after the two corpsmen had given the captain and his twenty-five officers and crew their shots, the party from the submarine saluted the quarterdeck and climbed back down the Jacob's ladder into the waiting boat. On the way back to the submarine, the coxswain from the *Kara Deniz* slumped over the tiller.

A sailor from the submarine gently pushed him aside and took the tiller. He turned the motorboat back to the *Kara Deniz*. As the officers climbed back aboard, they didn't seem surprised that no one came to receive them.

But then, no one had been expected.

38. CASTLE ROOKED
7 JULY 2008

THE COMMANDER OF THE THIRD REGIMENT, FIFTH DIVI-sion of the Army of the Republic of Texas, an aficionado of round figures, estimated the crowd at one million. The Forte family's *Houston Herald*, fully as partisan but per-haps more precise, put the number at 700,000. Whatever the truth, people filled the bleachers erected for the occa-sion and spilled over all the way to the edge of the *Alamo*'s mooring, five hundred meters away and in direct line with the reviewing stand.

The ceremony was typical Texas. There had already been a march-past of the Fifth Division, regimental com-manders riding in front of their units on matched palomino ponies. Bands from all over the republic both preceded and followed, some out of tune but all loud, mainly supplying background to the hordes of prancing, baton-twirling drum majorettes. Rodeo riders dashed to and fro, giving an exhibition of fancy horsemanship and roping. The Texas Air Force put on a display of high-speed aero-batics, resulting in only one midair collision.

The crowd ate it all up, and a lot more. Food vendors did a roaring business, liquor flowed in stupendous quan-tities, fistfights were not unknown, and everybody had a marvelous time.

And why not? This was the big turnaround. This was

the beginning of a new era for the Republic of Texas. Its oil had dried up along with its parched acres, and the cattle business had vanished with the lush range and winter forage, and for the first time in their lives Texans had began to think small.

What had kept them alive was the promise of fresh water in unlimited quantities. Water would change everything in Texas and *for* Texas. With its hand on the spigot, Texas would no longer be harrassed by jealous legislators from the forty-nine states back in Washington who were forever pressuring the infant republic to rejoin the Union. Texans of all political stripes resented that pressure. After all, they had *earned* the right to be free to make their own mistakes, to be free of the responsibility of paying for the mistakes of others. They had earned that right by the supreme sacrifice of Gwillam Forte, ten years ago to this very day, when he had saved both Texas *and* the United States from Russian domination.

This freedom they intended to keep. They had kept that resolution during the bitter days when their resources had dried up and blown away, and by God they were going to keep it now that the tide had turned and for a change they were holding trumps. The water that Texas initiative had brought to Matagorda Bay was going to awaken the sleeping green goddess of agriculture. Soon herds of cattle would home on the range, revived by Texas water. The wheels of industry would spin again, powered by the electricity that was already beginning to flow from the towering OTEC installations installed during the past two weeks atop the *Alamo*.

These pleasant circumstances were, naturally enough, the theme of the President of Texas, the Honorable "Cherokee Tom" Traynor, when, after the parades had passed and the warmth of the Monday morning sun and rivers of good bourbon had begun to course through the veins of his audience, he rose to speak.

"Mr. President," he began, inclining his head deferentially toward President Horatio Francis Turnbull, who sat to the right of the podium, "distinguished guests, ladies and gentlemen—and—and—" He paused, as if trying to remember something. A puckish smile appeared on his pleasantly ugly face, and suddenly he jabbed his finger at the crowd. "Oh, yes—" and bellowed: *"—and all you good ole boys and girls of our great and wonderful Texas."*

Pandemonium.

President Turnbull, sitting on the reviewing stand next to Secretary of Water Resources David D. Castle, turned to him and smiled. "Well, at least the drought hasn't affected the crop that made Texas famous," he stage whispered.

Cherokee Tom covered the microphone with his hand and glanced over his shoulder, smiling broadly. "I'd have thought that you, of all people, would appreciate how much political nourishment there is in a load of good old-fashioned corn."

The clamor died down, and Traynor shifted into low gear, starting his speech on a pedestrian level so that his thunderous peroration would seem all the more dramatic by contrast.

Turnbull tuned out, thinking about the coming election. The polls had been bettering projections of his margin of victory by one or two percentage points each week for the last six weeks. His lead over his putative Democratic opponent, David D. Castle, was now 61 percent to 34 percent, with the remainder undecided. Were the election held this week, he would surely win. But November was still four long months away, and empires had been lost in less time than that. Moreover, David D. Castle was a forceful public speaker, a faithful supporter of his fellow legislators both in the House and on the hustings, an able advocate of popular causes in the Congress, and an indefatigable and efficient administrator of the most mediagenic agency of the U.S. government, the Department of Water Resources. Under the proper conditions, he would be a hard man to beat.

Turnbull's adviser, William S. Grayle, had counseled him not to worry, insisting that in David D. Castle he had created a man with sufficiently powerful political credentials to win the Democratic nomination going away but not nearly enough voter appeal to defeat that silver-maned, golden-tongued man of the people, Horatio Francis Turnbull. Besides, they had taken out an insurance policy in case Grayle's plans went awry.

The insurance policy. Might not this be the perfect occasion to cash it in? He was pondering the matter when, through the mists of Cherokee Tom Traynor's oratory and a standing ovation, he realized that the President of Texas had finally concluded his speech and was calling on him to address the nation.

Turnbull rose to applause that was hospitable but scarcely thunderous. The tepid reception more than chilled him: it telescoped time. It made him see himself four months from that moment, when the fickle electorate might have become bored and restless. It was in this moment that his resolve faltered, that he decided to cash in his insurance.

"President Traynor, ladies and gentlemen, citizens of the Republic of Texas. As I think most of you know, I am a politician, and a politician, first and foremost, must think about the needs of the people he represents. My people are those of the forty-nine states, and their most pressing need—and yours—during these past four years has been water.

"When the shortage first became apparent, I was, frankly, astonished. I had always thought it limitless. After all, it covers nearly three-quarters of the earth's surface. In our oceans, lakes, and rivers there are 1.4 billion cubic kilometers of the stuff, plus another fourteen thousand in our atmosphere. And in the earth's crust beneath our feet lies yet another sixty million cubic kilometers, eighty times as much as is contained in all the world's rivers and lakes.

"Since man became civilized, water has marked his hours, ground his grain, powered his steam engines, carried his ships to far continents, irrigated his fields. The quantity he uses has even become the yardstick of his culture: Backyard societies can get by on forty liters per day per person, but fully developed countries such as ours require more than fourteen thousand for domestic, industrial, and household use.

"But abundance bred indifference. We wasted water—criminally. We polluted water—criminally. Then one day the crunch came, and we became aware of how utterly our lives depend on this all-too-familiar substance, suddenly no longer abundant.

"Why weren't we warned? Why didn't somebody tell us the peril we faced? Why didn't somebody *do* something about it?

"Well, somebody *did* warn us. He is with us here today. Somebody *did* do something about it, but he, I regret to say, is not. It is altogether fitting that the two men who combined forces to snatch our two nations back from the brink of ruin are native sons, one of the United States of America, the other of the Republic of Texas.

"Of Ripley Forte, who today lies seriously ill in hospital, I can only say that he deserves the esteem and thanks of all Americans for bringing the *Alamo* safely into port. We join President Traynor and his fellow citizens in praying for his speedy recovery.

"But what of David D. Castle, whose rare perception, indefatigable investigatory abilities, and inspiring leadership of the newly created Department of Water Resources first impressed upon the consciousness of Americans the danger we faced and who then did so much to resolve it—what of him?

"Clearly the American people need the continued services of such a man. In the Democratic Party, indeed, his name leads the list of aspirants to candidacy for president in the coming elections. It would be hard to imagine a better man to lead the Democratic Party, to which, according to the opinion polls, only a miracle can bring victory in November.

"Should he become the Democratic candidate, he will be a worthy opponent, and I will welcome him as such, for it is my duty as the incumbent to seek a second term. The record my administration has compiled, which includes, not at all incidentally, the creation of the Department of Water Resources and the appointment of Mr. Castle to head it, and the appropriation of funds which has allowed us together to bring this historic project to fruition, demands that I run and complete the work so well begun. That mission is to restore our nation to its former prosperity and world leadership.

"This task requires the best our nation can offer. It requires brains, imagination, perseverance, guts, and a record of accomplishment. All those qualities David D. Castle has demonstrated. So that we continue to enjoy the services of this exemplary public servant, I here declare that when, as I confidently anticipate, I am renominated as candidate for the presidency of the United States next month, I will ask David D. Castle to stand for vice-president as my running mate."

President Turnbull sat down.

The crowd was stunned. It had resigned itself to at least an hour of empurpled rhetoric and had heard instead a brief ten minutes of fact and common sense. It had been prepared to rain upon him a summer shower of polite applause. Instead, surprised by the magnanimity of President Turnbull's offer, it broke out in a storm of acclaim.

Equally stunned was David D. Castle. Even as the implications of what he had heard assailed him, President Traynor was at the podium waiting for the clamor to subside so that he could introduce the remaining speaker, Castle himself, stunned but not speechless—what politician ever is?

If he hadn't read the full text of his speech in the newspaper the next day, he would never have known what he had said. He stood up, acknowledged the expectant applause and President Traynor's gracious introduction, and gripped the lectern. Words flowed. They came by rote, a platitude from this speech of long ago, a banality from yesterday, a quotation, an apothegm, a joke. With all politicians, speech making is a reflex, like blinking in a strong light.

He listened to his own words with only half an ear, and his mind paid not the slightest attention. It was focused on the reply he would have to make to President Turnbull's high-minded offer before he sat down again.

The old bastard had really put him on the spot. He had *begun* his political career as Republican candidate for the House of Representatives from California's Sixth District, and only after he had lost that first election did he switch to the Democratic Party. If he now switched back to the Republicans, few would blame him: He would be perceived as the prodigal son returning to the fold. But flip-flopping yet again in order to campaign for the presidency as a Democrat in 2012, if he lost as a Republican vice-presidential candidate in 2008, would be political suicide.

On the other hand, what were his chances of succeeding if he gracefully refused President Turnbull's offer and pursued the Democratic nomination?

In a word, bleak. The President had an overwhelming lead already and would take full credit for bringing to North America the water that this very day would begin to flow to the parched Midwest. Even the Far West, from which he hailed and where he was viewed as a native son, was far from solidly pro-Castle, for he had failed to assure their independence of water supply by bringing the iceberg to San Francisco Bay.

But what if he did run as a Democrat and failed this year? Would not his chances of being the party standard-bearer be brighter in 2012? The dismal record of unsuccessful vice-presidential aspirants suggested that they would not. No, unless he ran as a Democrat and won, a very slim possibility, he had better not run at all.

Very well. What about his prospects should he accept Turnbull's offer to campaign as his running mate?

They were, in a word, very tempting. He had worked closely with Turnbull for the past three years, and the relationship had been cordial. His proven administrative ability and clout with his former colleagues in Congress were portents that he would be granted perhaps greater powers in the coming administration than any vice-president in history. And that experience, with Turnbull's support, would virtually assure him of election as a Republican President in 2012, when Turnbull would be ineligible to run again.

Moreover, with the two leading candidates running on the same ticket, there was no chance whatever that the Democrats could field a challenger who would have a prayer of election, especially given only four months to do so.

But by far the most important consideration was the copy of Turnbull's medical report that William S. Grayle had, with some difficulty, obtained for Castle earlier this year. According to the press reports issued immediately after his week of tests at Walter Reed Hospital, Turnbull was in robust health. But that was all a smoke screen. The secret report said that he had inoperable cancer and had only a 20 percent chance of surviving more than eighteen months. The puffed face was not a sign of good living but rather of the effects of steroids pumped into him to arrest the spread of the disease. The report intimated that he would be dead by this time next year. Whoever was vice-president would become president, with at least three and a half years to serve.

Castle dearly wished he could have consulted with Gideon Sorrow, international banker, political guru, and his handler and secret channel to the Kremlin. In such a vital matter, Sorrow would certainly have initiated urgent contacts with the Presidium itself, but David D. Castle was almost certain what their answer would be: Take the cash and let the credit go, nor heed the rumble of a distant drum.

That decision was the only one possible, given the conservative mentality of Russia's leaders. To them, revolution was only a catchword. They were careful men, hoarders of political capital, men who threw to the sharks anyone who rocked the boat. They would not want their best-concealed man in the western world to jeopardize his chances of becoming *their* man in the White House.

Then there was the matter of personal prestige. At the moment he was a colonel on the rolls of the KGB, the same rank Kim Philby had attained while in Britain's MI-6. Well, if he became President of the United States, they'd surely promote him. He would become at least major general—who could say, perhaps even *colonel*-general.

Seated on the platform behind him, President Turnbull entertained himself with the thoughts sure to be chasing each other through David D. Castle's mind. He knew all the arguments pro and con, all except the important one, for he had no suspicion whatever that David D. Castle had been recruited as a Russian agent during his days at Yale. He might have doubted it even had it been proved to him, for he was of the old school, a man who took for granted that even his most rabid opponents shared his patriotism, love of baseball, and tendency to shed a tear on hearing the national anthem or the mention of mother.

Sure enough, Castle finally came through. He would, he told the vast assemblage of indifferent Texans, be honored to serve his country as the running mate of the Honorable Horatio Francis Turnbull and work with him toward the greater prosperity of all Americans.

And so forth and so on, for although David D. Castle kept on talking, Horatio Francis Turnbull had ceased to listen. It was enough that Castle had agreed to follow in the footsteps of Daniel D. Tompkins, William R. King, Henry Wilson, Levi P. Morton, William A. Wheeler, and so many others who had been vice-president and then vanished utterly from the American political scene. Castle had obviously forgotten the inelegant but deadly accurate appraisal of the job by Franklin Delano Roosevelt's vice-president, Texan John Nance Garner, to the effect that the vice-presidency was "about as useful as a bucket of warm spit."

Turnbull wondered when the other shoe would finally drop: 2009, 2010? How long would it take the poor dumb son of a bitch to realize that the medical report had been a plant, that there was absolutely nothing wrong with Turnbull's health, that his doctor had given him another good twenty years to live?

Well, as Barnum once said...

39. FORTE VS. CASTLE
21 JULY 2008

"FOR A MAN DYING OF LUPUS ERYTHEMATOSUS," SAID Mansour, "you look extraordinarily fit."

"Habit. I die every morning before the coffee comes, but then I recover fast."

Ripley Forte eased himself into one of the rickety period chairs in the salon of the *Linno* and made a mental note not to make any sudden moves. Outside the snow was falling gently on the deck of the yacht, anchored in the Rio de la Plata off Buenos Aires; inside, in deference to Joe Mansour's thin Mediterranean blood, it was overheated. Forte pulled off his necktie and draped it across his sport jacket lying on an adjacent chair. He opened the collar button of his shirt and breathed easily for the first time since he had arrived in Argentina.

"I suppose," continued the dapper little Lebanese, "that you want an accounting, and rightly so, since I have rendered none since January."

"That's not what I came down here for, although it wouldn't hurt. I wouldn't want to overdraw my checking account."

Joe Mansour laughed.

"My dear Ripley, you couldn't do that if you worked at it forty hours a week. And since you're recovering from a severe illness and shouldn't tax your heart, if it's all the same with you, I'd rather not tell you what you're worth. It's a frightening sum and in two or three years, according to my projections, will be absolutely obscene."

"Yes, please, no obscenity. Remember, I'm an ex-Marine. Anyhow, I'm more interested in what Jennifer Red Cloud is worth."

"How do you like similes? In speaking of the finances of Raynes Oceanic Resources, you have a wide choice: not worth a tinker's dam, a brass farthing, a hill of beans, two cents, a row of pins, or a continental. Take your pick."

"As bad as that?"

"Just say the word, Rip, and I'll turn loose the bears. We'll eat Raynes alive."

"If you bought in today, how much would Mrs. Red Cloud's stock be worth?"

"Today? About 1.8 million."

"Next week?"

"What exactly do you want, Rip?"

"I want to bankrupt her. Put her out of business."

Joe Mansour pursed his lips and leaned back in his chair. He studied Ripley Forte's grim, weather-beaten face.

"I'd say you loved that woman a lot or hated her a lot."

"That's close enough. Answer the question."

"Oh, we could bankrupt her, all right, if that's what you really want. Instead of squirreling away some of her profits years ago in annuities or real estate, she plowed it all back into the company. Her stock represents everything she owns. But I'd need two weeks to set up everything and cover our tracks."

Forte nodded.

"That'll be just fine."

Japan was about as far as Jennifer Red Cloud could get away from the *Alamo*, and it was to her home in Kyoto that she repaired after she left the iceberg once it had become apparent that neither she nor the mysterious enemy who had thrice tried and failed to sabotage it was going to succeed. She needed the cultural isolation that Japan offered—she spoke not a single word of the language—and the tranquility of the rustic atmosphere of its ancient capital to think things out and decide how best to save Raynes Oceanic Resources.

David D. Castle made Jennifer Red Cloud's decision simple, for he brought with him proof that he was, after all, the man of her dreams.

"David, how lovely to see you again," she said warmly, taking him by the hand and leading him down the two steps into the salon. "How long has it been?"

"Too long," said Castle.

"I've missed you."

"And I've been counting the minutes until this moment, my darling," said Castle, unaware that they were in grievous danger of turning their meeting into a cliché contest.

She saved them by ringing a little silver bell for Manuel.

"A Bloody Mary for Secretary Castle," she instructed the white-jacketed Filipino, "and—"

Castle coughed apologetically.

"I'm actually drinking Campari and soda these days," he said, the memory of William S. Grayle's little pleasantry still fresh.

"Campari, then, Manuel. And the usual for me."

The butler bowed and left the room.

Jennifer Red Cloud was, Castle observed, as beautiful and desirable as always. She wore a simple, ankle-length black silk gown with a rope of pearls entwined in her upswept raven-black hair and a single pear-shaped diamond on a golden pendant around her neck.

"I've brought you a little present," said Castle, reaching into his inside breast pocket.

That was a novelty. Not since his gift of flowers at their first and only meeting when he had been a freshman congressman had he brought a gift. Since her proposal, especially, he had been relentlessly businesslike. She wondered what it would be. A diamond bracelet? An emerald brooch? Or pearls—a woman could never have too many pearls.

He drew out three Xeroxed pages stapled together and handed them to her reverently across the coffee table.

She took them, the sour taste of bile rising unbidden to her throat. She looked at Castle cryptically and then began to read the medical report.

Castle watched as her hard-set features softened. An expression of anticipation gave way to positive pleasure as she began page three. By the time she had finished it her face was glowing.

"But is this true? Can it be trusted?"

"A great deal of money was paid for that copy, and it's the only one which isn't under lock and key in the White House. You will note that it is signed by the President's personal physician and Bethesda's chief oncologist. They give him no better than a one in four chance of surviving through 2009. Which is another way of saying that come next summer, I will be the occupant of the Oval Office."

"And I?"

"You will be at my side."

"But what about Raynes Oceanic Resources?"

David D. Castle leaned back in his chair and made a steeple of his long, lean fingers. "Yes," he said. "I've been giving that some thought. Naturally, when we marry, you will have to divest yourself of all interest in Raynes. You can, of course, leave your shares in a blind trust. But there is, I think, a better way. Have your trustees liquidate completely and—yes, I know all about the depressed state of your stock," he went on hurriedly as Jennifer Red Cloud was about to protest. "Get out of the company altogether. It will work out better in the long run.

"Now, here's the way we'll handle it. Let your company continue to slide gracefully toward bankruptcy, meanwhile divesting yourself of all your stock. That will obviate any suggestion of ethical impropriety, which would be fatal to my campaign for a second presidential term. While this is going on, a second company will be formed, headed by an old and trusted associate of mine and prominent investment banker, Gideon Sorrow, to purchase Raynes's assets at, say, ten cents on the dollar. For that privilege, which you will accord him, and for my working behind the scenes to ensure that Sorrow's new company gets a solid grip on iceberg imports to the United States, he will set aside a large block of stock for us. By the end of my second term, the stock will have soared in value, and we will retire with more money than we could possibly spend."

"God, you're a devious devil," said Jennifer Red Cloud in frank admiration. "What a team we'll make."

Castle nodded and rose.

"We'll go over the details Monday."

Listening to him describe their coming coup had brought her Apache and Viking blood to a slow simmer, as it always did in the presence of an audacious maneuver involving risk and danger. All she needed now was the touch of a hand and it would boil over.

"Monday? That's two days away." She looked up at him provocatively through long lashes, "Let's, ah, *do* it. Now."

He reached across the coffee table and took her hand. He brought it to his lips.

His kiss was as cool and calculated, as make-believe as a senator's tax return.

She felt like punching him in the teeth but remembered how slow and stupid men could be. "The whole weekend ahead of us. I hoped I wouldn't have to spend it alone."

Castle released her hand and straightened. "I wish I could," he said uneasily, "but I'm afraid it's impossible. Turnbull's asked me to deliver a personal message to Premier Kawasaki, for which"— he consulted his wristwatch —"I'd better catch my helicopter to the airport or I'll be late."

"Tomorrow?" Jennifer Red Cloud said, still hoping, as

she walked Castle to the door.

"Tomorrow I must pay my respects to the emperor." He turned. "I don't think I mentioned how absolutely smashing you look in black, but I can think of a way you'll look even better."

"Yes?" she said, wondering whether he would frame his answer in stuffy lawyer's language or come right out and say how delicious her bare brown body would look against white satin sheets.

"Yes, on our wedding day, when you walk down the aisle in your long white wedding gown."

"Good-bye, David," she said through clenched teeth, and closed the door before he was halfway down the path to his waiting car.

Manuel thought that the caller had gotten the address wrong. The man was dressed in a red wool shirt, open at the collar, with worn dungarees and scuffed cowboy boots.

"I'm Ripley Forte," the visitor said.

"Yes?" said Manuel, and then, seeing the narrowed eyes in the strong, weather-beaten face, quickly added, "sir."

"Tell Mrs. Red Cloud I'm here."

The door began to close.

Forte put his shoulder to it. "Never mind," he said, barging through with Manuel trailing like a puppy at his heels, "I'll tell her myself."

He strode into the salon.

Jennifer Red Cloud was leafing idly through a house and garden magazine. She looked up.

"Why, Rip, how nice to see you."

Forte glanced over his shoulder at Manuel.

"Beat it!"

Manuel beat it.

"Sit down, Ripley," said Jennifer Red Cloud with a grand gesture. "Sit down and tell me all about your sordid little affairs. Since you left the *Sun King* with that fake— it *was* fake, wasn't it?—kidney ailment, I've completely lost track of what the masses are thinking."

"What I came to do isn't done sitting, not in Texas, anyway."

"And what *did* you come for, Ripley? Your telex was rather vague."

"I came to pay an old debt."

"Did you, indeed? I wasn't aware that you owed me anything, unless you're speaking of the pleasure of my company all those tedious months aboard that dreary iron ship."

"I owe you plenty, and today I'm going to pay you in full, and in kind, I might add."

"How mysterious. Would you care to explain?"

"Think back, Red."

"How far?"

"To July 1998."

"That's ten years. Ah, is it our anniversary?"

"In a manner of speaking. In the early part of the month my father was killed. In the latter part I was screwed out of my share of Raynes Oceanic Resources."

"Oh, *now* I see. You're here to gloat about Raynes having fallen on hard times."

"Your memory isn't so good, Red. Already you've forgotten what I just said."

"Refresh me."

"If that's acquiescence, your choice of verbs is wrong. What I said was, I came to pay you in full, and in kind."

She read it in his eyes. She had seen that look in men's eyes before. There was no mistaking it. *"Manuel!"* she shouted.

Forte just looked at her, not moving.

Manuel materialized, bowing nervously.

Forte turned around. "If I see your face again, Manuel," he said softly, "you're a dead man. Please believe me."

Manuel was a believer. He turned and fled.

Jennifer Red Cloud was lithe and fleet of foot, but she had taken no more than three steps toward the door when Forte's arm locked around her waist. She felt herself being lifted into the air and flung over Forte's shoulder like a bag of laundry. She kicked frantically and succeeded only in losing her shoes. He took no notice but strode to the foyer and then up the spiral staircase.

He opened the first door. It was a bathroom. He went

to the next. It was a bedroom with a huge circular water bed under a tentlike silken canopy.

She wanted to scream, but her heart was beating too fast and somehow seemed to have gotten stuck in her throat.

He walked in and kicked the door shut behind them.

She slipped out of the dream into reality, or was it the other way around? It had been like that ever since he had first grabbed hold of her, a delicious fantasy that had enveloped her, only to fade away into deep sleep and erotic phantasmagoria from which she awakened to sensations that she had read about but never really believed existed.

She stretched out her hand for more, but the place where Forte had been was empty. She rolled over on her back and opened her eyes.

He was on the other side of the room. He had just bent over to pick up his shirt from the floor.

"Where are you going?" she said, sitting up.

"Away."

"But, but why?" The late afternoon sun was slanting through the curtains, and a balmy breeze blew through the open window. "It's early. We've got all the time in the world."

Forte shook his head. "Time's run out, Red. I've done what I came to do."

She studied him through sleep-swollen eyes. "I don't understand."

He buttoned his shirt slowly. "Okay, I'll say it again. You and Ned Raynes diddled me good ten years ago. He's beyond reach, but today I paid you back, with interest. *Finito la musica*."

"You can't be serious."

"I'm serious. I've waited a long time for this. I've ruined your company, and I've given us both a taste of what might have been if you hadn't been so goddamn greedy."

She got out of bed and came toward him, her black hair floating around her shoulders, as light and lovely as swansdown on a summer breeze. She twined her arms around him. "But you love me."

"Who said so?" said Forte, standing perfectly still.

"*You* said so."

"Maybe I was lying."

"You weren't lying. I know it."

"Maybe not. Maybe so. What difference does it make?"

"It makes all the difference in the world. I know now that I want you, and I'm going to have you. I've waited too long for this. I'm not going to lose it."

He pried her arms gently apart.

"Sure. You feel that way now. You wouldn't be a woman if you didn't, and nobody ever said you weren't all woman. But tomorrow you'll be back scheming to knife somebody in the back, to take some kid's marbles, to take over the world. Well, Red, the world you're going to take over isn't the world I want to live in."

She stood back, her hands on her slim waist, defiance in her eyes. "I dare you to say you don't love me."

Forte shook his head sadly. "What's that got to do with anything?"

He turned and opened the door.

"Ripley, come back!" she called as she heard him walking down the stairs.

"*Ripley!*" she shouted. But there was no answer.

She heard the front door open and then shut.

A typical male trick. He was expecting her to run after him, panting with unrequited passion. And if she did, she knew she'd find him grinning at her from the bottom of the stairs.

She stayed where she was. When she didn't follow, he would return. She cocked her head, listening for his footfall. She waited, scarcely breathing.

She waited quite a long time, little realizing that she'd wait forever.

40. THE SINCERE FRIEND
22 JULY 2008

"*VYETEROK*," SAID KGB CHAIRMAN SERGEI BALIEV, leaning back in his chair and regarding the fluttering curtains with dreamy eyes.

"*Svezhest*," Premier Vasily Osipovich Korol corrected him.

"Well," said Prov Vaslav Navori, the great conciliator of the Presidium, "I think we must all agree, at least, that it is not a *buran*."

Whether the gentle wind ruffling the curtains was a mild *vyeterok* or a balmy *svezhest*, it certainly wasn't the cold, biting, black northeasterly *buran* out of Siberia, for it blew in from the west, bringing nothing but comfort and warmth. This day it brought not only uncommonly blue skies and shirt-sleeve weather to Moscow but the Brown-Ash Mark IX, which Premier Korol, at the window, was observing being unloaded in the inner courtyard of the Kremlin.

Around the rust-red container was a cordon of *spetsnaz* guards, automatic rifles with fixed bayonets facing outward against what menace Korol couldn't for the life of him imagine. Even the rats in the Kremlin sewers were reputedly required to carry security passes. Certainly nothing was going to happen here to that priceless piece of American technology. It had been sealed and spirited away from SD-1, Mr. Ripley Forte's secret underground arms factory in Houston, and it would remain thus sealed until opened in the presence of Lieutenant General Grigoriy Aleksandrevich Piatakov, chief of the First Chief Directorate, Foreign Intelligence, KGB. That would be part of Piatakov's reward for his superlative performance.

"A thoroughly professional job," said the premier.

"More than merely professional," added Navori reflectively. "It was in the nature of a complex military campaign conceived by one man and meticulously carried out by that same man down to the last detail. Our faith in Piatakov was not misplaced."

Korol nodded. There was no question that Piatakov, in the short space of three years, had become the first-ranking intelligence operative in the Soviet Union. Moreover, he had accepted with true party discipline assignment to what must have seemed a dead-end job—an exceptional demonstration of loyalty to the regime. Grigoriy Aleksandrevich had cheerfully thrown himself into his new duties. He had accepted the responsibility of completely reorganizing the First Chief Directorate and had done a magnificent job. He had obtained a late-model Brown-Ash Mark IX, which would revolutionize the information gathering and collating duties of Room 101, not to mention its role in national defense. Grigoriy Aleksandrevich had proved himself invaluable; more important, he was absolutely reliable.

"I wonder," said Premier Korol, turning away from the window and resuming his seat at the head of the conference table.

"Yes, Comrade General Secretary?" said Chairman Baliev.

"On the matter of the election of a new first deputy premier," said Korol, "I have observed that you have not favored us with your opinion, Baliev. Why not?"

Baliev was married to a cousin of Navori. He was a protégé of Yermolov. And Sedov knew of a certain event in his past that he hoped would follow him to the grave. "All three comrade candidates," he said finally, "have impeccable qualifications. It is not for me, their junior, to voice an opinion as to whose qualifications are best."

"A diplomatic reply," said Korol, nodding. "And in the coming phase of our history, as troubles multiply, diplomacy will be needed at the highest levels, *both in external and internal relations.*"

He glanced at each of his colleagues in turn. His meaning was clear, and so, as the others thought about it, was the good sense of his choice of Baliev to be first deputy premier and heir apparent to leadership of the Soviet

Union. Baliev was on good terms with the major power blocs within the Presidium. Once superseded at the KGB he would no longer have a power base of his own. His personality was that of a manager rather than an autocrat. He would be a balance wheel, when balance in the higher councils of the USSR was most needed.

"You see the difficulty?" Korol continued, turning to Baliev.

Baliev did indeed. He himself was an efficient, imaginative administrator of the *Komitet Gosudarstvennoi Bezopasnosti*, but *his* deputy, while an ideal number two man, did not have the brains or strength to succeed him.

Korol, having had his little fun, put Baliev out of his misery. "Gentlemen," he said, "we will vote, of course, but I personally believe Baliev is the best candidate for the post of first deputy premier. His skills and knowledge as KGB chief will, of course, be hard to replace. But in Room 101 we have an ideal successor: Lieutenant General Grigoriy Aleksandrevich Piatakov. Since a discussion of such an obvious choice would serve no useful purpose, I call for a show of hands on my nomination of Lieutenant General Piatakov to be new chairman of the KGB, to take effect on the election of Comrade Baliev as first deputy premier."

The vote was unanimous.

Lieutenant General Grigoriy Aleksandrevich Piatakov had put on his full-dress uniform, with medals, for this was a moment he would remember as long as he lived.

Standing at the door of the freight elevator, waiting for the arrival of the Brown-Ash Mark IX, he felt that he had reached the end of a very long road, a road that had led him through all the twists and turns of Ripley Forte's mind. For Ripley Forte's mind had been the key to everything.

Every Brown-Ash Mark IX in existence was guarded by regiments of troops behind barbed wire on American military installations, save one. That one was apparently even more inaccessible, for it was buried almost a mile beneath the earth in SD-1 in Houston, and fully as closely guarded. But there was a significant difference: It was under the control of one man, Ripley Forte. If Forte could somehow be persuaded to part with it, there would be no further problem.

Every man had his price. What was Ripley Forte's? To find out the answer had required study, and for months after Forte had come into possession of the Brown-Ash, General Piatakov had become a full-time student of that unsuspecting Texan. He compiled data on every aspect of Ripley Forte's character, his past, his dreams, his sex life, aspirations, associations, vices, prejudices, fears, friendships, idiosyncrasies, tics, weaknesses, affectations, loves, and hates. He assigned fifteen of his best agents, in Russia, the United States, and Texas, to discover what moved him to anger, made him laugh, made him cry, hurt his feelings, stirred him to pride.

After the first year, Piatakov knew with a high degree of accuracy what Ripley Forte would do in any situation. He knew that Forte could not be blackmailed, bought, persuaded, or tricked into giving up the Brown-Ash. Some more subtle strategy would have to be devised.

One element of that strategy was Forte's hatred and suspicion of Russians, whom he held collectively responsible for the death of his father. The emotion was useful because its direction was predictable.

Another element basic to Ripley Forte's character was raw ambition. He wanted to achieve in life at least as much as his father had done, preferably more.

And there was something else, perhaps most important of all: Ripley Forte was clever, and his cleverness was mixed with a love of irony.

Such were the elements Piatakov had to work with: Forte's hatred of the Russians, an Old Testament Talmudic lust for revenge against anyone who attempted to thwart or intimidate him, and a serpentine guile.

The rest might have been difficult even for a man of Piatakov's organizational ability, but the twelve wise men of Oyo—God bless them!—had made it easy. Thanks to his informants at the Oyo Experimental Farm Cooperative, he had learned full details of Project Titanic, the operation designed to sabotage the *Alamo* on its way to

Texas. Their first option had been anthrax, which would have wiped out the crew; their second the fire, which would have devoured the *Alamo*, the *Sun King*, and all its auxiliaries; and their third the atomic bomb, which would surely work had the other two attempts failed.

Forte, not knowing the source of the serial threats, naturally assumed they had come from Russia. The information he had obtained before the first attack would convince him that had he not received it in time, he must certainly lose the *Alamo* and all its crew. The message suggesting that, as decent compensation, he should give up the Brown-Ash for the information received, which alone had saved the *Alamo*, would only strengthen his determination to do nothing of the kind.

Nevertheless, the abortive aerial attack had demonstrated to Forte his impotence, and the triangle of fire had confirmed it.

Now came the hardest part, for Piatakov as for Forte: the long wait until the Texan came to realize that only one possible form of attack would prevail against the protection of the combined U.S. naval and air forces: an atomic blast. And the only feasible delivery system would be a mine, as a missile could be detected and reprisals immediately taken against its launching pad.

Forte had discovered the atomic bomb in time—Piatakov had been prepared to give him an anonymous hint, if necessary—and the rest had followed very much according to his predictions of Forte's behavior patterns. Forte had, as Piatakov had foreseen, prepared a decoy shipment and then spirited away the Brown-Ash through the tunnel to the old U.S.S. *Texas* berth, thence aboard the *Kara Deniz*, ostensibly for shipment to Japan.

And now the Brown-Ash was here.

The big steel doors slid back, and the rust-red steel container was trundled out on its dolly into the receiving area by six stalwart *spetsnaz* soldiers. The Brown-Ash was safe in its final resting place.

Lieutenant General Piatakov heard the tinkle of the telephone from the Presidium in the watch officer's cubicle.

"It's for you, sir," said the watch officer. "It's Premier Korol himself."

Piatakov walked over to the telephone. He listened to Korol's words of commendation for his splendid work, learned of the satisfaction of the entire Presidium, and then heard something about his promotion to head the entire KGB. He was sure he had heard wrong and respectfully asked the comrade premier to repeat that last sentence.

The premier did, with a solemnity that assured Piatakov that the premier wasn't indulging in pleasantry.

Piatakov nodded, in something of a daze thanked the comrade premier for his consideration and that of the Presidium, and hung up the phone.

He walked across the floor to where the technicians were waiting with blazing torches to cut through the metal door.

General Piatakov stood for a long moment contemplating the fruits of his victory. Finally he gave the sign to go ahead, and the cutting torches began their work. They worked slowly, pausing from time to time to let the metal cool so that the Brown-Ash would remain unaffected by the heat.

Who said there wasn't a God? thought Piatakov to himself. Not only was there a God, but a God with a marvelous sense of humor. For three years now Piatakov had been scheming and plotting and conspiring to bring off this coup, and he had succeeded brilliantly. He owed, it was true, a tremendous debt to the Israelis at Oyo, for had it not been for them, he would have had to devise a rather different stratagem. But whatever the means, he would have somehow managed to have an atom bomb delivered to Room 101, without the slightest suspicion of the masters of the Kremlin who awaited him, even now, in the conference suite.

Piatakov's calculations had been precise. He had anticipated Forte's reactions perfectly. And he had devised the perfect revenge for the Presidium's having robbed him of his freedom, his brilliant career, his faith in his leaders—Armageddon: instant annihilation in one huge ball of fire. For sentencing Grisha Piatakov to die slowly down here, he had sentenced them to die swiftly above. Forte's vengeance would be Piatakov's vengeance, too.

Now this: God twisting the knife, making him wish

that he hadn't been so damned clever, after all.

But what if he had made a mistake? What if Forte did not actually put the bomb inside the Brown-Ash? What if nothing but the Brown-Ash was in the big red container? Then he could board the elevator and in eight minutes rejoin the human race and live out his years in useful endeavor, elevated to a seat among the mighty.

The seal was cut, the door opened, and there stood the Brown-Ash Mark IX.

The technicians inserted a dolly beneath it and carefully extracted it from the protective steel container. Eager hands unwrapped the waterproof foil. The circle of interested spectators surrounding the computer grew to include nearly all the personnel on duty in Room 101.

The chief computer technician saluted. "Shall I energize it, Comrade Lieutenant General?"

For one wild moment Piatakov considered telling them to get the computer the hell out of here, that it was a Trojan horse that would destroy them all. But for what? He would be asked, How did he *know* the Brown-Ash was booby-trapped? How could he answer that? And what if it *didn't* contain a bomb? They would want to know why he suspected it *did*. There would be questions and unpleasant stimuli to encourage quick and accurate answers. And in the end?

"Yes." Piatakov was sweating now. "Hook it up."

"The test keyboard is ready, sir," the technician reported a few minutes later. "Would you care to make the first entry?"

"Yes, thank you."

Piatakov sat down in the chair provided him in front of the small green screen. A cursor blinked evilly at him.

Piatakov thought for a moment and then typed "Ripley Forte."

A short message appeared:

> Dear Sincere Friend:
> It is five minutes to midnight.
> Remember the *Alamo*!
> Ripley Forte.

Piatakov sighed and leaned back in his chair. He had quit smoking some years ago, but a cigarette wasn't going to hurt him now. He asked for one, accepted a light, and took a deep and heady draught.

Behind him the telephone rang.

"It's the premier again," said the watch officer. "He wants to know if the Brown-Ash Mark IX is working properly."

"Tell him it's working fine."

The watch officer reported what Comrade General Piatakov had said, then stood at attention as he listened.

"Sir. The comrade premier wants to know when you'll be joining them."

Piatakov thought for a moment and smiled. "Tell them I'll be up in a minute."

ABOUT THE AUTHOR

For 30 years Daniel da Cruz has lived and worked—as a diplomat, teacher, businessman, and journalist—in Europe, Asia, and Africa.

He spent six World War II years as a U.S. Marine volunteer, serving ashore, afloat (in 1941 aboard the *Texas*), and aloft in the three war theaters. A *magna cum laude* graduate of Georgetown University's School of Foreign Service, da Cruz has been variously a census enumerator, magazine editor and editorial consultant, judo master—he holds a second degree Black Belt of the Kodokan Judo Institute, Tokyo—taxi driver, farmer, public relations officer for an oil company, salesman, foreign correspondent, publishers' representative, vice-president of a New York advertising agency, slaughterhouse skinner, captain of a Texas security organization, American Embassy press attaché in Baghdad, copper miner and Adjunct Professor of Anthropology at Miami University.

Da Cruz has published twelve books, among them an American history text, a monograph on Amerindian linguistics, and three suspense novels for Ballantine Books, the most recent of which, *The Captive City*, was awarded a special "Edgar." He has written two other science-fiction novels, *The Grotto of the Formigans* (Del Rey, 1980) and *The Ayes of Texas* (Del Rey, 1982).